T0356544

"*Cinder-Nanny* is a definite must-read. This cute play on the age-old fairy tale will surely worm its way into your heart and leave you feeling all warm and fuzzy."

—*Harlequin Junkie*

"Wilson's ability to weave a sweet tale of two people, each of whom needs what the other has to offer, is magical."

—Bookreporter

The Paid Bridesmaid

"Combining a fast-paced plot with a slow-burning romance, this is sure to give readers butterflies."

—*Publishers Weekly*

"Wilson's (*Roommaid*) funny, sweet stand-alone about marriage, friendships, and mistaken identities is full of witty dialogue, endearing characters, and fast-paced narrative. Will appeal to fans of feel-good romances, rom-coms, and plots about weddings and social media."

—*Library Journal*

The Seat Filler

"Wilson (*Roommaid*) balances the quirky with the heartfelt in this adorable rom-com."

—*Publishers Weekly*

The Friend Zone

"Wilson scores a touchdown with this engaging contemporary romance that delivers plenty of electric sexual chemistry and zingy banter while still being romantically sweet at its core."

—*Booklist*

"Snappy banter, palpable sexual tension, and a lively sense of fun combine with deeply felt emotional issues in a sweet, upbeat romance that will appeal to both the YA and new adult markets."

—*Library Journal*

The #Lovestruck Novels

"Wilson has mastered the art of creating a romance that manages to be both sexy and sweet, and her novel's skillfully drawn characters, deliciously snarky sense of humor, and vividly evoked music-business settings add up to a supremely satisfying love story that will be music to romance readers' ears."

—*Booklist* (starred review), *#Moonstruck*

"Making excellent use of sassy banter, hilarious texts, and a breezy style, Wilson's energetic story brims with sexual tension and takes readers on a musical road trip that will leave them smiling. Perfect as well for YA and new adult collections."

—*Library Journal*, *#Moonstruck*

"*#Starstruck* is oh so funny! Sariah Wilson created an entertaining story with great banter that I didn't want to put down. Ms. Wilson provided a diverse cast of characters in their friends and family. Fans of *Sweet Cheeks* by K. Bromberg and Ruthie Knox will enjoy *#Starstruck*."

—*Harlequin Junkie* (4.5 stars), *#Starstruck*

Falling
OVERBOARD

The #Lovestruck Novels

#Starstruck

#Moonstruck

#Awestruck

The Royals of Monterra Series

Royal Date

Royal Chase

Royal Games

Royal Design

The Ugly Stepsister Series

The Ugly Stepsister Strikes Back

The Promposal

Falling OVERBOARD

SARIAH WILSON

 Montlake

Published by Montlake, Seattle

www.apub.com

Amazon, the Amazon logo, and Montlake are trademarks of Amazon.com, Inc., or its affiliates.

ISBN-13: 9781662514265 (paperback)
ISBN-13: 9781662514258 (digital)

Cover design by Hang Le
Cover image: © Alenik Eremeeva / Shutterstock; © ZeinousGDS / Shutterstock;
© Miro Kovacevic / Shutterstock; © Arif_Vector / Shutterstock;
© Victoria Sergeeva / Shutterstock

Printed in the United States of America

For Kevin

CHAPTER ONE

Lucky

"Everyone take a seat," Captain Carl said. The entire crew was gathered in the main salon, and part of me cringed as they settled onto the luxurious couches. I fervently hoped the engineer didn't have oil or grease on his pants, as I would be the one stuck scrubbing the stain out.

The captain cleared his throat and said, "As you may or may not already know, our chief stew left us last night. It's not ideal, given that we pick up our first charter tomorrow, but I know Lucky can fill in for us."

He nodded at me and I tried not to audibly gulp. I only had a year's worth of experience working on superyachts. I'd been on the *Mio Tesoro* for the last five months, starting off in the Caribbean. We'd recently crossed the Atlantic Ocean to spend the season in the Mediterranean.

I thought one year wasn't enough experience for me to be acting chief stewardess. I felt comfortable as second stew. I understood that position very well. I probably should have been flattered that Captain Carl was going to let me run things until he hired a new chief stew, but all I felt was an increasing sense of panic.

"And I know you all were worried about the yacht being bought by new owners," the captain said, and I felt my fellow crewmembers shift and grumble under their breath. Typically, when this kind of luxury yacht was sold, the new owners wanted to redecorate the interior and would have the ship return to a dockyard for upgrades.

Which usually meant they let the crew go.

We'd all been worried about having to find new positions, but I'd tried to take the fact that we'd traveled halfway across the world as a good sign. My best friend, currently the second stew, Georgia, had told me with her Australian sassiness that I didn't know what I was talking about, as I hadn't been around long enough to have been fired multiple times, and we might still be in danger.

She was right—I was a newbie. She had been in the yachting industry for years and probably should have been made the interim chief stew.

"I don't want it," she had told me after the captain called me up to the bridge to discuss me temporarily taking over. "I'm not interested in having the responsibility. I like the perks without the migraines."

My own head was throbbing, so I understood.

"I've spoken with the Cartwrights and they would like things to continue on as they are now. With one additional rule." Making certain that he had all our attention, the captain said, "There will be no hookups or relationships of any kind among the crew."

Emilie, the Canadian / our newest stew, gasped.

Casual hookups and noncommittal make-outs were fairly common on these kinds of yachts. Not with the guests, never with the guests. That was one of the strictest rules that existed.

But with the crew? It was always open season, even if there was a nonfraternization rule in place. Most of the crew were unreasonably attractive people in their twenties and early thirties and lived like we were in the last days of the Roman Empire.

Thomas, the British bosun, cleared his throat. "Could you explain exactly what you mean, Captain?"

"It's self-explanatory," Captain Carl quickly responded. "Keep your hands and lips to yourself."

This had been the rule on one of the other boats I'd worked on but not on the *Mio Tesoro*. Given the glum expressions and profound silence, none of my fellow crewmembers seemed very pleased about the change.

I wondered if Marika, our former chief stew, wouldn't be the only person to sneak off the yacht in the middle of the night.

"Lucky, you don't understand," she had told me last night as she'd packed her bag. "Krzysztof finally said he's ready to get married. I have to go back to Poland before he changes his mind."

Our former chief stew had been waiting seven years for her boyfriend to propose. While I understood her desire to return home and seal the deal before he could talk himself out of making a commitment, it left us in a bit of a lurch.

Specifically me.

I was the one who'd had to go tell Captain Carl that Marika had abandoned ship, and I was now in charge of the two stewardesses beneath me.

Captain Carl shook his head, as if annoyed with the crew's stunned reaction. "If any of you need anything, don't come to me. Deal with your problems by yourselves, like adults. Dismissed."

I stood up but the captain said, "Lucky? Stay behind."

My heart hammering in my chest, I sank back down on the couch. To distract myself, I studied his profile as he watched the crew depart the main salon.

Captain Carl was in his fifties and had dark hair shot through with silver. His face was lined and weathered from being in the sun so much, but he was still a handsome man. Georgia had often waxed poetic about him and said he was her favorite silver fox.

When the room was empty, he said, "I will need you to be chief stew for the next few months."

This was not a responsibility I wanted. I had thought I would be filling in temporarily. "But Georgia—"

He cut me off, his expression serious. "If I wanted Georgia to be chief stew, she would be. I want you to do it. I know you can rise to the occasion. And I know that the significant salary increase will be welcome."

My spirits lifted at his declaration. He was right. I was in yachting for one reason—I wanted to go back home and open a bakery in honor of my grandparents. This job paid a ridiculous amount of money, and I had a three-year plan to save up everything I needed to start my own business.

The captain said what my new yearly salary would be and I put a hand over my chest. My salary was going to nearly double.

This could turn my three-year plan into a two-year plan.

I could handle the stress for that kind of cash. "I thought you wanted to have four stews on the ship this season."

"If we need to hire another junior stew, we can. But we ran just fine with three in the Caribbean."

He was right. That was how things had been before he brought Emilie on.

As if he somehow sensed what I was thinking, he said, "I'm going to tell you the same thing I told Marika. I want you to keep an eye on Emilie. I need you to take responsibility for her and help her."

I stifled a groan. Emilie was Captain Carl's niece. She had apparently gotten into quite a bit of trouble back in Canada and her father had shipped her out to join us in hopes that his brother could teach her the value of hard work.

Or, more accurately, so that I could straighten her out and teach her how to work.

The problem was she was the laziest person I'd ever met, and yachting was about working hard for sixteen hours a day, every day.

While Emilie had aggravated me in the past, she hadn't been my problem.

Now she was.

My anxiety continued to mount despite my best efforts to cram it down and try to ignore it.

I nodded, to indicate that I'd heard and agreed to what he'd said even if I didn't have any thoughts on how to manage it.

"We're also getting a new deckhand today, Hunter Smith. He should be arriving soon. You'll need to order him a uniform. I'd appreciate you keeping an eye on him, too."

This was brand-new information. I had no idea why we would hire another deckhand. Who would not be in my department—so how did the captain expect me to look out for him, too? That's what the bosun was for.

"I'll need you to give him a tour of the boat. And I apologize—you know that I typically try to avoid coed sleeping arrangements, but you'll be sharing a room with him. I know that I can trust you to follow the rules and not get involved with him. I'm counting on you."

My mind buzzed with this information. It made sense—my cabin was the only one with an empty bed now that Marika had left. And there was no way to switch things around to get a female bunkmate. We had an uneven number.

I wasn't too worried about crushing on this new deckhand. Given the nuclear fallout from my last relationship, I couldn't imagine myself ever dating again.

Realizing that Captain Carl expected some kind of response from me, I swallowed and nodded. "I understand. I'll take care of it."

"Good." He got to his feet and stared down at me. "You know what I say. There is no *I* in 'team,' but there might be a *U* in 'failure.'"

He had such high expectations for the way the boat was run, how the guests were served. Marika had met them but I didn't know if I could do the same.

That buzzing feeling intensified as he left the main salon to return to the bridge.

You can do this, I told myself. It would be okay.

Then my phone beeped. I glanced at it and saw a message from one of my younger sisters.

Short on rent money. Can you send a thousand dollars ASAP?

I let out a shaky breath. It was always something with the twins. They often needed help and cash, and I was the only person left who could help them.

With a sick feeling in my stomach, I sent her the money.

A tiny voice in my head said I was never going to be able to save up enough. There would always be some kind of emergency. Things were not going to work out for me.

I was a failure at everything I tried to do.

My hands had started trembling and I realized that I was on the verge of a panic attack.

I needed to get outside. Far away from prying eyes. I didn't want the captain to think I couldn't do the job. I could. I had to. Especially now. With shaking limbs I made my way to the private area on the bow where the crew would hang out on breaks. When I arrived my legs gave out and I slid down against the ship's wall and landed with a thud on the deck.

All I could think about was all the ways this could go wrong. That I might be a terrible chief stew. That Emilie would somehow get worse and make my life even harder. That I would be so bad at this new position that the captain would have no choice but to fire me and I would ruin all my careful planning.

That I would never, ever get to open my bakery because I was a fraud and soon everyone would realize it.

It had been so long since I'd had a full-blown panic attack. Not since I'd found out that my ex-boyfriend had cheated on me. I did my best to keep the attack at bay, trying to make my breathing deep and even.

But my heart still raced, my stomach turned over, there were pains in my chest, and it kind of felt like I was going to die.

I tried to tell myself to calm down, that I was being ridiculous and overreacting, but my body did not listen.

"Are you okay?"

I shielded my eyes to look up, and a man I didn't recognize stood there, peering down at me. The sun shaded him from my view and I couldn't see him clearly. "Fine," I said between clenched teeth.

He crouched down next to me and said, "Are you having a panic attack?"

"Little bit," I managed.

"What can I do to help you?" he asked.

No one had ever asked me that before. My inclination was to tell him to go away but there actually was something he could do to help, even if it was weird. "Will you hold my hands?"

Without hesitation he offered me both of his large hands, encasing mine. His palms were warm and smooth, his fingers strong. For some reason having someone hold my hands when I was having a panic attack always made me feel grounded, and it was having that exact effect now. It was easier to catch my breath as he tethered me to the present.

I kept my gaze pointed down and gripped the man's hands tightly. "How did you know I was having a panic attack?"

"My sister used to have them. You've got this. It will pass."

His voice was calm and reassuring and just what I needed. "You're doing a great job," he added, and if I'd been able to, I would have laughed.

I was doing a terrible job of managing my emotions and anxiety. When I had an attack like this, I felt weak and pathetic. I shook my head to disagree with him. I again returned my attention to my breathing. I'd found that I could make the attack end sooner if I regulated the oxygen going in and out of my lungs.

His words were gentle and warm. "You're safe and I'll stay for as long as you need me to."

It was precisely what I needed to hear. He didn't think I was over-reacting or making it up to get attention, like my younger twin sisters had. He accepted it and encouraged me. It was so kind.

Just as he'd predicted, after a few minutes the attack subsided. My breathing evened out, the dizziness in my head went away, my chest stopped aching.

Then I made the mistake of looking up at the man who had helped me.

He had dirty-blond hair, longer on top with sun-kissed streaks. His eyes were a piercing sapphire blue, like the ocean in Aruba. He had broad shoulders with well-defined muscles in his upper arms.

And his face? It was like an Italian Renaissance artist had sculpted it and then immediately gouged his own eyes out because he knew he would never create anything better. Total symmetrical perfection—high cheekbones, strong jawline covered in stubble, sensual lips. Despite the fact that I had just spent the last few minutes getting my body back under control, my heart began to beat a fast, unsteady rhythm. A dimple formed in his left cheek when he smiled, revealing a row of perfectly white teeth.

It was like somebody had shoved an angel out of heaven and dropped him directly onto this ship.

CHAPTER TWO

Hunter

The woman crouched in front of me stared at me with her big brown eyes. I already knew her pale skin was soft from having held her hands, and she had long dark hair. I had always been a sucker for brunettes, and if we'd been at a club, I would have hit on her. There was something endearing and vulnerable about her that spoke to me, and I wanted to know more about her.

I wanted to help her.

It probably wasn't the best way to start out at a new job. If I was going to get my parents to believe in me, I had to impress them. I couldn't let myself be distracted.

Which meant I probably shouldn't have been ogling her long, lean legs.

She'd just had a major panic attack. My sister used to have them all the time. My heart twinged a little at thinking about her, like it always did.

"Does this happen pretty frequently?" I asked.

The woman stared at me for a moment before she answered. "I haven't had one in a long time. Not since my mother died two years ago."

That twinge in my heart expanded, became a dull throb of pain. I recognized the loss I heard in her voice. She let go of my hands suddenly and folded her arms against her chest.

I'd liked holding her hands but realized this would be a weird thing to admit. "I'm sorry about your mother. I lost my sister a couple of years ago, too."

There was so much sympathy in her eyes that the pain became sharper. "I'm sorry for your loss."

"Thank you," I said. Her cheeks were tearstained and it was having a strange effect on me. I reached into my pocket and handed her a handkerchief. "Here."

She held it between two fingers, like I'd just handed her a rotting carcass. "What's this for?"

I gestured at her cheeks and she flushed. I had to suppress a smile because I found her expression adorable. She mopped delicately at her face and then put the handkerchief into her own pocket. She stood up, wobbling, and I wanted to reach out and help her. I got the sense that she wouldn't have welcomed the assistance.

"Can I help you with something?" she asked. She was trying to be professional and it also struck me as cute.

I stood up as well and her eyes followed me, widening, and she took a step back. She was only a few inches shorter than me. I'd always liked taller women. "I'm Hunter Smith."

I clenched my teeth at the lie and wondered if she'd noticed. That had been part of my dad's conditions. I couldn't tell anyone my real last name. I had to be anonymous. Just part of the crew.

She cocked her head to the right, as if trying to recall something while also sizing me up. I wondered if she liked what she saw.

"Captain Carl is expecting me," I said, trying to keep the amusement out of my voice. She was attracted to me but was trying to keep it under wraps. She seemed the skittish type, though—like if I pointed it out she would jump overboard and swim away.

"Hunter Smith. Right," she said. "You're the new deckhand. Welcome. The captain is on the bridge. I'll take you to him. But you need to take your shoes off. We wear boat shoes or go barefoot on the deck. We don't want to ruin the teak."

It must have been obvious how green I was. I slipped my shoes off. "Right. Sorry."

Her gaze wandered down to my feet and then traveled up the entire length of my body. She let out a little happy sigh and I wondered if she was even aware that she had done it. Then she shook her head, as if trying to refocus. "This way."

I walked behind her and tried very hard not to notice the sway of her hips. We arrived at the bridge far too soon for my liking. I saw the captain standing in front of a navigational console, muttering to himself.

My father had explained everything to him. I hoped he wasn't about to blow my cover and ruin everything before it even started. "Hunter! You made it."

"I did." We shook hands briefly.

"Welcome aboard," Captain Carl said. "We have some rules. The first is that you don't do anything to embarrass me or embarrass the ship. I will not bail you out of prison and will only show up with a one-way plane ticket to send you back home. There is no drinking during charter, and no hookups with guests. And the new owner has instituted a rule that there won't be any sort of romantic relationship or fraternizing with your fellow crewmembers."

The last bit surprised me. I was going to have to call my father and ask what he'd been thinking. I turned around and glanced at the woman, regretful that I couldn't ask her out on a date.

"Understood," I said. I hadn't been this attracted to someone in a long time and disliked the idea that I wouldn't be able to explore the connection I felt.

"Good." The captain turned toward the girl. "You'll give him the tour, introduce him to everyone?"

"Yes. I'll do that right now." She stepped out of the room and I followed behind her. I told myself to stop looking at her but my eyes weren't obeying me.

She was off-limits and that had the unfortunate effect of making me want to pursue her even more. "You didn't tell me your name."

"Lucia Salerno. But everybody calls me Lucky," she said, glancing over her shoulder at me.

Lucky? Oh, that was just rife with possibilities for teasing. But before I could say as much, she said, "Please don't say anything about getting lucky. I've heard it all a million times before."

From this crew, no less.

"Wasn't going to." I absolutely had just been about to, but she didn't need to know that. I couldn't keep the smile off my face. "I don't think I can tease you. Especially since the captain just said that you're forbidden."

She tripped a little over her own feet, another adorable thing to add to the list. "Yes. Forbidden. As is everyone else."

I didn't care about anyone else. No one else on this ship could be anywhere near as interesting.

My dad had done this just to screw with me.

We went up to the top deck, where crewmembers were cleaning. Lucky explained that they had to chamois every surface and keep the exterior pristine because of how much damage the salt water could do.

One of the men stopped and immediately leered at Lucky. She looked disgusted and took a step away from him. It had been a long time since I'd wanted to punch someone but if he didn't stop looking at her like that I might not be responsible for my own actions.

He spoke with a French accent so thick that he sounded like a cartoon character when he said, "Belle Lucky, have you come to help us? I have an itch that I cannot quite reach. Maybe you can."

Lucky turned to me and said, "This is François. He's the first mate and sometimes engineer. He's from France and acts like he's not married with a child even though he is. He might be the reason for the new rule."

I could hear her distaste for him and hoped he was smart enough to keep his hands to himself. I had three sisters and it had always been my instinct to protect. I didn't have any right to protect Lucky but having come across her in such a vulnerable state . . . that response kicked in. I wanted to keep her safe.

Two other crewmembers joined us and Lucky continued the introductions. "This is Pieter and he's from South Africa. Kai is from New Zealand. Everyone, this is Hunter."

While I was shaking their hands, knowing I wasn't going to remember any of their names, a third man came over. "And this is Thomas, the bosun," she said.

I had no idea what a bosun was and didn't ask.

"From London," Thomas said, while pumping my hand enthusiastically. "Pleasure to meet you, mate."

I didn't get the same bad vibe from him, or the other two, as I did from the French guy.

"Where are you from?" Kai asked me. Where had Lucky said he was from? I couldn't quite place his accent.

"New York," I said.

"Another Yank! You must be happy about that," one of the crewmembers said to Lucky. She gave him a tight smile and I wondered what that was about.

I shifted my knapsack on my shoulders and Lucky said, "I should have let you put that down first thing. Let's go stow it and I'll show you to your cabin."

The bosun guy said, "Come find me after you've settled in and I'll show you the actual ropes."

That probably meant he was my boss. "I will."

Lucky took me through the ship, telling me about the rooms like I was a guest. I had to smile to myself that she couldn't appreciate the irony. But I didn't want to hear about Ming vases. I also didn't want to embarrass myself as I started this new job and sensed that she would be helpful if asked. "I'm terrible with names. Can you tell me the names of the crew again, and who is who?"

My memory had always been terrible, as had my ability to refrain from being distracted.

"François is the wannabe adulterer, short with dark hair. Pieter is the lanky guy with light brown hair. Kai is the one with the tattoos on his arm and black hair. Thomas has curly brown hair," she said.

I repeated the names to myself as we went down some stairs.

"Do I need to remind you of my name?" she asked, the teasing lilt in her voice unmistakable.

"Lucia Salerno. Lucky. It's not a name I'll ever forget." I didn't mean to flirt with her and so I felt bad when she missed the bottom step and nearly smacked into the opposite wall.

"Careful!" I said, again pressing my lips together so that I wouldn't smile. She was interested. I wouldn't be having this effect on her if she weren't. I couldn't see her face as I was behind her, and I wondered if she'd flushed that attractive shade of pink again.

We went into a tiny kitchen. She said, "This is the galley and that's our chef, Andre. He's from Brazil and makes the most incredible food you'll ever eat."

Another name. The chef glared at us and nodded as I said hello.

When we left the room, I couldn't help but lean in and whisper into her ear. "He seems pleasant."

She audibly gulped and then said in a tight, breathy voice, "He's your stereotypical temperamental culinary genius. And he's constantly aggravated because the captain won't allow him to have his parrot in the galley."

Interesting. Lucky was trying not to respond to me and couldn't seem to help herself.

"Understandable," I said with a nod, wanting to make things more comfortable for her. "That would be unsanitary."

"His parrot is named Preacher, and his favorite sound is a ringtone. He loves when he gets someone to fall for it and come into his cabin. So don't be fooled."

She was babbling just a bit. I probably shouldn't have enjoyed that, especially after the captain had explained the rules. So I tried to change the subject to something more neutral so that I wouldn't think about the curve of her neck. "Our crew is very international."

I heard the relief in her voice. "That's pretty typical for superyachts."

Lucky showed me the crew mess, where we would eat and the snacks were kept. There was a small living room that the crew shared. She turned to the right and went down a tight hallway and opened a door. "This is our room. You are on the top bunk."

Our room? That just seemed like cruel and unusual punishment. I was expected to share a room with a beautiful woman that I couldn't ever be with?

I threw my knapsack onto the top bunk and turned to face her. The room was incredibly small. Like a shoebox. It felt like if I leaned too far to one side my shoulders would hit the wall. We were practically touching just standing here and that was going to make things very difficult for me.

"We're sharing a room?" I asked. It was like locking a kid in a candy store and telling him he couldn't have any of it.

She nodded, looking a bit anxious. "I have the only empty bed. Which makes us bunkmates."

The desire to tease her, to make this not so awkward, returned. I smiled a little. "Bunkmates?" That made it sound like summer camp.

"Like I said, you on top, me on the bottom."

The image that created was like a swift kick to the gut.

Something she realized a beat later as she rushed to add, "I mean, you are in the top bunk and I'm in the bottom bunk. Separate. Not together. 'Bunkmates' doesn't mean sharing one bunk."

"Of course." Such a shame.

Lucky cleared her throat and said, "We share the closet, and the top two drawers are yours. That's the bathroom. The door locks. So you can have privacy and keep me out."

I wanted to tease her, ask her if I needed to keep myself safe from her, but sensed now was not the right time. I looked around and said, "I thought you had to be convicted of a crime to be put somewhere like this."

"It's not . . . ideal," she said and I wondered what specific part wasn't ideal for her. "I'll let you unpack. I'll be in the laundry room if you need anything."

She left in a hurry and I let out a small chuckle. The new rule probably existed because of me and my past but Lucky seemed to be taking it personally. Like I was some kind of temptation for her that she wasn't sure she could resist.

As I began emptying my knapsack, I realized two things.

One, that if she told me she was interested, I suspected that I wouldn't care about rules.

And two, these were probably going to be the longest and most frustrating six months of my life.

CHAPTER THREE

Lucky

Multiple loads of laundry were running and I grabbed the ironing board, plugging in the iron. I'd always found pressing the guests' bed-sheets had a calming effect on me, with its relaxing, repetitive motion. The feeling of accomplishment I got when the lines went smooth.

It gave me too much time to think, though.

I had told Hunter something I hadn't shared with anyone else on board, not even Georgia. I'd told him about my mother's passing. I didn't know why I had done that—what it was about him that made me want to tell him things.

I needed to figure it out, though. Because we were going to share a space that was approximately the same size as two telephone booths. Sleeping. Changing our clothes.

Showering.

The universe had apparently decided to test my willpower, because I wouldn't be allowed to kiss or date him. Then I decided it was ridic-ulous that my mind was even going there—he hadn't done anything to indicate he might be attracted to me. He definitely gave off a girl-in-every-port kind of vibe. So even if he was attracted to me, would it matter? I wouldn't want to date someone like that.

Georgia came into the laundry room. She was the kind of woman who had to fight men off with a stick. Poor Pieter was so desperately in love with her he practically swooned every time she walked by. She was petite, gorgeous, with light brown eyes and long blond hair that hung in waves. I had dark brown eyes and had inherited my nonna's thick, dark hair.

She was the kind of girl Hunter would most likely be interested in. They would be a matched set—like a real-life Malibu Barbie and Ken.

I found myself relieved that she couldn't hook up with him.

Like she'd intuited what I was thinking about, she said, "Who is the new yachtie hottie? To quote Popeye the Sailor, blow me down."

I should have known Georgia's man radar would ping and that she had managed to catch sight of him already.

"His name is Hunter. He's a deckhand." I was now officially pre-annoyed because I knew where this was about to go.

"Hunter," she repeated, musing. "What does he hunt? I would happily lie down in front of him and let him catch me."

So would I. I pushed the steamer button on the iron and pressed down harder.

She kept talking. "I should take him on a tour of the ship. Do you think he'd let me show him the bow thruster? Or the cockpit? I'd let him lash me to the mast."

"I've already given him the tour," I said, my tone a bit sharper than I'd intended.

"I'll bet you did," she said with a grin and hopped up onto the counter. As the new chief stew, I probably should have told her to get to work but I didn't. Giving directions to the stews, who were now officially under me, felt uncomfortable.

"He's so tall and big," she added with a sigh. "What size shoe does he wear?"

Her question caught me off guard. "I don't know. Why would I know that?"

"Don't you have to order his uniform from the provisioner?"

I did. I had completely forgotten.

"You know what they say about men with large feet," she said while waggling her eyebrows at me.

That annoyance surged again while I tried to tamp it down. "He's nice, too."

"So? Why would that matter?"

"I'm glad you're respectfully objectifying him," I responded.

"I try," she said with a shrug. "Do you think he'd let me respectfully objectify him later tonight?"

"What?" I asked in shock.

She started swinging her legs. "If he was my bunkmate, neither one of us would sleep until the season ended. Do you want to trade?"

While it might have been better for my peace of mind to have Hunter in a different cabin, I did not trust Georgia with him. Perhaps it was because he'd been kind to me but I felt like I owed him now.

Or maybe I was just jealous and didn't want Georgia to have him.

I decided the first reason sounded nobler and so settled on that one and then tried to change the subject. "I thought you were interested in Thomas."

She made a pshaw sound. "If that man ever had an original thought, it would die of loneliness."

Georgia wasn't wrong. Thomas was a hard worker and good at his job but he'd never struck me as particularly bright.

"You know how sea goggles work," she went on. "Men who are a four on land are a nine at sea because there's no other options. At least there weren't any until Hunter showed up. That man's a ten everywhere."

A ten? He was more like a twenty.

"Plus, Thomas doesn't know what to do with a woman once he has her. Hunter looks like he majored in it and graduated with honors."

Again, I wanted to fervently agree until I remembered where we were. Given the kind of luck I was having today, the captain was going to stroll by while Georgia was making inappropriate comments and we'd both get fired. I went over to close the door.

She jumped off the counter when she realized what I was doing. "No, wait!"

Then I saw the reason she was trying to stop me. There was a piece of paper taped to the back of the door. "What's this?"

At the top in Georgia's handwriting: *The sCrew List*, oh so cleverly combining the words *screw* and *crew*. Just below that she had written the number *100* and circled it.

She didn't have to tell me what it was because it was self-explanatory. All the male crewmembers were listed with numbers next to them. "Are these points?" I asked.

"Yes."

"How could you have this up already?" The crew meeting had only happened a little while ago.

Georgia didn't even have the decency to look embarrassed. "I work fast when I'm motivated."

"Did you not hear Captain Carl and the new rule?"

At that her eyes narrowed and I recognized that look. "I heard him fine." She hated being told what to do and had a very loose relationship with following rules.

Unlike me, who lived for them.

"The only people who ever shut the laundry room door are the stews. No one else is going to see it," she said, as if that made it better.

"Was this your idea?"

"Emilie and I came up with it together."

I should have known that it was both of them. I was pretty sure that cannibals were less man hungry than those two.

And Emilie and Georgia made some bad decisions when left to their own devices.

Like posting a list with points for sleeping with crewmembers.

"This is why two blondes don't make a right," I muttered and she just grinned at me. Then I noticed the name on the bottom. "You have Captain Carl on here."

"Yeah, I do. He is a sexy, sexy man. Anybody who can single-handedly control a one-hundred-and-fifty-foot superyacht deserves to be on this list, and I'm sorry you can't see it."

"The captain is married and has a son the same age as you."

Another shrug. "What can I say? I have daddy issues. But you'll see that we gave him fifty points because of the unlikelihood of it happening. Especially with his new rule."

I sighed. "François has a negative number next to his name."

"We should lose points if we sleep with him. Too easy and gross."

She wasn't wrong. That guy was a three-time gold medalist in the Jerk Olympics. "This list is going to get you fired."

"Only if I get caught, which I won't."

Such an unwise thing to do, but both she and Emilie were adults and could make their own truly terrible decisions.

Georgia moved around me and added Hunter's name to the bottom of the list and gave him twenty-five points.

There was a strange surge in my gut that felt a bit like jealousy and I immediately pushed it down. I couldn't afford to get fired, so there was no chance that anything could happen between Hunter and me.

"What do you get if you reach a hundred points?" I couldn't help but ask.

"Besides the physical satisfaction that I'm assuming I'll personally receive? Probably an indeterminate prize of very little value. We haven't decided yet."

I could feel my anxiety welling up inside me at what she and Emilie were planning on doing, what they were risking for nothing. I reminded my swirling stomach that this wasn't my issue.

"You could join us," she said.

I let out a short bark of laughter. "You know that's not me. I don't break rules and I don't hook up with people. I've only had like, two boyfriends."

"This week?"

"No, ever."

A look of pure horror crossed her features. "I've had a million! The key is to lower your standards. The lower your standards, the higher your average. Although that might not work with you. Someone told me once that the smarter a woman is, the harder it is for her to find a man."

"That's sexist." After a beat I added, "And I must be a genius."

Now it was her turn to laugh. "You don't see your own value, Lucky. As your name suggests, every man on this ship would be lucky to be with you."

I tried not to roll my eyes and instead just shook my head.

"What?" she demanded.

"With all your plotting and rule-breaking, I'm just wondering how you sleep at night."

"Hopefully not alone," she teased. "But usually some combination of wine and sleeping pills."

I was glad the door was shut. I knew she was joking but somebody else might not realize it.

She slid the pen back into her skort pocket and said, "I have some dust to vanquish in the primary cabin."

"I would say 'have fun,' but we both know neither one of us will." Being a stew on a yacht was exhausting, backbreaking work, but the money made up for it.

When she was gone I found myself thinking that her and Emilie's plan to hook up with as many crewmembers as possible was something Marika was going to have to deal with until the moment I remembered that I was the new Marika. It was my responsibility.

My anxiety flared up again because I didn't know how to tell my friend to knock it off. I had the worried feeling that this might become an issue and hoped that none of this would blow back on me.

Speaking of responsibilities, Hunter needed a uniform.

When I returned to our cabin, I didn't know if I should knock or just enter. It was also my room, but would it be more appropriate to give him some sort of heads-up?

Before I could decide, the door opened and Hunter stood there. My heart sped up and I didn't know if it was my concern over Georgia's game plan or being near him again. "Lucky, you're back!"

I told myself to ignore his gorgeous smile and piercing eyes and be calm and collected and treat him like every other person on board. "I need your shoe size," I blurted out.

Wow. Great job.

Given his quizzical expression I quickly offered an explanation. "I need to order your uniform."

He said he wore a slim extra large and size fourteen in shoes.

Georgia was going to pass out.

I sent a text to the provisioner and she immediately responded that she'd have it sent over the next morning. I told him as much.

The next thing I knew, Hunter was taking my phone from my hands. I was so surprised that I initially didn't react.

Finally I managed to say, "What are you doing?"

He finished up and gave it back to me. "You said I could ask you if I needed anything, and I thought it'd be easier if I could text you instead of traipsing around the ship trying to find you."

While that logically made sense, the only thing I could think was that I had Hunter's number and that already-crushing teen girl inside me was giddy.

"I should go find . . . Thomas, right?" he asked.

"Yes. Down the hall, up the stairs, and you'll see the deck from there."

"I remember how to get there. Directions I'm good with. It's just names that give me some difficulty, Lucky Salerno." He winked at me and every bone in my body dissolved. I had to lean against the wall for support.

Georgia and Emilie were wrong.

Hunter Smith was worth a lot more than twenty-five points.

CHAPTER FOUR

Lucky

There was always more to do than we had time for on the yacht. It was easy to get caught up in my never-ending to-do list and I tried hard to push thoughts of Hunter away but was unsuccessful. I kept glancing out of windows hoping to catch sight of him.

When there were no guests on board, our workday ended at six o'clock. Everybody headed downstairs to the crew mess, where Andre had prepared us a Thai-inspired meal that smelled divine. My stomach grumbled loudly as I followed the scent.

The crew mess had two side-by-side tables with a long wraparound bench for us to sit on, like a booth at a restaurant. I was one of the last to arrive and almost everyone else was already eating. I grabbed a plate and sat down next to Pieter, who was slurping up noodles while also keeping his puppy dog eyes on Georgia, who was whispering something to Kai.

Poor Pieter.

And maybe this was the reason for the new rule. We didn't need the drama and distraction that inevitably accompanied romantic entanglements among the crew.

My heart did not get the memo, though, and nearly beat out of my chest when Hunter came into the room with Thomas.

That thumping got worse when Hunter sat down next to me, on the very edge of the bench. There really wasn't room and I had to scoot over to accommodate him. His broad shoulders very nearly touched mine.

"Hi," he said with a smile, and my throat closed in on itself, preventing me from responding.

He didn't seem to notice and started eating. I was busy watching the way his mouth moved as he ate, admiring the lines in his throat when he swallowed, memorizing the appreciative noise he made when he tasted his food.

I forced my eyes forward, well aware of my own patheticness. Then his right knee brushed against mine and my kneecaps started melting like they were made of ice and he was a blowtorch. My nerves jangled and I could feel my leg tingling. I expected him to apologize and move his leg away but he didn't.

Like he wasn't even aware that he'd done it.

I was having some kind of physical and existential crisis over here and he was oblivious.

That felt like a very obvious indication that he was not interested in me. That he could touch me and not even be aware of it.

I wanted to groan. It had been way too long since I'd been on a date, given how I was overreacting to something so small and innocuous.

Everyone continued to chat and eat, and by all accounts it was just a typical crew dinner.

I was the only one being weird.

Despite my best efforts not to, I couldn't help but watch Hunter out of the corner of my eye. It was like everything he did fascinated me. He took a second helping and all of his attention was focused on demolishing his food. I felt a little lightheaded as I imagined what it must be like to have him concentrating all his energy on me.

"Are you not hungry?" Hunter asked, his voice rumbling from deep in his chest, surprising me.

Yes, I was hungry. Just not for food. Which was the problem. "I'm full."

"Should we go upstairs and have a beer?" Thomas asked the group, and almost everyone enthusiastically agreed. The captain didn't mind if we had a couple of drinks the night before a charter so long as we were bright-eyed and bushy-tailed the next morning and ready to work.

As everyone stood up and cleared their plates, I considered my options. I could hide out in my cabin and avoid everyone. That was my first inclination. I'd always been a fan of the run-and-hide method for dealing with my problems.

But I knew it would be worse if I didn't go. I was supposed to be watching over both Hunter and Emilie and I couldn't do that from inside my cabin.

Plus, I had to figure out a way to keep Georgia and Emilie from trying to score points from their list, and the only way to rain on their parade was with my actual presence.

I had a blue ribbon in being a wet blanket.

"Are you coming?" Hunter asked as he stood up, and I nodded, getting my plate.

We went into the galley and Georgia took our plates so that she could scrub them. Pieter had put himself on drying duty in order to stand next to her.

"Hunter, help me bring this ice chest upstairs!" Thomas called out. Hunter went over to help.

I headed abovedeck and Kai was right behind me. We walked in silence to the sundeck, where Hunter and Thomas were setting up the drinks. I sat down on one of the outdoor couches. Kai grabbed a couple of bottles of beer and came over to where I was sitting. He offered me one but I waved it away. Given the precarious state my hormones were in, I needed to keep all my wits about me. My body did not need the excuse to act out inappropriately.

Kai sank down next to me, opening his bottle and taking a deep swig. He sighed and leaned back.

"I've never seen you so flustered by someone before," he said, nodding his head in Hunter's direction.

"I'm not flustered," I denied, far too quickly, judging by the smile on Kai's face. "It's just . . . he's new. And I'm unaccustomed to him."

That sounded weak even to my own ears.

"He's definitely green," he said.

"I know. I felt his hands," I responded and realized too late how that sounded.

"You what?" He was far too entertained. Kai had been on the ship since I'd arrived and it had always amused him that I was the only crewmember not trying to find a one-night stand in every port we partied in.

Something he never had an issue with.

"It's not what you think."

"You don't know what I'm thinking," he said from over the top of his beer bottle before he took another drink.

I let out a sigh of annoyance. I did not have to explain myself to Kai. "You know what the rules are."

"I do. But rules are made to be broken."

"Rules are made to be kept and followed or else the entire world devolves into anarchy and chaos," I retorted and Kai laughed.

There was a prickly, heated feeling at the base of my neck and I turned to see Hunter watching me. He had a bottle in his hand and was seated on the couch across from us, with Emilie on one side and Thomas on the other.

"Well, hopefully your man will catch on quickly. He tried today but we don't really give gold stars for effort here. Captain might get rid of him if he's not up to the task."

Why did that make me feel like someone had plunged an ice pick into my chest? It might be a good thing for my weak will if Hunter had to leave. Would Captain Carl really send him packing if he couldn't meet the ship's standards?

Thinking of Hunter being fired turned my thoughts back to Georgia and Emilie's list. I briefly toyed with the idea of telling the captain about it but worried I'd only make myself look bad. Like I couldn't handle my junior stews.

It seemed better to pretend that I knew nothing about it and keep my head down and just work hard.

Lots and lots of hard work and no thinking about Hunter.

But it didn't help matters that I was so aware of where he was the entire time. Who he was talking to, the way he smiled, and how his eyes danced when someone said something he liked. The rich, deep sound of his laughter and how I wished that I were the reason for it.

This was so, so bad.

I had to find a way to get a grip. I blamed my anxiety spiral from earlier for putting me into a vulnerable emotional state. I would feel this way about anybody who had tried to assist me. If it had been François, I would have . . .

Nope. I couldn't finish the lie. I would have sent François away. I would have sent all of them away, including Georgia. I wouldn't have let any of the crew see me like that.

I didn't know why I had let Hunter stay.

Emilie leaned her whole body toward Hunter while Thomas told him some story that had the bosun gesturing wildly. My blood pressure rose when Emilie moved in and put her hand on Hunter's upper thigh.

But without making a spectacle or drawing attention to it, he gently took her arm by the wrist and put her hand back on her own lap in one smooth, fluid motion.

I could see the shock on her face from here. Emilie was also very blond and very pretty and I was fairly certain that this was the first time she had ever been rejected.

She did not seem to be enjoying the experience.

It probably wasn't a good thing that I was.

Because my job now was to find a way to put Hunter into the "friend" and "coworker" categories in my mind and keep him there.

It was just hard when he looked like he should have been walking the red carpet in Cannes instead of cleaning the yacht sitting in the Old Port.

François called Kai over. Kai stood up and then said to me, "He keeps looking at you, in case you were wondering."

Now I knew my cheeks were red because I could feel my face heating. Kai smiled again and went to see what the first mate wanted.

The idea of Hunter stealing glances at me should not have filled me with so much hope.

Kai's empty spot was immediately filled by Georgia. She let out a loud sigh. "Hunter is so pretty. Mother, may I?"

"No, you may not."

"You're not my mother," she said and then added, "You don't understand. I need him biblically. Or as they say, in a way that will be concerning to feminism."

"I—" How could I respond? I couldn't reprimand her when I was over here thinking the same kinds of thoughts.

"He seems like the kind of guy who would willingly sacrifice himself for the noble cause of female hedonism, right?"

I hope so.

François came over, strumming on a guitar. "Do you have any requests?" he asked, trying to make deep eye contact with Georgia.

"Do you know 'Not Now' or 'Go Away'?" she retorted.

He took her words in stride with a smile and walked over to where Hunter and Emilie sat with Thomas.

She went right back to her soliloquy on Hunter. "It's fine. He'll be mine once I break out the heavy artillery. I'm going to hit him with both barrels."

There was a long pause before she added, "Unless there's something you want to tell me."

I couldn't even protest that I didn't know what she was talking about. She was giving me an opening. Admit that I had an unsuitable crush on our newest deckhand. It wasn't a big leap. Even Kai had noticed.

But I wasn't interested in staking a claim.

"You should get rid of that list and do what Captain Carl asks," I settled on. At least it would allow me to ease my guilty conscience. I would keep quiet and let her make her own decisions but I didn't have to be party to it.

"We both know that's not going to happen," she said with a grin. "Time for me to get my weapons ready."

She stood and pushed her shoulders back. Given the predatory looks on both her and Emilie's faces, it was like a sickly gazelle had accidentally wandered into the lair of a couple of starving lionesses.

"I'm going to bed," I announced, not sure if anyone even heard me over François's singing and their general merriment and seduction plans.

It was still very early in the evening but I did not need to witness Georgia making her move.

Mostly because I was worried about what I might do to try to stop her.

CHAPTER FIVE

Hunter

Lucky had been watching me. It hadn't been my imagination or wishful thinking. And it seemed like it had been against her will, like she was trying not to. When she disappeared a part of me hoped that it was some kind of silent invitation.

I tried to figure out just how long I had to wait before following her down to our cabin without appearing creepy. I would much rather hang with her than anyone else here, but I (1) didn't want to freak her out and (2) had to follow that idiotic nonfraternization rule.

The rules didn't say that she and I couldn't be friends. Who couldn't use another friend?

I just had to be sure that I didn't think too much about how we'd met. There was a switch in me that flipped when I saw someone in need. Especially someone dealing with the same issues my sister Harper had. My heart twinged as I thought of her. I wondered if the grief of losing her would ever go away.

Our cabin was empty, which surprised me. Maybe I had misread the situation and she wasn't interested. I wondered where she had wandered off to but decided I was not going to be a stalker and would not go looking for her.

Instead I got ready for bed and climbed into my bunk. I pulled the blanket up to my chest and started scrolling through my phone. I knew I was completely addicted—one of my therapists had told me that social media gave people with ADHD hits of dopamine. I supposed that was one good thing about coming here. I couldn't compulsively be on my phone all day.

Then the other good thing about being here walked in through our door.

"Hi," she said, sounding nervous. Her gaze kept dipping down to my shoulders. Did she like what she saw or was she bothered that I didn't have a shirt on?

"Hey." I put my phone down. She was far more interesting. "I thought you said you were going to bed."

I grimaced. She was definitely going to think I was a stalker.

Her gaze came back up to my face and she flushed slightly, like she was embarrassed that she'd been staring. Interesting.

"I was. I am." She fumbled her words and I thought her flustered reaction was adorable.

"Where have you been?"

"I was fixing the guest cabins. Emilie didn't do a very good job. There's clean and then there's superyacht clean. Every surface has to be polished, buffed, and detailed to the highest degree possible. There was dust everywhere. Streaks on the shower door. The gold-plated fixtures hadn't been properly dried, which could lead to serious damage." She sucked in a deep breath. "Sorry. I'm not a gossipy kind of person. She just gives me twice as much work to do."

Friends. I could do this. "Why don't you say something to her?"

"It doesn't do much good."

I heard her collapse onto her own bunk.

"Couldn't you speak to the captain?"

"No, because she's his niece. He wants us to rehabilitate her and teach her how to work, and so far she spends all of her time on her phone and she's completely exhausting and I have no idea how I'm supposed to motivate or teach her. She's so unreliable. She's like an airline in person form."

I stuck my phone under my thigh, making sure I wouldn't accidentally pick it up since it bothered her. I wasn't sure what to say and so I decided to channel my therapist. "That sounds rough."

"I'm sorry. I shouldn't be complaining to you. That's not the kind of person I am."

"No, you seem like the kind of person who likes to bottle things up until you have a panic attack."

My teasing worked and she laughed. The sound made my chest feel warm. "Thank you. I needed to laugh."

"I aim to please."

Then I didn't let my brain get distracted by the many ways that I could offer to please Lucky. It was entirely inappropriate.

She didn't respond and suddenly stood, grabbed something from her drawer, and went into the bathroom. Was that a hint to leave her alone?

The only thing that distracted me more than my phone was a pretty girl, and Lucky was gorgeous. I'd already seen that French guy make a pass at her. I wondered if she spent her time pushing men overboard after they hit on her.

My phone buzzed under my leg. I pulled it out and saw a message from my mom. It was another long explanation as to why they thought I wasn't responsible enough to start up a residential center in Harper's memory, that they loved me and wanted to support me, but given my track record . . .

It wasn't anything I hadn't heard a million times before.

Lucky came back out of the bathroom in an old T-shirt and flannel pajama bottoms that somehow made her look even sexier than she had in that little skort, and it was like getting kicked in the stomach. I forced my gaze to stay on my phone.

"Are you okay if I turn out the lights?" she asked.

I would be okay with her doing any number of things, but instead I just answered, "Yes."

She climbed into her bunk and I let my phone fall into my lap so that I could put my hands over my eyes. I was hyperaware of where she was in the darkness and wanted to make things okay between us again. To get back to that friendly vibe.

"Were you avoiding me earlier?" I asked. Better to get straight to the point.

She answered my question with a question. "Why would I avoid you?"

Still avoiding. Intriguing.

Maybe Lucky didn't want us to be just friends.

No other way to find out than to step up to bat and swing away. "It seemed like you were watching me up on deck and then you were just gone."

It took a few beats, but then she said, "Captain Carl asked me to keep an eye on you."

I couldn't resist teasing her. "Just an eye? Is there anything else you wanted to put on me?"

Please say yes, an inner voice chanted, and I told it to shut up.

Her voice was high and tight and tinged with regret. "No, thank you."

I couldn't help but laugh. It sounded like she'd had to convince herself to turn my joking invitation down. I should probably change the subject. "Which one is Emilie again?"

"The one who tried to grope you earlier."

"Ah." I'd never had an issue getting feminine attention but that had been overkill. "That gathering tonight made me feel a little like fresh meat being tossed into a lion's den."

She didn't answer. Had it bothered her? I probably shouldn't have hoped that it did.

I also didn't want her to stop talking so I said the first thing that popped in my head. "Georgia seems nice."

She sounded a little deflated when she responded. "She is. We're friends. But I can tell you she has a problem following rules and has no filter. Which is probably why the captain didn't offer her the chief stew position. She can only fake her happiness for so long before she says something blunt to a guest."

I knew that they were friends but there was a definite note of jealousy this time. Did she think I was attracted to Georgia? I wasn't.

Then she added, "She's the best but she is absolutely that friend you have to explain to people before you introduce them and then apologize for afterward."

I laughed and I liked that Lucky was funny. "And now you're the one in charge of them."

"Not by choice. Our former chief stew ran off in the middle of the night to go marry her noncommittal boyfriend and the captain decided to promote me instead of replacing her. And I don't know if I'm going to do a good job of it." She paused to let out a deep breath. "I'm a hard worker but delegation's not really my strong point. I'd rather just do the work myself."

"Fiercely independent?"

"By necessity, yes." She stopped herself and I wondered what she'd been about to confess. She went back to what we'd been talking about. "Being in charge of them is a challenge I'm not quite sure I'm up for. It's like trying to herd kittens. Cute and sweet but they totally ignore you, and if you leave them to their own devices, they will get into things they shouldn't and claw stuff up."

I could definitely see that. "So how do you herd kittens?"

"The only way I know how is to set the example. Which means that I have to follow the rules and do whatever the captain and the guests ask of me and hope that Georgia and Emilie will do the same."

Wow. Message received. She couldn't have been clearer. I told my bruised ego it wasn't an actual rejection. That she was just very invested in doing her job well. I understood that. I was trying to do the same thing.

I tried to keep the disappointment out of my voice. "I see."

But then I realized that she had just revealed something important about herself. I wanted to understand her better. "Rules are important to you, aren't they? I thought I heard you saying something to . . ." What was that dude's name? "I want to say Kai."

"Yes, Kai," she confirmed.

"You told Kai that you think rules are important so that the world doesn't devolve into chaos."

"I did tell him that."

Rules had never been my thing, but it sounded like they made her happy. Maybe that would be a strong enough incentive to behave. "I respect that."

I might not have liked it, but I would respect it.

"And," I added, "you can do this. Herd kittens. I have faith in you."

It felt like she needed the boost.

Which she confirmed with the way she said, "Thank you."

"You're welcome. Good night, Lucky."

"Good night, Hunter."

I heard her roll over and I stared up at the ceiling above me.

When I had agreed to this, no one had mentioned that I would be sharing a room with a tempting, sexy woman who made me laugh, and who I admired and respected. I wondered if my parents had done this deliberately. To make sure I failed.

Because if there was anyone who could distract me from what I wanted to accomplish, I suspected it would be Lucky Salerno.

CHAPTER SIX

Lucky

When my alarm beeped the next morning, I quickly shut it off. Hunter was lightly snoring above me and it made me smile.

Not so perfect after all.

Nope, couldn't let my thoughts go there. I had just been feeling vulnerable yesterday. I would get over it. I would get used to his flawless face and we would be fine.

I kept running last night's conversation through my head. It had seemed like Hunter cared whether or not I was willing to break rules. I decided it was due to my overwrought imagination and to stop interpreting our interactions through my touch-deprived filter. I'd just been out of the dating scene for so long that I was no longer fluent in subtext and could easily misunderstand.

The best thing for me to do would be to throw myself into mindless cleaning and burn off my inappropriate feelings with hours of physical labor.

But then I stood up and saw him. He was curled on his side in a ball with his blanket tucked in around him. His hair was messy and his expression soft. It was one of the most endearing things I'd ever seen and the sight of him knocked the wind out of my sails.

I found myself reaching out to push back some hair that had fallen over his eyes. I immediately retracted my hand, told my percolating hormones to stop their unbridled ogling, and whirled around, grabbing my clean uniform from the closet.

As I got ready for the day, I kept telling myself that this was because so much had changed so quickly. I was now chief stew, we had a new charter season starting, new owners of the boat—everything was different.

There was upheaval and uncertainty. It made sense that I would be reaching out to hold on to something just to anchor myself. Someone who had been nice and helpful.

That's all it was—nothing more.

I went into the laundry room and started multiple loads, throwing in Hunter's handkerchief, and then headed over to the galley, where Andre was already prepping for the day. Captain Carl had gone over the guests' preference sheets with us and I was pleased to see that Andre would be catering to their pescatarian wishes.

We were welcoming Robert and Donna Carmine in honor of Donna's seventy-fifth birthday. Robert was a movie studio executive and they had attended the film festival in Cannes. They would be celebrating her birthday here on the yacht with four friends. They had requested a pink and gold theme for the party and I'd already put in a call to the provisioner for decorations and costumes for the stews.

I reminded Andre about the cake and he made a growling sound. Most yacht chefs despised baking. I would've offered to make it for him but he would have taken that as an insult to his culinary skills. I scooted off to the stew pantry because it was in dire need of cleaning and reorganizing before the guests arrived.

Thomas found me while I was cleaning the coffee maker. "Have you seen Hunter?"

Frowning, I put my cloth down. "He was still in bed when I got up."

"He's not in his cabin. I forgot to give him a radio yesterday. If you see him, tell him to come find me so that we can get that sorted and discuss the schedule."

"I will."

Thomas will find him, I told myself. I didn't have to get involved. The bosun was more than capable of tracking Hunter down.

But I didn't listen.

I found Hunter in the gym, where he was doing pull-ups on a high bar. The way his muscles flexed and contracted in his arms stole my breath.

And unfortunately for me, he noticed me before I had a chance to stop staring.

"Hey, Lucky! Are you here to work out?" He hopped down and walked toward me. He had on a tank top and I realized that I could have built my entire life on those perfect, broad shoulders of his and I swallowed hard. The closer he got to me, the drier my mouth became.

All I could think about was the way he'd said "I aim to please" last night and how my overwhelming lust had urged me to climb up into his bunk and drape myself over him.

I hoped that he'd never say those words in front of Georgia, because she would try to prove the veracity of his statement.

Much as I wanted to do right now.

Then I realized how long I had gone without responding and it made me finally able to speak. "Not allowed!"

"What's not allowed?" Why did that sound like an invitation?

I had to clear my throat to keep talking. I made sure to keep my eyes trained on his so that his muscles would stop distracting me.

But his face was every bit as distracting.

I shifted from one leg to the other, tapping the fingers of my right hand against my leg. "We can't work out in the gym during a charter. It's off-limits for us. Only the guests can use it."

Did I sound nonchalant? Probably not, because I was feeling overly chalant at the moment.

He threw a towel around his neck. "Technically the charter hasn't started yet."

That he was the kind of man who would be looking for technicalities to avoid following rules was not good. I was afraid I'd be too willing to jump on board. "It will start in a few hours. Thomas is looking for you. He has your radio and wants to discuss your schedule. And your uniform should be here soon."

"Aye, aye," he said with a salute that was somehow adorable. "I'll have to figure something else out then when we have a charter. I have ADHD and exercising to burn off excess energy is helpful."

I had to press my lips into a thin line because my body wanted me to offer alternative ways to burn off excess energy, perhaps together. Instead I said, "One of my younger sisters has ADHD."

"Then you get it," he said with his dazzling smile and I felt weak-kneed. "I'm just focusing on getting myself shipshape."

I couldn't help but let out a small groan. "Please tell me I don't have a bunkmate who is a fan of nautical puns."

"Well, I could tell you that but then I'd be lying." He smiled at me again and there was this moment between us, this pulse that seemed to envelop me.

I wondered if he felt it, too.

Then I noticed a bead of sweat running down his right temple. It should have been a turnoff but it was not. Without thinking I reached out and took the edge of the towel still on his neck and patted the spot dry.

"You're sweaty." I whispered the words and then immediately let the towel drop. I wanted nothing more than to touch his skin, to taste the saltiness of it. To have him press his slightly damp body against mine.

He seemed to move closer, like he was leaning toward me. His gaze slipped down to my lips and he flexed his hands at his sides. Like he was going to reach for me. Then he seemingly changed his mind as he cleared his throat and said, "Right. I'll go shower and then find Thomas."

He left and I was so caught up in images of him standing under a stream of water that I didn't register what he'd said. That wasn't really how things worked here—he should have gone and found Thomas first and then worried about showering. Chain of command and all that.

But at the moment that was not my primary concern.

I told myself for what seemed like the millionth time that nothing could happen between me and Hunter.

This was going to be the longest season ever if I couldn't remember that.

~

There were approximately five bajillion things to do before the charter guests arrived, and I caught Emilie on her phone in one of the guest cabins and not doing the tasks I had assigned to her.

"We need to work together as a team," I told her. Because now I was going to have to come behind her and fix all of this. Georgia was upstairs working on the guest communal areas and couldn't help me.

"Oh, I agree," she said with fake enthusiasm. "Just tell me what I need to do and I'll get it done."

That was a lie but I figured it was probably safer for my current career if I didn't say as much. I didn't need her tattling to the captain that I was being mean to her. "Please go make sure the crystal bowls are filled with candy and nuts in the main salon. Then head to the laundry room and after you get some more loads going, do a quick clean of the crew mess."

Her expression dropped and she didn't try to hide her annoyance. "Everybody uses the crew mess. We should all have to help clean it."

My internal temperature began to rise. Everyone did clean up after themselves but it was specifically the duty of the interior crew to do the deeper cleaning.

And things were different before, when Emilie had just been an extra set of hands. It didn't really matter if she didn't pull her own weight because the rest of us could manage fine without her.

But now we were in a position where she had to complete the daily tasks I'd assigned to her or it was going to seriously affect me and Georgia.

"That's what I need you to do," I said, trying to mimic what Marika would have said if she'd still been here. She probably would have been a lot harsher but I hated hurting people's feelings. I tried to avoid it as much as possible.

"Fine," she said, not bothering to pull her false enthusiasm back up again. She walked off, still typing on her phone. I had to hope she would do what I asked because I would be the one Captain Carl would come down on if things weren't done properly.

The next couple of hours flew by quickly—we loaded on provisions and Georgia helped me get everything I'd ordered put away. I left Hunter's various uniforms on his bunk and radioed him that they had arrived.

Instead of responding over the walkie-talkie, he texted me.

Thanks for bringing that to my yacht-tention.

The smile that broke out on my face was immediate and unexpected. Kai happened to be walking by and he raised both of his eyebrows at me.

"Hunter?" he correctly guessed but I just shook my head at him. He let out a laugh and went abovedeck.

Getting the text was nice because another message came in immediately after that from my sister Lily.

Chauncy needs surgery and the vet says it's going to be like five hundred bucks. Can I borrow that from you? I promise to pay it back!

Lily usually promised to pay me back. She never had but at least she made the effort, unlike Rose, who just asked for the money.

My fingers hesitated above the keys on my cell, and for a brief second I considered telling her that I was not going to send her money.

But I was all my sisters had. I missed the way our relationship had been before our mother had died. We had just been a family then and now I felt like I was little more than an ATM to them. I sent her the money via an app and slipped my phone into my pocket. I went to check on Emilie, and to the surprise of absolutely no one, she was taking selfies and sending them to people and only one dryer was running.

"Did you finish up Captain Carl's formal shirt?" I asked. The captain had specifically asked me about it right after I'd finished putting away the provisions. He was expecting it for the guest arrival.

"It's in the dryer," she said, not even looking up from her phone.

Which would mean it still needed to be pressed. "You need to get more laundry going. These machines should be constantly running all day."

But when I opened the dryer door, I saw that everything was covered in streaks of blue.

Including the captain's shirt. I held it up and Emilie finally stopped typing long enough to look at me. "What?"

Could she not see the stains? "Did you check the pockets before you put everything in the washing machine?"

I had told her approximately thirty times to do just that. It was one of the first rules when it came to doing laundry. There must have been a pen in somebody's pocket. Probably the captain's.

She rolled her eyes. "I don't have time to go through every single pocket. I'd never get any laundry done."

Given the empty machines, she wasn't getting any laundry done now, either. Swallowing back my anger, I reached into the dryer and began pulling out linen napkins. All ruined.

The one positive was that the captain had another dress shirt and we had extra table linens. I could order replacements. I'd go up to his cabin and get his dirty one and launder it myself. Maybe he wouldn't even notice and he'd never have to know what his niece had done.

But despite my name, luck never quite seemed to be on my side.

The captain came into the laundry room. "Is that my shirt?"

CHAPTER SEVEN

Lucky

Captain Carl reached over and took the shirt out of my hands. "What happened?"

It would be so easy to throw Emilie under the bus. She was the one responsible, after all. But when I saw the stricken look on her face, I remembered what the captain always told us—the buck stopped with me. I was her department head and it was my job to train her.

If she didn't listen, unfortunately, that was on me as well.

"That's my fault. I'm sorry," I said. "I'll order you a new one."

He gave me a disapproving look, one saying that I had let him down.

My anxiety spiked, jangling my nerves, and I started envisioning exactly what he would say when he fired me, as he was so obviously going to do now.

But all he said was, "Let me know when the new one arrives."

I let out a sigh of relief. "I will. Thank you. And it won't happen again."

The captain nodded and headed toward the galley.

Emilie said, "I so owe you one."

"Just be sure to always check the pockets from now on," I reminded her. My adrenaline began to dissipate, causing my limbs to feel hollow but jittery. I tried to focus on some deep breathing so that I could calm down.

It didn't work well but I still held out hope that someday I'd become a breathing expert and would be able to prevent myself from getting so wound up and upset.

"I will," she promised. "I will always check the pockets. And I'll get some more laundry going."

Hopefully fear of her uncle would help get Emilie in line. It also occurred to me that I had something I could hold over her head now. While I didn't know all the details of why she had joined the *Mio Tesoro*, I knew she was worried her family would cut her off financially. Working for Captain Carl was her last chance.

I'd never much liked rich people but technically Emilie was poor now so I could make an exception.

I dug through the piles of clean laundry on the countertops until I found Hunter's handkerchief. I needed to return it to him.

Even though part of me was urging me to keep it as some kind of weird souvenir.

That made it more imperative for me to give it back.

The few hours we had left flew by in a haze of cleaning and prepping. A new shirt for the captain arrived at the dock. There was going to be a hefty surcharge but I was grateful it had arrived. As soon as I gave it to him, he radioed the rest of the crew to tell everyone to change into our whites, or our formal white dress uniform shirts. The men would put on dark slacks and the women would wear black skorts.

I stopped by Emilie's room to tell her that I needed her to prepare a tray of champagne for the Carmines and their guests. Still eager to please after this morning's incident, she assured me she would take care of it.

When I got to my own cabin, I realized that I needed to shave my legs. My dark hair grew so quickly and was very noticeable against my fair skin. I went into the bathroom and grabbed a razor and shaving cream and put my leg into the sink.

I lathered up my left leg and had shaved about half of it when the bathroom door suddenly swung open, nearly hitting me.

Hunter stood there and his gaze quickly settled on my leg, following the line from ankle to knee.

"Oh," he said. "Sorry. I didn't realize you were in here."

That tension was back, the one that made me feel like the air around us was electrified and I was waiting for the moment I would get zapped. "I should have locked it."

He continued to look at my leg and then shook his head, as if remembering himself. "Right. Sorry."

Then he closed the door.

I stood there with my razor pointed up in the air. Had that just happened? There was no mistaking where his eyes had lingered. But had that just been from his surprise at finding me that way? He saw my legs all the time. Our skorts were very short.

Why would this be any different?

There didn't seem to be any other alternative but to chalk it up to my heated imagination. I couldn't let myself get caught up in such flights of fancy, like that Hunter had been overcome by his lust at the mere sight of my half-shaved leg and was doing all he could to restrain himself.

Ridiculous.

When I finished up and came out into the cabin, he was gone. I noted that his bed had been made, while my covers were still wadded up at the foot of my bunk, like always. I quickly changed my uniform top and grabbed a scrunchie for my hair.

I had taken a bit longer to get ready than I'd anticipated and had to hurry out to the deck to welcome our guests. I ran past Emilie, who was at the bar in the main salon getting the champagne flutes ready. I was pleased that she was doing what I'd asked her to do.

When I got onto the deck, I went to stand in the line that had already formed. Hunter had been between Pieter and Kai but he came over to stand right next to me.

My heart beat rapidly in response. There was nothing preventing him from being next to me other than the exterior crew usually stood together, as did the interior. There wasn't a rule I could specifically point to and tell him to go back to his fellow deckhands.

Plus, I liked having him next to me.

"You have more stripes than I do," he said, looking at my shoulders.

"I outrank you," I told him.

"I'm not sure how my fragile masculine ego feels about that."

He was teasing and again I found a smile popping up. "I have a feeling that it will survive."

"I don't know. I may not recover."

I would happily play nurse, my overeager hormones said, and I was so glad I didn't say the words out loud. "I think you'd find a way."

"That's true. I do like a bossy woman."

Flirting? Statement of fact? There was no way to be sure. I took the scrunchie off my wrist and gathered it around my hair. I couldn't see my reflection but I knew how bad it looked, especially in comparison to Georgia. She looked stylish and cute with her low ponytail while I resembled . . .

"It must be nice to put your hair in a ponytail and not look like a founding father," I grumbled.

Hunter raised his eyebrows at me. "You do not look like a founding father."

"I know that I do."

He leaned his head in slightly. "I'd pledge allegiance to you."

Okay, that was definitely flirting, right? It had been so very long I could no longer tell. I probably shouldn't automatically assume that nice compliments had flirtatious overtones.

"I'm not a flag," I responded, trying to quash my own hopes. "Or a country."

He shrugged. "I think Lucksylvania sounds like a wonderful place to visit."

I tugged on my hair in response, grimacing. I was not going to answer about my fervent desire to spend my next vacation in Hunternesia.

"Why do you do your hair that way if you don't like it?" he asked.

"Protocol for the stews."

"Aren't you the chief stew now? Can't you change it?"

Huh. I absolutely could change things. That had been Marika's rule. "You're right."

I took the scrunchie out and pulled my hair up high and immediately felt better.

I'd been so worried about the responsibilities of my new job that I'd forgotten about some of the perks beyond just the money.

The universe gave me approximately half a second to enjoy that realization before bringing it all crashing down.

Emilie walked onto the deck and immediately dropped the tray of full champagne flutes. There was a long moment of shocked silence and then I immediately started calling out directions.

"Georgia, go grab a container to put these shards in. Thomas, we're going to need rags." Did champagne stain teak? I couldn't remember. "Maybe the spot cleaner, too. Emilie, go back inside and get another tray ready. The guests will be here soon."

Everybody sprang into action and I bent down and started picking up shards of glass. The one thing I had going for me right now was that Captain Carl hadn't come down yet. This would displease him greatly.

Hunter was next to me, helping me gather the glass. I briefly noticed just how large and strong his hands were.

"What do you need from me?" he asked.

"To keep doing what you're doing."

"You have a cool head in a crisis," he said in an admiring tone.

"On the outside, but internally I'm panicking and considering every possible way things could go wrong. Like a guest stepping onto a shard we missed with their bare foot and bleeding all over the deck which would not be good for the guest or the wood and then what if the wound is bad and they sue us or worse, don't leave a tip, and then all my dreams go poof and the captain fires me and . . ." I let my voice trail off, exhausted by my own fears.

"Have you tried not overthinking everything?"

He was teasing me but I answered him seriously. "I have anxiety. I don't have any other kind of thinking available to me."

"My therapist would say to use a positive affirmation to stave off negative thoughts."

Hunter didn't seem like the kind of guy who would see a therapist, even though I knew that wasn't a fair judgment to make. People had a lot more going on under the surface than they let the rest of the world see.

He'd already told me that he'd lost his sister—I didn't know what other kind of trauma he might have dealt with.

"Something positive?" I asked. "Well, it could have been worse. It could have been red wine."

"That's not quite what either I or my therapist had in mind."

Georgia returned then and helped us pick up the rest of the pieces. She also brought out cleaning putty, which we could use to make sure we hadn't missed any tiny bits of glass.

We quickly got everything dried and cleaned and swept up. I heard Captain Carl's footsteps heading toward us. Georgia stowed all our supplies under the outdoor bar and lined up next to me.

Emilie walked out with the tray of champagne flutes just as the captain arrived. I saw that she was being careful to use her fingers against the bottoms of the flutes to make sure she wouldn't knock them over again.

The Carmines and their elderly guests arrived at the passerelle, the gangway that led from the dock to the yacht. Pieter had rushed down to instruct them to remove their shoes and place them in the basket we had put there for that purpose.

Hunter whispered to me, "That looks like heaven's waiting room down there."

Again I smiled, but when I realized that the captain was looking at me, I pressed my lips into a line. "Shh," I said. "Just smile and nod. Our first charter is about to begin."

CHAPTER EIGHT

Lucky

Our guests came on board, led by the primaries, Robert and Donna Carmine. The captain shook hands with them, introducing himself and welcoming them.

"What are their names again?" Hunter asked me.

If he had been anyone else, if we had been anywhere else, I would have assumed that he was coming up with things to ask me so that we would keep talking. But in this instance I knew it was that he really didn't remember.

"The Carmines and their friends." I told him each individual's name but recognized that he might struggle with it. "I think it'll be good enough if you remember the primaries' names, and 'Mr. and Mrs. Carmine' will work. My sister uses visual images to recall stuff like this. So think of a car and mine. The kind you find in the ground."

"Like a bomb?" he asked while the Carmines greeted François.

"Yes, but a mine. Please don't call them the Carbombs."

"I'll do my best but I make no promises," he said with a wink and my knees might have wobbled slightly.

Why, why, why was he so sexy?

Maybe it was the forbidden-fruit angle. I might not have been so attracted to him if I could have acted on it.

That wasn't true. He would still be this hot even if I could have declared open season on him.

"Why are they all so wrinkled? Have they never heard of Botox?" Emilie muttered.

"Have you never heard of people being in their seventies?" I retorted and then told her to be quiet. The last thing we needed was one of our guests overhearing.

"Do you think she meant 'boat-tox'?" Hunter asked me.

"That's not funny."

"Beg to differ."

My mood shifted from vexed with Emilie to wanting to laugh. I'd only known him for a short time but he made my soul feel lighter.

This was concerning.

Then the Carmines were introducing themselves to Hunter, and Mrs. Carmine said, "Aren't you a handsome one! I suppose you could rescue us if we sink."

He really did have that I'll-save-your-life vibe going on. It was probably the muscles.

"Absolutely," he agreed, shaking her hand. "I hope your husband won't mind, but I'll be sure to rescue you first."

Mrs. Carmine's cheeks turned faintly pink and it reminded me that I didn't know Hunter very well. A part of me had hoped that I was the only one he was saying possibly flirtatious things to but it turned out not to be true.

Nellie Fitzgerald, standing behind Mrs. Carmine, asked in an anxious voice, "Does that happen often? Yachts sinking?"

"It's usually just the once," Hunter quipped, and Mrs. Fitzgerald's eyebrows shot up her forehead.

"He's kidding!" I reassured her. "He's such a jokester." As if he and I were old colleagues who had done a thousand charters together. "I'm Lucky and I'm the chief stew. I will take you on a tour of the boat and the deckhands will bring your luggage on board for you."

Then I would have to send Georgia and Emilie to unpack those suitcases and get the guests' clothing put away, pressing and cleaning whatever needed to be taken care of. The Carmines and their friends would be with us for a week, and we would give them the highest level of service possible.

After I'd shown them the entire ship, I offered to take them back to the sundeck and get them some cocktails while they watched the *Mio Tesoro* pull away from the dock. The captain and the exterior crew got underway and headed toward the ocean. Our trip would end at Saint-Tropez with lots of stops along the way.

When I got into the main salon, I noticed that Emilie hadn't done the pillows the way I'd asked her to. I stopped to fluff the throw pillows and put them in the correct position.

"What are you doing?" Hunter asked.

I glanced up at him. He was holding two suitcases, obviously on his way to deliver them to one of the guest cabins.

"They need to be evenly fluffed and the zippers have to be face down and placed at the correct angle."

He lowered the suitcases to the lush carpet. "And what happens if the pillows aren't done that way?"

That had me pausing for a second. "Nothing happens. This is just how things are done." It was how Marika had taught me, how her chief stew had most likely taught her, and so on.

"More rules?"

"More rules," I confirmed.

"It doesn't allow for a lot of spontaneity."

I finished my task and went over to the bar and started grabbing bottles of alcohol and crystal tumblers. "Spontaneity is overrated."

He came over and leaned against the bar like he was a cowboy in the Old West. "Romance comes from spontaneity."

I uncorked the rosé that Mrs. Carmine had asked for and tried to ignore the effect his words had on me. "It's important on a yacht for things to be orderly and precise."

"The basket of junk you keep in the cabinet under the sink says otherwise."

"My personal space is a different story," I said as I finished pouring. I had a lot of products, like moisturizers and serums and cleansers and toners, and not quite enough space to keep them organized.

Not that I would keep them organized, but it seemed like a convenient excuse.

"I noticed."

Why had he noticed? I'd never had a man make any kind of remark about my slovenly ways. To be fair, I'd never shared living space with a man before.

It didn't seem to bother him—he said it more like he thought it was adorable that I was a neat freak in public while being a private slob.

While I reminded myself that I wasn't allowed to have that fluttery feeling I was currently experiencing, my body was making a very convincing counterargument about why some rules should be ignored.

It's not just that he's hot. Which he is. Like, surface-of-the-sun hot, my body said. *He's funny and nice and you know that usually the universe doesn't give with both hands.*

Which was true. Thinking of Hunter being nice reminded me of our first interaction. I reached into my skort pocket and got his handkerchief and handed it to him.

"Here. And thank you."

He took it from me and put it into the pocket of his shorts. "You could have just left this in our cabin."

I should not have had a thrill that he called the cabin ours. It was ours. That was just a statement of fact.

But when Hunter said it? It made me feel like I was a part of something with him. "I don't get why you have a handkerchief. How old are you?"

"Twenty-five," he said. "And you?"

"Twenty-four. And we are both too young to be carrying something like that around."

He grinned at me. "It's a good thing to do because you never know when a beautiful woman might need one."

I nearly knocked over the wineglasses I had just set on the serving tray.

Thomas entered the main salon and his gaze immediately landed on Hunter. "There you are. Stop chatting up Lucky and get those suitcases downstairs. The captain will make anchor and I'll need your help assembling the floating deck."

"Sure thing," Hunter said and went back over to the luggage. Thomas stepped out onto the deck and my brain was still scrambling as it tried to parse out precisely what Hunter may or may not have meant with his statement. Did that mean he thought I was beautiful? Or did he mean he might need it for a future encounter with an unknown beautiful woman?

And I couldn't even go and talk to Georgia about it because I knew she was interested in him. Would she see it as a betrayal? Friends weren't always easy to come by on superyachts. She was the first friend I'd made over the last year and I didn't want to lose her.

She already knows you're attracted to him, that insistent voice inside me said. *She would probably back off if you told her that you were interested.*

But what would be the point?

Captain Carl strode through the main salon and nodded to me before passing into the dining room on his way to the bridge. I put a hand over my stomach. What if he'd been in here just a couple minutes earlier? If he had seen Hunter and me together, what would he have thought? Would he have disciplined us?

It was like a cosmic reminder that nothing could happen with Hunter even if we both wanted it.

Which was still debatable.

I knew how things would go and so I had to find a way to stuff down my raging hormones or I was going to lose my job.

CHAPTER NINE

Lucky

While I was distributing drinks, Mrs. Carmine thanked me and then said, "My friend Irene has a hankering for some homemade vanilla ice cream and I was hoping you could arrange that for us. She prefers it over store-bought."

I kept my features even, trying not to react. "Of course. I'll get the chef right on that for you."

But I knew what Andre would do when I told him. He was currently in the midst of creating a charcuterie board and vegetable and fruit trays for the guests to snack on. He wouldn't be happy about having to make ice cream because he hated disruptions to his routines. He liked things to be fairly predictable.

I'd never understood why he'd gone into yachting, which was the total opposite of predictable. You never knew from one hour to the next what was going to happen or what the guests would require from you.

When I got to the galley, I let Andre know about the request in a very calm tone. He pressed his lips together in a thin line, which I knew meant that he was displeased, but thankfully, he didn't yell or throw any pans. I counted that as a win.

"You can take those upstairs," he said, pointing at the trays he'd prepared. Every single one looked like a work of art. I radioed Georgia and asked her to come help me so that we could bring all the serving trays upstairs at the same time.

The chef pulled the eggs out of the walk-in to start the base for the ice cream. He might have slammed the door a bit harder than was necessary but again, all things considered, it could have been much worse.

Georgia helped me with the trays, which the guests oohed and aahed over. I told Mrs. Carmine, "The chef is working on the ice cream and I will bring it up as soon as it is ready."

"Take your time, dear."

Then my afternoon turned into running back and forth from the deck to the galley to update the Carmines on Andre's progress. I offered multiple times to refresh their drinks or to bring them more snacks but they always demurred. As those hours went by, we reached our anchorage point and the entire boat trembled slightly as the crew lowered the anchor into the water.

I wondered if Hunter was helping them.

Not long after that Andre announced that he was done and served me up a bowl of vanilla ice cream with whipped cream and caramel lace tuile. I knew it killed him to not do something extra or over the top for the presentation, but it was already more than enough for a last-minute and unexpected request.

When I got to the sundeck with the ice cream, I noticed that all of the female guests were at the stern of the boat, staring down. I went over to join them.

What had they seen? A dolphin? A whale? Sightings like that were rare in this area of the Mediterranean but it wasn't unheard of.

Not a marine mammal. They were staring at Hunter.

Who had his shirt off.

He was setting up the floating deck so that the guests could use the Jet Skis and other water toys.

One of the women sighed and I completely understood. I had only glimpsed paradise last night when I'd seen the barest hint of his shoulders. But this?

I had been admitted to the promised land and it was Hunter Smith's glorious chest.

It was like watching a masterpiece come to life, every muscle and sinew moving and flexing, the strength on display making me feel a bit woozy.

I fanned my face with my free hand. He was making me overheated.

He had to put his shirt back on. He was going to give these poor women a heart attack.

He was going to give *me* a heart attack.

Plus, it was against the rules. Thomas and François must have been setting up the waterslide or else they would have told him it wasn't allowed. I was the only person who could tell him to cover up.

I wished that I could yell at him from here because it would be much safer with all this distance and these elderly people at my side to keep my piping-hot libido in check. But I couldn't make a scene in front of the guests.

"Ice cream!" I announced, and Irene reached for it without taking her gaze off Hunter. I glanced over at their husbands, who sat on the couches in the shade and wondered what they thought about this. I gave her the bowl and then turned immediately to go down the stairs that led to the back of the ship.

"Hunter!" I hissed his name, worried about getting too close because there was every possibility that my hands might have minds of their own and wind up on his chest.

"Lucky! To what do I owe this honor?"

Then, to my horror, he came over to where I was standing, so close that I could see every freckle, every vein, every blond hair on his tanned chest.

I felt dizzy.

"Why is your shirt off?" That wasn't what I meant to say. I intended to reprimand him but it was like my mouth was trying to delay the moment that he put his polo back on for as long as was humanly possible.

He shaded his eyes so that he could look at me. "Because it's five hundred degrees out here."

"Ship rules. You can't take your shirt off." To the dismay of the female half of the Carmine party.

And myself.

"Seriously?"

"Yes, seriously. You need to put it on. We have to keep our entire uniform on whenever we're on charter."

He grabbed his polo from where he'd left it and seemed to be moving in slow motion. So much so that I was worried I was about to do something reckless. "Please hurry, we have an audience."

Hunter glanced up at the gathered women and waved. I couldn't be sure but I thought I heard someone giggle in response.

"Aren't we supposed to be making the guests happy?" he asked, still moving at a maddening pace that had the effect of making my heart rate triple.

"Yes, but not by flashing them."

"I'm not flashing anyone," he said and then finally, finally put his shirt back on. I let out a deep breath that I hadn't realized I'd been holding.

"Well, that's not fun," I heard someone say above us, and I completely understood her disappointment. Him putting his shirt back on was like throwing a tarp over a museum-quality painting.

"Lucky, are your cheeks a little pink?" he asked.

My hands went to my face. Why did he notice everything? "Like you said, it's hot out here," I finally managed to say.

His grin let me know that he did not believe my explanation.

Nor should he.

"Well, thanks for giving me a *stern* talking-to," he said. "Get it? Because we're in the stern of the ship?"

"I got it," I said quickly.

"I'm sorry for being such a pain in the boat."

"What did I tell you about the puns?"

He glanced up, like he was trying to recall just what I'd said. "That you love them and I should share them as often as possible?"

Despite the fainting spell I was fighting off, that made me smile as I shook my head. I wanted to stay here. To keep talking to him and hear what new nautical pun he might come up with. I couldn't linger, though. His chest being covered up would hopefully make it easier for me to leave. "I should get back to work."

He nodded. "Me too. Tell the Carbombs I said hi."

"That's not funny," I told him. "You're going to slip and do that for real and people don't like it when you don't remember their names."

"If I have to explain to you why it is funny, I would be happy to. I can cite references if you'd like. I would include the fact that I've made you both smile and laugh, which is enough evidence that what I'm saying is correct."

"That's not evidence," I sputtered. I did think he was funny. He amused me. I wanted to hear what inane thing he would say next, and that was bad because humor was one of the main things I looked for in a man.

I couldn't be considering Hunter that way.

"It is evidence. Good enough for a court of law. The judge would rule in my favor." Why did I like his teasing so much?

"I have to get back to work," I repeated, as if it were some kind of magical phrase that would make my feet move away from him when they didn't want to. I had a job to do, guests to check on who had paid a lot of money for me to be at their beck and call.

They weren't paying for me to ogle my bunkmate.

Thomas's footsteps on the stairs behind me got me to finally move. "Hunter, come help me unload the water toys."

I brushed past the bosun and made my way back to the upper deck. The women were just where I'd left them, still watching Hunter.

Irene handed me her bowl of ice cream. "I'm sorry. I didn't get a chance to eat it in time."

"I'll take care of it," I said immediately. "Would you like more?"

"No, I'm fine," she said.

I took the bowl back down to the galley to be washed.

I looked down at the soupy mess.

Me and the ice cream. Both of us completely melted because of Hunter.

CHAPTER TEN

Hunter

After I'd changed into the black pants and button-down shirts called, appropriately enough, "blacks," Thomas sent me to the upper deck to find Lucky and help her. He hadn't had to tell me twice.

The interior crew had on pink dresses for Mrs. Carmine's birthday, and I did my best not to objectify Lucky, who looked incredibly sexy. The dress fit her perfectly, outlining every long line and curve, her long black hair up in a ponytail that swayed back and forth as she moved.

It had become apparent to me that she had no idea how hot she was, and I found that personally offensive.

"Thomas said I should come help you," I said, realizing that standing there and watching her was not exactly the behavior of a friend.

She thrust a package of pink balloons at me. "Here. Blow these up."

I took one out. "Do balloons ever strike you as strange? 'Happy birthday, here's a rubber sack filled with my breath.'"

Her smile made my chest feel too tight. "Don't make jokes. This needs to be perfect. Her entire group has been so lovely and patient. You have no idea how rare that is."

I should have blown up the balloon but instead I watched her as she climbed onto the table to attach some pink and gold streamers to the top of a pole. I told myself that I shouldn't be looking at her butt.

My staring turned out to be a good thing because the boat rocked sideways and she lost her balance. Because she had all my attention, I was there to catch her before she fell. Her back was against my chest and all my blood rushed south. She was so soft. She fit perfectly in my arms and smelled amazing. I wanted to bury my face in her hair.

"Are you good?" I asked, and I didn't know if the question was for me or her.

She trembled slightly and I could hear how quickly she was breathing. From the almost fall or because I was holding her?

My heart thudded low and hard. What would she do if I turned her around and kissed her senseless?

"I'm good," she said in a low, breathy voice that made my brain shut off entirely. She didn't help things by turning slowly around.

I wanted her.

And I couldn't have her.

She swayed toward me and I wondered if she even realized it. Her dark eyes met mine, and then lowered down to my mouth.

I wasn't alone in this. She felt it, too.

Lucky is off-limits, I reminded my body.

My hands were still on her waist and I reluctantly pulled them away. I had balloons to blow up. Although it seemed like a poor substitute for what my lips wanted to be doing.

After a moment she went back to decorating but something had shifted between us. The air was charged and there was a heated heaviness there that pressed into me, urging me to stop being a coward and kiss her.

When she finished she asked me, "Do you think they'll like it?"

I had been busy imagining the kinds of sounds she'd make when I sucked on the pulse point I'd seen rapidly beating at the base of her neck, so I didn't respond the way I should have. "It's very pink."

Then I saw my screwup. She looked disappointed. She had wanted me to tell her she'd done a good job.

Before I could correct my mistake, she ran her hands over her thighs to smooth her skirt, making me wish I were the one doing it. "It's what Mrs. Carmine asked for. Which is why I'm wearing something you'd drink when you're nauseous."

"I think you look . . ." I racked my brain for a word that wouldn't scare her. *Sexy. Delectable. Good enough to eat.* I settled on, "Cute."

She looked so offended that I almost laughed. "You should be glad that we didn't have to put you in a Speedo to serve the guests."

"You've done that?" I would not imagine her in a bikini.

"I haven't. Have the men in the crew? Absolutely." Her eyes lingered on my chest when she said that. I got the sense that she would have liked to see me in a Speedo. She hadn't been able to keep her eyes off me earlier, when I'd been shirtless. It had made her flush a soft pink. And it had made me wonder what I could do to keep her skin that color.

And how far her blush went.

One of the stews came in with silverware and handed everything to Lucky. I understood that she was doing her job but I was annoyed by the interruption.

She all but batted her eyelashes at me and said flirtatiously, "Hi, Hunter."

What was her name? I took a shot. "Hi, Emma."

Her face fell. "It's Emilie."

I felt bad. "I'm sorry. I meant Emilie."

But my poor memory came in handy as it caused her to leave, clearly pissed.

"Uh-oh," I said. "I think I screwed up."

"She'll be okay," Lucky said as she started placing silverware. "Emilie we can afford to make angry. It's the guests we have to worry about."

"Yes, we wouldn't want to aggravate the Carbombs."

Her lips twitched like she wanted to laugh. She held up a butter knife and thrust it toward me and I imagined her as a sexy pirate, threatening me with her cutlass. I would easily walk the plank for her.

"You really don't want to do anything to annoy any elderly people," she said, pulling me out of my fantasy. "The older they get, the less a life sentence in prison is a deterrent. So you better behave and use the right name, especially since our tip could be on the line."

I laughed and pointed at the knife. "Lucky, are you threatening me with a deadly weapon?"

"Do you know how hard it would be to kill you with a dessert knife?" she said as she set it down.

"You seem the persistent type. I think you could do it."

"Probably true, and then I'd have the room to myself, with no one to comment on whether or not I was a slob."

"You are a slob," I said. And then betraying where my mind had gone, I added, "But if I wasn't there, who would fight off the peg-legged and eye-patched pirates when they storm the ship?"

I was grateful that she didn't ask why I was suddenly talking about pirates. There wouldn't have been a way to explain.

She said, "I don't think we'll be visited by Blackbeard anytime soon."

Lucky focused on putting out the knives and forks and I wanted her attention back on me so I reverted to the thing I knew would work. A joke. She couldn't resist them, no matter what she said. "Do you know the way to make a pirate angry?"

"Steal his doubloons?"

"No, take away the *P*."

I saw the moment when she realized that I meant the letter *P*, turning *pirate* into *irate*. And she grinned at me and made me feel like I could defeat an entire boatload of pirates by myself. "I like making you smile."

It wasn't something I'd wanted to admit to, but it was true. I wondered if she would confess that she liked me making her smile, but she stayed silent and finished setting the table.

Feeling a little like I'd been dismissed, I asked, "What else do you need me to do?"

"You could go down and wash dishes," she said. "The dishes are never-ending, just like the laundry."

Wasn't there someone on board for that? "Don't we have a dishwasher?"

She looked at me like I'd just spouted nonsense. "Yes. You."

I was a dishwashing virgin and had no idea how to do it. "I've never washed dishes before."

"I can show you," she offered. "I'm really good at it."

Which led me to wonder what she would say if I offered to show her the things that I was really good at.

Another stew called over the radio, "Lucky, Lucky. The guests are ready to come up."

She glanced around and said, "Copy. Send them up."

The Carbombs and their guests came upstairs, and Mrs. Carbomb seemed thrilled by her birthday decorations and kept thanking Lucky. "Everything looks so wonderful."

"I'm glad you like it," Lucky said and I was happy that she looked so happy.

The French guy had set up an audio system and started playing songs from the 1950s and 1960s and two of the couples started to dance. I knew I should go but I liked watching Lucky getting her accolades.

Mrs. Carbomb came over and patted me on the arm. "Why don't you dance with Lucky?"

I saw the twinkle in the older woman's eye. She had done this deliberately. I wanted to kiss her on the mouth. Throw her a ticker-tape parade. Thank her profusely.

Lucky looked like she was about to refuse so I hurried over to her and held out my hand. "We have to do what the guests want, right?"

"You're right. We can't disappoint Mrs. Carmine. Especially since you've already promised to save her in case of an emergency," she said, giving me her hand.

I whirled her once and she laughed in surprise before I pulled her close. She wrapped her hands around my neck and I settled my hands at her waist again and was surprised at the relief I felt. Like this was what I was supposed to be doing—touching her.

But I didn't bring her in as close as I wanted to, thinking a bit of distance might keep me from doing something entirely inappropriate in front of the guests. We swayed together and I saw the way she kept swallowing, felt her fingers fidgeting against my neck, how she wouldn't meet my gaze.

Then I did something stupid. I leaned in to whisper, "What are you thinking about?"

She tilted her head and shivered against the sensation of my breath on her ear. I shouldn't have asked her but I wanted to know if she was thinking the same things as me. Had to know if I was the reason for the rapid rise and fall of her chest.

"Nothing," she said.

"I don't believe you," I murmured.

Lucky cleared her throat and then said, "I was thinking about how much work I still have to do."

"That's not true, either. I think you're thinking about me." I finally provoked the reaction I wanted, her dark eyes indignantly meeting mine, that pulse point in her neck that was already a fan of fluttering.

"I am not thinking about you." She tried hard, but there wasn't any conviction in her words.

I knew I should give her an out. "You are. You're thinking about how much you're dying for me to make another boat pun."

One of her gorgeous smiles lit up her face before it disappeared. "I'm not interested in your puns. I'm afraid that ship has sailed."

"Lucky!" I said, delighted. "I am impressed. And you can protest all you want but I know you love my ex-port-ise of nautical humor."

She laughed. We fell quiet after that, listening to the music and continuing to sway together to the slow beat. It wasn't an awkward silence. I was soaking in what it was like to be close to her in a way that the captain couldn't find fault with. A heady warmth flooded my body and I had to fight off the urge to move closer. My limbs felt too heavy. Like I needed to lie down.

Preferably with Lucky.

I said her name.

"Yes?" she answered.

This might have been a bad idea, but I did it anyway. "You're the one I'd save from the sinking ship first."

She didn't seem to know how to take my declaration. "Mrs. Carmine is going to be so disappointed."

I wanted to be able to tell her what I really thought. How much I liked her. How beautiful I thought she was. Now I was the one swallowing hard, my breathing unsteady, my fingers digging slightly into her back.

We came to a stop, no longer moving. I forgot about the party, about the music, about the guests.

Everything except her.

This couldn't happen.

"I should go wash the dishes," I said. Could she hear how shaky my voice was?

"You should," she agreed. But she didn't move away from me. She didn't let go.

Neither did I.

I had to force my feet to move, my hands to drop. She crossed her arms over her chest, her expression disappointed.

There wasn't a choice here. I had to go. I turned on my heel and left. I let out a deep breath.

She was going to get me fired.

Or, more accurately, I was going to get myself fired.

CHAPTER ELEVEN

Lucky

The rest of the party went well. The guests danced and laughed and the entire crew came up to sing "Happy Birthday" to Mrs. Carmine. I tried not to make eye contact with Hunter, as I figured that was the safer choice.

Especially with Captain Carl here, singing loudly and off-key.

I had come so close to doing something totally embarrassing before Hunter had left to do dishes. It had felt so good to be close to him and I'd craved more. If he hadn't gone when he did . . . I didn't know what might have happened.

After they ate the cake, Mrs. Carmine opened her present from her husband, which was a tennis bracelet with diamonds so big you could see where the *Titanic* had hit them. The guests drank another round of champagne in honor of the birthday girl and then finally called it a night.

Mrs. Carmine thanked me again. "This was so lovely. Thank you."

She was an extremely wealthy woman. She had probably had birthday parties lavish enough to rival most people's weddings, but I appreciated her gratitude. "It was my pleasure."

And it really had been.

Georgia was on lates, meaning she would stay up to finish the cleaning and be available in case one of the guests needed her. She would also need to get everything ready for breakfast the following morning.

I could have gone to bed but I felt too keyed up to return to my cabin. Especially if Hunter was there in some state of undress. I didn't have enough control over my rebellious hormones yet. Work would help.

Georgia and I took down the decorations while Emilie carried the dishes and silverware down to the galley to be washed.

Probably by Hunter. I wondered if someone else had shown him how to wash the dishes. It was self-explanatory but I imagined that Georgia might have taken advantage of the situation and found a way to wrap her arms around him to demonstrate the exact strokes he should make when scrubbing the china.

Trying to think about something else, I noticed that my second stew seemed grumpy, which wasn't like her. "Are you okay?"

"It is so annoying cleaning up after people so old their birth certificates are probably expired."

"Georgia!" I said, looking around to make sure that no one had overheard her.

"What?"

"It's bad enough that I've got Emilie doing that. Don't you start."

She frowned. "It's not my fault Mrs. Carmine went to her prom with Abraham Lincoln."

I tugged at a streamer and it fluttered down to the deck. "They are so nice. Stop it."

After a moment's hesitation she let out a deep breath and said, "You're right. I'm sorry. They are nice. I think it's just a defense mechanism that kicks in when I'm tired and hungry. It makes things easier if I can be angry with the charter guests. They're usually so awful that if I make fun of them in my head it makes the work not seem so bad."

In a way that made a strange sort of sense to me. "That's fine but keep it in your head and not coming out of your mouth."

"That's never really been my strong suit," she said. "You know that I say exactly what I'm thinking."

"I do know," I agreed, gathering up the streamers to put them into the trash bag she had brought up to the deck.

"And as an example of always speaking my mind, what is going on with you and Hunter?"

I hadn't been expecting that. I froze, gripping the edges of the trash bag tightly, wishing I could disappear. For a moment I couldn't speak, my throat closed off. Then I finally managed to sputter, "Nothing. Nothing is going on with me and Hunter. Why would you ask me that?"

Was I being that completely obvious? Did the captain know?

No, he couldn't possibly be aware of my crush or he would have said something about it to me already.

"I saw the two of you dancing and I've seen love scenes in movies with less heat."

My eyes widened, my anxiety making my heart throb. Had the rest of the crew seen us? "The Carmines requested that we dance together." My voice was practically a whisper, I was so worried.

"Did they?" She said it like she didn't believe me. ·

"Yes," I said, forcing the word out. "Why else would I have danced with him?"

"Because he's God's gift to women and you would have been a fool of the highest degree to miss the chance to dance with him?"

She wasn't wrong. He had been so strong and warm and dreamy and . . . I shoved the streamers into the trash bag with more force than was necessary. "It only happened because the guests asked us to."

"Uh-huh." She didn't believe me and I didn't blame her because I didn't believe me, either. "I think you're trying to earn points."

I had to refrain from rolling my eyes hard enough to capsize the yacht. "I'm not participating in that nonsense you and Emilie have going on, and I think you should take that list down and knock it off. If the captain found out . . ."

"He won't," she interjected. "You worry too much. Has anyone ever told you that?"

"My mom, my grandparents, and every man I've ever dated," I said.

"Add me to that list."

"No more lists!" I said and she laughed.

"You know, it would be very easy for you to hook up with Hunter," she said as she deflated another balloon. "With you two sharing a cabin and all. No one would know."

She pointed up at the camera that was facing the sundeck. There were cameras all over the ship, and the viewing screens were in the bridge and the crew mess. It was a way for the crew to keep tabs on the guests and their needs when we took breaks.

It also meant that the captain could see us most of the time. The only private places without cameras were the guest and crew cabins.

"I would know," I told her.

"Why do the new owners have a rule about not having a root and then put a man and a woman in a cabin together? That doesn't make any sense."

Having a root? It must have been Australian for hooking up. Most of Georgia's slang words were about sex. "Probably because they think we can control ourselves." I was perilously close to that statement not being true but Georgia did not need the encouragement.

Emilie came back onto the deck at that moment with a spray bottle and washcloths and had apparently caught the tail end of our conversation. "I'll trade rooms with you, Lucky."

It didn't require much imagination to figure out how that would end up. "I think we'll keep things the way they are now."

She looked very disappointed.

I said, "Emilie, why don't you go ahead and head down for the night. I'll see you at six tomorrow morning." She immediately set down her cleaning supplies and hurried downstairs.

A few seconds later François ran past us, saying something into his walkie-talkie, looking frantic.

"What was that about?" Georgia asked and I shrugged. No idea.

When Thomas emerged from the main salon, she went over and blocked his path. "What's happening?"

"Some of the stabilizers stopped functioning. The engineers are working on it. It will be fine. I'm sure they'll get it fixed quickly."

Would they really get fixed soon or was he trying to reassure us? The seas weren't too choppy and the skies were clear, but I did notice that the boat was rocking a bit more than normal. I'd been so busy chatting with Georgia about Hunter that I hadn't realized it.

"Are you going to be okay?" she asked and I nodded.

I lifted my wrists. "I've got my bands on." I always wore them.

"You should go take your meds before it gets worse."

She was right. It was fairly late and I knew I should go to bed, given that I'd also have to be up at six o'clock. I had wanted to use this time apart from Hunter to regain my composure, to remember myself and my position and what I was doing all of this for.

"You've got this?" I asked.

"I do. Go to bed. I'll see you tomorrow."

The rocking on the boat became stronger as I headed down to my cabin. I again debated over whether I should knock but decided that Hunter and I were going to have to figure out a way to coexist in our space and not treat it like we were guests in our own cabin. He might not even be in there. With the stabilizers malfunctioning they might have needed him in the engine room to help.

I went inside and shut the cabin door behind me. I let out a sigh of relief when I realized the room was empty. I reached for the bathroom door but it swung open on its own.

There stood Hunter, a towel slung low on his hips, just out of the shower.

I could only gape as my heart exploded against my rib cage. My mouth went utterly dry.

Water dripped from his wet hair, his chest and arms still damp with drops creating tiny streams on his skin.

If someone had asked me if he could have somehow become even sexier, I would have said no. Such a thing didn't seem possible.

But just-out-of-the-shower Hunter was proving me completely wrong.

There were so many things I wanted to do at once—I wanted to run my fingers across his wet skin, lick those drops away, drag my lips across his muscles.

Why was the cabin so hot? Was it always this hot?

He seemed utterly unaware of the fact that he had disconnected my limbs from my spinal column. "Hey, Lucky. What are you doing?"

Thinking of ways to ravage you.

I had to swallow twice before I could form words. "I was, uh, that is to say, um . . ."

Why had I come down here? And why was he standing there like he didn't have a care in the world? Did he not know how he looked and the effect he had on mortal women?

And if he made one wrong move, that towel would slip off completely and then . . .

"Medicine!" I practically shrieked the word. "I came down here to get medicine. My medicine. For . . . medicinal purposes."

He gave me a slight smile and stepped into the cabin, letting me into the bathroom.

I hesitated, though, because I didn't trust myself to walk by him without doing something that most likely would alarm him.

My hormones were chanting *do it!* while reminding me of all the flirtatious things he'd said to me. That he seemed like he might be interested in me if not for the rules.

Which felt ridiculous because I was not the kind of girl men gravitated toward. I wasn't a troll or anything, but I knew I wasn't as pretty as Georgia and Emilie. I'd had a couple of boyfriends, I'd dated, but I wasn't the woman who walked into a party and made heads turn.

Men with torsos that would make Greek gods weep in envy dated women like that. The prettiest girls in the room.

Right now you are the prettiest girl in the room, my body whispered, and it was hard to argue with that logic.

He took a step forward, clearing the path for me. He was probably misinterpreting my reluctance as something else and was doing the gentlemanly thing and moving as far out of the way as he could.

Then the boat pitched hard to the right, and given how little control I currently had over my body, I realized that I was about to hit my head hard on something.

But then Hunter was there, grabbing me and bracing us against the wall, holding me in place so that I wouldn't fall. Saving me again. He easily matched his balance to the movement of the ship while I would have been unconscious on the floor if not for him.

"Thank you," I whispered.

"You're welcome." He was finally pressed against me and I felt his words rumbling up from his very bare, still wet chest. It was the most incredible feeling in the world and everything I had hoped it would be.

His nose barely grazed the tip of mine, sending my pulse into overdrive. That had to have been an accident. It had only happened because we were so close, with him pinning me up against the wall so that I wouldn't fall down.

What was that scent? He used the same soap and shampoo as the rest of us. He must have brought some kind of expensive-smelling cologne with him. Something masculine and delicious. I wanted to bury my face in his strong neck and get a good whiff.

Blood rushed through my ears and I knew I was breathing faster and harder than normal. My core tightened, my nerve endings exploding with excitement and anticipation.

I couldn't help but glance down in hope that his towel had perhaps slipped farther or fallen off completely but it was firmly in place. He must have superglued that thing on. I tamped down my ridiculous disappointment.

It was then that I noticed that, just as I'd feared, my fingers were flat against his abdomen muscles and I didn't remember putting them there.

I jerked my fingers away, as if he'd scalded me, and let my hands drop down to my sides. "Sorry."

He gave me a slow, sexy smile that made butterflies take wing in my stomach. "Don't be."

CHAPTER TWELVE

Lucky

Don't be? What did that mean? That he was okay with his bunkmate manhandling him? Or that he didn't care about what I had done because it was no big deal to him?

I found myself hoping that there was even a tiny chance he shared the overwhelming attraction I felt—the one that made me feel like I was drowning.

He gave me another sexy smile and then his gaze dipped down to my lips before meeting my eyes again.

"The boat's not rocking as hard anymore." He said the words softly and it made my insides even meltier.

The boat had been rocking?

My fuzzy mind determined that his words seemed correct and a good explanation as to why I was currently in this situation but all I could think about was how warm Hunter's lips looked and I wanted to kiss him more than I'd ever wanted anything in my entire life.

"You needed some medicine?" he prompted, that amused look not leaving his bright blue eyes.

Like he knew something I didn't.

And I needed medicine? For what?

I forced my brain to turn over and start up. Every moment I passed in silence was more humiliating than the last. "Seasickness," I finally managed to say. "I get seasick."

"Seasick?" he repeated. "You work on a yacht and you get seasick?"

Was there a way to permanently meld myself to him so that we never had to be apart again? "I do. That's why I wear these."

Somehow I managed to lift my wrists, which was harder than it sounded. I was just so off-kilter that it was like I'd lost complete control over myself. It was difficult to get my body to respond the way I wanted it to.

"Elastic acupressure bands," I added unnecessarily. "I also have over-the-counter meds for it in the bathroom. For if the seas get rough."

"You should go get that," he said but he didn't release me.

"I should," I agreed. But no part of me was in any hurry to move away from him. Including my brain, who had been convinced by my body that it was a good idea to stay put.

"Or I could get it for you," he offered and I felt his hand flatten against my back, as if he would somehow pull me closer.

"No, that's okay. I can do it." The fact that I was still upright and able to speak felt like a modern miracle.

"Lucky . . ." His voice trailed off and I held my entire body still, waiting to see what he would say next.

What he would do.

He didn't make a move, though. He just kept holding me and I saw his Adam's apple bob, how he tightened his jaw, and his mouth opened slightly. As if he intended to say something.

Or do something.

But if I stayed here, caught between him and the wall, I was going to make the biggest of mistakes.

I put my hands up on his chest. This time it was deliberate and I pushed gently against his very firm, very warm pectoral muscles. He immediately released me and backed up. I did my best newborn-fawn impersonation with my unsteady legs as I tried to make my way into the bathroom. I didn't have very far to walk but it felt like I was crossing an entire football field, his eyes on me the entire time.

When I entered the bathroom, I shut the door behind me and leaned against it, trying to breathe deeply and unable to. My skin was prickly and flushed, my stomach turning and twisting.

It wasn't anxiety that had me falling apart, though—it was unbridled lust. Hunter was too attractive.

I had probably been sweating again, and with my luck, he'd seen it.

Groaning softly, I pushed away from the door and opened the medicine cabinet. As I rummaged around for my pills, I wondered if there was an anti-Hunter medicine that I could take to clear him from my system.

I located my medication and popped a couple of pills in my mouth, leaning down to drink from the faucet. I had a water bottle in the cabin but I wasn't ready to go back out there yet.

In large part because I needed to give him the chance to get dressed. I was worried I might turn into some kind of feral vixen if I returned to our room and he was still in a towel.

When I straightened up water dripped from my mouth into the sink and it immediately made me think of how Hunter had looked when he'd walked out of the bathroom. I stared at my reflection in the mirror.

Enough, I said. *This is over-the-top ridiculous. You can control yourself. He is a nice man and doesn't deserve to have you throwing yourself at him and putting both of your jobs in jeopardy.*

I waited until I had sufficiently calmed down before I put my hand on the doorknob. It occurred to me at the last moment he might not be dressed. "Are you decent?" I asked through the door.

Because I can wait until you're not.

For a second I was afraid I'd said the last part out loud, but given that he hadn't run from the room screaming, I figured I had managed to keep it inside.

"Not usually," he responded.

My grip tightened. "That wasn't what I meant."

"If you're asking if I'm dressed, then yes, I am."

That should not have been such a disappointing prospect. I opened the door and he was standing by the closet putting a T-shirt on. I got one last glimpse of the perfectly sculpted muscles in his abdomen before he slid the material down.

"How was your first day?" I asked, my voice sounding strange to my own ears. Like I'd forgotten how to have a normal conversation.

"It involved more clothing than I'd anticipated."

My stomach fell to the floor and my head was instantly woozy again. "Oh?"

Masterful response, Lucky, I chided myself.

He grinned at me. "I find most activities infinitely more fun the less clothing that's involved."

I wholeheartedly agreed with him. I closed my eyes and summoned up a mental image of Captain Carl to remind myself why nothing could happen here. There was a rule. I liked rules. I followed rules. Rules were important.

But when I opened my eyes and looked at Hunter, I couldn't remember why rules mattered.

When I didn't respond to his teasing, he added, "My first day was easier than I'd expected."

"You should come work in the interior," I said, grabbing some pajamas to change into.

He nodded. "I definitely think you all have it worse."

I pointed at the bathroom. "I'm just going to—um, did you need to . . ."

"It's all yours," he said and climbed up into his bunk and settled in. I hurried back into the bathroom and locked the door. I got ready for bed and tried to figure out what I was going to do when I returned to the cabin.

There was no way I would be able to fall asleep, despite how tired I was. It had taken me so long last night to finally drift off. I usually checked emails, scrolled through social media, and read texts from my sisters asking me for money. I didn't think I'd be able to process what I was reading. My brain was being uncooperative.

I decided to watch one of my favorite musicals. Nonna had absolutely adored old Hollywood musicals and we had spent so many Sundays viewing them together.

They always made me think of her and tonight I could use some of her strength.

I reentered the cabin and put my dirty uniform into the hamper, then grabbed my laptop and headphones. I didn't offer to turn off the lights because I thought the darkness might prove too tempting. I got into my bunk and pulled my covers up, then opened my laptop. I searched for the movie I wanted.

It wasn't until the opening score blared into the cabin that I realized I had forgotten to plug my headphones in. I hurriedly tried to get the jack in but my fingers were not cooperating. It took a few attempts but I finally managed it.

Hunter's head dropped down to my right and I gasped, startled. He said something, but I had the movie up too loud. I paused it. "What?"

"Are you watching *The Court Jester*?"

My mouth hung open. "How could you possibly know that?"

"I've seen it many times. It's one of my favorites. Would you like some company?"

"I—" At this point somebody was going to have to take me to a hospital, considering the kind of heart palpitations he gave me. It probably wasn't a good thing for it to be beating so hard so often.

I knew I should tell him no. But too many things had happened in rapid succession—dancing with him at the party, our earlier interlude where I was introduced to the marvel that was his chest, being held close against him while the ship rocked back and forth, finding out that he liked musicals and him asking to join me.

Honestly, I felt powerless to resist. And I didn't want to. "Sure."

His head disappeared and a second later he jumped down to the floor and looked at me expectantly.

"Oh. Right," I said, scooting over.

We probably should have gone out to the crew mess and watched it there. Then we would be in a public place where absolutely nothing could happen.

I didn't offer to do that, though.

It felt like my skin was literally pulsating as Hunter climbed into my bed next to me. That feeling only increased the closer he got, accompanied by zinging tingles. The mattress shifted with his weight and I held my breath.

My bunk was a bit wider than his. I probably should have offered it to him when he arrived, given how much bigger he was than me, but I had seniority.

It meant that there was enough room for both of us. Barely. He was stretched out alongside me, close but not touching. I could still feel his warmth and wanted nothing more than to turn and nestle into his side, letting him hold me while we watched Danny Kaye pretend to be a jester and the Black Fox.

"What's this?" he asked, reaching under his lower back. He pulled out my stuffed penguin that I took with me everywhere.

"That's Randy. My dad bought him for me at the aquarium." I put out my hand and he handed it over. If he thought it was childish of me to have a stuffed animal, he didn't say so.

The other men I'd gone out with had.

"Why are you looking at me that way?" Hunter asked.

Oh no, what way was I looking at him? I was afraid that it was in the "please ravish me" way. "I was just thinking that you don't seem like the kind of guy who likes musicals."

Would he believe that? *Please let him believe that.*

"Then how else would I know the chalice from the palace has the brew that is true?"

I smiled. "Okay, you passed the test. But that's not an explanation."

His expression dropped. "My sister adored musicals. She wanted to be an actress on Broadway. She would make me watch them with her."

A lump formed in my throat. "That's the sister that passed away?"

He nodded. "I used to hate these movies. But I would give anything to be able to watch one more with her."

"I know exactly how that feels." I wanted to put my hand on his, to comfort him, but I didn't trust myself. His pain made my heart ache.

"Should we start the movie?" he asked, folding his arms over his broad chest.

"Yes." *We should. We definitely should start the movie and not sit here and think about climbing on top of him and kissing away his sorrows.*

I pushed play and he tapped me on my arm. When I looked at him, he pointed at my headphones.

He must have thought I was such a disaster. Why couldn't I be less of a mess around him? I unplugged them so he could hear the movie, then had to immediately adjust the volume so that we wouldn't bother our fellow crewmembers.

Hunter shifted, causing my mattress to sink in slightly, and I had to be careful to keep that tiny sliver of space between us.

"What we need now is some popcorn," he said.

No, what I needed now was a defibrillator.

"I'm too tired to make any," he added, and I didn't offer because I couldn't climb over him and retain my last shred of willpower.

We watched the movie and I wasn't able to pay attention to it. Instead I was keenly aware of Hunter and everything he was doing. When he would laugh and smile, how much he seemed to be enjoying himself.

When it was over I closed my laptop and he said, "Thanks for that. Good night."

"Good night," I echoed, keenly disappointed that he was leaving my bunk to climb back into his own. He turned off the light and I heard the bed above me creaking as he settled in.

A few minutes later he was fast asleep, already gently snoring.

Meanwhile, I hadn't moved. I realized that watching the movie with him was the best night I'd had in a very, very long time and I didn't know if that was a good thing or an extremely sad remark on what I had let my life become.

CHAPTER THIRTEEN

Lucky

After my close encounter of the potentially catastrophic kind with Hunter, I knew my best bet would be to steer clear of him. The next morning I got up quietly, got ready, and then went into the galley, desperate for coffee.

I grabbed a couple of muffins and filled a disposable cup, intending to go watch the sun rise. Deciding to be nice, I filled an extra cup for Emilie and added three sugars and some cream, the way she liked it.

But as I was walking by my cabin, I heard Hunter's alarm going off. Maybe he was in the bathroom and couldn't reach it.

I went inside and he was lying on his bunk, unmoving.

Setting down the coffee and muffins, I walked over and nudged him, making sure not to let my hands linger. "Hunter, your alarm is going off."

He groaned into his pillow and the sound did strange things to my abdomen. "Tired," he grumbled.

"Here." I held out the extra coffee. I'd get Emilie another one. He pried one eye open and then pushed himself up on his elbow to take it from me. He had been wearing a shirt when we watched the movie, but he must have removed it before he'd gone to sleep. Bare chested.

Again. I smothered a sigh and instead said, "A little starter fluid for the morning impaired."

"Plank you very much," he said.

I rolled my eyes at him, but I did smile.

"This is a little sugary," he said.

"That's probably because I didn't make it for you. It's how Emilie likes it." When he raised both of his eyebrows in surprise, as if he didn't think I should be getting coffee for my junior stew, I rushed to add, "My job is to anticipate the needs of people around me, including the crew."

I handed him one of my blueberry muffins. He gave me a weird look that I didn't know how to interpret initially, but then I started putting two and two together.

"You're not one of those guys who doesn't eat sugar, are you? I don't understand why people are so against it. Who was there for you when things went bad in your life? Comforted you? It wasn't kale."

He gave me a sleepy grin and took a sip. "I like to eat sweet things."

Air solidified inside my lungs. I very much wanted to be devoured by him.

"I'm a little surprised you eat muffins," he added.

"Of course I do," I said, trying to ignore the way my heart had jumped into my throat and was fluttering wildly. "Eating muffins is a way to basically have cake for breakfast without people asking you if you're okay."

That earned me a lazy laugh from him. "The last woman I dated wouldn't eat carbs at all."

My feelings very quickly shifted from excitement to not knowing how to respond. What did that have to do with anything? Obviously his last girlfriend and I were not in the same category. To quote *Sesame Street*, one of these things was not like the other.

He had to have meant it as a general observation that he was applying to all women. Not to women he wanted to date. Because he and I were friends. Bunkmates.

Nothing more.

"That's sad," I finally said, my brain still parsing through all the possible interpretations of what he'd just said, regardless of how improbable my conclusions might be.

Hunter had another sip of his coffee. "She was obsessed with being a size zero."

That was one thing I had going in my favor. I did not care about my size or whether I was too fat or too skinny for someone else. I was just me.

I had my nonna to thank for that. "A waist is a terrible thing to mind."

Another chuckle from him. "Why do we have to get up this early again?"

"We need to be ready to go before the guests wake up."

"Why don't they sleep in? Aren't they on vacation?"

An excellent question. "Even if they sleep in, we still have to get up early just in case."

He took a couple of bites of his blueberry muffin and then placed it and his coffee on the built-in shelf behind him. He turned onto his back, putting his hands behind his head. His blanket caught and was pulled down as he moved, the top resting on his hips.

I had to tear my eyes away from his chest. That had felt deliberate. Like he'd done it on purpose just to torment me.

He said, "Despite the ungodly hour, this day is starting out pretty well. A movie date last night, her bringing me breakfast in bed this morning."

"That wasn't a date," I quickly countered, ignoring the way my heart seemed to be skipping beats.

"We watched a movie together and then wound up back at my place. I'd consider that a successful date."

I knew he was teasing me but I couldn't return his banter. It felt like if I went along with his joke, he might think I was pathetic enough to hope that it had been a real date.

After a beat, like he had been waiting for my response, he turned on his side and reached for a medicine bottle and his water container.

He took a couple of pills out and swallowed them, chasing it down with water.

"Adderall," he offered. "For my ADHD."

"Did you disclose your medications to the captain?" Maritime law required that he do so. It was absolutely none of my business, and he would have been well within his rights to say as much to me.

He didn't.

"Yes, I told the captain."

"Good. I wouldn't want you to be fired."

Now he hit me with the full, blinding glare of his perfect smile. "Is that your way of saying that you would miss me if I was gone?"

I hadn't known him for very long but I realized that I absolutely would miss him if he was let go. He had somehow found a way to sneak into my heart and steal a tiny piece of it for himself. He had made himself matter to me.

I liked him.

But it would be ridiculous to say as much.

"You should get up," was what I settled on.

He grinned again, with that look of his, as if he knew exactly what I was thinking even if I didn't speak the words. "I will."

Nodding, I grabbed my breakfast and coffee and turned to go.

When I opened the door, he said, "Can we watch another movie together tonight?"

I would love that more than anything in the whole world.

"Sure." Feeling the need to protect my too-easily-swayed heart, I added, "But it's not a date."

"Whatever you say, Lucky."

~

I was looking forward to establishing a new routine with Hunter, going back to our cabin at the end of the night to watch a musical together.

Thomas inadvertently put an end to that.

As the greenest deckhand, Hunter was assigned to the late-night anchor watch. I could have given myself that same shift but Emilie still needed supervision around guests and for someone to make sure that she was actually working.

Georgia did not supervise Emilie when the two of them worked together. So it had to be me.

Hunter and I were, for lack of a better term, two ships passing in the night. He would have been so proud.

Over the rest of the week, I found myself often wondering whether or not Hunter and Georgia were taking advantage of all those quiet late nights together. Those thoughts caused a pang of jealousy so deep and so sharp that it surprised me. In former relationships I'd never been the jealous type, even when I'd had reason to be.

Which was a pretty big indication to me that this new schedule was for the best. I had dreams, a plan, and I needed to be working toward that. To help get us the biggest tip possible.

I shouldn't have been thinking about Hunter.

He didn't help matters, though. He made an effort to find me and spend time with me during my dinner breaks. Those breaks were never consistent—my routine was based entirely on the guests' wants and needs—but every time I had the chance to grab myself a bite to eat, he was there. Asking me about my day, how things were going, telling me what he had been working on. He always sat next to me and pretty much ignored the rest of the crew.

Our conversations were superficial, surface level, but I still enjoyed talking to him. The puns he'd throw my way. The way he would tease me.

I told myself it was a coincidence that we ate dinner at the same time, but deep down I knew it couldn't be.

Then I went and broke the superficial rule. "What do you and Georgia do when you're up late together?" I found myself asking.

"Work."

"What kind of work?"

"The kind on the lists that you and Thomas leave for us to do." He studied me for a moment and then asked, "Lucky Salerno, are you jealous?"

"What?" I quickly responded, hoping my cheeks weren't currently betraying me. "No! Why would you think that?"

"My mom always says if it walks and quacks, it's a duck."

I was very much a duck but didn't tell him that.

And if the dinner conversations weren't distracting enough, I found that him just existing was enough to send me into overdrive. I would wake up early in the morning, hurrying to turn off my alarm so that it wouldn't bother him. When I stood up I always stole a glance at him. His hair tousled, his face relaxed, his marvelous torso on display, and more times than I could count I had taken a very cold shower and stood in the stream until my heart calmed back down. The shock of that water on my heated skin was the best solution I'd found so far.

Hunter Smith was the very definition of the word *temptation*.

Drop-off day came quickly. We were heading to the harbor at Saint-Tropez. During our midmorning snack half of the crew decided to go out that night to Paddy's Pub on the marina. We wouldn't pick up another charter for a couple of days, so this was their chance to party.

I intended to celebrate the end of this charter by staying in my cabin and eating chocolate while watching a movie.

Captain Carl came in the room and we all fell silent, but he'd obviously overheard us. "You're intending to go out tonight as a group?"

Kai was the one who nodded and answered, "We are."

"Good, good. Crew unity is important. It's something I used to always tell Marika. You should be looking for ways to bring the crew together." Now the captain was pointing his remarks specifically at me. I remembered Marika complaining about it on more than one occasion, but she'd never done anything to fulfill his request.

"I clean the boat and wait hand and foot on his guests. I don't need to be the cruise director for the crew, too," she had grumbled.

I straightened my shoulders, ready to do as he'd asked. I would find a way to make us more united. Organize some kind of team-building activity. Maybe tomorrow.

But it meant I would have to go out with the group tonight. I couldn't make them run some obstacle course or climb a mountain if I wasn't willing to go to a bar with them.

Hunter wasn't there so I decided to find him and let him know about our plans. In part because I knew I'd be more likely to go if he was going, too.

That probably should have concerned me.

I could have called him over the radio but didn't. I wanted to see him.

And I got my wish. He was in the garage with the water toys, shirt off, doing pull-ups on an overhead bar. It was a glorious sight, all those powerful muscles contracting and tightening. I could have set up a booth and sold tickets and raised all the money I needed for my bakery in a single day.

Realizing that I was currently bordering on stalkerish, I cleared my throat to let him know that I was there.

He hopped down and grabbed his shirt, putting it back on. "I know, I know. Shirts on during charter."

That suddenly seemed like a stupid rule.

"I just like exercising," he added.

My unthinking response was, "I can tell."

This was what happened when I let my body run the show. We said bonkers things.

"Do you like exercising?" he asked.

I liked watching him exercise. Did that count? "I do crunches sometimes. Cap'n in the morning, Nestlé at night."

He laughed and came over to me. "To what do I owe this honor?"

"The crew is going out tonight and I came to invite you along."

"Lucky Salerno, are you asking me out on another date? I don't know, things seem to be moving pretty quickly between us."

I would not be baited. He loved tormenting me. "Ha ha. Everyone is going. Not just me."

"You say everyone is going, I say it sounds like a date."

"Not a date. We're leaving at nine o'clock, where we'll then go out and drink our body weights in alcohol."

"I'll be there, ready to dock and roll."

"No puns," I reminded him.

"There's nothing I can do about that. I'm already giving you the best that I've yacht."

I let out a little groan while he laughed. "Nine o'clock," I reminded him.

"Nine o'clock," he repeated. "For our date."

I shook my head and left the garage. Despite me repeatedly assuring him this wasn't a date, my heart was currently beating like it was.

CHAPTER FOURTEEN

Lucky

We were approaching the dock and the exterior crew were on their radios calling out distances to the captain as he brought the yacht in.

"Fenders!" I heard Thomas say as the *Mio Tesoro* came to a slow crawl. Sometimes the interior would assist in tricky situations, like when the yacht was being narrowly positioned between two other ships. No one had called for us to help lower the inflatable cushions this time.

They probably should have. I had just finished helping Georgia and Emilie with packing up the guests' luggage when I both heard and felt a loud crunching noise as we made contact with the dock, hitting wood and concrete.

Captain Carl's extensive litany of expletives filled the primary cabin and I turned the volume on my walkie-talkie down as I ran up to the deck.

All the guests were watching Thomas and François as they circled around Hunter, who had apparently failed to get his fender down in time, resulting in the ship smacking into the dock. I leaned over the side to get a better look.

This had happened once before, on one of my previous ships, but that had been a much harder hit. The damage to the *Mio Tesoro* looked to be mostly superficial, though it would cost a few thousand dollars to repair it.

It could have been much worse.

The fender was put into place and the deckhands began throwing their lines so that they could be tied off by the dockworkers.

Once everything was secure, Captain Carl came down to where Thomas, François, and Hunter waited.

I half expected the captain to lose it in front of the guests, despite the fact that I'd never seen him do so before. This was a very big screwup.

Icy darts pierced my heart and lungs. He was going to fire Hunter.

And while I knew this was how yachting worked, it didn't make it any easier. I had already decided that I wanted Hunter to stick around. I liked spending time with him.

I wasn't ready to let go of him.

To my surprise, the captain didn't yell. I was close to the guests and would have been able to hear him if he had. I didn't know if he was refraining for their benefit, but I was glad for it.

Or maybe that quiet anger would be worse once the guests had departed.

The exterior crew went to retrieve the luggage to take it to the cars waiting at the dock. I checked with the guests to see if they needed anything before they departed.

"I could use a stiff drink," Mr. Carmine said, and the sentiment was echoed by several other people. I called for Georgia and she helped me get whiskey to everyone who wanted it.

Then the captain radioed for the crew to line up to say goodbye to the guests. I was eager to stand by Hunter this time, to check on him and make sure that he was okay.

He stood farther away from me, next to his fellow deckhands.

I wondered why, my feelings slightly hurt. He had just been joking about going out on a date with me and now he was avoiding me?

The guests came out and thanked each member of the crew as they moved down the line. Because I was paying such close attention to him, I heard what he said to Mrs. Carmine.

"Since you're leaving I suppose this means you're not going to run away with me." His voice sounded like it normally did, with that flirtatious and playful lilt there.

"Not this time," she said with a laugh.

"Your husband is a lucky man."

"And I know it," Mr. Carmine said, enthusiastically pumping Hunter's hand.

When Mrs. Carmine reached me, she hugged me tightly and said, "Lucky! Thank you so much for everything. We had a fantastic time."

"You're very welcome. We hope you'll come back."

"As do I." She paused a moment and then leaned in to say to me, "You should give that young man a chance."

I was stunned. "What young man?"

"Hunter. He likes you."

I tried to smile but it wasn't working. "He's just that way with everyone." *Including you.*

"As someone who has been alive for much longer than you have, please believe me when I say that's not true."

Mrs. Carmine did not know what she was talking about. He had literally just joked about running away with her.

"Thank you again for your wonderful service, Lucky. It was very much appreciated," she added, with a knowing expression on her face.

"It was my pleasure," I responded automatically, stealing a glance at Hunter.

Who was not looking at me.

I wasn't quite all there as I said goodbye to the rest of the guests. Mr. Carmine handed the captain a thick envelope, which was a good sign. Then they walked down the passerelle, put their shoes on, and climbed into their waiting car.

"Go get changed and let's get the boat turned over," the captain said. "We'll meet up later to talk about the tip."

I wanted to make sure that Hunter was okay but I still had a job to do. I grabbed Georgia and Emilie to let them know what we needed to accomplish after they changed into their day uniforms. Hunter headed downstairs, probably to our cabin. After I'd quickly outlined our tasks to the girls, I followed him.

He had changed out of his dress whites and had already put his day T-shirt on. It was a good sign that he wasn't packing.

"What happened with the captain?" I asked, closing the cabin door behind me.

"He whisper-yelled a pretty impressive number of profanities at me and then told me to never do something like that again."

The relief was instant and overwhelming. He still had his job.

Hunter shook his head. "I don't even know what happened. I was ready and then I got distracted and next thing I knew the ship was hitting the dock. I feel like such a tool."

"I thought he was going to fire you."

"Me too." He looked very, very worried.

It made me wonder why he needed this job. Everyone on board had their own reasons for agreeing to work these ludicrous hours and do the constant, extreme physical labor. Like Georgia, who supported her elderly grandmother's nursing home costs by herself.

Money was usually the primary reason.

"I can't be distracted like that again," he said.

"You can't," I agreed. "Distractions are dangerous in yachting."

He was silent for a moment, his face somber, and he said, "I'm learning that the hard way."

So was I.

~

Hunter had hogged the bathroom, so I was running a bit behind in getting ready for the crew's evening out. I ran upstairs in my bare feet, carrying the high heels I planned on wearing. I only had a couple of dresses appropriate for a night on the town and tonight I'd worn the black one.

When I got to the deck, almost everyone was there. The first thing I noticed was that Hunter was whispering something in Emilie's ear and she was giggling. She sat so close to him that she was practically in his lap.

He's a flirt, I reminded my disappointed gut. *You knew that.* This was a natural state of being for him.

I had to get over this attraction I felt for him and find a way to just be his friend. It could work. I liked hanging out with him. I would have to make some internal boundaries so that I could keep myself on the right side of propriety.

Kissing him could only lead to disaster. Not only for my job but for our friendship. Because the last time I'd let myself fall for someone, it had destroyed me. I didn't want that to happen again. Hunter didn't seem anything like my ex, but I knew that appearances could be deceiving.

It didn't matter how hot and sweet and funny Hunter was. I couldn't imagine myself ever being in the market for a boyfriend again. My heart had been destroyed too many times already.

Everyone was pregaming, as the Carmines had left a large amount of expensive champagne behind and yachties were notorious for not letting a single drop of liquor ever go to waste.

Georgia handed me a flute. "Lucky! Are you actually coming out with us?"

"Yes." I took a small sip.

"Does that mean the apocalypse is nigh? Should I be praying and going to church to save my soul before it happens?"

"*You* should probably be doing that anyways, apocalypse or no," I teased her and she grinned at me.

"Who are we waiting on?" she asked. "I'm usually the last one."

I glanced around to see who was missing. "François."

"Did someone say my name?" the first mate asked as he walked out of the main salon.

"Yes, we were complaining about you taking so long," Georgia informed him.

"This beauty does not happen naturally."

She rolled her eyes. "I can't believe I have to be on the same boat as him. I need to drown my sorrows. I am going to get so dehydrated tonight." Then she turned and loudly said, "Let's go!"

A large van was waiting for us. When I got to the dock, I attempted to put my shoes on and cursed myself for picking ones with ankle straps.

"Here." Hunter offered me his forearm so that I could balance more easily.

"Thanks," I said, ignoring how warm his skin was, how strong he felt.

After I had my shoes firmly on, I accidentally let my hand linger on his arm for a beat too long.

That was exactly the kind of thing I had to stop doing.

And I found myself making inane conversation. "The taxi has probably been waiting for a while. We're late, so we should get going."

Ugh. I internally grimaced.

"Boat-ter late than never," he responded just as Emilie walked up and looped her arm through his.

This is none of your business, I told myself. I marched toward the van, determined. I was going to behave. That would probably mean limiting my intake. I couldn't overdrink because when intoxicated, I had a tendency to become very friendly with men I was attracted to. I would probably be the only one being careful—the rest of the crew would be on a mission to drink enough to drown an elephant, like the world would end if they didn't consume all the alcohol in France tonight.

Hunter could sit with Emilie and flirt with her to his heart's content. I didn't care.

I couldn't let myself care.

I climbed in and went to the back row.

To my surprise, Hunter entered the vehicle a second later and, despite the fact that every row was empty, ended up sitting right next to me.

It made me entirely too happy.

CHAPTER FIFTEEN

Hunter

This wasn't the best idea, choosing to sit so close to Lucky. If I'd been smart, I would have gone into one of the other seats, but I was just naturally drawn to her. Today I had made a superyacht hit a dock because I'd been thinking about her and the way that she had smiled at me over her shoulder, tossing her hair to one side . . . it was like something out of a toothpaste commercial and too cheesy to ever admit to, but one second I had a fender in my hand and the next I had cut my inheritance in half.

The captain had chewed me out, as he should have, and so I told myself to put some distance between me and Lucky. I'd already screwed up royally—I didn't need to do it again.

But then she'd held on to my arm while putting on those strappy little shoes and here I was, choosing the seat next to her.

And pressing myself close to her side to make room for everyone else.

She smiled up at me and said, "If you sit any closer to me, you're going to have to buy me dinner."

The air felt thick and heavy. My chest constricted too tightly for a moment and I found myself responding, "I'll buy you dinner anytime you'd like."

I was trying to sound casual and suspected that I'd failed miserably.

Thankfully the rest of the crew got into the van, including the chef and his parrot, who was making a ringtone noise. I wondered if the bird ever tried to escape. I wanted to joke with Lucky about it but everything felt too serious at the moment. I did want to take her to dinner.

And then back to our cabin.

I stifled a groan. I had to think about something else or things were going to get very embarrassing very quickly.

One of the stews got in the van—I was pretty sure it was Georgia—and so I turned to Lucky and said, "Georgia mentioned that you don't usually join in on these outings."

I wanted to know why. I wanted to understand everything about her.

"I'm worried about spending too much money because cocktails can get expensive. Living on the yacht, we get a definite taste of the high life, and suddenly purses from Walmart aren't good enough and you want a designer bag, like the ones you see every day. And it doesn't seem like that big of a deal, you've got plenty of money, but then next thing you know you're broke and you've got to sign up for another year to try and earn it back. It's a vicious cycle. I'm trying really hard to save up as much money as I can."

There was a reason. "Why—"

A bunch of hollering and whistles cut me off. I turned to see the guy from New Zealand kissing the other stew. Emma. Emilie. Something like that. They were going at it, and it annoyed me for two reasons.

The first was that the captain had been pretty clear about his rule and these two had just forced the rest of us to be their accomplices.

The second was that I was jealous as hell that I couldn't kiss Lucky like that.

Someone closed the van door and we set off. I still wanted to know why she was trying to save up. "So is spending money the only reason you don't like going out?"

"You know how other people have FOMO? Fear of missing out? I have the opposite. JOMO. Joy of missing out."

That made me grin. I loved the way her mind worked.

And I definitely loved being pressed against her. She was so soft and warm.

And utterly distracting.

"I don't know why people have to go to a bar to have fun," she added. "Have they ever tried watching movies and eating ice cream with no pants on?"

"Most of my favorite activities don't involve pants," I said as seriously as I could. I was joking but also not joking.

She ignored it and answered my initial question. "But money is probably the biggest reason why."

"You got six thousand dollars today," I pointed out.

"Sometimes it can be feast or famine when it comes to tips. Most charters won't be like the one we just had. The Carmines were very easy and pleasant."

"So the tip wasn't typical." I hadn't thought much about the tip, but it mattered to her and I was discovering that the things she thought were important had suddenly become important to me, too.

"It depends. Usually it ranges from about fifteen hundred to thirty-five hundred for a week. There are some that leave more. I worked with a girl on my last ship who earned her entire year's salary in one tip from a three-week charter. But there are other guests who don't leave tips at all."

She still hadn't told me why the money was important.

The stew I had decided was definitely Georgia called out, "We're almost there!"

"Do you know where we're going?" I asked.

"Paddy's Pub. It's an Irish pub."

"We're going to an Irish pub in a French beach town?"

"The drinks are cheaper, and there's more locals and yacht crews than tourists. Plus, Thomas likes a girl who works there, Siobhan. He's the one who made the call. And nobody else cares where we go as long as there's liquor. Thomas keeps waxing poetic about the joys of pub crawls. I've asked if we can do a bakery crawl but nobody else wants to."

I laughed. "This is our date, so you can choose whatever you want to do and I'll happily go along with it."

Whoops. I hadn't meant to say that. There was just something about her that made me want to tease her relentlessly.

With my words and . . . in other ways.

"Are we back to that?" she asked and had the cutest exasperated expression on her face. Instead of discouraging me, it made me want to do it more. "I don't think it's a date if there's seven other people here."

"We haven't defined the relationship yet. You're free to date five other guys at the same time if you want."

I knew it wasn't a date. But I wanted it to be.

We pulled up to the pub and we were the last two to get out. I stretched, as it had been very cramped back there, and then I offered her my hand to help her. I was pretty sure she was going to twist her ankles on the cobblestones in those ridiculous shoes.

She hesitated for a moment and then slid her hand in mine and I felt that touch everywhere. I loved the way our hands fit. I held on to hers for a moment longer than I needed to and then turned to shut the van door. She made me feel like I was fifteen again, getting overheated from just a hand touch. I pulled my shirt away from my body several times, trying to get some air circulating.

When I saw her noticing what I was doing, I attempted to come up with a believable excuse. "It is so hot. I don't understand why people like summer so much."

"I have a theory about that," she said as we walked behind the rest of the group.

"Do tell."

"Because it was the only significant time we had off from school when we were younger. So after twelve years it was ingrained in us to like it. The actual season is terrible."

"Another thing we agree on," I said as I rushed over to hold open the door to the pub for her. She made me want to lay down my cloak so that she could safely cross over a mud puddle. Or slay a dragon.

Lucky had turned me into a character from a fantasy movie.

The pub was a little hole-in-the-wall, like it had been carved out of a castle dungeon. Stone walls and a ceiling so low I felt like I was going to hit my head. The crew sat at a large table. Lucky took a seat and I sat on her left.

A barmaid arrived to take our orders, and Lucky asked for a club soda. Kai, if I was remembering his name correctly, asked for several bottles of wine and told the server, "In true nautical fashion, we plan on getting wrecked."

I couldn't help but grin at Lucky. I enjoyed puns no matter who made them, and I saw that she was also smiling. Like we shared a private language.

The crew were all talking to and over each other, and while they all seemed like very nice people, I wished they would disappear and that Lucky and I could have the date I had teased her about.

She was thinking seriously about something—I could see it on her face. Did she daydream about me the way I did about her?

It had been a long time since I'd felt this way about a girl and not had her feel the same way. It was probably good for my ego to be on unstable ground. Things had become so predictable and routine, boring, that I had situationships instead of relationships.

I knew I shouldn't chase Lucky, but I wanted to, and the prospect of winning her favor really, really appealed to me.

After the waitress brought our drinks, Lucky suddenly said, "Hey everyone, I thought we could go on a walking tour tomorrow morning as a bonding activity. And we can have lunch after. On me."

The reactions were immediate and entirely negative.

"Noooo!"

"Why?"

"Not for me."

"In the morning?"

"On purpose?"

"Don't they have ticks here?"

Georgia said, "The world is our playground and you want us to go on a hike?"

"Not a hike," she said defensively. "A walk."

"Tomorrow I'm going to lay on a beach and drink until I can't remember my own name," Georgia responded. "The only walk I want to do here is a wine walk."

"A what?"

"That's where I walk the streets of Saint-Tropez at night with my glass of wine."

Lucky frowned. "That's called drinking in public and it's against the law."

"You and your rules," the other stew muttered, reaching for her wineglass.

"That's France's rules. And I'm trying to unite the crew," Lucky said, and she sounded so defeated that I wanted to hug her until she felt better.

Georgia, who had made her interest in me very obvious, took a drink and then made eyes at me. "I know how I'd like to unite with the crew."

"Not like that. This is like, a team-building exercise," Lucky said.

"The whole reason we work on a yacht is so that we don't have to do that sort of garbage office team-building corporate junk. We already bond. We get pissed together every chance we get," Georgia retorted.

"I don't think getting drunk in yachtie bars is what the captain had in mind," Lucky responded, and again I was struck with the urge to help her. "It's required. Thomas, back me up here."

The bosun was watching the bartender and ignoring Lucky. He took a deep swallow of his beer and slammed it down on the table. "She doesn't know it yet, but that woman's about to get Union Jacked!"

What did that mean? Thomas went over to the bartender, and when she saw him, her whole face lit up.

I again suppressed my jealousy. I nudged Lucky's shoulder and pointed at her club soda. "Why aren't you drinking?"

"I'm allergic."

That was unexpected. "Really?"

"Uh-huh. When I drink I sometimes break out in handcuffs."

I immediately started laughing and Georgia seemed determined to ruin it. "It's because Lucky isn't any fun."

Ha. I knew that wasn't true.

Lucky sat up primly in her chair. "Just because I'm choosing not to drink doesn't automatically mean I'm not any fun. That is a separate choice that I have also made."

I laughed again. "I think you're a lot of fun."

"You must not get out much."

"Too much, unfortunately." I had done a lot of stupid things after Harper died. Lots of regrets.

Someone across the bar was checking Lucky out, and I put my arm along the back of her chair. I wanted to send a clear signal.

While I understood that I had no claim over her, I was pretty sure that if anyone here tried to hit on her, I would knock them out.

I didn't know what it was this woman had done to me that made me go all caveman. I hoped I would get to figure it out. It didn't seem to matter how many times I reminded myself about the captain's rule.

I'd never had an issue talking to women or asking them out. Rejection wasn't really in my wheelhouse, as I didn't have much experience with it.

But I was actually a little afraid she'd say no if I asked her on a real date, just the two of us.

I had no idea how to make this happen.

CHAPTER SIXTEEN

Lucky

I couldn't read Hunter's expression. He seemed more serious than usual. He had put his arm on the back of my chair and it was almost like he was touching me.

Georgia stood suddenly and grabbed me by the arm. "We're going to the loo."

Before I could protest she was pulling me behind her, forcing me to follow.

"What are you doing?" I asked when we got to the bathroom and she practically pushed me inside. The room was tiny with a couple of stalls, which were both occupied.

"Tell me what is going on with the hottie yachtie. Who saw who naked?" she asked.

"What?" I asked, alarmed.

"There is this level of awkwardness with you two and I'm assuming that one of you walked in on the other while changing."

I could feel my cheeks flushing, a fact that didn't escape Georgia's notice.

She crowed, "I knew it! Who was it?"

"I saw . . ." I let my words trail off.

"You saw him in all his naked glory? You haven't shared any of this with me yet and you call yourself my friend? Spill, now. I want every sordid detail."

This wasn't any of her business, especially when I knew she was interested in him. I wasn't going to fuel her imagination. "There aren't any sordid details because I've only seen him without his shirt on a couple of times. It's no big deal."

Even though it had been the biggest of deals.

She gave me a disbelieving look, and rightfully so. "You like him."

"Of course I like him. He is a nice person and a good bunkmate." Was I being casual enough?

Apparently not. She shook her head. "You're a terrible liar. Are you at least kissing him?"

"No. Captain Carl was very clear about that."

"Well, you already know what I think about his rule." She opened her clutch and pulled out her lip gloss, reapplying it in the dingy mirror. "I'm not kissing him and neither is Emilie."

That filled me with a relief that I hoped wasn't evident on my face. It must not have been, because she kept talking.

"If none of us are kissing him, that means Hunter isn't kissing anybody and that seems like a crime that should be punishable by the Hague."

"I think he'll survive a few months of not making out with his coworkers," I shot back, more sarcastic than I intended.

She finished up and put the lip gloss back into her bag. She pulled out her phone and began scrolling through it. "Somebody should be getting some action. The closest I've come to it so far was François asking me earlier if I wanted to be the mother of his second child."

"Gross," I said with a frown. "What did you say back?"

"I said given that I hadn't had a full-frontal lobotomy, the answer was no." She paused whatever she was doing and said, "This one has potential," before swiping right.

"Are you on a dating app right now?" I asked, looking over her shoulder.

"Yes. And they should come with a drop-down menu so that you can indicate how desperate you are." She looked up at me. "I'm assuming desperation is part of your problem. I know you are a Goody Two-shoes who loves rules more than she loves anything else, but you've been without Vitamin D for so long that you're going to implode if you don't at least make out with somebody soon."

It took me a second to figure out what she'd meant by "Vitamin D," but given that it was Georgia, it didn't take long.

And she might have had a point. "I think it has been too long since I kissed someone." There was a reason for that. One Georgia didn't know about.

"Yes, you bloody dag," she said affectionately.

I'd heard her call people dags before and knew it meant that she was questioning my intelligence.

"And you like Hunter," she added, expecting me to confirm it.

I couldn't help but do just that. Although there had to be a rational explanation for why I liked him. "Maybe it's like that Florence Nightingale effect. He helped me during a medical crisis, so now I'm attracted to him." I'd told her all about my first encounter with Hunter.

I could have sworn I heard her repeat *bloody dag* under her breath, but she said, "Go on and tell yourself whatever lies you need to in order to sleep through the night. Which also seems like a shame, by the way. That you share a room with that scorching spunk and you spend your time sleeping. I would—"

I cut her off. "I know what you would do."

Talking to Georgia about this situation had made me feel worse, not better. I had openly admitted to another person that I found Hunter attractive. Which made me feel like my defenses were weakening.

Erasing my boundary lines.

He was making me want to forget all about my past and take a chance on someone new. As if this relationship would somehow be the only one that didn't end in despair and heartbreak. I hadn't told Georgia about the losses I'd suffered because I didn't think she'd understand. She might want me to get over it and use Hunter to do so.

I changed the subject. "Speaking of people not seeing what's right in front of them, if you're not going to date him, you should put poor Pieter out of his misery."

"You want me to shoot him?"

"No," I said with a laugh. "I personally think you should give the man a chance, but if you're not into it, let him know."

A bunch of women entered the bathroom at once, crowding us. It made me want to get out of this place.

"Maybe I should go back to the boat," I said, also worried about what might happen if I prolonged my exposure to Hunter in a more laid-back environment without the distraction of work.

"If you do, make Hunter take you back. We're in a country full of Françoises." She pulled the bathroom door open and I followed her back to the table.

And it seemed like Hunter's whole face lit up when he saw me. That was a dangerous sight.

Georgia and I retook our seats and he returned his arm to the back of my chair. If it had been anybody else, it would have seemed like a possessive move. As if he were telling the other men in the pub to back off.

I was not going to read into things.

Starting *now*.

Pieter leaned across the table to talk to Georgia. It sounded like he was asking her to go on an official date. I felt bad for him that he liked her so much and she wasn't going to give him a chance. He was cute and nice. She wasn't holding herself to the captain's rules, so that wasn't the reason.

But from the stories she had shared with me, it seemed that she preferred men who treated her badly and I wasn't sure why. She was an amazing, fun, witty, warm person and deserved to be with a man who recognized that and appreciated her.

"I don't think you and I are a good idea," Georgia said in the nicest way possible.

"Are you sure I don't meet your koala-fications?" Pieter asked playfully, but to his dismay, she leaned across the table and ruffled his hair like he was her pet.

"You're sweet," she said.

Hunter let out a small groan. "That's the death knell."

"Was that your influence?" I asked. "The koala thing?"

"While you two were in the bathroom, he asked me the best way to flirt with women."

"And your advice was puns? That was bad advice."

He shrugged one shoulder. "It works."

I wanted to argue with him, but truth be told, it was working on me. I thought it was adorable.

Our food arrived and I dug in, suddenly starving. But to my disappointment it was only okay. I'd had much better.

"You look bummed," he observed.

Like he was always paying close attention to me. "I can't wait until we have a charter that gives us a night off in Italy. I'm in a committed relationship with pasta."

"You're saying my rival is spaghetti?"

"Better hope not, because you'd lose."

He was about to reply when a girl at the bar lost her balance and tumbled to the ground from her stool. He immediately got up and went over to help her.

I shouldn't have been impressed by this—it was just a decent, human thing to do—but none of the rest of the crew had even noticed.

After he made sure that she was okay, he came back over and sat down.

"You are so nice," I said, unable to help myself. "That's so unfair. Nobody should be nice and hot and have two ways to get free stuff."

He leaned back in his chair, his eyes dancing. "You think I'm hot?"

Realizing what I'd just admitted to, I immediately tried to down-play my admission. "Relax. You, of all people, do not need to go fishing for compliments."

"Would you let me catch one if I was?"

"You are not the kind of man who needs to be complimented." He had a mirror. He knew how he looked.

"Everyone needs that, Lucky. Like you should know that you have one of the most beautiful smiles I've ever seen."

I was simply going to ignore the way my heart was currently flopping around wildly inside my chest, like a gasping fish on land. I couldn't acknowledge him saying kind things to me. I knew where we would end up. "Georgia says that constant compliments turn guys into raving egomaniacs."

"Do you think that about me?"

"No, which is why I said the nice thing."

The waitress brought our check and Pieter grabbed for it. I guessed he was trying to impress Georgia but she didn't even notice.

With dinner done I knew exactly how the rest of the evening would go.

"Let's go to a club!" Emilie said.

Right on cue.

Everybody was standing up and I got my purse and followed the group out. I hung back, creating some distance between myself and the others.

Hunter noticed and slowed down to walk alongside me. "Where are you going?"

"Back to the ship," I said. I registered that he was the only one who'd figured out what I was up to. Nobody else seemed to have even realized that I was gone.

"Can I walk with you?"

"I'm a big girl. I don't need you to watch over me." Then I remem-bered Georgia's advice that this was a country full of Françoises and took his offer. "But if you need to go back, we can walk together."

"I have to get to bed," he said. "I've got a hike in the morning."

That made me smile and I saw that had been his intent. "Okay. But it's not a hike. Just a walk in nature that will end up back in the main part of town."

"You don't want to say goodbye to anybody?" He nodded toward our crewmembers, who were getting farther and farther away.

"I already told Georgia earlier that I was going to duck out." We took a left at the corner, walking toward the docks.

"So you're a fan of the Irish goodbye and the Irish hello."

I blinked in confusion. I knew what an Irish goodbye was—leaving a party without saying anything. "What's an Irish hello?"

"That's where you don't even go to the party."

I laughed. "You're right, I am a fan of that. I've always been a bit of a homebody, and currently the yacht is my home. Plus, I know how this night will end up for the rest of the crew."

"Oh?"

"Dinner and drinks, then off to a club to drink the place dry, and then stumbling back to the yacht, where they will finish off that champagne in the hot tub while playing drinking and kissing games. Like they're still in middle school."

It had never held any appeal for me, and even less so now that Hunter would be in the mix. Even if I couldn't date him, I also didn't want to watch him make out with Georgia or Emilie because someone had dared him to do it.

Not only because my newfound jealousy might prompt me to do something possibly felonious but also because I didn't want to be party to the crew so flagrantly breaking the rules. I had no desire to be in a position where I would have to lie to the captain if he ever asked me about it. It was better for me not to know.

Hunter turned the conversation to more neutral subjects—asking my opinion on the pub, what was (or wasn't) happening between Pieter and Georgia, about past charter experiences that I'd had.

And when he closed the cabin door behind him, and despite the fact that this thought should have occurred to me before, I realized that I wasn't going to be alone tonight. He wouldn't have anchor watch because we were docked. I was used to him not being here in the evenings.

"What's the plan now?" he asked.

I did not have a plan. I had end goals. Like staying away from tempting boys and keeping my job. "I, uh, was going to watch a movie."

"Which one?"

"I was thinking *Guys and Dolls*." There was an awkward silence and I felt obligated to invite him to join me. "Do you want to watch it with me?"

"Yeah. But I'm going to shower first. Walking around in that heat . . ." He let his voice trail off as his gaze flicked over me. He took a step toward me and there was a look in his eyes that I hadn't seen before.

It was . . . smoldering.

He pointed his thumb toward the bathroom. "Do you want to—"

And suddenly I was terrified of what he was going to say next. My anxiety wrapped itself around my throat like a giant snake. I couldn't find out how he intended to finish that sentence.

"I'm going to get snacks!" I announced and left the cabin as quickly as I could.

As I went into the crew mess and started gathering up chips and popcorn, I wanted to kick myself. I had totally overreacted in that moment. He had probably meant to ask me if I wanted to use the bathroom first.

But a part of me was absolutely convinced he'd been about to ask me if I wanted to join him.

And I didn't know what my answer would have been.

CHAPTER SEVENTEEN

Lucky

As I made my way back to the cabin, my arms laden, I had convinced myself that I had imagined the whole thing. I was definitely conjecturing.

This was another situation where we probably should have gone into the crew mess to watch the movie, but the captain was still on board, and if he saw us sitting in there alone together, he might come to some incorrect conclusions. Not to mention that everyone would return wasted at some point and I didn't want to deal with them.

When I got back to our room, I heard the shower still going. I dumped the snacks onto my bed, pushing them down toward the foot so that he wouldn't crunch them when he joined me.

This entire evening might have turned out differently if I weren't weighed down by my past, if I hadn't loved and lost so many times. I would have been excited by the opportunity to get to know Hunter better. To see if we could become something more.

It wasn't only the captain's rules that made me keep Hunter at arm's length. My own screwed-up past played a very big part.

I was setting up the movie when he came out of the bathroom with only a towel on.

Again.

My stomach clenched. Did he not understand the way that he pushed my willpower to its absolute breaking point?

He went over to the closet to grab some clothes. A still-working part of my brain noted that he could have initially brought the clothes in with him so that he could get changed in the bathroom, but he didn't.

I always took my things with me into the bathroom so that I could change after I showered.

Was he just so comfortable with himself and with me that it didn't matter if he paraded around in a towel in front of me? That was a foreign concept to me.

Did the man not realize the potential danger he was placing himself in?

This was why I couldn't consume alcohol around him. When he'd asked me earlier why I wasn't drinking, the words *the better to keep my hands to myself, my dear* had popped into my head. And I still wanted to go a little Big Bad Wolf on him.

He got his clothes and went back into the bathroom. I let out a very deep breath because I'd apparently stopped breathing the minute he'd walked into the cabin. I was relieved he was changing in there.

And not out here, where I was pretty sure I would have watched even though I knew I shouldn't.

My phone beeped and I had a message.

From François. I frowned.

Lucky????

What do you want, François?

This is Georgia! Where R uuuuuuuu????

Why do you have François's phone?

It took a bit before she could respond and I wondered if she was having a hard time hitting the buttons correctly, as she had most likely drunk more than her fair share already.

> I dropped my mobile in the harbor so I had to borrow François's which probably means I have HPV now.

Not able to help myself, I laughed.
She asked again:

> Where R U?

> On the ship watching a movie with Hunter.

> Are you having, as the French say, ze sexytimes?

> Yes, we are having all the sex.

I added some laughing emojis so that she would know I was joking. Then I added:

> I told you I was going to leave early.

> Right. Okay. Have fun and I will see you later. Or not.

That made me feel worried, given her earlier statement regarding desperation and dating apps.

> Be careful. Stay safe.

> I am in my garden implement phase of life and can make no such promises.

"What's got you smiling?" Hunter asked as he returned to the room with damp hair, his clothes slightly sticking to him.

Perfectly outlining everything that I was missing out on.

"Georgia just texted me from François's phone. She lost hers in the ocean, apparently."

He got into the bed next to me and I realized that he had put on his cologne. The scent filled my senses and I had to make my entire body go rigid so that I wouldn't reach for him.

"The crew really have a 'work hard, play hard' thing going on, don't they?" he asked.

"More like 'work hard, then destroy your liver.'"

He rewarded me with a laugh, and that warmth from earlier spread through me again.

"The hangovers they're going to have tomorrow will not be pretty," I said.

"You know the trick to curing a hangover, don't you? Don't stop drinking."

Now it was my turn to laugh, but the sound died when he pulled a length of rope out of his pocket.

"Why do you have that?"

"Thomas and François have said my knots aren't up to par. I'm supposed to practice."

"I can help you with that. I have good knot-how."

"Lucky Salerno, was that a pun?"

"No, that's what yachties call it," I told him, taking the rope. I showed him the bowline, the most important one; the eight knot, which was the easiest; the clove hitch; the square knot; and the cleat hitch. I completed the knot first, explaining what I was doing, and then handed him the rope so that he could try it for himself.

And I got to see why Kai had told me that Hunter had to step up his game. Knowing how to do those five basic knots was highly important in sailing. I moved his fingers and the rope to make sure he was getting it properly. It was not easy to concentrate on the task at hand because every time we touched, which was frequently, zaps of electric energy surged through me until my whole body felt like one giant buzz.

"How do you know all of this?" he asked, exasperated after his bowline came apart for the fourth time. He handed it back to have me demonstrate again.

"You pick things up being on the yacht. Although this is a skill that has no real-world application."

"Depends on what you're into."

It was clearly a joke, but that didn't stop my mouth from going dry, my core from clenching.

I had to change the subject right away. "Just practice and you'll get it. It does make me worried about you because you're terrible at this. Is there anything you're good at?"

"I'm not allowed to show you what I'm good at."

That made all the air completely leave our cabin. My lungs stilled in my chest, my heart vibrated with tension and want, my stomach heated. I handed the rope back to him, no longer trusting myself.

"Let's start the movie," I said. My voice sounded strangled and weird.

"Sure. You can feel free to take your pants off, if you'd like."

For one completely panicked moment, I didn't understand why he'd said that to me. Then I remembered earlier, when I'd told him my idea of a good time involved watching a movie with no pants.

"Ha ha," I said back, setting my laptop on both of our legs so that we could see it.

"You never did tell me why you like musicals so much," he said.

"They make me happy. I don't understand why Hollywood thinks everything has to be some depressing, dramatic story about a dysfunctional family."

"Why do they make you happy?"

"Because they make me think of my nonna. After my stepfather took off, my mom had to work like, three jobs to try and make ends meet and my younger sisters and I spent a lot of time with our paternal grandmother."

"Do you still get to see her as often as you'd like?"

Pain lanced my gut. Despite believing that certain wounds had finally healed over, all it took was one question like that to open them back up again. "A couple of years ago, she died from pneumonia."

"Lucky, I'm so sorry. Your mom and your grandma. That's rough. Where was your dad through this?"

This wave of pain didn't feel quite as fresh or intense, probably because it had been so much longer. "He had an aortic dissection right after my twin sisters were born. He was driving with his dad at the time and crashed the car and they both died."

He was silent for a moment, and I was sure he was tallying up all the people in my life that I'd lost.

Then he did what I'd wanted to do when he talked about his sister. He took my hand in his and held it.

It wasn't a romantic gesture, but a soothing and affectionate one. "I'm so sorry for all the loss that you've experienced."

"Thank you." My words were little more than a whisper.

"How do you . . ." His voice trailed off, as if he didn't want to finish his question.

"How do I deal with it?" He nodded, letting me know that I'd guessed correctly. "I don't know. You just put one foot in front of the other and you keep going. You keep living and do the best you can with the circumstances you've been given."

I also kept my heart locked up so that no one else could hurt it. Because with as kind and gentle as he was being right now . . . it felt like I could fall for him. I was so grateful for the nonfraternization rule. I didn't want any more heartache.

"I know how hard that can be to do," he said.

"It is," I agreed. "It makes me cling to the things that I want, the things that I care about. And the anxiety probably comes from the loss."

I'd never seen a therapist, but it was as good an explanation as any other.

"Have you dealt with depression? Anxiety is often comorbid with depression."

"I don't have time to be depressed." Realizing how that sounded I hurried to explain. "I'm not trying to make light of it or sound flippant, and I know how debilitating it can be for so many people, but I've had to work multiple jobs since I was fourteen to help my family. Like I said, I had to keep putting one foot in front of the other because there wasn't another choice."

He was quiet for a long time. So quiet that it made me wonder if I'd said something that had offended him.

Just when I was about to apologize, he turned his head toward me. "You're a really strong person."

"I don't know if I'm strong. I don't feel very strong." Hot tears welled up in my eyes, surprising me. "I really don't want to cry right now."

"It would be okay if you did."

Another reaction I was unused to. Most of the guys I'd dated got upset if I cried. One had even accused me of using it as a manipulation tactic. I nodded and closed my eyelids and felt two tears quickly falling down my cheeks.

"Would it be all right if I hugged you?" he asked.

"Yes." I desperately needed to be held.

He turned his body toward mine and took me in his arms. I pressed my face against his shoulder. Everything about him exuded not only strength, like he could protect me from anything, but a sense that things were going to be okay.

It had been a very long time since I had felt as safe as I did in his embrace.

Definitely dangerous.

His cheek settled on the top of my head, and when he spoke, his words seemed to echo inside my skull. "My sister Harper used to say she had sharp edges because she had been broken and then tried to put herself back together. She was worried it made her rough with other people, so she kept them at a distance."

"That's how I feel." I related so much to that statement. In pushing people away and in feeling irretrievably broken. "I've tried to dull some of my edges."

"I hope you don't. I like your sharp edges."

This felt like more than a friendship. It felt like the beginning of something. Like there could be a romantic relationship between us if we both let it.

But I had to remind myself that he was a genuinely nice guy who responded to people in need. Probably because of his own loss—it had made him a more compassionate and aware person. He was kind.

I needed to remember that.

And why I had been avoiding romantic entanglements for so long.

He started rubbing his hand up and down my back. It was meant to be in a soothing way, but it wasn't soothing me. It was getting me riled up.

I had to put those barriers in place. Erect the protective walls.

"Thank you. I'm glad you're my friend." I said it more for myself than for him.

His arms tightened around me. "Me too."

There. He had just confirmed it. Only friends. He wasn't interested and only saw us as friends.

Which was what I wanted. What I needed.

So why did it feel like my heart was breaking all over again?

CHAPTER EIGHTEEN

Lucky

Later that night I lay in my bed, reviewing how Hunter and I had spent our evening. I'd had to disentangle myself from his hug once I realized how much I wanted to stay right where I was. It wasn't good for either one of us for me to behave that way.

We had heard the crew return and their shrieks and laughter, the sounds of them running down the hall and eating loudly in the crew mess.

But none of them came into our cabin.

Until much later on.

Hunter had returned to his own bunk and quickly fallen asleep. I envied his ability to do that.

I was lying awake, reminding myself of all the reasons my job was important to me, how horrible my relationships always turned out, when the cabin door started to slowly open. It was kind of freaky—like something out of a horror movie. My heart accelerated and I looked around for something I could use as a weapon.

That sensation fled when Emilie came into our room, wearing a nightie that left absolutely nothing to the imagination.

She began to creep over toward our bunks. She put her hands on Hunter's bed and that's when I spoke.

"What do you think you're doing?"

Emilie froze like a statue. "Lucky?"

"Yes."

"You're awake?" I could hear the panic in her tone.

"That's why I'm talking to you."

"I . . . got lost."

Lost. Ha. "This isn't your cabin. Go back across the hall."

"Sorry," she said as she let go of his bunk. "I must have gotten turned around."

"That can happen when you're trying to seduce a deckhand against the captain's rules." I hoped I sounded firm and not at all like a hypocrite.

Because that was how I felt.

She didn't leave. Instead she mumbled, "You had him to yourself all evening. You're so selfish."

Was she drunk? "You shouldn't be speaking to me that way. I'm your chief stew."

That shut her up. I could feel her eyes on me. She finally turned and closed the door softly. Had she actually intended to hook up with him in here while I was sleeping? So foul.

"Thanks," Hunter said above me.

Stunned that he was awake, it took me a few beats before I could respond. "You're welcome."

I wondered how much of that encounter he had heard. There had been the slightest hint of delight in his thanks, like it amused him that I had assigned myself the job of watchdog.

The captain had asked me to keep an eye on him, and it turned out he'd done so with good reason.

Even if sometimes I felt like a fox assigned to guard a henhouse.

~

I was the first one up the next morning. Hunter was still snoring. I drank the sight of him in briefly and then hurried off to get ready.

Given the fact that not even the mice were stirring, since the whole crew had been struck with a case of hungoveritis, I took it as a sign that I'd be doing my activity alone.

So much for unifying the team.

Maybe Georgia had the right idea and I should go out more with them when they were partying. That would probably bond us better.

It would also have the added bonus of keeping me from spending time alone with Hunter. Being surrounded by a group of people seemed like a safer bet. He tempted me into forgetting all my resolutions regarding staying away from men.

I went to the aft deck with my coffee and watched the sun creeping its way over the horizon. I loved this time of day—the quiet, the tranquility, the beauty.

Even if my life was filled with a lot of hard, manual labor, I was grateful for moments like this one.

"That's some sunrise."

I turned in surprise to see Hunter standing behind me with a backpack on. He came over to join me at the railing.

I said, "I think the rest of the crew forgets that we're in the Mediterranean and how amazing it is here. Don't you think it's beautiful?"

"I do."

But when I glanced over at him, he wasn't looking out at the horizon.

He was looking at me.

A knot formed in my throat and my vision went a bit hazy. Something was happening.

Or I just really wanted something to happen despite my best intentions.

It was impossible to tell. I turned my gaze back to the ocean. My heart was attacking the inside of my chest, my lungs constricting. "What are you doing?" I asked.

He didn't seem to understand that I was asking him to name what was happening between us; he failed to pick up on the desperation I was feeling. There was an impossibly long moment before he finally answered. "I thought we were going on a hike."

Just the tour, then. Nothing else. I wished I could flip a switch that would make my heart beat normally again. To be as indifferent as him. "Was anyone else awake downstairs?"

"No."

I set my coffee down and pulled out my phone. My hands shook slightly as I sent a text to the group chat, asking if they were coming. I waited for a bit, trying to calm my nerves, but there was no response. That wasn't good. I put my bag over my shoulder. "I guess this means it's just the two of us."

He grinned. "If you wanted to go on a date with me, Lucky, all you had to do was ask. You didn't have to go to these extremes."

"I'm not dignifying that with a response," I told him and headed for the stairs. I was still fighting off the disappointment he'd caused by being oblivious.

Or maybe he wasn't oblivious. I'd been telling myself since he arrived that he wasn't interested. I thought I should probably start believing it.

I should also remember that it was a good thing there wasn't any romance between us.

"Yes, you will. You can't help yourself." He had no problem keeping up with me.

And he was right. "It's not a date. And it's not a hike."

I could hear the smile in his voice. "Whatever you say."

As I stepped onto the dock, he asked, "Are we meeting someone? Didn't you say this was a guided tour?"

I held up my phone. "We're going to follow an app. It will tell me the path to take. The whole thing is . . ." I peered down at the screen. "Like six kilometers. I don't know how far that is."

"It should take us about an hour and a half to walk that. So long as you're not slow."

Why did he enjoy baiting me so much? "I don't do anything slow."

"That's a shame."

He's teasing you, I had to remind my frenzied libido. I was glad we were going for a long walk. My body needed the exercise so it could work off some of this lust. "This way."

We began our walk through the narrow cobblestone streets of Old Town, surrounded by yellow, ochre, and orange buildings that were covered in green leaves and bright pink flowers. The streets were quiet, mostly empty.

It felt otherworldly. I reached out to let my fingertips graze the building closest to me. It was cool to the touch, but I guessed that once the sun rose high enough, the stone would warm up.

"Why do you think people stopped saying 'take a hike'?" he asked.

If someone had asked me to predict what he might say, that would have been dead last. "What?"

"Think about it. It's such a great way to tell someone off. Completely dismissive without being crass. Telling somebody to go away and experience the wonder of nature for a little while and leave you alone."

One of the bells from a nearby cathedral rang briefly—as if it had been hit by mistake. "I suppose it is the ancestral form of 'go touch grass.'"

His smile lit up his whole face. It seemed very unfair that he was pretty enough to distract me from our surroundings.

And my inattention was so great that my phone began to beep at me, letting me know I'd missed the street I was supposed to turn left on. I turned around and doubled back until I reached the corner and went the correct way. "Ancient people could navigate by the stars and I'm about to get lost while having GPS."

Hunter laughed as we walked together in companionable silence. We'd had our share of awkward moments so far, but that was mostly due to me and my overactive imagination. He seemed perfectly content to be walking in the quiet with me, not rushing to fill it in.

And for the first time in forever, I didn't feel compelled to fill it, either.

We had just reached the outskirts of the city proper and were headed along a route that took us past beaches, neighborhoods, and through areas with rocks, tall grasses, and trees.

It was strange to be in such a lush, green area and know that there were white-sand beaches with bright blue waters just beyond them.

There was movement to our right in the underbrush and I came to a stop, the hairs on the back of my neck standing up. "What is that? Do you think there are bears in France?"

"I don't know. If we see one, we'll ask him. Did you bring bear spray?"

"What's bear spray?"

"It's like pepper spray for bears. You should always use it if a bear attacks you because you're going to die anyway so it's better if you make the bear really and truly mad so that he'll maul you faster."

His silliness made my fears ease. "Have a lot of experience with bears, do you?" A cat came out from the underbrush, stared at us for a moment, and then left. Feeling ridiculous, I shook my head and started walking again.

"I'm actually quite the outdoorsman. I'm an avid bird-watcher and have a secret talent for identifying them."

"Oh?" There was a small brown bird singing in the treetops not too far from us. "What's that one?"

He peered at it, shading his eyes while he studied it. "Yep. That one's easy to classify. It is definitely a bird."

I laughed, scaring the little creature away.

"All jokes aside, I really do love being outside," he said. "It's one of the best things about this job. The constant nature."

"Same. Why do you think I chose this as our activity?"

He moved closer to me. "Your mind always goes to the worst possible scenario, doesn't it? Like automatically assuming a noise you hear is a bear?"

My skin prickled at the uncomfortable sensation he caused. It was like he saw through me so easily, so clearly. "It does. I'm always worried about what bad thing is going to happen next."

"Considering what you told me, that makes sense. You've had more than your fair share of bad things. I understand why you'd always be bracing yourself for the next one."

It was the most profound and correct thing that anyone had ever said about me.

Which meant I had no idea how to respond to it.

CHAPTER NINETEEN

Lucky

I settled on pivoting around and pressing forward without answering him. He seemed to correctly sense that he might have pushed me a bit too far out of my comfort zone and didn't ask me anything further about my catastrophizing everything.

I was considering what he'd said, recognizing the truth in it. I'd always thought envisioning the worst possible outcome was the smart thing to do so that I would be prepared. Being caught off-guard by a doomsday event was awful.

Something I knew all too well.

It occurred to me that I was always holding my breath, waiting for terrible things to happen, because they always had.

The stress that constant fear caused—the pressure that I put myself under—it wasn't good.

Hunter started whistling "Luck Be a Lady," one of the songs from *Guys and Dolls*, as we continued down the path and it felt pointed.

Like he was making a pun with the song. Only I didn't catch the meaning.

Maybe he just liked the song and liked to whistle.

It didn't feel that way, though.

He abruptly stopped and then said, "Tell me something I don't know about you."

What, he didn't want to keep making wild but accurate guesses? "You don't know most things about me."

"That's not true. I know lots of stuff. I know you sometimes have panic attacks, that you've lost a lot of your family, that you're a hard worker charged with keeping the yacht clean even though you're a messy person. You're extremely loyal, protective, and you always follow the rules. You're smart and funny and probably too generous with your time. Your anxiety is difficult to deal with but you do it anyway. You're kind and thoughtful, especially with the guests. You have excellent taste in movies. I make you laugh even though you want to pretend that I don't. And you have freakily good balance—you can carry several plates on your arms up and down narrow sets of stairs on a swaying ship."

There was another moment, just like I'd had earlier, where it felt like he was laying my soul bare and correctly calling out everything he saw.

I didn't want to dwell on that, this feeling of being so seen. Because that was another thing that hadn't happened in a really long time. "I love to bake."

"You do? That works out well for me because I love to eat."

I'd seen him eat and that was a hundred percent true. I still got a little hot and bothered when I thought about how he devoured his food, the hunger, the focus.

Wanting to redirect myself, I announced, "I want to open a bakery."

The confessions just kept rolling on. I had never said that out loud before, not even to my sisters. It felt like such a foolish and impossible dream, like something that couldn't ever happen.

"That's why I'm yachting," I added on. "My nonna used to have an Italian bakery. She and my nonno immigrated to America from Naples and that's where I spent all my time with her. My dream is to reopen it and carry on her legacy."

"What happened to her bakery?"

The path had narrowed and I had to push some tall grass out of the way to continue on. "It got foreclosed on and everything inside was sold off. She had battled cancer for a few years and was really deeply in debt because she took out all these loans to pay her bills. She never told us."

"I'm sorry. That sucks." He must have been able to hear the pain in my voice.

Was it weird that his empathy was one of the most attractive things about him?

"What about you? What's your dream job?" I realized that most of the time we'd spent together, it had been him asking me questions.

In part because I was afraid to get to know him better. I suspected that if I did, I would like him even more.

What I already knew, that he was funny, kind, compassionate, goofy, quick-witted, comforting, and implausibly handsome, was bad enough.

He didn't answer for a bit and I wondered if it made him uncomfortable to talk about himself. That definitely would have set him apart from every other man I'd ever met. "I told you about my sister Harper passing. What I didn't tell you was that she died from an overdose. She had struggled with depression and anxiety for most of her life and dealt with suicidal ideation. My parents think she took her own life but I think it was an accident."

That stopped me in my tracks and I turned toward him. "Hunter." Without thinking I walked over to him and wrapped my arms around his waist. I realized after the fact that I probably should have asked him first, but he returned the hug, holding me close.

"I'm sorry," I said. My inclination was to rub his back the way he'd rubbed mine when I told him about my family, but I knew that nothing good would come from that. "Are you okay?"

"I am. Like I said, I had a lot of professional help after the fact. I mean, once I stopped acting out."

Let go of him, my brain was chanting, registering how embarrassing this was. My arms were reluctant to move but I finally managed it. I took a step back so that I'd stop crowding the poor man. "Acting out?"

He turned his gaze toward the ocean, visible from our vantage point. "I blamed myself after Harper was gone. I thought that I should have reached out more, checked in with her. Maybe I would have figured out she was using again and could have done something. But I was busy with life and school and I'll always regret that I didn't. And my way of coping was to get blackout drunk as often as I could and drop out of law school."

I heard his voice break, saw him swallow a couple of times, watched the way his jaw set.

"Law school?" I asked, wanting to change the subject, as it seemed like talking about that time in his life was hard for him. "Isn't the law like, all memorization?"

"That and arguing."

He had that last one down, at least. "You have a hard time remembering names."

"Case law is different."

"How?"

"It just is," he said with a shrug. "That's how my brain works. I don't know how to explain it."

"That's how I feel most of the time. I know I'm being irrational and I know the things I worry about aren't going to come true but it's just what my mind does."

He nodded, his gaze still on the horizon. "But to answer your question, my dream is to open a residential treatment center to help people like Harper."

That seemed pretty spot-on for him. And it had the effect of further weakening my poorly constructed defenses. "Did you go back to law school?"

"No." There was something heavy there, something he left unsaid.

"Well," I said brightly, "you've come to the right place. To earn money and to maybe find potential investors for your residential treatment center. We're dealing with the wealthiest people in the world and you might be able to make some connections. I know a lot of yachties who have gone on to some great jobs or started their own businesses because of the friendships they made with the owners or the guests. Or you could take the path one of my former chief stews did."

Hunter raised his eyebrows as a question.

"She married the owner of the boat. He is forty years older than her, and she's very happily spending as much of his money as quickly as she can."

"Is that your plan? To find a rich guy to marry?"

The question felt completely insulting. "I'd rather french-kiss an electric eel than end up with somebody rich. Rich people took my nonna's bakery." Which was a whole other story I didn't want to get into—how furious I felt at the bank executives who foreclosed on her bakery without even giving me the chance to make things right.

A strange expression crossed his face. "But you spend your days serving the rich."

"The irony is not lost on me. And I do worry sometimes that it makes me a bit of a hypocrite. But a prospective date telling me he has money would send me screaming in the opposite direction. Rich people are the literal worst, and I know that even more now because of my job. I'm going to save up everything I need and then I'll reopen her bakery."

Another pause. "So you're not looking for an investor, but why don't you take out loans?"

"I'm never going into debt," I said firmly. "I saw what it did to my nonna and my mom and I'm not going to put myself in a position where a bank can take everything I've worked so hard for."

"Given how you feel, you really did pick the worst possible job to go into."

"Like I said, I recognize that. But the money we can earn here is ridiculous, and I'd be a fool to miss out on that. I'm hoping to earn fifty thousand dollars in tips by the end of this season. And I try not to think about the 'rich' part with our guests and focus on what works for me. I like taking care of people. I think it's why I like baking so much. It's a way to take care of someone with sugar and chocolate."

We were close to the beach that was the turning point for our walking tour. I started down the path again and he was close behind me.

"I can't believe you were almost a lawyer," I said.

"Not quite. There were a lot more steps before that point."

"It explains why you're constantly contradicting me."

"I don't do that."

I glanced over my shoulder and saw him grinning. We broke through the grass line and it emptied onto a quiet beach. There were only a handful of people there. The sand was white but littered with gray rocks.

I went over to the shore and stared out at the sea, at that color that exactly matched Hunter's eyes.

"It's funny," I said. "I'm constantly surrounded by the ocean but I never, ever get tired of it."

He came over next to me, his arms folded across his chest. "I know what you mean."

We stood there for a long time, quietly watching as the tiny waves lapped onto the shore. The sun continued its ascent in the sky and the edges of the waves sparkled like diamonds in the bright light. The air smelled of brine and sea salt and suntan lotion.

It was a perfect moment.

Hunter looked like he was deep in thought.

"What are you thinking about?" I asked.

"I was thinking that I'm really glad I'm here. Thank you for sharing this with me."

My breath caught at his words. I had intended for this to be a group activity that we would all enjoy but I discovered that I was so, so grateful that he and I were here alone.

CHAPTER TWENTY

Hunter

An internal alarm had been sounding inside me ever since Lucky had told me she hated rich people. *Tell her, tell her, tell her,* it said, over and over again.

I didn't say anything and I probably should have. She was going to be pissed when she found out.

But I had never gone out with a woman where I hadn't wondered whether she was really interested in me or my parents' money. This was a golden opportunity to see if Lucky could like me without my background overshadowing that.

She had to get to know me first, and she would lose all interest in doing that if I told her the truth. And my parents had already told me I wasn't allowed to tell anyone who I was, so that made it easier for me to rationalize.

I would tell her eventually. Just . . . after.

When we got back to Old Town, I asked, "Is there somewhere we can grab breakfast? That's hopefully French this time?"

"You're in luck," she told me with a teasing smile. "Almost every restaurant here is French."

I laughed and we found a café that had tables set up on the sidewalk. It felt quintessentially French, and we found a table and sat.

The waiter came over and greeted us in English, immediately pinning us as tourists. He handed us menus and said he would be back.

"Is it that obvious that we're American?" she asked.

"Maybe it's obvious that you are. I'm an international man of mystery," I said with a smile as I glanced at the menu. "Although I don't even know what part of America you're from."

"Connecticut. What about you?"

"New York." A different server came over and left us glasses of water while I was busy internally grinning at the fact that we didn't live too far apart.

"It's too bad we don't have Andre here. I think he speaks some French," she said.

"Or François, who is fluent."

"Ugh. No thanks," she said, scrunching up her face.

I laughed again. "Not a fan?"

"He's gross. I don't like men who treat their commitments as something negotiable. He's the reason I don't want to learn the language—I don't want to know what he's been saying to me. I only know one phrase in French, and I would never repeat it around him because my understanding is that it's an invitation to my bed and I would never, ever let that happen."

My skin suddenly felt too tight for my body. I wanted her to French phrase me more than I had wanted anything in my life. "Just with François?"

She'd let me into her bed. In a platonic, harmless way that had nothing to do with French phrasing.

But before she could answer, the waiter returned to ask if we had any questions about the menu. I internally cursed at him for interrupting us. "We haven't really had a chance to look at it yet."

The waiter gave us an imperious, annoyed look and said he'd return.

"Let's hurry up and choose," she suggested. She didn't like to rock the boat and it didn't surprise me that she didn't want the waiter to be annoyed with her. I wanted to explain to her that his reaction was also very French but instead looked for something to eat. Maybe I could sublimate my desire with food.

When the waiter came a third time, she ordered the crepes and I got the same thing. Because I wanted to taste whatever it was that she was putting into her mouth and I recognized this was a very strange desire and so stayed quiet.

"Copying me again?" she teased as we handed our menus back to the waiter.

"I'd already decided on it after all your talk about sugar and chocolate this morning." If she wanted to put herself on the menu, I'd much rather order her. I guessed she would be even sweeter.

"Do you speak any foreign languages?" she asked.

How could I explain what I knew without sounding like a total dirtbag? "Just some phrases in a few different ones. Like 'where is the club' and whether a woman wants to . . ."

French phrase me.

Her cheeks colored slightly, another interesting reaction. "What kind of women do you date?"

Hope bloomed in my chest. There could only be one reason for her to ask me that question. I considered being honest with her and just telling her that I was attracted to her.

But she seemed so skittish, so scared. I didn't want to push things, so I did what I always did when I was uncomfortable. I made a joke. "It depends. I have very Pacific taste."

She let out a small groan and I laughed.

"What about you?" I asked, even though I knew I shouldn't. "What kind of men do you date?"

"Cheating jerks, mostly," she said with a shake of her head.

"That sounds like there's a story there."

"Not a very interesting one. The story is both of the men I dated for a few months cheated on me. The last one, Robb, with two *B*s by the way, which should have been a giant red flag, ended our relationship by impregnating my best friend. That was the last time I'd had a panic attack. It's the other reason why I got into yachting. I needed to escape my hometown."

This poor woman. "That must have been hard, to lose your boyfriend and your best friend at the exact same time."

I saw tears well up in her eyes and it took everything in me not to shove this tiny table aside and hold her close. When she cried it tore me apart. I wanted to make everything okay for her.

"It wasn't fun," she said, and I could see how she was fighting to keep it together. "I've given up on dating. I'm tired of being hurt, tired of being cheated on, tired of losing people I love. I'm just going to concentrate on my sisters and my bakery and not worry about romantic things."

I would never do that to you.

The words popped into my head and I wanted to say them to her.

Before I could, the waiter returned with a basket of croissants. He set it down and she grabbed one. "Do you know how much I love bread?"

Had she sensed what I was about to say? It felt like she was trying to lighten the mood and so I played along. "As much as you love pasta?"

"Hmm. If I'm in a relationship with pasta, then bread is my mistress."

I laughed and got my own croissant. I took a bite and might have moaned slightly. I tried to stay away from carbs but this had me rethinking things. "You're right. These are amazing."

"Stick with me. I'll never steer you wrong."

I grinned. "Another nautical pun, Lucky Salerno. I'm so glad I'm being a good influence on you." I knew I should keep things light and easy but I still had unanswered questions. "Earlier you mentioned your mom being in debt. Can I ask what happened?"

If my abrupt subject change surprised her, she didn't show it. "I told you how my dad and nonno died right after my twin sisters were born. My dad didn't have a life insurance policy because he didn't see the need for one, given that he was so young. My mom was raised in foster care and didn't have any family. She worked to support us, with my nonna helping. A year after my dad died, she met my stepdad."

The waiter interrupted us, bringing us our crepes. We both thanked him and I dug in. I'd never had crepes this good before. "You were saying?"

She took a deep breath. "Long story short, my stepdad left when I was fourteen. I think he'd met someone else. My mother had been a stay-at-home mom while they were together but they'd never married, so when he took off, she didn't have any rights to alimony. She worked a bunch of jobs to take care of us and I pitched in. She ran up credit card debt and could only make minimal payments. Things never got better because of it."

Her stepfather abandoning them was another major loss for her. I had to put my fork down. If Lucky had been beautiful to me before, she was even more so now. Harper's death had nearly destroyed me. I couldn't imagine what Lucky had gone through—continually losing the most important people in her life but persevering in spite of it. I admired her so much. She was incredibly strong.

It made me feel like I wasn't good enough for her. I needed to try harder and be better. Maybe I could become the man she deserved.

Instead of giving any indication of where my thoughts had gone, I went back to her story. "And I'm guessing you helped out a lot with taking care of your sisters."

"I did. And I was glad to do it. I liked that I could do something to make my mom's life a little easier."

I could have guessed that she had done whatever she could to help her mom. I wanted to tell her how much I liked her and how incredible she was. She was being so honest with me. Maybe I should do the same. Tell her about my family and my situation. Ease her into it. "Did I tell you that I have two younger sisters, too? Not twins, though. They're eighteen and sixteen."

Her phone buzzed and she glanced down at it. Her face fell.

"What is it?" I was ready to slay dragons again.

"One of my sisters needing money. They only ever text me when they need something. It's six thousand dollars this time to fix their car."

That was our entire tip from the Carmines. Did they know that? My gut told me that they were taking advantage of her. She had dreams and needed money for it. I told myself that I didn't have enough information and needed to back off.

I wanted to protect her. But she hadn't asked for my help or my advice. I couldn't rush in and try to rescue her. Harper had often teased me about my white-knight syndrome and told me that I couldn't save everyone.

If Lucky wanted my perspective, she would ask for it. That didn't mean I couldn't point out what was happening. "Do they do that a lot? Ask you for money?"

She shrugged. "I guess. I'm the only family they have left."

"But you're saving your money for your bakery."

"It might delay me a little bit, but they need my help. Plus, now that I'm chief stew, my base pay is higher, so I'll be able to save up faster. I have a three-year plan."

A plan that would never happen if she kept bailing her family out. "How old are your sisters?"

"Twenty-two." I heard the defensiveness in her voice.

I needed to tread carefully. "I understand wanting to help, but sometimes it stops being help and starts being taken advantage of. Especially someone like you."

"Someone like me?" The defensiveness had turned into anger.

I held up both of my hands, not wanting her to misunderstand. "Someone who is generous and thoughtful. I understand why you want to help them. I'm overprotective of my younger sisters, too."

She stayed quiet and I was hit by a wave of tiredness and frustration that I couldn't help her out of her situation. I covered up a yawn.

"Am I boring you already?" she asked.

"No, somebody kept me up late last night."

"Me?"

"You talk in your sleep," I told her.

"What do I say?"

"It would be ungentlemanly of me to repeat. But it works out well for me because I like to listen in my sleep."

"I don't know how it would be possible for you to hear anything, Mr. Kettle. You snore like you swallowed a chain saw."

Before I could tease her back, a wasp darted directly at her and she gasped, standing up and knocking her chair over. This I could help her with. I grabbed a napkin and swatted it away from her.

Not a dragon, but close enough.

"Maybe this is why I always think the worst is going to happen. A wasp just tried to take me out!"

"My mom always says that who you are when a wasp gets close to you is the real you."

She picked up her chair and sat back down. "You haven't really mentioned your parents before. What do they do?"

I hadn't mentioned them deliberately. They were worried that I would use their name to try to get out of my responsibilities, but I had no intention of doing so. And despite my earlier resolution, I couldn't tell Lucky yet. I needed more time. "I'm a disappointment to my parents."

True but not too much information.

"Are they upset that you are a deckhand?"

"No, they're not upset about that." It had, in fact, been their idea.

The server came by to fill our water glasses back up to the top. We couldn't keep talking about my parents. So when the waiter left, I said, "Lightning round."

"What?"

"You said we don't know each other well, so let's do a lightning round so we can get to know each other better. Favorite color?"

"Pink. You?"

"Black," I said, looking at her hair. "Favorite holiday?"

"Duh, Christmas. What's yours?"

"Easter. It's a big deal in my family. Favorite season?"

"Winter."

"Spring," I said. "Hobbies?"

"Musicals and eating."

"Same," I said with a grin.

I found out her favorite type of sports (none), her favorite type of music (pop), her favorite kind of book (romance), the name of her high school boyfriend (some tool named Wesley), her favorite animal (cat), her favorite dinosaur (stegosaurus), and a hundred other things that it probably would have taken me months to learn about her if we were actually dating.

The waiter returned with our bill and she grabbed it. I was not going to let her pay. Especially not if she was sending her sisters thousands of dollars. She insisted and I recognized that it would hurt her pride if I refused, so I swallowed and nodded.

"Should we head back?" It wasn't what I wanted. I would happily stay out here all day with her but we did have things to do on the ship.

She stood. "I kind of don't want to. This has been like a movie date montage."

"What do you mean?"

"This wasn't a date because I don't see myself doing that again anytime soon. You and I are just friends." It felt a little like she had just headbutted me with that friends thing. "But I always wanted to have that date-like situation with a guy that's something from a movie. Where it's just easy and fun. In real life my dates are usually awkward, awful, and full of dread."

"It sounds like you've been dating the wrong guys."

"That's for sure."

If she would just give me a chance . . . I put my arm on her so that she would stop walking. "Maybe you should try dating the right ones."

CHAPTER TWENTY-ONE

Lucky

My heart galloped in my chest and my mouth went dry.

Like you?

"You're right," I said with a fake smile. "Maybe someday, when I find a pot of gold and hell has frozen over, I'll think about dating again."

"Not all men are terrible," he said. "And you only have to find the right person once."

He made me want things I couldn't have. Had told myself I didn't want to have. I tried to brush off what he was saying. "Maybe I will try to date the right kind of guy when I'm done with yachting. Until then I'll be too busy. Plus, the rules."

I walked a bit faster toward our destination. Hunter was being a friend to me. Kind and caring. It would only make sense for him to tell me to stop dating losers when that had been the only type of man I'd dated so far.

But I yearned, literally yearned, for his words to mean something else. For him to be saying that I should date someone like him.

Or that I should just date him.

Hunter asked, "What is everyone else doing today?"

"Since we have a charter tomorrow, we won't be able to go out tonight. We'll just have a couple of beers on deck, like we have before. It's a working day. When we have a whole day free, Andre likes to rent a car and explore. You could do something like that, too."

"Oh no, I can't rent a car."

"Why not?"

"I may have the tiniest bit of a road rage issue."

"That must make it hard to get places," I said.

"Not really. Living in New York City means it's not a problem."

"Personally, I find it hard to imagine that you're not actually perfect." He was like someone a romance novelist had dreamed up.

His mouth pressed into a thin line. "I'm the furthest thing from perfect."

"I don't believe you," I told him as I took off my shoes, ready to board the *Mio Tesoro*. "I don't want to compare, but of the two of us, I'm willing to bet you have your life much more together than I do."

"In what way? We're both doing the same job."

Fair point. "For starters, I'm guessing that you don't suffer from crippling impostor syndrome."

"What are you an impostor at?"

"Life," I told him.

"You can't be an impostor at life," he said as we walked down the stairs toward our cabin.

"You can. I feel like I never know what I'm doing and I'm faking everything."

"Lucky, that's adulthood. None of us know what we're doing. We're all faking it and trying to do our best. Nobody has to get it perfect because nobody can."

We entered our cabin and I wished that his words were true. It would have been nice if I could believe that everyone around me was struggling as much as I was. I always felt completely alone and the odd person out.

But he made me feel like I wasn't.

I needed to get out of this room—it suddenly seemed way too small.

"You can shower first," I offered. I set my bag down and went to the aft deck to sit in the sun for a little while. I had to stop thinking about my bunkmate all the time. I felt like I was getting obsessive.

"Lucky! Ahoy, mate!"

I looked up and saw Georgia sitting on a lounge chair with a flute of champagne. I went over and joined her.

"You do know it's too early to be drinking champagne, right?" I said.

"Technically, this is a mimosa. I put a drop of orange juice in it. And I hate that we have these restrictions about when we can drink things. I feel like half my life is wondering if it's too late to drink coffee and the other fifty percent is figuring out if it's too early for alcohol."

She was going to be hungover and unhappy tomorrow when the guests arrived.

We were expecting a bachelorette party and I hoped things would stay on this side of utter chaos.

"Sorry I didn't show up this morning," she added before taking another sip of her "mimosa."

"I know you're not outdoorsy."

"What do you mean? I'm outdoors right now drinking champagne on the deck!" she said with a grin, toasting me with her flute. "I'm sure you didn't miss me, though. You must have enjoyed having Hunter all to yourself."

I had. But I knew better than to say that to her.

"Are you two official yet?" she asked. "And you can lie to me all you want, but I know you think he's cute and you might shank someone if it meant he'd be your boyfriend."

Also true, which made me feel anxious. "I can't think of him that way."

"You can and you should."

I shook my head. "You have no idea how much I . . ."

Despite me not finishing my sentence, since I realized I was saying too much, Georgia got it. "I'm guessing you think about him all the time."

Now that I had opened the door just a crack, I found that I wanted to unburden myself. I had no one else to talk these things through with. "I've told myself I'm never dating again but he makes me want to change my mind. I am so tired of having the same internal conversation. That we're just friends and to stop wanting inappropriate things and misreading everything he's saying."

"Well, I'm not going to be any help because I would tell you to read way into it and be totally inappropriate."

"There are rules."

"You should be tired of saying that, too. Captain Carl is an unreasonable person. You shouldn't have to keep rules unreasonable people make. If you lived in a country run by a dictator, nobody would blame you for rising up in rebellion."

"This is not a dictatorship," I told her. "We're free to leave anytime we like."

She shrugged. "Whatever. To give you the heads-up—you should probably make a move on Hunter soon. I think you'll regret it if you don't. And he might get tired of waiting."

My life was full of regrets. I was too afraid to try to add Hunter to the list.

If he got tired of waiting, he was free to date anyone he wanted.

Just not me.

~

There was always something to do on a superyacht, some chore that needed to be completed, some porthole that needed to be detailed. It was easy enough to keep myself busy and away from the cabin.

I even skipped dinner, which wasn't a hardship because Andre was making it in honor of Pieter and it involved pizza with grilled bananas, bacon, and garlic.

I knew I was running away from my problems and felt like a coward. It wasn't the first time I'd done it. I'd always found it easier to leave than to face romance-related issues head-on.

Why couldn't I just get over this infatuation? Relegate Hunter to the friend zone in my mind and keep him there? All the exterior crew were attractive men. I didn't feel this pull toward any of them. I hadn't had even a smidgen of a crush where they were concerned.

But Hunter was unlike all the other men on board.

When I was certain the crew had finished eating and gone up to the sundeck to have a few drinks, I snuck into my cabin. I breathed a sigh of relief that it was empty. I would just live my life like normal and hope that my stupid and inappropriate feelings would catch up to reality sooner rather than later.

After I got ready for bed, I grabbed my laptop and headphones and crawled into my bunk, intending to block everything out with a good movie.

I'd just put my headphones on when the cabin door opened. "There you are!"

Hunter.

My heart literally leapt up at the sight of him. He was here. Here with me.

Not out there with Georgia and Emilie. He had chosen me.

He had a bag of microwave popcorn in his hand and kicked the door shut with his foot. "What are we watching?" he asked.

Then he climbed into my bunk, and for a moment, I was too stunned to respond. "I . . . I haven't chosen anything yet."

He opened the bag and the air was briefly filled with the scent of artificially buttered popcorn. "I vote *Singin' in the Rain*. That was Harper's favorite."

"Okay." I was not going to read into this situation and think it was significant that he was sharing his sister's favorite movie with me. I did a quick search and found the movie, starting it up. My stomach grumbled because I hadn't eaten. I reached for the bag of popcorn but he pulled it away.

"You love pasta, I love popcorn," he said as an explanation while grinning at me.

"There's no way you love popcorn the way I love pasta."

"Debatable. Generally, as a rule, I don't share food." Then, in defiance of his own proclamation, he offered me the bag.

As I took out a handful, I told myself, again, to not mistake his gesture for something it wasn't.

It was advice I should have taken to heart.

Because one minute we were watching the movie together and the next I woke up to sunlight streaming in through the porthole.

I didn't remember turning the movie off. Gene Kelly had been dancing and singing in various types of weather and then suddenly it was morning. It took me a second to get my bearings, to come fully awake.

Then I realized that Hunter was asleep next to me.

There was a momentary sense of utter panic but it quickly subsided. Despite all of my protests that we were only friends, I was glad he was here. That we had felt comfortable enough with each other to fall asleep together.

He wasn't touching me—he had fallen asleep on top of my blankets, while I was underneath them. He was softly breathing in and out, his face relaxed and vulnerable. I turned onto my side so that I could study him.

It really was unfair how unbelievably handsome he was.

Then it occurred to me how weird this might appear. What would he do if he woke up to see me staring at him?

I reached over and pressed against his shoulder. "Hunter."

He didn't respond—his breathing stayed even.

It probably didn't help that I didn't want to wake him up. I wanted to stay here with him, in this little warm bubble where nobody else existed. Where there weren't any rules to worry about, no guests, no Georgia and Emilie trying to snag him, no terrible past weighing me down.

Just us.

I shoved a little more forcefully this time. I couldn't even get out of bed unless he was awake—he was closest to the door. We only had a few hours before the charter guests arrived.

He finally awoke with a start, his eyes unfocused, his hair flopping over onto his forehead. He pushed it out of the way.

"Lucky?" He sounded so disoriented.

"I think we fell asleep watching the movie." My laptop was wedged between the wall of the ship and my bunk. I hoped I hadn't broken it by sleeping on it.

"Oh." He breathed the word out and I felt it against my face, washing over me. "I'm sorry about that."

He absolutely did not have to be sorry. I was happy. So I echoed the words he'd once said to me. "Don't be."

We lay there, facing one another, our chests slowly rising and falling together.

"I should get up," he said, whispering the words.

I wished I could tell him he didn't have to.

But the real world existed beyond that door. Guests were coming, the captain had expectations, we had jobs to do, I couldn't date him.

"We should both get up," I agreed, but neither one of us moved.

Until we heard someone yelling in the hallway. That got him on his feet quickly.

He looked down at me and I could have sworn that what he wanted in that moment was to climb back into bed with me.

But then he disappeared into the bathroom and left me alone, wanting and aching for him. I rolled onto my back and put my hands over my face.

So, so bad. This was all so bad.

CHAPTER TWENTY-TWO

Lucky

We had made it through the week—this was the last official night of the charter. Our bachelorette party had been a total nightmare. Not just in their constant demands, which seemed to change on an hourly basis, or their nightly drunken fights, where the bride fired the other six women as bridesmaids and then reinvited them at breakfast the next morning, or their staying up every night until three and getting up at seven after completely trashing their cabins, or the way they demeaned us all, as if we weren't people.

No, the nightmare was that they kept finding new ways to be horrible and make our lives as difficult as possible. These malnourished, high-strung, sociopathic socialites had been acting like they were auditioning to be on a Bravo reality television show for the last six days.

And despite the fact that they had told us the first night that they were all in relationships, they had been on the exterior crew like Kodiak bears on spawning salmon.

Hunter, most of all.

I kept reminding myself that there was only one day left as I went into the primary cabin, only to find Emilie standing in the bathroom, texting on her phone. Nothing had been done. "What are you doing? Why haven't you cleaned any of this?"

She should have been nearly finished by now. The guests were upstairs at dinner, pretending to eat their food, and the cabins needed to be cleaned and the beds turned down before they returned downstairs.

Something had shifted between the two of us the night I caught her sneaking into my cabin. She was more belligerent, more defiant, lazier.

Whatever goodwill I had earned by protecting her from her uncle had disappeared.

"I'll get it done. Calm down. Why are you always riding me?" she asked.

"Georgia and I have been picking up your slack for the last week. It's going to stop, and you are going to pull your weight." Could she hear how my voice was wobbling? It was hard for me to lay down the law like this. She probably couldn't take me seriously when I couldn't even take myself seriously. "Now get this cabin done."

She picked up a rag and began to listlessly move it in circles on the countertop. I left and wished I had it in me to inspire her to do more. I had tried begging. I had tried asking nicely. I'd done my best to be motivational. I had tried offering to show her precisely what needed to be done. Bribing her.

Nothing worked.

If I weren't so afraid of Captain Carl, I probably would have gone and tattled on her. Maybe he would have sent her packing back to Canada and we could have picked up a new stew who would actually do the job.

When I got to the crew mess, Thomas and Kai were staring at the monitors. I went over to see what they were looking at, and it was the guests at dinner. Everything had been served and Georgia had cleared away all their plates. Now they were just drinking and yelling at each other. The volume was turned down so that we couldn't hear them, but it was easy to see how angry they were.

The bride, Sasha, stood up and threw her glass of red wine in her maid of honor's face.

"It's going to take forever to get that stain out of the deck," Thomas said nonchalantly, in the same sort of tone he might use to comment about the weather.

It was probably because we had all become numb, resigned to our fate where these guests were concerned.

I had done everything in my power to make them happy, all to no avail. I had brought on manicurists, pedicurists, hairstylists, makeup artists. I brought on some French stylists, but all of their clothing options were declared to be "trash." I offered to get the guests some aestheticians but that had only offended them.

"Do we look like we get Botox and fillers?" Sasha had demanded angrily, and I did my best to keep my gaze off her injected lips and the way her forehead didn't move despite her fury.

I said, "Of course not!" and only worried momentarily about my pants catching on fire and then having to jump into the ocean to put them out.

I'd then arranged for a couple of massage therapists to come on board, which was nice for me because I'd been training in Swedish massage with the intent of getting certified. Increasing my skill set would potentially put me in a position to ask for a salary increase.

My attempt at getting the guests to mellow out through the power of massage failed and had only led to another screaming fight between them.

The one time the guests didn't fight was when they were sunbathing nude on the sundeck. The exterior crew did their absolute best to be professional under the circumstances, but the women seemed to particularly delight in hounding them and trying to make the guys uncomfortable. The guests didn't want Georgia, Emilie, and me to serve them when they were on the sundeck—just the men.

I didn't do what they had asked. I didn't trust them to not maul the crew if given half a chance. I just put a big, fake smile on my face and apologized profusely, telling them the exterior crew were far too busy doing other things and that I would do my absolute best to take care of them.

The one thing I did that they actually seemed to enjoy was when I set up the bachelorette party and hired some local male strippers. I was glad that Georgia was on lates that night. So was she, as she'd managed to hook up with one of the strippers, and then proceeded to argue loudly with Emilie that he should count as a temporary crewmember since he had been working on the yacht, which meant Georgia had earned extra points. Emilie strenuously disagreed.

They had been so loud I'd had to shush them for fear of the captain overhearing.

It was like the bachelorette guests were rubbing off on us, making the entire crew snippy and irritable.

Except for Hunter. He'd been the one shining light in all of this.

It started the very first night of the charter, when I had returned to our cabin and was surprised to find him in his bunk.

"What are you doing?" I had asked. "Why aren't you on anchor watch?"

"Pieter offered to take the night shift." Pieter had been sexually harassed the least so far out of all the crew, so it was probably a safer choice. "I think he's doing it to be on the same shift as Georgia. To try and win her heart."

"I don't know if that will work out for him," I said. "She's the one who told me her heart was black and shriveled and incapable of feeling."

I knew she'd had a spectacularly bad breakup before she'd joined the *Mio Tesoro*, and so a part of me understood why she'd come up with the list. She didn't want to care about someone again.

And I understood it because I was in the same boat.

Literally and metaphorically.

"Regardless of whether or not his plan will work, it's probably better for me to hide out in here for the week," Hunter said. He was right. We didn't want to make the guests feel bad by pointing out that they couldn't treat him like a side of beef because it might compromise our tip.

We also couldn't let our crew be compromised. Hiding seemed to be the best option to avoid an ugly confrontation.

So for the last week, that was what we had done. Hunter and I had watched a different musical together every night, laughing and talking and staying up way too late. I'd been so tired in the mornings but it had been worth it just to be with him.

We didn't bring up the night we'd fallen asleep together. It was a topic we both avoided.

Which was good because it was better for me if I didn't dwell on it. It was bad enough that I thought about it every night as he slept above me. What it was like to wake up with him, to have him so close.

To exist with him in a place where the buzzing in my mind turned off and I wasn't constantly worried about what terrible things might happen.

I had just felt . . . peaceful. Content.

Maybe even happy.

But being around him made me feel things in specific places in my body where I was busy trying not to feel anything.

I kept hoping he would do something, anything, that would be a turnoff. Clip his toenails in front of me. Stink up the bathroom. Forget to put on deodorant. Something that might gross me out and give me the ability to move on.

Only it hadn't happened.

He was considerate and clean and respectful and in every way imaginable an excellent bunkmate. He had even started making my bed for me in the morning. And I hadn't decided whether that was just thoughtful or a message that he was annoyed with my messiness.

Regardless, his wonderfulness just made everything more difficult.

"Oh no, now what?" Thomas said, bringing me out of my Hunter reverie. I focused my attention on the screen in front of me. Hunter had been walking past the guests until Sasha waved him over.

The bosun leaned in and turned up the volume so that we could hear what they were saying. The bridal party was hooting and hollering at Hunter.

Georgia was passing by and came to a stop, staring at the monitor with us. "What is the Sisterhood of the Traveling Implants doing now?"

I didn't even shush her—I was just worried for Hunter. It was like he'd just wandered into a pool filled with starving piranhas. They were going to strip him to the bone in less than five minutes.

"Come here and give me a lap dance, you sexy thing!" Sasha shrieked at him, waving her hands high above her head.

"Take your shirt off!" someone else shouted.

"And your pants!"

They were all so drunk.

Hunter tried to beg off, saying he had some work to do, but they weren't listening.

Sasha then peeled off her expensive couture dress and threw it at his head. He reflexively caught it.

Time to save the day. I spun around on my heel and headed for the deck. Those women were seriously objectifying him.

As was I, but I only objectified him in my brain. I didn't announce it to him out loud.

It was called manners.

By the time I reached the deck, the women were fighting over who was going to dance with Hunter first and he was standing there, his eyes glazed over, his expression a bit frightened.

"There you are!" I said to him. "The captain asked me to escort you to the bridge. Ladies, is there anything else I can get for you?"

"A new stripper," somebody muttered. They all looked mutinous.

Just a few more hours and they would be gone. I had to remember that. "I'll be back to check on you," I said.

I would tell Georgia to limit the amount of caffeine she was putting in their espresso martinis.

And maybe I'd grind up some sleeping pills to add to their martinis so that they would just go to bed.

I let out a sigh. I knew things were bad if I was even jokingly considering spiking the guests' drinks.

Just a few more hours to go, I repeated to myself.

We would survive this.

CHAPTER TWENTY-THREE

Lucky

"Does the captain really need to see me?" Hunter asked when we entered the main salon.

"No. It looked like you were in danger."

He shook his head. "You don't have to keep rescuing me. I can take care of myself."

"I don't doubt that for a second," I said. "But it's better to keep you out of the way than to make you stay in a situation where you have to somehow extract yourself while also not offending the guests. Besides, it's fun playing the white knight for once."

He smiled at me, then handed me the bride's dress. "Sasha wanted this to be put in the washing machine. She spilled something on it. Then she asked me to bring it back to her cabin when it's done."

Hmph. I bet she did. "This isn't machine washable."

"I'm guessing anything's machine washable if you don't care about it enough."

"Unfortunately, we have to care. I'll hand-wash it and figure out how to get the red wine out without ruining the dress." I might have seen this as a fun challenge and not just aggravating if the dress had belonged to anyone else.

"You can radio me when you're finished with it and I'll bring it to her."

Nope. "Let me handle this," I said.

He gave me a half smile. "Are you still in white-knight mode?"

I nodded. I was. He deserved to be protected from the ravenous horde upstairs. "Unless you want to go back out there and see what they have in store for you," I said.

The look of panic on his face made me laugh. "No, thank you."

"All those wealthy women? Does this mean you aren't a fortune Hunter?"

"Lucky! That was puntastic."

We couldn't just stand here grinning at each other. This dress needed to be cleaned and I needed to stop awkwardly flirting, so I headed to the laundry room. Instead of going back to whatever he'd been doing before, he followed me. When we arrived I started pulling supplies to clean the dress and get the stain out.

There was a crashing sound and Thomas calmly called out, "Lucky? The guests have gone aggro and are slapping each other around. They've knocked the centerpieces off the table."

Had they broken anything? I hoped not. "Georgia?"

"On it!" she called back.

She would be able to sort this out and maybe even convince them to go to their cabins and sleep it off. Cabins that I hoped Emilie had finally finished cleaning.

"Can you imagine spending a quarter of a million dollars just to fight with your best friends for a week straight?" I asked.

"I cannot," Hunter said, jumping up onto the counter and watching me work. The buttons on his polo shirt strained, as if they could barely contain the muscles underneath. "So what else is going on? Besides the guests being terrible? It seems like something is bothering you."

Other than the fact that I wanted him to shut the laundry room door, throw me up onto the counter, and kiss me senseless? I had to rack my brain for a second to remember the other reasons why I was in a not-great mood. "Oh. Emilie is up to her old tricks again. Spending all her time on her phone and not cleaning the guest cabins."

"I've seen how much extra time you've had to spend following behind her to make sure things are done right."

He paid close enough attention to me to realize that? I wasn't sure how to take what he'd said.

"You shouldn't have to be doing practically everything by yourself," he added. "You should be able to delegate. I know you don't like doing that because of how independent you are."

That was true. "Georgia's been a big help."

"Do you have the power to fire Emilie?"

I briefly let myself fantasize about what it would be like if I did. "Only the captain can fire people. Chief stews can make recommendations but he has all the authority. They're family, so I can't replace her. I'm supposed to be helping rehabilitate her."

"She doesn't seem to want to be rehabilitated." Then, with a shake of his head, he said, "I don't like it when people take advantage of you."

I wouldn't mind if you took advantage of me. I pressed my lips together so that those words wouldn't come out accidentally.

Despite the fact that all the washing machines and dryers were running, we heard yelling in the hallway. I stuck my head out of the laundry room and heard the guests screaming at each other. Thomas and Kai had gone upstairs to deal with it. Hopefully they'd escort everyone to their cabins.

Good. Maybe they'd finally fall asleep. Just as I was headed back into the room, Hunter came bounding out to see what was going on and I nearly smacked into him.

He had to put his hands on my shoulders to steady me. "Careful!"

But his touch didn't help my balancing situation. If anything it left me even more off-kilter. We stood there for several beats, staring at each other, my pulse ricocheting around inside my wrists.

"Are you okay?" he asked.

"Just a bit . . . lightheaded."

"Seasick?"

I couldn't tell him the actual reason why I was suddenly dizzy, so I just nodded.

He let out a little laugh and gazed at me like he thought I was adorable. "Working on a yacht when you get seasick is like being afraid of heights and becoming a pilot."

Then he released me and I fanned my face with my hand, trying to cool down. Why was I not used to him yet? Why did my face flush every time he touched me?

"Is it bad to say I feel sorry for the groom?" he asked over his shoulder, unaware of my predicament. "I'm pretty sure she's going to wipe him out in the inevitable divorce. Maybe we should start a GoFundMe for his legal fees."

"This is supposed to be a once-in-a-lifetime event, and it's sad that the bridal party isn't going to have any good memories from this trip."

"Once in a lifetime? Statistics disagree," he said.

I shook my head at his joke. "When the world elects me as the Supreme Leader, I'm going to outlaw weddings because they turn normal people into frothing psychopaths."

He came back into the laundry room. "You don't want to get married?"

"I don't know if I can see myself doing it. My parents and my grandparents had really happy marriages, so I know it's possible, but it seems like this mythical thing that only a few people actually get to experience. I only fall for men who have an allergy to it. I think I might consider it if I did meet the right person, but it seems like it only happens to a lucky few."

"Then I guess it's a good thing you have the name that you do. Like I said, it only takes once."

I sucked in a deep breath, wanting to ignore what it seemed like he was insinuating. "What about you?" I asked in a too-bright voice.

"'Commitment' is not a four-letter word in my family. I come from a long line of disgustingly happy and in-love couples, and so yeah, I imagine I'll get married. Someday."

It felt surreal to be having this conversation with him. Especially because my brain was frantically envisioning a beach wedding with him starring as the groom.

Hunter turned to shut the door behind him. Alarmed, I started toward him. I wasn't sure what I was going to do but I had to keep him from seeing the list.

But I wasn't fast enough.

"What's this?" he asked.

I ran through various untruths in my head but realized two things simultaneously—the first, that it wouldn't do me any good because it was self-explanatory and the almost lawyer would figure it out, and second, and probably more importantly, I didn't want to lie to him.

"It's a competition. To see who can kiss slash hook up slash fool around with the most crewmembers," I said.

It was the first time I'd seen the list since I'd initially found it. There were various handwritten points listed next to everyone's names.

Even François's. Ew. Which one of them had kissed him?

The word *stripper* had been written in, crossed out, and rewritten again probably a dozen times.

But there were absolutely zero points next to Hunter's name.

"Are you a part of this?" he asked, sounding highly suspicious.

"No!" Had I said that too forcefully? I modulated my voice. "I mean, no. I'm not. This is just Georgia and Emilie's thing."

He looked relieved.

Why would he be relieved by that?

"You know, Kai mentioned some competition. I just didn't realize it was like this. And I'm part of it?"

"They're both pretty determined to score from you."

"That won't happen."

"Oh?" That was far too hopeful. I didn't repeat it in a more uninterested tone, as I decided that would draw too much attention to it.

"You're not the only one who needs to follow the rules."

He had joked in Saint-Tropez that he was an international man of mystery, and I was believing it. There was something he was leaving unspoken, and it felt important. I wanted to solve the puzzle he'd just dangled so temptingly in front of me.

Before I could ask him about it, he continued on, "Plus, I'm not interested in either one of them."

"Oh?" Now my voice was shaking, I was repeating myself, and so I forced myself to go back over to the dress so that I would have something else to focus my energy on.

Because I was giddy. Utterly giddy that he wasn't interested in either one of my stews.

He might not be interested in you, either.

I brushed that annoying voice of mine away. I was going to live in glorious denial until he said something to the contrary.

Not that we could act on it, but just the fact that there was some small glimmer of hope was enough to make me feel like I was being lit up by 1.21 gigawatts of electricity.

Then I went and found a way to destroy that feeling. "But you made a face."

His quizzical expression told me that he had no idea what I was talking about. "I what?"

"When Kai and Emilie kissed in the taxi. You made a face. I thought it was because you liked her."

"It was because I didn't think it was okay for them to be doing that in front of the rest of the crew. We were all given the same rules by the captain. They put all of us in an awkward position. Nobody wants to snitch on them but they made us their accomplices."

The fact that he was a rule follower made him even more attractive. Bad boys had never held much appeal for me.

He folded his arms and continued his TED Talk, gesturing toward the list. "You've said that Georgia is your friend. But if she was, she wouldn't be doing stuff like this. Putting you in a precarious position."

"She is my friend. But yachting makes relationships different. It's a 'let's be friends until one of us quits or gets fired' sort of situation. Everything in our lives is temporary. You might keep in touch on social media, but it's never the same as when you worked together."

"So you make friends thinking that things will always end?" he asked.

"They do end. The impermanence is why the captain's rule is a good one. Nobody here is going to wind up with a happily ever after. I mean, you do hear about it happening, and those people go off and work on yachts together as a couple, but that is more the exception than the rule. Relationships are usually short lived."

"But not always."

"Not always," I agreed.

"That seems . . . sad."

Realizing that I was neglecting Sasha's dress, I started dabbing at the stain. "It's our life here. We have to live in the present and enjoy our days the best we can because we never know when it might all change."

"That's true of life in general," he said, taking his spot on the counter again. "It kind of sounds like college. You have these friends and roommates you see every day and then college is over and everything changes. It was a strange adjustment."

I ran lukewarm water in the sink to wash the dress, grabbing a mild detergent. "I wouldn't know. I didn't go to college. I wanted to, but obviously there wasn't any money for it."

"College hasn't gone anywhere. You could still go. You'd do amazing."

I liked the way he talked. Like the world was still full of possibilities for me. Where I saw doors that had been shut, he saw a way to open them up again.

He made me feel like I could say the things I felt and he wouldn't turn away from me. That he would listen and understand.

My heart began to pound as I thought of telling him how much I liked being with him.

That I didn't want our situation to be impermanent. How a piece of my soul hoped that our friendship would last long past our time on this yacht.

That maybe we could be something more. Someday.

"Hunter, there's something that I—"

CHAPTER TWENTY-FOUR

Lucky

But before I could share the innermost parts of my psyche and my deepest desires, Thomas interrupted us over the radio.

"Hunter, Hunter, Thomas."

He grabbed his walkie-talkie. "This is Hunter."

"I need your assistance on the sundeck."

"Copy. I'll be right there." He jumped off the counter and smiled at me before he left.

I fought off the sinking disappointment I felt. This was better. I could concentrate on the task at hand and didn't have the chance to vomit words all over Hunter. I hadn't humiliated myself.

Now there was no chance of him putting his hands on my shoulders and saying, "Lucky, you're a really nice person but I don't think of you that way." That would have been horrific. World-ending. Nuclear apocalypse bad.

Why had I been so ready to tell him that I liked him? To risk that kind of rejection?

The stain had lifted out and the dress was clean. Marika had been a wizard at finding the most incredible products for laundry and cleaning.

I wondered how the exterior crew was doing with the stained deck while I rinsed the dress, wrung out the excess water, and then put it between two fluffy towels to dry quickly.

I went into the galley to see what we still needed to finish for the night. By the time I completed everything there, the dress had dried completely. I went to Sasha's cabin and knocked on her door.

She answered it naked.

And from the expression on her face, I was not who she had been expecting.

I held the dress out to her while averting my eyes. "Here you go! All clean."

This was a first for me, so I wasn't sure of what the protocol here was. Sasha took the dress and carefully checked the edge where the stain had been.

Figuring I should probably go, I said, "Have a good—"

"Where is my champagne?" she demanded. Like she was angry that the stain was gone and so she had to find something else to be mad about.

"Did you request champagne?"

"Did I request . . . yes. I told the taller blonde to bring me champagne." She was talking about Emilie.

Who had dropped the ball, again.

"I'll get that for you right away," I said.

Sasha was obviously very comfortable with her body, as she continued to stand there and yell at me. "It should have been in my cabin waiting for me!"

"You're right, my apologies—"

But she cut me off. "And my bridesmaids' cabins were not cleaned. What is wrong with you and your staff? You literally have one job. How much of an idiot do you have to be to work here? Do you have to fail an IQ test?"

I knew she was drunk. I knew she was angry. I knew she was frustrated. But instead of being able to rationally excuse her lashing out, my anxiety was making my entire body shake, telling me that she was right about everything she was saying.

"I'll get you the champagne and I'll clean their rooms—"

She interrupted me again. "It's too late. They're already in bed. Do better. I can't believe how terrible the service has been on this trip."

Sasha slammed the door shut and I gasped a little, the sound shocking my system. I hurried to the galley to get the champagne. I knocked on her door and she threw it open, still naked, and grabbed the bottle from my hands before slamming the door a second time.

She was going to tell the captain. She would tell him how incompetent I was and he would fire me and then I would never reopen my nonna's bakery. Everything would be gone because Emilie couldn't be bothered to do her job, because Sasha couldn't be a nice human.

And after I got fired, I would never get to see Hunter again.

I was nauseous; I needed to get to a toilet. I hurried to my cabin and went immediately into the bathroom.

Kneeling over the toilet, I felt sweat pouring down my back and a stabbing sensation in my chest. I was on the verge of a panic attack, which I very much did not want to have. I sat on the floor of the bathroom and began my breathing exercises.

I wished Hunter were here to hold my hands. I closed my eyes and pictured it and somehow it helped. My breathing got easier and my legs stronger, so that I was able to stand up and splash water on my face.

The cold shock of the water also made me feel more myself, reminded me where I was. Grounded me.

I glanced up at the shelves and saw his cologne bottle. I picked it up and took off the lid, taking a deep sniff. It so reminded me of him that I found it calming me down even more. He chose then to come back into our cabin. I began fumbling the bottle and it was a minor miracle that I didn't drop it and douse the entire bathroom.

"Lucky?"

I got the bottle back onto the shelf and quickly checked my fingers to make sure I hadn't accidentally spilled any. There would not be a logical way for me to explain why I suddenly smelled like him.

Not detecting any rogue scents, I came out into the cabin.

"There you are. What did Sasha . . ." His voice trailed off as he looked at my face. "What happened?"

He sounded a bit angry. I told him everything, how mean she had been, what she had said. His jaw got tighter and tighter.

"The Carmines jinxed us by being so nice," I said. "The universe needed to rebalance by giving us nightmare guests."

"That bridal party are all starving," he interjected. "It's why they're so terrible."

I tried to smile. "Pasta really does make the world a better place." I let out a big breath. "Then I got Sasha the champagne and was worried that I was going to have a panic attack so I came back here. I didn't have one, though, because I thought about . . ."

My earlier resolve to tell him how I felt was completely gone. Especially after Sasha's attack. I felt too raw to be rejected.

"What did you think about?" he asked in a quiet voice.

As if he knew.

Again, I had that pang of wanting to be honest with him. I couldn't, though. So I settled on, "Something that made me feel better. I'm just worried she'll go to the captain."

"Even Captain Carl can see how awful these guests are," he said.

"He's not supposed to," I countered. "We live by 'never let them see you sweat.' Everything can go completely wrong just so long as the guests and captain never know."

"The guests know how they're acting. I'll go and say something to that bride right now," he said, his jaw still tense.

I put my hands on his arms to stop him from leaving. "No! That would be the worst thing you could do. We've all had to put up with so much from them. Let's not fumble this at the one-yard line."

"A football reference?" One corner of his mouth quirked up in a half smile and I felt the tension leave his body.

"Yes, football. I'm trying to speak to you in a language you'll understand."

He nodded. "I also would have accepted 'loose lips sink ships.'"

Now I was the one smiling. "Sasha's not worth losing our jobs over. I do hate how small she made me feel. That I let her make me feel small and didn't just let her words roll off my back."

His clenched jaw returned. "Understandable, given how horrible she was being to you."

It was then that I realized I still had my hands on him and dropped them back down to my sides.

"Do you know what would cheer you up?" he asked. "*White Christmas.*"

He was right. That would cheer me up.

"Get ready for bed and meet me in your bunk when you're done," he said. I hurried and changed, knowing that he was off to make some popcorn.

I was already in bed when he returned. Sure enough, he'd microwaved some popcorn. He climbed in beside me and offered me the bag first.

It was a sweet gesture. I took a handful and started the movie.

And everything was going just fine until the retired general entered the dining hall where all his former troops were waiting for him as a surprise. The expression on the actor's face . . . I knew exactly how it would look, but it still managed to make me tear up every time.

Well, almost every time. This time it had the effect of making me sob.

"Hey," Hunter said, sounding worried.

I was crying too hard to respond. It was like everything that had happened that evening, along with all the other stuff I'd been internally wrestling with, the longing, the pining, the desperate wanting while knowing nothing could ever happen, came pouring out of me.

And I absolutely did not want to cry in front of this man, but it was like I couldn't help myself. I had to get it all out.

Without saying another word Hunter hugged me to him, holding me. He seemed to understand that it was exactly what I needed.

By the time the characters were singing the last song of the movie, I finally managed to calm down. Hunter reached over and shut my laptop.

"I'm sorry I keep crying in your arms," I said against his shoulder.

"That's what they're here for," he said, and flexed them against me. It made me laugh-cry at the same time.

"It's better than a panic attack, right?" I tried to match his light tone.

But then he switched things up on me and got all serious. "However you need to process what you're feeling, you should do it." He paused and added, "And I'll be here to help you in any way that I can."

That last line made me feel worse. Like he saw himself as needing to support me because I was such a mess. "Crying like that makes me feel really weak."

His words were making me feel weak, too. In more ways than one.

He reached up with his hand and turned my face so that I was looking into his bright blue eyes. "Lucky Salerno, I don't think you're weak. You are one of the strongest people I've ever met."

Our gazes locked and I saw the moment when his eyes lowered to my lips, and felt his arms tighten around me. My heart fluttered with excitement, my stomach squeezed with anticipation, my nerve endings sparking with joy.

This wasn't my imagination.

Hunter wanted to kiss me.

CHAPTER TWENTY-FIVE

Hunter

Kissing had often felt like something to get what I wanted. A marker that had to be hit before moving on to the main event.

But with Lucky?

I knew that I could spend all night kissing her and it would be enough.

Because it would be different with her. I instinctively understood that.

That there was more between us and it wouldn't feel like it had before. That I could so easily sink into a pool of sweet desire with her and never want to find my way back out.

A hot spike of longing pierced my gut, pinning me in place. My chest burned with an emotion I didn't quite recognize. I became acutely aware of her. The way her silky hair caressed my arms. The smattering of freckles on the bridge of her nose. How her breathing sounded faster and shorter. That light tropical scent of hers.

Only one sense left—I needed to taste her.

My lips ached to touch hers. I had to know what it would feel like. My skin prickled with a need for her that made it painful to stay on my side of the bed.

"Lucky," I said softly, hoping she would hear what I couldn't say.

I leaned forward and heard the way her breath caught, saw her eyes widen. I went slowly, giving her the chance to stop me.

Which she did. "We should call it a night," she said in a whisper that made my stomach clench.

Okay. Message received. I did my best not to look disappointed. "Good night."

It was hard to let her go but I did and scooted to the edge of her bunk. To my shock she reached out and put her hand on my arm, sending a bolt of crackling pleasure through me. My pulse thudded at the contact. Had she changed her mind?

"Stay," she said and it made that emotion from my chest head straight into my heart.

I must have misheard her. "What?"

"Don't go."

There was no more oxygen in this room.

"If you want," she added, sounding embarrassed.

I wanted. I wanted so badly that I was nearly shaking from it. Desire curled and twisted low in my gut.

It couldn't happen. I knew that. I stood up.

I saw on her face that she thought I had rejected her. Didn't she know that I would give her anything she asked for? Would do anything for her?

I turned off the light and then locked the door.

She gasped when she registered that I wasn't going anywhere. I lifted the covers and slid into bed next to her. It took every single ounce of willpower that I possessed not to reach for her. I had to take things slowly. I shouldn't even be doing this at all. I should remember my plans and what I had promised to do.

But being this close to Lucky blocked all that out.

We faced one another. Her breathing still hadn't settled and neither had mine. I wasn't touching her, wasn't kissing her, wasn't doing anything that I wanted to do, but somehow this felt intimate to me. She was so sweet and warm and it was killing me to stay put.

"Good night, Lucky."

"Good night, Hunter."

I had no idea how I was going to survive this.

~

When I woke up the next morning, it was to discover that she was watching me. I wondered if she liked what she saw.

Then I realized my hand was on her waist. That had happened unintentionally.

Unintentionally in the sense that I hadn't agreed to it, but it was completely intentional on my body's part.

That I had sought out a connection with her while we were sleeping. "Why do you always wake up so early?" I grumbled.

Her smile was pure sunshine and it chased away my grumpy mood.

"Maybe because it's a day full of possibilities," she said.

Then she leaned toward me, as if she intended to kiss me. Like it was something we had already done a thousand times.

At the last possible moment, she suddenly seemed to realize what she was doing and ended up smacking her forehead into my nose.

"Ow!" I took my hand from her waist and rubbed my nose. Like it already wasn't bad enough that I couldn't be with her—now I was getting assaulted.

"Are you okay?" Her voice wobbled, as if worried that she had permanently damaged me.

I wished I could kiss her frown away. I settled for teasing her. "I'm fine. I just didn't know you were this clumsy in the morning."

If I stayed in this bunk any longer, I worried that I was going to do something I'd regret. She had the prettiest, pinkest lips and it felt like a crime that I didn't get to kiss them. I went into the bathroom and wondered if there was enough cold water on this ship to calm my raging heartbeat.

I looked at myself in the mirror. I felt like a coward. *I should just talk to her.*

If she said she wasn't interested, that was fine. I was a big boy. I could handle it.

But if she said she wanted something more . . .

All my thoughts about taking things slow went away and I came back into the cabin. She was still lying in bed and the only thing I wanted to do was climb back in there with her. She looked so uncertain and worried and I wanted to make things better.

Thomas's voice came through on the walkie-talkie, calling my name.

He had the worst timing. I grabbed it and responded. He said he needed me on the aft deck. I said that I'd be there soon, watching her the whole time.

"Lucky, I—"

"You should go," she said, pulling the blanket up to her chest. "It might be important."

I doubted it but I heard what she wasn't saying. She needed some space. She wanted to think about what had almost happened last night.

She was concerned about breaking Captain Carl's rule.

I got ready and left with her still in her bunk. I had some thinking to do, too. Mostly about how everything might change once she knew who I really was.

Would she be understanding? Or would she freak out?

I knew I should tell her everything.

But there was a part of me that held back, not wanting to lose her.

The mindless physical labor didn't help my situation. If I'd been doing something that engaged my brain, maybe I would have been able to keep thoughts of her at bay.

That wasn't happening now.

While I scrubbed the teak deck, I took a picture of it and sent it to her.

She responded so quickly that it made me smile.

What is this?

I texted back:

> I'm sending you unsolicited deck pics.
> Signed, Your Favorite Buoy

I could imagine her laughing, the way her whole face would light up and my heart would swell that I was the one responsible for it.

There was a twinge in my chest and I rubbed it. I realized that I could very easily spend the rest of my life making Lucky happy.

~

The bachelorette party from hell finally left and screwed us on the tip. Everybody wanted to go out and celebrate that they had gone but the captain put a stop to that.

He told us to meet him in the main salon. When I arrived, Lucky was already there. And I grinned at her like I was coming home from war.

I told myself that someone was going to notice, but I didn't care.

Especially not when she lit up the way that she did.

Thomas was seated next to her and I told the bosun to move. He was in my spot.

She smiled at me and then briefly laid her head against my shoulder. Like a sort of hug. And it made me want to melt all over this expensive couch.

Which would've been a shame, because she would have probably been the one stuck scraping me out of the fabric.

I was so whipped.

The captain came into the room and sat down in an armchair. "Our next charter has been canceled."

Lucky looked upset and I knew why. We were scheduled to pick up three accountants and their wives. She'd said after the demons masquerading as a bridal party that the universe owed us a nice, boring charter. And the group had planned stops in Italy, somewhere that she was desperate to go.

The captain added, "But we have arranged a couple of last-minute charters. We will pick up the first one tomorrow in Nice at ten o'clock in the morning, and the guest should be with us for a week. So if you made any plans for tonight, cancel them."

The crew groaned. We were supposed to have had two days free to do as we liked. The captain didn't seem to like the response and glared at everyone before leaving.

Kai threw up both of his hands. "Is he serious? We don't get to go out?"

The exterior crew got into a heated discussion about how angry they were.

This worked for me. There was only one person I wanted to spend time with. I leaned toward Lucky and my lips might have accidentally brushed against the shell of her ear. I took great satisfaction in the way that she shivered.

"Movie and popcorn?" I asked.

"Yes, please." Her voice was rough with longing.

I imagined her begging me with those words while writhing underneath me and it briefly took away my ability to stand.

"I'll meet you in bed," I said. I didn't wait to see her reaction, and I used the two and a half minutes that it took the popcorn to cook to calm myself down.

Lucky had suffered so much in her past. I couldn't be one more person who let her down. I had to respect what she wanted.

Problem was, I had a pretty good idea of what she wanted but she wasn't letting herself go down that path.

I didn't want her to get fired. I didn't want me to get fired.

That was what I needed to remember.

She didn't help things by being so unbelievably sexy in her pajamas. I'd never found flannel appealing before but it did things to me now. I handed her the popcorn and she started the movie while I concentrated on keeping my hands to myself.

When the movie ended I asked her the only thing that I cared about. "Am I going to stay here?"

Last night might have been a one-off.

Or given the time it had accidentally happened, a two-off.

There was a long pause and then she said, "You don't have to. No worries either way."

I suspected that she was worrying both ways plus a secret third way. I searched her face, trying to figure out what it was that she needed in this moment.

So I gave her honesty. "I know I don't have to. I . . . I'd like to."

"Then yes, I want you to stay."

Despite the fact that we were nowhere near a church, I was fairly certain I'd just heard a choir start to sing the "Hallelujah" chorus.

"Every night?" I clarified. I needed to know where the line was.

"If you want."

Not that again. She couldn't say that to me or else I might slip up and tell her just how much I wanted.

"I'll be right back." I went into the bathroom to give myself some breathing room and get ready for bed.

This was enough. Whatever she had to give me was enough.

And I'd be thankful that I got to be close to her.

CHAPTER
TWENTY-SIX

Lucky

Our next charter guest, Rodney Whitlock, was what my mother would have called an odd duck.

He had arrived on the yacht precisely on time and totally alone. He visibly startled when he was introduced to Hunter, a reaction I completely understood, as I wanted to do the same thing every time I saw Hunter.

Especially when I woke up to him in my bed.

I'd never been on a charter where there was only a single guest. And I had mistakenly thought it might involve less work, but there was always plenty to do.

Rodney spent most of his time reading in the main salon. He didn't want to go to shore or have any excursions, didn't want to use any of the water toys or head into any ports.

He was happy to stay put in the middle of the ocean and read. He took all his meals in the salon as well. He had requested that Andre make him the exact same grilled steak (but without grill marks) and baked potato dish every night. The chef highly disliked not being able to flex his creative muscles and I got an earful in several languages every night at dinner.

There was only one more night left on this particular charter, so I wouldn't have to put up with Andre's exasperation for much longer.

It wasn't too upsetting, though, because other than Andre, the week had gone extraordinarily well for me. Hunter and I had stuck to our routine of watching a movie when we got off shift and then sleeping together in my bunk.

Every morning when I woke up, I felt like a princess out of a Disney movie. Like woodland creatures should have come and assisted me with my chores because everything in my life felt so magical.

My feelings for Hunter deepened at an alarming rate. This was part of sea goggles, too. Everything happened quickly on a yacht because of that impermanence thing. People developed feelings faster than they might normally.

That also meant they went away quicker, too.

I didn't know if I could risk my heart that way again. I was afraid that losing Hunter would be a million times worse than when my other relationships had ended. Because he was such a better person and I liked him so much more.

I really wanted to keep Captain Carl's rule, wanted to remember that relationships never worked out for me, but it was getting harder with each passing night.

I adored Hunter Smith. I might have even been a bit in love with him.

We had both been able to call off a bit earlier than normal, as Rodney went to bed at like, nine o'clock in the evening. We weren't going to have an early evening tonight, though, because Thomas had asked Hunter to come help detail the Jet Skis. The bosun was taking advantage of the fact that Rodney wasn't a demanding guest to get deeper cleaning done.

I was doing the same thing. I'd assigned additional jobs to my stews, which Emilie had grumbled about and basically ignored.

It was getting pretty old doing her work. Especially because she took an equal share of the tips.

Whenever I complained to Hunter about my Emilie situation, he would listen. He wouldn't offer suggestions unless I asked for them, something I appreciated. Men I'd dated in the past had always wanted to fix things and thought they had some brilliant insight that I couldn't have possibly come up with on my own. Not Hunter.

I knew the situation annoyed him, and he sometimes might say as much, but he treated it like it was my problem and he would respect whatever decision I made.

Only I wasn't making a decision. I continued to just do it myself and be upset about it.

Since Hunter wouldn't be off shift until later, I decided to watch some massage therapy technique videos. I had some coursework that I probably should have been reading but I had always been a visual learner. Watching people do the work was the most helpful.

I got into bed and found a video from one of my favorite YouTube channels. They were doing some deep tissue massage and the woman on the table seemed to be very enthusiastic about them digging into her back.

My cabin door swung open and there stood Hunter.

"What are you watching?" I heard the delighted implication in his voice that I might be watching some kind of naked movie. I hurried to hit the pause button, but because his presence was flustering me, it took a few attempts.

"A massage training video."

"Why?"

"When you're a stew it's good to learn new skills. Lots of owners want to have a massage therapist on board. It might even lead to a pay bump. I'm taking an online massage course for stews. And after this season is over, I'll use my vacation time to do my five days of practical training in order to get my certification."

He kicked his boat shoes off and wriggled his toes. "You would spend your vacation getting certified in massage?"

"I already travel the world as my job. I don't mind spending my vacation time doing something practical. And I need to learn."

"If you ever want to practice on someone, let me know."

"I do!" I blurted it out quickly. Way too quickly. "I mean, I do need to practice." And I tried to tell myself that this was just about working on my techniques and not about getting to run my hands over those magnificent muscles in his back.

This was for . . . science. Yeah, science.

"But I don't have a massage table," I added.

"We'll just do it on your bunk."

Then he took off his shirt and I had to stifle a gasp. He climbed onto the bed and lay face down, waiting.

Gorgeous. Those lines and curves and hard planes all over his back . . . I might have slightly salivated.

Apparently I was just going to ignore the fact that I'd basically picked up a stick doused in gasoline and held it above an open flame.

There was only one way this was going to end—with me being burned.

This was a bad, bad, bad idea.

Just because it's a bad idea doesn't mean it won't be a good time, a voice that sounded remarkably like Georgia's said inside my head.

The good-time part was the problem.

"Lucky?"

I realized that I'd been quietly sitting there contemplating what I was about to do for an uncomfortable amount of time. "This is a weird angle," I finally said. "I'd probably need to . . ." *Straddle you* did not sound appropriate, so I went with, "Sit on you."

"Okay." He said it like I had made a reasonable request. Did he not understand the magnitude of what I had said?

"I don't want to squish you." That wasn't the reason I was afraid to climb up on top of this man. I was far more worried that I wouldn't be able to remove myself later.

He turned to look at me over his shoulder with an expression that said "be serious." "You won't."

I knew he was right. I wouldn't. I could have put an actual armored tank on his back and he would have been just fine. I had been desperate for an excuse. So before I could reason my way out of it, I moved over and then sat at the base of his lower back. I was allowed to touch him. My fingers tingled.

But that might have been due to how badly my hands were shaking at the prospect.

Be a professional, I told myself. And I tried. I really did. Unfortunately, the second my hands made contact with his warm skin, I was lost.

I attempted to focus on the different muscle groups and pressure points that I'd learned about, but all I could think about was how firm he was, wanting to outline the light brown freckles on his shoulders with my fingers, making constellations.

It didn't help matters that he seemed to be enjoying what I was doing. There were soft sighs, happy murmurs, little imperceptible half groans as he relaxed into the mattress.

His sounds did not help with my situation.

"Is that okay?" I asked in a slightly strangled voice.

"What?"

"The . . . everything. The massage." *Me rubbing my hands all over your back, touching you in the way I've wanted to since the first time I saw you without a shirt.*

"It's really, really good," he rumbled in a sexy tone that made my pulse thump and my bones melt.

It also made me want to find out what else I could do that would make him say that again.

I realized then that I was gripping the sides of his torso with my thighs. I tried to slacken my hold, all too aware of the masculine strength that lay beneath them.

What if he rolled over? Ran his strong hands up my thighs and then up my torso until he reached my neck and then he would pull me down to him, crashing his lips against mine and then . . .

My stomach throbbed with want. I had to shake my head hard to get those images to stop. My imagination was always getting me in trouble one way or another.

A few months ago I had given meditation a go in order to help with my anxiety. But I'd spent all my time feeling anxious that I was doing it wrong and would somehow mess it up, so it did not help. It had taught me about developing a mantra, or a word or phrase to repeat to help distract my overactive mind.

Nothing can happen was the phrase I decided to use. *Nothing can happen, nothing can happen, nothing can happen.* Over and over until it was the only thing in my mind. So I would stop thinking all the things I shouldn't be thinking.

The next sound he made caused my mantra to falter.

He was snoring.

I had put the man to sleep. Well, I guessed I knew exactly how much appeal I had. So sexy and desirable that he could drift off in the middle of me touching him. If I hadn't been so bummed about it, I might have laughed.

Would he wake up if I moved? I had to. I couldn't just drape myself across him like a blanket and fall asleep that way.

Even though I very much wanted to.

Get up, I told myself.

But instead of lifting my leg to move away, I found myself studying his face. It was one of my favorite things to look at. The next thing I knew, I was leaning down and kissing his cheek.

Horrified, I immediately pulled my head away and hit his bunk. I rubbed the top of my skull and finally rolled away from him.

Not okay. Not okay. I couldn't do anything like that again.

My lips were scalded. I lifted my fingers up to make sure they weren't actually on fire.

I had kissed him. Put my mouth on his skin. When he wasn't even awake. That felt wrong. I regretted what I had done. I wished he were awake so that I could apologize.

Maybe that was a small blessing, though. He wouldn't know. He wouldn't have to give me the "you're a really great girl" speech.

We could continue on with things as they were. Nothing needed to change.

Even though I hadn't meant to do any of it, it was like I had crossed some bridge and the way back to the other side had completely washed away.

～

"Lucky."

I gradually became aware of the fact that someone was pressing small, warm kisses along my throat.

"Hunter?" I asked groggily.

"You made me feel so good. Now let me make you feel good," he murmured against my skin, and I was instantly awake.

"What?"

"I'm going to kiss you."

It was both a warning and a promise. A still-functioning part of my brain registered that he was giving me the opportunity to stop him.

When I didn't speak he turned my head toward him and crushed his lips to mine. I was so shocked that for a moment I couldn't react. He moved his mouth against mine in a rhythm that had my body pulsing in time to the motion and my nether regions tingling.

Then I had the presence of mind to put my hands against his shoulder and push slightly. He immediately broke off the kiss and looked down at me.

"I don't understand what's happening," I said. My body was urging me to shut up. And my fingers, of their own volition, began stroking the skin of his pectoral muscles, marveling at how warm and strong he felt. The shirtless sight of him made me breathless and I didn't know why. I had seen him this way a million times.

Maybe it was because I was finally allowed to touch him.

His right hand went over mine and he brought it up to his mouth for a butterfly kiss. I curled my fingers in against the sensation.

"I want to be close to you," he said.

"We are close."

I felt his smile against my hand. "Closer." His velvety voice did something unspeakable to me.

Why had he suddenly decided to rewrite the rules?

Then he was slipping his arms around me, bringing me flush against him. He held me tightly and kissed the underside of my jaw, that sensitive spot just behind my ear. I shivered and he smiled at the effect he was having on me. His right hand began to travel down. Along my ribs, squeezing my waist, and then settling on my hip.

He dug his fingers in, gripping me toward him, and I sighed.

The heat from his fingers was scalding me and I found myself desperate to know what it would be like without any clothes between us. His lips explored every piece of my skin that he could reach—my throat, my jaw, my face, my eyelids. He had me aching and burning and nothing had even really happened yet.

My heart kept up a steady beat of his name, *Hunter, Hunter*. I wondered if he could hear it.

And then he finally returned his mouth to mine with a hunger that both surprised and thrilled me. I hadn't known that it could be like this between us. My lungs felt like they were going to burst, my skin throbbing and heated, like I had a delicious sunburn.

His tongue slipped into my mouth, fitting and stroking against my own, and I moaned at his sensual caresses. Streaks of intensity shot through me and an undeniable pressure began to build.

Then his fingers were at the hem of my T-shirt. "May I?"

Him asking made the moment even hotter. I wasn't sure I could have denied him anything. "Yes."

He had it up and over my head in one swift motion. I only had about two seconds to worry about my ratty sports bra before he moved over me and pressed himself against me. My softness against his hardness, our burning skin moving and creating the most amazing friction as he kissed me over and over until I was dizzy and breathless and lost to everything but sensation.

His mouth went back to my throat. "You are so sexy. I have wanted you for so long."

While his touch and kiss were incredible, his words did me in.

I melted. I wanted everything he had to give me, and he had so very much that he wanted to share. Sweet fire raced through my veins, making me burn so hard for him. His mouth was hot on mine and his hands were everywhere and I couldn't even register what was happening because I could only feel.

Like I was about to drown in pleasure.

Everything was happening so fast and all I knew was that I wanted him and wanted this and I didn't care about anything else.

He pulled himself away from me and I whimpered in protest, only to realize that he had his fingers on the waistband of my pajama pants. He looked at me and I nodded.

And as he began to tug them down, I became aware of the fact that someone was calling my name.

CHAPTER TWENTY-SEVEN

Lucky

"Lucky?"

I jerked awake. The cabin door was open, light spilling in from the hallway.

"Yeah?" I responded, not really knowing what was going on.

"I need you," Georgia said. "In the galley."

"What time is it?" I mumbled.

"Three in the morning," she said. "Please hurry."

She left, closing the door behind her. My first thought was that something had to be seriously wrong for Georgia to come in and wake me up in the middle of the night.

My second thought was that I had not actually been making out with Hunter. It had been a dream. A very vivid one that had felt way too real.

My third was that Hunter was still snoring away next to me, shirtless.

A fact my second stew couldn't have failed to notice.

Letting out a soft groan, I tried to climb over him as carefully as I could, but some bodily contact was inevitable if I didn't want to fall onto the floor. He made a sound and then rolled to his left, into the spot I'd just vacated.

Like he was searching for me.

Had I made any sounds in my sleep? If I had, my second stew was never going to let me hear the end of it.

I came out into the galley, bleary-eyed and not feeling at all prepared for whatever Georgia was about to do.

"What's going on?" I asked, blinking against the bright lights of the galley.

"That was my question for you. What is going on? Why is Hunter half-naked and sleeping in your bunk? Are you two . . ." She lowered her voice to a whisper. "Becoming one?"

I was too tired to figure out what that meant. "What?"

She let out a sound of exasperation. "I was trying to say it in whatever flowery romance language you use. Are you having sex with the man?"

Other than in my dreams? "No!"

"Ugh. Such a waste."

My hormones and overactive imagination agreed with her. "Nothing is going on. We do sometimes sleep together but in the most platonic sense of the word. Just sleeping. We don't cuddle or anything. We haven't even kissed."

Other than that smooch I'd laid on him a few hours ago.

But I knew she wouldn't count that.

Or maybe she would. And she might count my feverish dream. Which was reason enough not to tell her.

"That's very disappointing," she said.

"Why did you wake me up? It wasn't to grill me about Hunter." Even though that was something she would absolutely do.

"Rodney wants homemade chocolate chip cookies."

I blinked several times, not sure I'd heard her correctly. "What?"

"He hasn't gone to bed yet and he's up in the main salon looking very sad. I asked him if there was anything I could bring him and he asked if someone could make him chocolate chip cookies."

We'd certainly had weirder requests in the middle of the night, but until today Rodney hadn't been that kind of guest.

"And I was afraid that if I tried to wake Andre up he would shank me and then Preacher would ring loudly enough to wake everybody up," she added. She wasn't wrong on either count. The captain had complained on more than one occasion about the parrot. I didn't want him to have a reason to get rid of Preacher. Andre would leave and we needed him. Talented yacht chefs were hard to come by.

"Good call," I said. "I'll make them."

"I figured."

Pieter came into the galley and went over to Georgia, putting his arm around her waist and squeezing her once before he went over to grab a cup of coffee. He was whistling a merry tune as he filled his mug up and then left the galley.

"What was that about?" I asked.

She waved her hand nonchalantly. "Oh, we might have hooked up a couple of hours ago."

"Georgia!"

"What?"

"You're on shift!" I reminded her. How was I supposed to respond to this? What would Marika have done? Honestly, she probably would have laughed about it and asked Georgia for details.

"Trust me, it didn't take long. Although he surprised me a couple of times. Especially when he—"

I held up one hand before I went over and turned on the espresso machine. I needed more caffeine than mere coffee could provide. "I don't need to know more. Why now?"

She shrugged. "I was bored, it was dark, and my ovaries were desperate." She watched as I took eggs and butter out of the walk-in refrigerator. I was going to have to write down everything I used for when Andre had to restock.

"That's not really a good reason."

"I think you should make a move on Hunter," she announced, and I nearly dropped the eggs I was carrying.

"You also think Vegemite tastes good, so forgive me if I don't make decisions based on your opinions." I was teasing her to get away from what felt like a very serious subject matter, but she wasn't interested in letting it go.

"I wouldn't push you in that direction if there were other options. Normally I'd tell you that there's plenty of fish in the sea, but you and I know better since we work here. The ocean is overfished and full of garbage."

I laughed.

"And this ship?" she went on. "Is a shallow pond and not at all suitable for fishing."

"Yet you seemed to have landed one." I was going through a cabinet filled with baking supplies, hoping that Andre had some chocolate chips.

"A little one that I'll have to throw back."

"Your call," I said, triumphantly finding some semisweet chips on the bottom shelf. "But Pieter is nice to you. I know you're not used to that, but it is okay to let a man be nice to you."

"He does kind of worship me, doesn't he?"

I liked how nice Hunter was to me. I was also unused to it.

As I tossed the chocolate chip bag onto the counter, Georgia's phone rang.

"Who is calling you this time of night?" I asked as she glanced at the screen.

"My grandmother, who does not understand the concept of time zones no matter how many times I explain it to her. She also keeps sending me all-caps texts about how I'm going to hell for 'fornicating.'

I told her that I'm never getting married, so technically I'm not having premarital sex, but I don't think she was amused."

"Go to bed," I said with a laugh. "I've got this."

"Are you sure?"

"Yes, get some rest. Once I'm up, I'm up." I couldn't have gone back to sleep even if I'd wanted to.

Although it would have been nice to just lie awake next to Hunter and listen to him snore.

"Okay, I'm off. See you tomorrow. Or, later today."

"Good night," I called after her and then finished gathering up the ingredients I needed. I turned on the oven to preheat it and searched for the silicone mats and the baking half-sheets.

I fell into an easy rhythm. I missed baking like this. I had never dared infringe on the sanctity of Andre's galley before. I would have to clean up really well so that I wouldn't have him yelling at me when he woke up. Things fell apart completely on a yacht when the chief stew and chef didn't get along.

It was then that I noticed it was raining. If I'd been on an upper deck, I would have realized it sooner, but the rain must have shifted direction and was falling sideways and hitting the porthole in the galley.

It didn't take me long to finish mixing the wet ingredients. I added the dry, stirred, and then put in the chocolate chips. I rolled dough into balls and put them on one of the trays. I got the first batch in the oven, and only then did I grab myself a cup of espresso. I stared out into the inky blackness just beyond the porthole. It was a cozy moment and I found myself wanting to share it with Hunter.

Then he came into the galley, like I'd accidentally summoned him.

"What are you doing up?" I asked, shocked.

Not only because he was awake but because I still had burning, detailed images in my head of him kissing and undressing me.

Just like I had, he blinked against the harshness of the galley lights. "You got up. And I can't sleep when you're not there."

He casually lobbed that emotional nuclear bomb at me and I had nothing shored up to protect myself against the cuteness and depth of it. What did that mean? It felt like my legs had been disconnected from my spinal column, and I had to lean against the counter to stay upright.

"You're making cookies?" He phrased it as a question even though it was pretty obvious what I was doing.

"Y-yes." I did not need to start stumbling over my words now.

"Do you need help?" he asked. He reached over and took a bunch of cookie dough and popped it into his mouth.

I pointed my wooden spoon at him. "What are you doing? That's not for you!"

He licked some of the dough from his finger. "You can't tease a man with the smell of baking cookies and not let him have one."

I moved the bowl away from him. "You should have enough willpower to refrain."

"You have no idea how much willpower I have," he grumbled more to himself than to me.

Not willing to let my brain make another dangerous leap to an illogical conclusion, I said, "It's also bad to eat cookie dough."

"I like to live dangerously. Bring on the raw eggs."

"Salmonella's not pretty."

"Given what I'd just tasted, it would be worth it." Then he reached for my cup of espresso and took a drink. "Decided to have a little bit of coffee with your caffeine, did you?"

"Ha ha."

"Someday soon we're going to have to discuss your chemical dependence on coffee. You might have a problem," he teased.

"I don't have a problem with coffee. I have a problem without coffee." I turned around and got a clean mug. "Speaking of, do you want one?"

"Yes, please."

Not that I'd minded that he'd taken a sip from mine. I liked sharing things with him. "How strong do you want it?"

"Strong enough to show up on a drug test."

"Double shot of espresso, coming up."

When I handed the mug to him, he thanked me and then asked, "Are you coming back to bed?"

How he said it—like we were a real couple—knocked my breath clean out of my lungs. The way his words made me want things I couldn't have . . .

My knees were weak all over again.

For a moment my throat felt too tight, like it was going to prevent me from being able to speak at all. I coughed. "I can't. I have to stay here until the batter end."

He grinned at my pun, the way I knew he would. It helped to lighten that heavy, thick tension I'd been feeling.

But only a little bit.

"Are you sure you don't need help?" he asked right before he snitched another piece of dough.

"I'm good. Chocolate chip cookies are easy. If it had been macarons, you would have found me in a ball on the floor, crying."

"Why are you making cookies?"

"The guest requested it." The bell dinged and I took out the batch in the oven and set it on the stove to cool. I put in the next tray and reset the timer.

Hunter frowned slightly. "Did he say why?"

"No," I said, flicking a bit of dough at him.

He looked at me in mock outrage. "Don't start something you're not willing to finish."

I laughed and then immediately modulated my tone, remembering that nearly all our fellow crewmembers were currently sleeping in their cabins nearby. "Do you cook?" I asked.

"I have the repertoire of a diner chef, but not the skill."

"Honestly, I'm not that great at cooking regular food, either. But I love baking. The precision of it, the science involved. It has to be done correctly, all the ingredients interacting perfectly, and the end result will always be the same."

"So you like it because there are strict rules."

That made me pause. "I guess so. I hadn't thought of it that way."

"If it's basically science, does it turn out perfectly every time?"

"No! So many things can go wrong. Even if you do everything exactly right, it might not turn out."

He studied me and then said, "I would think that would upset you."

Fair point. "Even less-than-perfect chocolate chip cookies taste pretty good. And if I need to start over again and hope things turn out better the second time, I can." I put a couple of cookies on a plate, sprinkled on some sea salt, poured a glass of milk and then a glass of wine.

"Wine this late?" he asked.

"It's raining outside. The yachtie motto is 'when it rains, we pour.' I'm hoping it will make him sleepy."

So that I could go back to bed with Hunter. The idea sent warm tingles racing along my nerve endings.

I set the tray for Rodney off to the side so that I could put the final batch of cookies in the oven.

"You should hand those extras over," Hunter said. "So I can test them and make sure they're not terrible."

I grabbed a handful of flour and chucked it at him. It hit him square in the chest.

His mouth opened to an O and then he looked up at me in surprise.

"You're not allowed to question my baking abilities. I'm willing to finish this," I said, getting another handful.

Mischief filled his eyes and he set his mug down. "Oh, you think so?"

"Not the eggs!" I screeched, seeing what he was reaching for. "Do you know how hard that is to clean? They harden like cement!"

Since I had the container of flour, he grabbed the sugar and flung a bunch of it at me. I immediately tossed white, powdery flour back at him and we started pelting each other, giggling and laughing while trying not to wake everyone up.

He looked like a ghost, his hair completely coated in flour. He moved closer and closer to me, backing me into a corner. Then he dropped the sugar and lunged, grabbing my arms and putting them behind me, pinning me against the counter. He pressed his body against mine.

"Got you!" he said.

The laughter died in both of our throats at the same time as we realized the situation we were in. Our chests were heaving against one another, and while my heart had already been pumping hard during our food fight, now it was jackhammering against my ribs. His gaze dropped down to my lips and I ached for him in a way I didn't know was possible.

I saw the lines in his neck, the tension in his jawline, the heat in his eyes.

"Lucky . . ." He breathed my name out. "I want . . ."

CHAPTER TWENTY-EIGHT

Hunter

This was getting out of control. One second we were laughing and flinging ingredients at each other and the next Lucky was in my arms, looking up at me with those beautiful eyes of hers, her chest heaving against mine, and I was overwhelmed.

I honestly couldn't remember the last time I had wanted someone this much. And it wasn't just because she was unbelievably sexy, which she was, but because of how intensely I liked her as a person. Spending time with her was the best part of my day.

Scratch that. Sleeping next to her was the best part.

When she'd woken up, the bed had felt too empty without her. I needed her next to me.

I didn't know what that meant.

What I did know was that if I didn't kiss her soon, I might spontaneously combust from all this thwarted lust. Sugar sparkled on her neck and the desire to lick it and taste how sweet she was solidified the air in my lungs.

Blood rushed away from my head, pooling in my gut, and I was breathless and desperate and bent my face down toward hers.

I needed to tell her what I wanted. I had actually started to but couldn't finish.

This wasn't okay. I couldn't do this. Especially not with Rodney on board. He was making me self-conscious. I wasn't ready for her to find out. Not yet.

The oven timer beeped, and the sound broke through the haze. "You should get that. We don't want them to burn."

She only stared up at me, apparently as unable to move as I was to let her go. My throat felt too tight, my pulse throbbed. Everything said to hold on.

I had to let go, though. I made myself release her and took several steps back. There was a major internal battle happening inside me right now, and I was afraid that I might lose. I had a sick feeling in the pit of my stomach. My frustrated libido was not happy with me and I physically felt the pain of stepping away.

The only thing left to do was joke. "If there's one thing I remember from training, it's that fires on boats are very bad."

She had a deer-in-the-headlights expression on her face. If I'd been more insecure, I would have worried that she didn't feel the same. But I knew that she did. I had proof of it now.

My guess was that she had decided not to act on it. It was the smarter decision.

The one I should have been making.

But when it came to her . . . all she had to do was ask. I would have burned down this boat for her if that was what she wanted.

It took her a few moments to spring into action. I tried to make my breathing go back to normal while she took the cookies out of the oven and turned off the timer.

I had never been in a situation like this before, and so I had no idea how to navigate it. I wanted to sweep her up into my arms and go back to our cabin and show her how much I liked her.

"I'll clean this up," I said, looking everywhere but at her.

"Right," she said, folding her arms over her chest. "I'll help."

That was the last thing I needed. She had to go away or else I was going to start kissing her and never stop.

Lucky was special and it was killing me to stay away from her.

"No, take Rodney his cookies. I'll get this cleaned up and then I'll go relieve Pieter." I couldn't have her climbing into bed with me at four in the morning and pretend like things were the way they had been before. I got a broom and dustpan and started sweeping.

"I can clean, too," she said. "Let me just—"

"Lucky." I ground her name out in warning, my entire body tensing. She swayed toward me.

"Just go," I said, feeling very defeated.

She grabbed the tray and had to walk past me. I shoved my body against the cabinets so that she wouldn't accidentally brush against me. I was so weak for her right now that I didn't think I could take even something that small.

Then I felt bad when I saw the expression on her face. She was disappointed, confused, and relieved all at the same time.

As soon as she left, I missed her again. Now I was worried that I'd hurt her feelings, and that was the last thing I wanted.

So I bounded up the stairs after her, intending to make sure that she was okay.

She had already entered the main salon, and I heard Rodney sheepishly say, "I'm sorry to have woken you up."

"That's literally what I'm here for," she said in an upbeat voice. She worked so hard for her guests. I wondered if they even knew.

Or appreciated her.

"You probably think this was a strange request," he said.

Lucky laughed and my gut clenched at the sound. I loved her laugh. Then she listed off a bunch of requests she'd gotten from other charter guests that included illegal drugs, zoo animals, and an insane amount of toilet paper. "So no, cookies aren't too strange a request."

He made an appreciative sound. "This is delicious. Did the chef make this?"

"No, I did."

"You're a wonderful baker," he said, and I had a strange swell of pride in my chest. Rodney was extremely picky.

That's my girl.

She thanked him and then asked him why he had requested cookies.

"Because of my wife." Rodney and his wife had been friends with my parents, but I'd never really known him that well. I knew his wife dying had utterly destroyed him and that's why my parents had offered him the boat. "On our first date, two of the tires on my car had gone flat, so I was an hour late picking her up. I grabbed some packaged chocolate chip cookies from a gas station as an apology. She didn't give me a hard time about it but said that she would make me her world-famous chocolate chip cookies to let me know what I'd been missing out on."

I'd heard that story a bunch of times. He had told it at the funeral.

"That's sweet," Lucky said.

"And every year since then, she made me those chocolate chip cookies for our anniversary. Today would have been our fortieth wedding anniversary. She died last year."

Lucky said how sorry she was.

"Thank you. My wife loved the ocean. That's one of the reasons why I came here. Hank offered it to me last minute and I agreed because she would have loved this. I like to think she's still here in spirit, enjoying it with me."

It was obvious how sad he still was. I could hear it in his voice.

"I'm sure she is," she said.

"You know, I hate to say this, but I think your cookies might be almost as good as hers. Her dream was to open a bakery in Paris when we retired. Now it's time for me to retire and . . ." I could hear him clearing his throat a couple of times. "I'm sorry, I'm not usually this much of a watering pot."

"It's okay," she said. "Would you tell me about her?"

He sounded surprised. "Really?"

"Yes, really. My dream is to open a bakery, too, so she sounds like someone I would love to hear more about."

And Lucky just sat there with him. Letting him talk about his wife, pour out his heart to her. I glanced around the corner so that I could see her sweet face. This wasn't trying to placate him for a bigger tip. She was someone who had experienced a lot of loss, and it had made her more compassionate. Kinder.

Definitely too good for me.

I went back down to the galley to clean it, like I'd told her I would. As I started sweeping I thought about Rodney and his wife. Growing up, it had always been evident how much they had loved each other.

My heart painfully constricted in my chest as I realized that I wanted what he'd had. I wanted Lucky. But this thing with her was about so much more than just sex.

She and I could laugh and play and talk and chill. She was funny, adorable, loyal, sweet, and a million other good things. We were friends and she was retina-burning hot. I'd never really had something like that before with anyone.

These warm feelings that flooded into my chest every time I thought about her . . . I suddenly realized what they meant, and it was like a semitruck had slammed into me going a hundred miles an hour.

My heart raced so quickly that I couldn't catch my breath.

I was in love with Lucky.

I let out a groan because I had no idea what to do next.

~

Drop-off day arrived and I was glad to see Rodney go. He asked for Lucky's cell number and promised to send her some of his wife's recipes. He shot me a conspiratorial wink before he left, and I was grateful that he'd kept my secret. I had to figure things out before I spoke to Lucky. Part of me wanted to tell her everything and confess that I had fallen for her, but my brain convinced me to keep quiet and try to go back to how we'd been before.

She needed me to go slow and I was willing to do that for her.

Rodney left each of us ten thousand dollars, and the crew acted like it was burning a hole in their pockets. They made plans to go out, and Lucky reluctantly agreed, probably because the captain had told her to unify the crew and she'd decided that drinking with them was the best way since they'd refused to show up for her planned activities.

We were in an upscale restaurant in Nice. I was nursing my beer because alcohol would loosen my tongue and I would tell her everything.

"Why hasn't anyone passed that bread basket down here?" she demanded.

I asked Kai for it and then handed it to her. "There you go, my little carbivore."

Whoops. I shouldn't be calling her pet names. Instead I started telling her a story about the night me and my fraternity brothers had stolen a cow from a farm in upstate New York and had brought it to the second floor of our frat house. It had been a problem because apparently cows could go upstairs but not downstairs.

She nearly choked because she was laughing so hard, and all I could think about was how much I loved her.

I probably had a goofy grin on my face.

"Let's go back to the ship and get in the hot tub!" Georgia yelled out, interrupting us.

Lucky in a swimsuit? Yes, please.

"Do you want to?" I asked.

"Sure!" she agreed enthusiastically, and my heart rate doubled.

I wanted to get back to the ship as quickly as possible.

"Is everyone ready to go?" Thomas asked the table, and we all started standing up.

Because I had to control so many of my urges, sometimes they would slip out. Like now, when I leaned over to her and said, "It is getting late. You should probably take me home with you."

She shook her head but I saw her cheeks flush, her pupils dilate. Heard how she caught her breath.

I was playing with fire and didn't much care if I got burned. I knew that I should worry.

But I just didn't.

We poured out from the restaurant onto the sidewalk. Georgia had her arm looped through Pieter's. Relationships could happen on the yacht, no matter what the captain or my dad said.

"See? I told you. Puns work," I said.

Because despite her relationship issues and fear of loss and love of rules, things could work out between us.

I just needed her to give me a chance.

CHAPTER TWENTY-NINE

Lucky

Could Hunter and I have what Georgia and Pieter did? I wanted it so badly that I couldn't respond to his observation. We hung back a bit behind the rest of the crew. Emilie kept sneaking glances at us over her shoulder, even though Kai had his arm around her.

I looked up at the dark sky, studying the bright stars above me that reminded me so much of the freckle patterns on Hunter's shoulders.

"Do you know anything about constellations?" I asked, desperate to stop my brain from remembering with perfect clarity what his back and skin had felt like when I'd massaged him.

"Of course."

"What's that one?" I pointed right above us.

He studied it for a moment and then said, "That is clearly a constellation."

I elbowed him while he laughed. "That wasn't what I meant!"

"I may not know the constellations, but I know what that heavenly body is right there." He pointed at a bright star. "That's my lucky star. Beautiful, isn't it?"

His words rendered me speechless. And I couldn't bring myself to ask the questions I wanted to.

Was that deliberate? Had he said that because of me?

There was a noise off to our left and we both turned to see that an elderly woman had dropped her large bag as she struggled with her dog, who was straining against its leash.

She was yelling at her dog in Italian and Hunter ran over to help. He picked up the bag, handed it to the woman, and then crouched down to talk to the dog. The dog started wagging its tail and then sat down on the ground, staring up at him adoringly.

Whatever he'd said seemed to have worked. The older woman kissed him on both cheeks and then hurried off down the street. The whole scene was so cute it made my uterus hurt.

"If that was for my benefit, I'm not impressed," I joked as he walked back over to me.

It was a complete lie. I was very impressed with his kindness and thoughtfulness and how even unruly dogs fell in line just to please him.

He teased me right back. "This is just how I am. If you're impressed, that's on you."

That was a true statement. It was just who he was. He was the kind of man who saw a need and took care of it.

Was he doing that with me? He sensed how I needed him and he was being that guy for me?

I didn't like that idea. Better to keep things light and not think about depressing stuff. To remember that relationships never worked out for me. "I do like that you don't try to impress me."

He smiled. "I aim not to please."

"I don't believe that. I think you love to please."

His eyebrows shot up his forehead, and I suddenly realized how that might have sounded. Then he gave me that infuriating secret smile of his that had me feeling like one of those fainting Victorian-era women.

Before I could launch into what most likely would have been a very weak and pathetic explanation, my phone buzzed.

Saved by the bell.

And again, Lily had the uncanny sense that I must have felt happy and wanted to wreck it.

> I'm a bit behind on my credit card this month. Could you send me another six hundred dollars? I promise I'll pay you back!

"What is it?" he asked.

"You get two guesses and the first one doesn't count," I said before I put my phone back in my pocket. I would deal with her later.

"Isn't that like, the sixth text from them this week?"

"Yes."

He put his hands in his pockets as we continued our stroll back to the yacht. Hunter didn't have to say anything. I knew what I needed to do. Put my foot down and tell them that they were adult women and needed to start paying their own bills.

"I'm scared of losing them," I confessed. Another thing I'd never actually said aloud before. What was it about this man that made me want to share everything with him?

"They're your sisters. The only family you have left. Do you really think that if you stopped giving them money, they would stop loving you?"

I was afraid of exactly that. Hot, unshed tears clouded my vision. I didn't want to keep crying in front of him. I never did this. I had always had to be the strong one. The one who took care of everyone else and made Mom's life easier. I didn't get to fall apart. Ever.

But he made me feel like I could and then he'd be there to help me put myself back together again.

Somehow he alone seemed to be in possession of a key that could unlock this emotional side of me that I kept hidden from everyone else.

He wrapped his arm around my shoulders and squeezed me gently, to offer what comfort he could. He probably didn't realize that he comforted and soothed me just by being here.

"What's your favorite thing to bake?" he asked, and I realized that he was trying to distract me. That he somehow knew it was what I needed in this moment, to help me not fall apart.

"I don't know if I have a favorite," I said, trying not to sniffle. "There is one thing I can't master no matter how many times I try. Sfogliatelle. It was my nonna's signature item, but she didn't leave the recipe behind. I've tried it a million different ways and they never turn out like hers."

He considered this information while I noted that his arm was still around my shoulders. This was something friends did. Right?

I just loved how warm and safe it made me feel. Like he'd fight off every bad thing that came my way.

"What is sfogliatelle?"

"A Neapolitan dessert that kind of resembles a lobster's tail but it's made of these buttery, crispy, thin layers of pastry. Sometimes it has fillings like orange and vanilla-flavored ricotta, or almond paste or whipped cream. I've asked so many chefs for tips, including Andre, but no one can tell me anything that makes them taste right."

"Is there anyone else who might know the recipe? Maybe before she came to America?"

"My nonna told me once that she worked in a bakery in Salerno owned by a married couple. Arturo and Giovanna Mascarelli." She had loved them like family and had talked about them often while I was growing up. "I'm guessing they've passed on. Maybe their kids or grand-kids took over? I don't know. As far as I can tell, they aren't on social media. It's why I was bummed our original charter got canceled. We were supposed to have spent the whole trip on the western coast of Italy. At some point I was hoping to go into Naples. I could have talked to some of the bakers there. Maybe they'd be able to figure out what I'm doing wrong."

"And you'd get to eat the pasta," he added.

"I can't even imagine," I told him with a sigh. "I bet it's like eating tiny bites of heaven." I'd never been to Italy before.

He smiled at me and we walked along the docks, only a few steps behind the others now.

"You didn't drink very much tonight," he observed.

So I don't launch myself at you. "Neither did you."

Did it mean something that we were aware of each other's alcoholic content? I couldn't have said how many shots Thomas had taken or how many bottles of wine Georgia was personally responsible for demolishing.

"After Harper, I told you that I got out of control. That included a lot of blackout drinking. One time I fell and broke my foot, something I have no memory of. When I woke up in the hospital, all I could think about was my sister being in the same hospital and how terrible my decisions had been. It made me want to turn my life around. Plus, as my therapist was fond of pointing out, copious amounts of alcohol can interfere with my meds. And people with ADHD are more likely to become addicts because of how our brains are wired. It didn't get to that point for me, but it's better to be safe than sorry."

"I don't think anyone here shares your concern," I said as Kai very nearly stumbled into the water, almost taking Emilie with him.

"Do you ever worry that our fellow crewmembers are a bunch of lushes?" he asked jokingly.

"Constantly. But then I worry about everything."

He smiled. "I find life is better for me when I do things in moderation."

That's disappointing, my inner Georgia-esque voice said.

"This crew is allergic to moderation. They prefer to participate in stuff that ends with them being bailed out of jail." I was about to climb up onto the passerelle when Thomas peered down at me from the deck with an unfocused grin.

"Don't worry, Lucky! We won't do anything stupid or felonious tonight."

"History suggests otherwise," I told him, and he broke into peals of laughter.

"Meet us in the hot tub in five!" Georgia called out as I came on board, disappearing downstairs with Pieter.

Hunter and I went back to our cabin and I grabbed my suit and then headed into the bathroom to get changed first. I was cursing the fact that I had brought mostly practical swimsuits. I had thought I'd be using them to go swimming or diving. I'd never imagined hot tub nights.

I came out into the cabin and grabbed my cover-up and realized that Hunter had left.

Maybe he'd gone into one of the guys' cabins to get changed.

I made my way up to the sundeck and the hot tub, which I could hear bubbling all the way from the stairs. When I got there, Georgia was alone and drinking a flute of champagne.

"Lucky! Come and sit with me."

I took off my cover-up, climbed in, and grimaced slightly. The water was very warm. I knew I would get accustomed to it. I sank down next to her and let out a sigh of relief. The lights of Nice twinkled at me from the shore.

I felt the warmth of the water seeping into my bones and sighed again. I knew it would stop being relaxing when everybody else arrived, so I planned on taking advantage of the next few minutes.

My quiet was short lived, though. I had just closed my eyes when Georgia said, "So when, exactly, were you planning on telling me that you and Hunter are dating?"

"What?"

"Lucky, I know. It's okay. You can tell me."

"I do not understand what's happening right now," I said.

She mumbled something under her breath that I automatically assumed was *bloody dag* and then said, "I'm just glad you finally came to your senses. I know that's not an easy journey for you to make. Somebody should give me a medal for encouraging you to go after him. I'm a bloody American hero."

"You are neither American nor a hero," I said, my brain still scrambling to make sense of what she was saying. "And Hunter and I are not dating."

"Lucky, I'm possibly quite drunk, and so you should be honest with me because the odds are I won't remember this tomorrow."

"There's nothing to tell."

She patted the water next to her, like she was patting a spot on a couch for me to sit on. "I accept your implied apology."

"For what?"

"Because I was right and you were wrong."

This conversation felt like it was spiraling out of control. "Georgia, I'm not dating Hunter. I think I would know." Given how closely I paid attention to him, there was no way I would have been able to miss the fact that we were boyfriend and girlfriend.

"It's your lie. You go ahead and tell it however you'd like. But even Professor Plum and Colonel Mustard are happy you finally caught a clue," she said.

"I'm telling you the truth. Hunter and I are not together."

She frowned. "I caught you in bed with him."

"Where nothing happened. I told you I haven't even kissed him." It literally happened only in my dreams.

"I just assumed you were lying to try and cover your butt. Which I respect because I wouldn't want you to get fired."

"Georgia." I got her attention before I went on. "Why are you so sure that he and I are dating?"

She blinked slowly. "Because Hunter told me you were."

CHAPTER THIRTY

Lucky

"Hunter told you we were dating?" I shrieked. "We're not!"

Everything was taking on a surreal sheen. I knew what the truth was, but her assured ness was making me question myself.

Now Georgia looked alarmed. "Don't get upset. I believe you! You guys are not dating."

I knew why she was concerned. I usually kept my freak-outs private.

You don't keep them from Hunter.

That was a problem for another time. Right now I had to worry about the fact that she had either misunderstood him or was drunker than either one of us realized and had made it up.

"Hunter told you, used the actual words, that he and I are together?"

She nodded.

Did the rest of the crew know about this?

More importantly, did the captain know?

"I distinctly remember that he said you two were . . . 'involved.' That was the word he used." She nodded, pleased with herself.

"Why would he do that?"

She shrugged. "I don't know why he would tell all of us but not you."

If he thought we were dating, I probably should have been the first person he told.

"This doesn't make any sense," she added.

It did not. Although it did explain why Emilie was being so openly hostile toward me. She must have thought I was trying to get the highest-point guy on the sCrew List for myself.

Then another thought occurred to me. "What if Emilie tells her uncle?"

"I don't think she will. It would draw too much attention to what she and I are doing. We're all better off if he doesn't know that anyone is hooking up."

But she couldn't be certain. Why would Hunter potentially put both of our jobs in jeopardy? "I don't understand why he did this."

"Maybe he wanted me and Emilie to back off," she said. That was a reasonable explanation. Neither one of them had been very shy in their attempts to land him.

While I was considering this, she said, "Have you seen those rom-coms where couples pretend to date? They call it . . . fake-dating. That could be what's happening."

"I don't know if it can be fake-dating if only one person is aware of it." I was going to have to get to the bottom of this.

"You know what happens whenever people fake-date in the movies, don't you? They always fall in love." She had a dreamy look on her face.

Nobody was going to fall in love. That I might have already fallen was beside the point. I had to protect my heart and I knew what a danger Hunter would be to it. "Everyone knows?" I didn't know why I was asking a question she'd already answered.

It was like I just needed to hear it all more than once so that I knew it was real.

"Oh yes. Whenever the two of you sneak off to your cabin instead of hanging out with us, everyone assumes that you two are . . . what is a nice way of putting this . . . expressing yourselves through the physical act of love."

"I . . . we . . . that's not . . . I . . ."

"It's called a complete sentence, Lucky. You should try it."

Oh, I had a complete sentence, all right. "I'm going to make him set everyone straight."

She took another sip of her champagne. "I figure that there's only one way to resolve this. Kiss the sexy man you live with."

That was so far from where my mind was at that it threw me off. "How is that a resolution?"

"You need to see if there's a spark there. If you aren't attracted to each other, then you're just stressing about nothing."

That was so not an issue on my end. "Stressing about nothing is kind of my specialty. And kissing him won't solve anything."

"Disagree. If nothing else, you can tell me about it and answer the burning questions that I have regarding whether or not he's a good kisser."

I had no doubts on that front. The fact that I was ready to combust every time he got close to me said that if we did kiss, I would probably just dissolve into a million tiny pieces and scatter all over the ocean.

I did still have that tiny fear of mine. That he was such a nice guy, wanted so much to be of service to others, that he might kiss me because he could tell that I wanted it. "Hunter wouldn't kiss me just to be nice, right? Like, what if he kissed me just because he didn't want to hurt my feelings?"

She shot me an incredulous expression. "Have you met men before? They don't do that."

We couldn't continue our conversation because Thomas and Pieter suddenly splashed into the tub, getting water all over the deck.

"We'll clean that up later," the bosun mumbled before he reached for Georgia's champagne bottle and drank directly from it. She smacked him on the arm and told him he was gross.

A few seconds later the rest of the crew showed up, including Hunter, and everyone climbed into the hot tub.

I felt very strange—I was both angry with him for lying to the crew and yet still had the urge to plaster my mouth over his.

Maybe Georgia was right and the only way to work things out was to kiss him.

But I needed a bit of time to process what she had told me before he and I had our inevitable confrontation.

Because he was going to explain why he had done it.

And why he hadn't seen fit to clue me in.

Emilie slid down into the hot tub so that she was right next to Hunter. She was wearing what looked like dental floss with a couple of lace doilies to cover her bits. My black tankini made me feel like a nun in comparison.

And even though I was mad at him, I did wonder what Hunter would think if I wore a swimsuit like hers.

Despite my inadvertent modesty, his eyes were constantly on me. I felt his gaze even when I was speaking to someone else. I had to remind myself of his lie because I was melting from his intensity.

Everybody was getting progressively drunker and wilder. François had put some music on and the thumping bass seemed to shake the entire ship. The crew were dancing and kissing and it was quickly headed in an out-of-control direction. Sometimes they made me feel like I was a passenger on a floating brothel.

"Let's play Truth or Dare!" Emilie said as she looked at Hunter. Now that she'd gotten him into the hot tub, she obviously planned on taking advantage of it.

"We're not eleven," I said to Georgia. "And if Captain Carl comes out, he's going to fire all of us."

"That's part of what makes it so fun," she said. "The thrill of possibly getting caught."

"I'll go first!" Kai said, and although I wasn't sure, he looked a little annoyed about the way Emilie was watching Hunter. He dared Thomas to go down and run naked back and forth on the passerelle.

The bosun didn't need to be asked twice and ran down the stairs, nearly slipping and falling twice, but ran the short length with his trunks completely off, to the delight of the crew.

When he returned, trunks back on, he made François twerk in Andre's face, something neither one of them seemed to enjoy. François asked Emilie, "Truth or dare?"

"Truth."

That seemed out of character.

"Who do you fancy on the ship?"

"Hunter." Her answer was immediate. No hesitation. That green-eyed monster inside me bared its teeth.

"Somebody should get that girl a thirst aid kit," Georgia stage-whispered to me. I wondered if her pun was a result of Hunter's influence, and I also wholeheartedly agreed with her assessment.

Emilie either didn't hear Georgia or didn't care. She said, "Hunter, truth or dare?"

"Dare."

I winced. Bad choice. Given her answer, she was obviously going to dare him to make out with her or something equally terrible. I was going to have to scour my retinas after. Maybe it was time to make a break for it. I didn't know how committed he would be to following through with a dare. He might have been the kind of guy who would do whatever the other person said, or he might blow her off. I could not sit here while they kissed.

I wasn't interested in ending my night in a French prison.

Then she did something surprising. She turned toward me and said, "I dare you to kiss Lucky."

There was a combination of protests and cheers. I heard Pieter say, "That doesn't count! They're already dating!"

Hunter looked alarmed, and I wanted to say, "Yeah, the jig is up," and make him explain. But so many other people were talking that I just pretended like I hadn't heard.

Emilie's expression was sharp, calculating. She'd made this dare as some kind of test. Maybe if we were awkward about it, like we were sure to be, given that we'd never done it before, it would be confirmation that we weren't together.

Or she might have wanted to see our reactions to her demand. She obviously suspected something was up and was using this as a way to test her theory.

"Choose something else," he said, sounding casual.

And like he thought her request was ridiculous.

Rejection, humiliation, burned me from the inside out. He told everyone we were dating and then he didn't even want to kiss me?

None of this made any kind of sense, and now my anger was easily outweighing my lust.

"Kill the music!" Georgia suddenly called. François switched it off and she told everyone to shut up.

We all went silent and listened and there was definitely the sound of a door opening.

"The captain! Scatter!" she said, and everybody scrambled to get away. We all headed out in different directions to return to our cabins. I ran through the main salon with Hunter right behind me.

We got to our cabin and he slammed the door shut. We both leaned against it, listening, breathing hard.

I was struck with a desire to laugh until I caught sight of his expression.

And despite the fact that he'd just publicly said "No, thanks" to kissing me, he looked like he was now seriously considering it.

"Alone yacht last," he said. He wasn't going to charm his way out of this situation. I didn't care how beautiful he was or how cute his puns were.

I was keenly aware of how little clothing we were wearing, how warm he was, how much skin we were both showing, and the way his chest was currently glistening from the still-evaporating water. I would not let myself get distracted by his shiny body.

Would. Not.

"Lucky." He said my name so softly, and I told my nerve endings to stop exploding with excitement. "We didn't get to do our dare."

Yes, because he hadn't wanted to and had let everyone on this ship know that he wasn't even a tiny bit interested in me and that kissing me was the worst thing in the entire world.

"I know how much you love to follow rules, and the rules of that game say that we have to . . ." His voice trailed off, his eyes moving down to my mouth.

His head moved toward mine. He was definitely going to kiss me. Because of a game?

I deserved better than that.

And I deserved to be kissed by someone who wanted to kiss me, not by someone who felt socially obligated.

I didn't trust myself to put my hand on his chest to stop him, so instead I took a step back. "Are you drunk?"

He looked confused, like he didn't understand why I would ask that. "Not even a little. Why?"

"Because I want to make sure that you're sober enough to understand how mad I am at you."

"Mad? Why would you be mad at me?"

Did he really not know? Although to be fair, now there was more than one reason to be upset.

I backed up against the bunks to put some space between us. It didn't help much because this room was too small. I needed distance because my body and lips were making a very convincing argument as to why I should ignore everything that had happened before and take Georgia's advice and just kiss him.

Maybe there wouldn't be a spark there and then we could just be friends. It might help me to get over this crush I had on him and move on.

But I needed him to explain first.

"What's this I hear about you and me dating?"

CHAPTER
THIRTY-ONE

Lucky

"Georgia?" he asked, and I nodded to confirm his suspicion that she had been the one to tell me.

I expected him to deny it. To say that I must have misunderstood or that Georgia had.

"I'm sorry. I did say we were together." He looked sheepish, rubbing the back of his neck.

"Why would you do that?"

"To get Georgia and Emilie to leave me alone. Unlike some people, I know when I'm being flirted with."

Who was he talking about? Me? Implying that I didn't know when I was being flirted with? That was not the point right now. "Look, I understand how they are but—"

"You're not the only one who needs to follow the rules," he interrupted me. "I've spent too much time not doing that. I need to be a better man. And I knew you wouldn't make a move on me."

That throbbing humiliation returned. "So I'm safe. You don't have to worry about me."

Poor pathetic little Lucky. Of course I wouldn't be bold enough to go after what I wanted. Like I wasn't even tempting enough for him to consider me a problem, like he did the other girls.

Then he took that pain away with what he said next. "No, you're the one I have to worry about the most."

I heard my own blood rushing in my ears. Before I could ask him to clarify, he went on, "After I saw that list they made, I doubled down on the lie. And it's a harmless lie, isn't it? It doesn't hurt anyone."

I told white lies all the time. In this industry it was a requirement. I might as well have told the guests, "Yes, there's nothing I love more than cleaning your stinky toilet immediately after you've used it! I live to serve!" I wouldn't be a good stewardess if I were a hundred percent honest with our guests. We had to tell them what they wanted to hear.

But this wasn't a tiny white lie. This was a shimmering, multicolored disco ball of lies.

All those times when I had thought he might be flirting with me, had actually fooled myself into thinking he might be interested in me, they were all meaningless. This was why he had done it. He'd had to keep up the facade, the pretense that he and I were together.

It was why I had thought he wanted to kiss me. He'd never actually wanted it. It had all been in service of his lie.

That broke my heart a little. "It's not harmless. What if word gets back to Captain Carl? We'll both be fired."

"We're not actually dating." He said the words slowly, like I didn't already know that.

"If he believes we are and the crew verifies the lie you told them, we could be in trouble."

"It seems to me like the crew constantly breaks most of the captain's rules and so they have a vested interest in keeping quiet. Mutually assured destruction."

"Maybe. But you're gambling with my future."

He took a step toward me, his arms out, as if he intended to hold me. But he dropped his hands. "You're right. I'm sorry. That was selfish of me."

His immediate confession and sincere apology helped to melt the edges of my anger away. "It means a lot that you're being honest with me and didn't deny it."

There had been many, many people in my past who had not. Who had continued to lie even when confronted with actual evidence.

Lines of worry etched into his forehead. "Lucky, I haven't been completely honest about—"

Our cabin door flew open and all of the exterior crew stuck their heads in our room. They'd obviously hoped to catch us doing something illicit and let out groans of disappointment that we were only talking.

"It's all clear," François told us. "No sign of the captain. We're going back to the hot tub if you want to come with us."

Hunter turned toward me and raised an eyebrow. I shook my head slightly.

"No thanks. We're going to call it a night," he told them.

Those were the wrong words to use, as it caused the boys to break into loud and suggestive catcalls and comments. Hunter had to shut the door on them.

"They always say there's no such thing as a secret on a boat. Except this one, apparently," I said. And it was such a good secret that I had been entirely unaware of it.

"I can go and tell them the truth," he offered. "I'll shut it all down."

On one hand, it would be like declaring open season on him. Emilie would be relentless. Possibly Georgia as well if things didn't turn out with Pieter.

But on the other, I didn't want it to get back to the captain. I wasn't sure what to do. "We can figure that out later."

He nodded. "Can you forgive me?"

What he'd said was true. The crew would risk their own bad behavior being exposed if they went to the captain. And he had managed to make both Georgia and Emilie back off, using me as his shield. I didn't mind that part. I could get over the lie that had given me the benefit of not having to watch him kissing either one of my stews.

I was upset that he didn't like me and I had fooled myself into thinking he did. But that wasn't Hunter's fault. "I can forgive you."

"That's because you're such a kind person."

I knew he'd meant it as a compliment, but it felt a little like a rejection. I was the nice girl, his buddy. Not the woman he wanted to be with. Kindness didn't get a guy's motor revving.

I pushed my wet hair off my shoulder. "We should go take a shower." My cheeks turned hot as I realized what I'd just said. "I mean, I will take a shower alone and then you'll take a shower, also alone. Separately. At different times. I didn't mean . . ."

He was grinning at me, obviously amused. He closed some of the space between us.

"We didn't get to finish upstairs," he said. "It's my turn. Lucky, truth or dare?"

What was he doing? His eyes were serious. He really wanted to keep playing? What information was he hoping to get out of me? Did he want me to confess to my crush? Maybe what he'd told the crew about us wouldn't seem like such a big deal if I openly admitted that I did have feelings for him. But the truth felt dangerous right now. "Dare."

And before the words even came out of his mouth, I knew what he was going to say and I both feared it and desperately wanted it. "I dare you to kiss me."

"We're alone," I said. "We don't have to play games."

"I feel like we've been playing a game with each other since I got here." He moved closer to me again.

"But you don't want to kiss me."

That got him to stop moving. "Why would you think that?"

"In the hot tub? Emilie dared you to kiss me and you practically made a gagging sound."

217

He smiled. "That's not what happened. I told her to pick something else because the first time we kiss will not be in front of an audience."

Desire for him pooled in my stomach, mixed with confusion. "You want to kiss me?"

I had thought it was to sell his story. But then I thought about the times almost kisses had happened.

And it was always when we had been completely alone. In our bunk, in the galley.

Never in front of anyone else.

"Why do you want to kiss me?" I added, grasping for something, anything, to keep him at arm's length because I was quickly losing this battle. The closer he moved the more my resolve wavered.

"Why?" he repeated, sounding far too amused. "Because there's this hunger, this burning, every time I'm around you. Do you know how much it has tortured me to lie in your bed, so close, but not able to touch you?"

"Yes." I breathed the word out. I knew exactly what he meant. The desire I felt began to pump hotly through my veins. "So you want to touch me?"

I wanted to groan. Why was I saying these things?

He grinned and somehow got even closer. "Very much."

"And what else?" I managed to get out, my throat closing in on itself.

"Everything else."

I couldn't make a sound, couldn't even breathe.

And there was nowhere else for me to escape to as my back was now flat against the closet door. His skin had long since dried, and while we both should have been cold, given the air-conditioning and our damp hair, I felt nothing but heat.

Especially from him.

"I've tried really hard to just be your friend," he murmured. "And I'm failing."

"You don't want to be my friend?"

"I want more."

My mouth dropped open slightly and my heart pounded so hard it was going to bruise my ribs. "No one else is here. You don't have to pretend."

"I'm not pretending, Lucky. I've never pretended with you."

That was a missile being launched directly at my heart and I could feel the impact of it exploding, blowing up the defenses I'd been hastily trying to construct.

"May I?" he asked, and for a second I didn't know what he was asking permission for. Then I realized that he had his hand outstretched next to my arm. Not kissing. This was okay. It wasn't kissing. As long as we didn't kiss, I could keep my job. And my sanity. Which I was sure I would lose if I were ever foolish enough to be in another relationship again.

I nodded my head and he reached out and ran his fingers along my arm, from my shoulder down to my hand. My bare skin prickled in response and I audibly gasped.

This couldn't happen. I couldn't let it. I had to stop it before things went too far. Before we crossed that line.

"You're my lucky star, you know." As if he were answering the question I'd been too afraid to ask earlier.

And with that one sentence, he almost obliterated what little resistance I still had.

"Hunter, wait." This time I put my hand on his chest and it was as firm and warm and strong as I remembered. I had my palm just over his heart and I could feel that it was beating faster than normal, his chest moving quicker as he breathed harder. "I don't want to complicate things."

He put his hand over mine, holding it in place, and it was the sweetest and most romantic gesture. "I'm not a complicated man."

Who would have ever guessed that I would be the one to make the speech? "You're such a great guy—"

"I am. I have references," he interjected and I smiled. "And before you finish that sentence, what do you want?"

"What I want is irrelevant."

He shook his head. "What you want is the only thing that matters right now."

Sharp, tingling heat coursed through me and I couldn't think.

"I want . . ."

This time I was the one who couldn't finish my sentence. Because the end of it was *everything*. I wanted everything.

"Lucky," he said, and I wondered if he was feeling at all impatient. Because I certainly was. "I know you want to kiss me because you already have."

CHAPTER THIRTY-TWO

Hunter

Lucky made a sound at the back of her throat. "I did not! I would remember if I had!"

She had. Even if she didn't want to admit it. I tried not to smile. "Last night. On my cheek."

The expression on her face was one of guilt. Was that because of the rules or because she'd thought I hadn't been awake? I didn't need an apology.

I only needed her to do it again. But in a different spot this time.

And I couldn't get over the fact that she had thought I didn't want to kiss her. It was all I ever thought about. It was amazing that I could still manage to do my job at all.

"That is . . . neither here nor there," she said, raising her chin slightly.

If she hadn't been wearing so little clothing, I probably would have recognized that she was trying to give herself an out. But we'd been handed a golden opportunity to break the rule in a way that we technically couldn't be held responsible for, and I didn't want to waste it. "That's confirmation. Why won't you admit to it?"

"Because I can't." Her voice broke. "I can't kiss you and you can't kiss me and that's just how things are. And that cheek kiss was unintentional."

"How do you kiss someone unintentionally?"

"By not intending it. It just happened."

I couldn't stand the distance between us. I put my hand on her waist and tugged her forward. She came very willingly. "And why did it happen?"

"Because . . ."

Because she had wanted to kiss me for as long as I had wanted to kiss her. She needed to know that. "I've been imagining kissing you for weeks, Lucky. I want it more than almost anything."

"Why didn't you mention that earlier?" she demanded as our chests collided with each quick inhale and exhale. She was so soft that I was having a hard time focusing.

"You spook easily."

"I'm not a horse. And I'm sorry, I shouldn't have kissed you like that."

"Yes, you should have." I let go of her hand and cradled her face, running my thumb along the lower edge of her lip. "I think you should kiss me more."

She made a noise at the back of her throat that made my knees go weak.

"But it's your decision," I said. I would walk away if that was what she wanted, even if it killed me. "Whatever you want, I'll respect it."

"You just said you have to follow the rules."

I nodded. "I do. But right now I don't care."

I was past caring. She made me feel like I was getting dragged out to sea by the tide and I should just go along with it and not try to fight. I should give in.

But this was deliberate. This was a choice. One we were both going to make together.

I leaned in so that my mouth hovered just above hers, not touching. She was unbelievably tempting and someone should have given me a medal for keeping my lips and hands to myself for so long. I had to gulp back the sensations I felt in my attempt to keep a clear head.

I reminded myself that this was her decision and I would respect it.

But it didn't mean I might not try to sway her a little. "I promise not to tell the captain."

"That's not the point. I would know." She was trying to sound determined but she had already decided.

I couldn't stop the eager grin that spread across my face. "Yes, you will most definitely know when I'm kissing you."

"I don't want us to get in trouble."

"Everybody else is doing it." I murmured the words while nuzzling my nose along her wet, dark hair.

"To quote my nonna, just because everybody else jumps off a bridge doesn't mean that I should."

That put an image in my head that I had to share with her. "It will feel like that between us, you know. Like we're free-falling, not able to catch our breath. Our stomachs will swoop, we'll be in sensory overload, dizzy and weightless, that spike of adrenaline making it thrilling and terrifying at the same time."

"Terrifying?" She said the word so sweetly that a bolt of desire shot up my spine and I had to lean slightly against the door so that I didn't fall over.

"You're terrifying, Lucky Salerno. You scare me to death. The things you make me want, the way you make me feel . . ."

She reached up then to run her fingers along my cheekbones, and her touching me, wanting to touch me, ignited my blood, setting me on fire.

Then she said the one word I had been waiting for.

"Yes."

I would go slowly. I would. I would not freak her out. I watched as her eyelids drifted shut and she waited. I wanted to remember this moment. The last one before I kissed her.

After this, everything was going to change.

I lowered my head slightly and softly brushed my lips against hers. It was so light that there was barely any contact, but it was like I'd licked a live electrical wire. I felt that small kiss in every corner of my body, lighting me up like a Christmas tree.

Then she did something that almost destroyed me.

She moaned.

And that sound fizzed hotly in my blood. It made my hands tremble when I moved them up to her hair, anchoring her against me.

I used the tip of my tongue to lick her lips briefly, needing to taste her.

"You taste so sweet." I groaned the words against her, not knowing how I was still capable of speech. "Like you still have sugar on your skin from last night."

"I washed it all off," she said, her breath catching.

"Then it must just be you."

Not able to help myself, I returned my lips to hers. I kissed her as thoroughly and tenderly and gently as I could. I needed to tell her with my kiss the things I couldn't yet say. Her mouth moving against mine . . . it made me shiver and I felt the heat and sweetness of her lips all the way down to my toes. It made me want to forget all of my resolutions.

I had no idea that my lips were connected to so many nerve endings in my body. Every single one of them was exploding.

Something she seemed to be feeling, too. She wrapped her arms around my neck and pulled me closer. Urging me to do more.

Not yet. I had to retreat. I pulled my head back. "Slowly. I'm going to enjoy this. I intend to savor it. Savor you."

I saw what my words did to her. Her hungry expression was doing unspeakable things to me. She tried to challenge me. "Says the man who stole cookie dough because he didn't want to wait for the cookies."

"You said I couldn't have a cookie, so I took what I could get."

I wouldn't give in to temptation. I would take things slowly. I would learn every one of her sighs, the way her body felt against mine, all the different ways her mouth could kiss.

If I had thought I was being tortured before, I had been wrong. This. This was torture. The most exquisite kind imaginable. Especially because all I wanted was to rip this swimsuit off her and take her over to our bed and sink into her, but there would be time for that later.

My body began to argue with me that this was a bad idea. I felt like I'd crossed a desert, desperate for water, but was only allowing myself one drop at a time. It was delicious and I'd been dying for it, but it wasn't enough. I wanted to guzzle it down, have it spilling from my mouth, drink so much that I would never feel thirsty again.

But I was pretty sure that my thirst for her would never be quenched.

I started to trace the shape of her mouth, lingering and exploring. I kissed her thoroughly, with a devastating slowness, and she arched against me, panting and pleading. The kisses that passed between us were intimate and sensual and my bones were melting. My fingers didn't get the message from my brain that I was moving at a glacial pace because they were teasing and feeling and exploring and she shivered against me.

"Please," she begged, and it broke something inside me. My body was rigid with restraint, desperate for her, and I lost my self-control.

She opened her mouth and I slid my tongue inside, stroking hers. She collapsed and I grabbed her by the waist, pinning her between me and the door. She arched her back when I sucked her tongue into my own mouth and made the sexiest sound I'd ever heard.

Liquid heat pooled at the base of my spine and then exploded outward.

She was the best hit of dopamine I'd ever had.

I felt everything I had promised her—my stomach swooped, feeling hollowed out, my senses overloaded, adrenaline spiked inside me, I was dizzy and weightless.

"I didn't know it could be like this," I said to her, dazed, and she nodded, her lips swollen, her hair a beautiful mess.

"Neither did—"

I took her mouth again before she could finish her sentence. Each stroke of her tongue against mine was electric, traveling along my synapses and frying my nerve endings, sending me into a frenzy of wanting.

I loved this woman so much.

She melted against me, hot and soft and pliable, and I was determined to wrench every moan, every wave of pleasure, from her body, to watch her fall apart while I—

There was a pounding on my door. "Lucky? It's Captain Carl."

CHAPTER
THIRTY-THREE

Lucky

Hunter and I broke apart immediately, our chests heaving, our breathing loud and thick with mutual desire and disappointment from how the captain had just single-handedly brought things to a halt.

Did the captain know? This was exactly the kind of thing that always happened to me. I had broken the rules and now I was going to have to pay with my job.

Totally worth it, my hormones said, and I couldn't completely disagree.

Hunter grabbed some clothes and jerked his head toward the shower. I nodded and got a shirt, throwing it on over my swimsuit, running my fingers through my hair.

When he closed the bathroom door, I opened the main one. "Yes, Captain?"

He was talking but it was like being underwater while someone from above the waterline spoke—muted and distorted. My head was still spinning from kissing Hunter and it was all I could think about.

Which was obviously a problem because the captain had never come to my cabin before. My fuzzy brain did note that he didn't seem angry, so he didn't possess some secret power that alerted him that I had just broken his rule.

As my senses started to return to my control, I worried about how I looked. Was my hair a mess? My lips swollen? My cheeks flushed a bright pink?

Did I look like a woman who had just been kissed so thoroughly and so expertly that I was now worried I'd never be able to kiss another man ever again, for fear that they'd always fail to measure up to the unbelievable ecstasy that I'd just experienced?

"The chocolate sauce? For the ice cream?" the captain repeated slowly, which was fair, given my total lack of response to his apparent question. "Do you know where it is?"

"Yes!" I hurried into the galley. It was odd to go from something so transcendent, so completely life-altering, to the pantry to search for chocolate sauce.

He couldn't have radioed me like a regular person? Why had he interrupted the greatest thing that had ever happened to me for an ice cream topping?

I came out of the pantry and handed it to him, and the entire time I behaved as if the man had X-ray vision and bore personal witness to what had been going on between me and Hunter. I needed to calm down, to get a hold of myself, or I would raise his suspicion.

"The new owners are our next charter guests," the captain said.

It was probably the one thing Captain Carl could have announced that would have brought me completely out of that fuzzy half world I was currently living in.

"The owners?" I repeated. Why hadn't he told us sooner? There was so much to do.

Not that I'd been lax at my job, but if the new owners were coming, this ship had to be beyond perfection.

"I kept it from the crew because I didn't want them to panic." Understandable, given that that was exactly what I was doing now. Not to mention that the last time we'd had a VIP, the well-known crown prince and princess of a specific nation, Kai had spent the entire morning throwing up and Thomas had been so anxious he'd run a Jet Ski into the ship. The crew had nearly fallen apart on that trip.

I didn't want that to happen again.

"I'll let Thomas, François, and Andre know tomorrow morning," Captain Carl added. "But I'm counting on you to get everyone prepared and make sure everything is perfect."

No pressure. "I will."

As I walked back to my cabin, I thought over not only what the captain had said but how close Hunter and I had come to being caught.

The owners arriving felt like some kind of sign. A reminder that I needed to be on my game and that wouldn't happen if I was focusing all my attention on Hunter.

That kiss had been a mistake. The best one I'd ever made, but still a mistake.

When I got to the cabin, Hunter was already done with his shower. He had pants on, but no shirt, and was towel drying his hair.

I flashed back to that kiss and it made me feel weightless, like I was being shoved from the top deck into the ocean. Even the memory of it was better than almost anything else I'd ever experienced.

"Is everything okay?" he asked, sounding concerned.

His tone helped to strengthen me. We both needed our jobs. We couldn't mess that up. "It's fine. He wanted me to help him find something in the galley."

"Good." He studied me and I wondered what he saw. He inclined his head toward the shower. "Your turn."

I had to avert my gaze from him while I gathered up my things because if I didn't, I was absolutely going to launch myself at him and hang on tightly, like a baby koala.

After I'd locked the bathroom door, I undressed and stepped into the shower. When I turned the water on, I saw that it was already set to freezing.

Looked like I wasn't the only one in need of a cold shower.

I finished up with everything I had to do in the bathroom, practicing the words I would say to him when I went back into the cabin.

When I came out he was standing next to the closet, waiting.

"I wasn't sure if it was okay for me to be on your bed," he said. The note of uncertainty in his voice was beyond endearing.

Was he regretting things now, too?

"We should talk," I said. I made sure to lock the door and then I sat on my bunk. I patted the spot next to me so that he knew it was okay to join me.

His movements were hesitant, so unlike the confidence and surety he'd shown me just a few minutes ago.

Like he also knew we had crossed a line we shouldn't have.

"I thought you might run away from me," he said as he settled against the hull, one of us on either side of the porthole.

I blinked in surprise. Normally that was exactly what I would have done. I would have slept in a guest cabin or convinced Georgia to let me share her bunk. Relationships terrified me so much that I tried to avoid them at all costs.

But this time? It hadn't even occurred to me. I knew I had to come and talk to him.

Maybe I was growing as a person.

I hated that this was the reason, though.

"I'm not running," I said. "But we can't kiss again. We might not have cared in the moment about the potential consequences, but we have to care now."

He was silent.

And I rushed to fill in the quiet, to explain so that he would understand where I was coming from. "Don't get me wrong, I . . . *enjoyed* seems like such a weak word for what it was, but I really enjoyed it."

"So it's just over before it even gets started? You can just turn it off like that?"

I hadn't been able to turn it off since I'd first laid eyes on him. "We have to, don't we? What if Captain Carl had walked into our cabin? He would have caught us."

More silence.

"You said to me that Georgia was putting me in a dangerous position by not following the rules when she came up with that list. And that if she was a good friend to me, she wouldn't do it. This is worse." And if we were each other's friends, which we were, we wouldn't do it to each other.

"Message received. I'll stay away from you."

He started scooting forward and I darted out my hand, stopping him. "I don't want you to stay away from me. But we can't kiss. I'm sorry, I know I probably sound selfish, like I want to have my cake and eat it too, but I'm not trying to be unfair. I'm trying to do what's best for both of us."

"Us being kept apart is not what's best for me," he said, putting his hand on top of mine. "I don't want to stay away from you, either. So the line is no kissing?"

I nodded.

He laced his fingers through mine. "Now that I've touched you . . ."

My breath caught.

"I don't want to go back to not being able to touch you. It was torture before, and it would be hell now."

My heart flew up and permanently lodged itself in my throat. It was the most romantic thing anyone had ever said to me. I couldn't imagine any of the men I'd dated before saying that not touching me would be hell.

"Touching is okay," I said in a strangled voice.

"Good." His hand tightened around mine. "And now that I know you won't get scared, I want you to know that I care about you."

His velvety tone made my skin heat while my pulse beat wildly out of control.

"I care about you, too," I admitted, even if it wasn't the smart choice. Even if I was laying my soul bare in front of him, practically begging for him to ruin my life like every other man before him had.

He grinned, the first one I'd seen since we'd been interrupted by the captain.

"What about holding?" he asked.

Like a hug? That seemed innocent enough. "Sure."

"And sharing a bunk?"

I definitely did not want to give that up. "I think it'll be fine as long as we remember to lock the door."

"Good. Let's go to bed," he suggested, and my thighs almost burst into flames at the invitation.

We moved and situated ourselves, and as I was getting comfortable, his arms went around me, pulling me to him. I was a bit surprised at first until I realized that he had asked if this would be okay for him to do.

I nestled into the spot at the base of his shoulder and wrapped my arm across his chest. He had his left arm around my shoulders and put his right hand on mine. He rested his face against the top of my head.

And my body was just one giant tingle as so many were happening all at once, over and over again.

It was the best feeling in the entire world. I ignored that warning sound inside me, the one that tried to prevent me from getting hurt.

"This is special," he said softly. "What we have. I don't want to lose it."

"Neither do I."

He squeezed me softly and told me good night.

I closed my eyes and my brain suddenly filled with memories and feelings of what it had been like to kiss him. I tried very hard to think about anything else but it wasn't working. Especially not when I was cuddled up next to him like this.

Despite how sublime kissing him had been, I knew we couldn't do it again.

But I was worried I wouldn't be able to give it up completely. It was like swearing off chocolate. If someone had never tasted it, it would be very easy to not have it.

Hunter was like the most delicious, luxurious, refined, expensive chocolate that I'd ever had, and so now I knew exactly what I would be missing out on.

There had to be a way forward for us. I just had to find it.

~

When I woke up the next morning, Hunter was spooning me. I was lying on his left arm and he had his right draped across my waist. He was a warm, firm wall behind my back and I felt like a very foolish woman for not doing this the entire time.

I rolled over to face him and his right arm subconsciously tightened around me. I could tell that he was still sleeping, given his light snoring. I fought off the urge to kiss him good morning. I wondered if that impulse would ever go away.

It was more difficult to get out of the bunk, as we were so completely entangled with one another, but I finally managed it. I got up and used the bathroom, got dressed for the day, and then went out into the galley, where I grabbed a couple of cups of espresso for both of us.

I returned to the cabin and sat next to him on the bed. I nudged him awake. "Hunter, time to get up."

His eyes drifted open and he smiled lazily at me and then put his arm around my waist. "There you are. I missed you."

He hadn't even known I was gone. He was too romantic for his own good. I shook my head as I handed him the mug. "Double espresso."

He sat up and took the mug from me. "Thank you. I lo—" There was a strange pause, and then he hurried to finish his sentence. "I love coffee."

I told my rampaging heart to chill out. Hunter had not been about to say that he loved me. We had only known each other for a few weeks. We weren't dating. We'd only kissed once. That was ridiculous.

Giving him a tight smile, I said, "I'm off to clean. I'll see you later!"

I hurried out of the cabin and went to find Georgia. I needed her insight. I couldn't figure this out on my own. She was still in her cabin, which wasn't surprising.

She was also alone, and that did surprise me. Either Emilie had gotten up early like she was supposed to and had started on her chores or she had hooked up with one of the deckhands and was currently in their cabin.

I would have wagered good money on the second.

"Georgia?" She was on the bottom bunk, sprawled out completely.

"Mmph?"

"I need to talk to you."

"Lucky?" She groaned. "What time is it?"

"It's seven o'clock."

Another groan. "Can't this wait until a more humane hour?"

"It's about Hunter and how I kissed him."

That got her attention. She sat straight up and reached for my espresso, drinking almost the entire thing in one gulp. "I'm going to use the toilet and then I'm coming straight back here and you're going to tell me everything. Don't go anywhere."

She went into her bathroom and I turned the cabin lights on. I knew she was the person I needed to talk to for a couple of reasons—(1) so far she had been right about everything between me and Hunter and so I was hoping she would have helpful wisdom that would assist me in moving forward with him, and (2) there was no one else for me to talk to.

I wanted to confide in her, for us to be closer. I suspected that I had kept Georgia a bit at arm's length deliberately—that I was always so worried about losing people I cared about that I sometimes closed myself off so that I wouldn't care.

If things were going to change in my life, if I was going to let people in, it seemed easier to start with Georgia. I knew she would help me figure out if he'd been about to say that he loved me. Because despite all my fears, all my concerns, all my doubts, I thought I might love him.

And if we loved each other—then why stay on this ship? We could apply as a couple to a new vessel and start over somewhere together. There could be a future for us where we didn't have to sneak around and worry about getting busted or angering our captains.

A future where I was brave enough to take a chance.

Georgia returned, looking way too happy. "I feel like I should buy life insurance because you kissing him is like the third sign of the apocalypse. And I am shocked . . . that it took this long. Okay, tell me everything."

"I can trust you, right? You'll keep this a secret?"

"Did you know that Thomas and Kai both hooked up with the same woman within an hour of each other a few months ago?"

"What? No!"

She looked smug. "That's because I didn't tell anyone. I can keep a secret."

"You're telling me now."

"Statute of limitations has passed," she said with a wave of her hand. "So for at least the next three months, I can guarantee that my lips will be sealed."

Three months from now I might be on an entirely different yacht with Hunter. We might be able to take a chance on actually being together. I was again struck with that mixture of dread and longing. I told her everything, from the first day I'd met him. I didn't leave anything out, including all the ways I'd embarrassed myself. Every thought and feeling I had, all the things we'd said to each other. I wanted her to have the full picture.

I even told her about the deaths in my family and the boyfriends who had obliterated my self-esteem and belief that a relationship could ever last.

When I finally finished she sat there blinking at me. "Let me see if I have this correct. The man who looks like he was the first one assembled at the handsome factory is your best friend and you love being with him. You spend all your free time with him. You sleep together, and I mean that in the most boring sense possible, on the regular. He got up at the crack of dawn to go hiking with you. He watches musicals with you almost every night. And you're asking me if I think the two of you are in love with each other? And whether or not you could have a successful relationship?"

When I nodded she started laughing. And it lasted so long that it was kind of starting to hurt my feelings.

"I'm sorry," she said, wiping tears from her eyes. "That bloke of yours is bloody brilliant."

"What do you mean?"

"Did I ever tell you that my grandfather had a ranch in the outback?"

What did that have to do with anything? "No."

"He did. And he used to tell us this story about how to catch wild horses. That they were skittish and afraid of new things, so the ranchers would put up one length of fence at a time. When the horses were used to it, they'd put up another and another until one day the horse was trapped inside the fence."

"You think Hunter trapped me?"

"No, I think he got you accustomed to him in small doses so that when you did kiss, when he told you he cared about you, you didn't freak out and try to swim back to America."

"You think he did this on purpose?" Like as a manipulation? That didn't seem like something he would do.

She shrugged. "I'd guess no. He probably just instinctually understood who you are, fabulous but neurotic, and so he gave you what you needed."

I nodded and then asked the question I had most wanted to ask her. "Do you think I'm in love with him?"

"Is my grandmother Catholic? The answer to that is yes, by the way. And before you ask, yes, I think he loves you, too."

That filled me with giddy, effervescent bubbles, like somebody was mainlining champagne into my bloodstream. "Should I say something to him about it?"

"Probably not. My advice would be to shag the beautiful man and go from there."

"I can't!"

"Oh, you can."

"This is your great wisdom?" I had been hoping for more.

She let out a small sigh. "You're a grown woman. You can figure out what you want and what you are or are not willing to do just fine without my input. The person you should be talking to is Hunter. Feel out where he's at, and then I think you'll know what to do next."

"Okay, that was actually good advice," I said.

"I'm the best," she agreed. "Now get out of my room so that I can get up and start cleaning for rich people who don't appreciate it."

I hugged her and then went off to do the same. There was a lot to fill my time but it did not occupy my mind. I couldn't think about anything else but him. The only future I wanted to imagine was one where we left the boat together, where I could put down my cargo ship–size baggage and let myself be vulnerable and happy with him. It would be terrible to stay put and have to keep things as they were now.

Because I was pretty sure Georgia was right and I was in love with him. I'd had past relationships, but the feelings I'd had for those men paled in comparison to how I felt about Hunter. Like holding up a light bulb next to the sun and asking which one was brighter.

I came across him tying up some lines. "Look at you with that bowline!"

He grinned at me and I knew he wanted to hug me or take my hand. He folded his arms across his chest instead. There were cameras everywhere—it wouldn't have taken much for the captain to catch us in the act.

"Despite what you might think, I am good at things."

I had a very personal and intimate experience of just how good he was at stuff. I hoped I wasn't blushing. "I know you are."

He took a step closer. "Do you also know the reason why I couldn't do the knots when you showed them to me?"

"Why?"

"It was because you made it impossible for me to concentrate on what you were doing because you kept brushing your fingers against mine. I can't think when you touch me or kiss me."

He left me with that emotional drive-by and went up the stairs to the sundeck.

Hunter made it so that I couldn't think, either.

And if neither one of us were thinking . . . that would only lead us to some very rule-breaking places.

CHAPTER THIRTY-FOUR

Lucky

As we settled into our bunk that night, I suggested *Calamity Jane* for our movie and he agreed.

This was the first time he had held me while we watched something together, and it was so much better than just sitting side by side. Another thing I should have been doing since the beginning.

As I searched for the movie, he was playing with the ends of my hair with his free hand. He said, "Today was a really beautiful day. I wish we could have called in sick and played hooky together."

His words made my stomach flutter. That he talked about us like a couple and all the ways I imagined we could play hooky. It made me believe that we would work out and ride off into the sunset together.

"Yachts don't really do sick days," I told him. "Unless something's broken or we're in need of surgery, we have to soldier on. I personally wish there were such things as calling in healthy. 'Sorry, Captain, I'm not coming in today because I feel great and I don't want to spend my time scrubbing a toilet with a toothbrush.'"

He smiled and I turned my face up toward his. He reached over and brushed his knuckles against my cheek. "I'm trying very hard to respect your rule but you're making it extremely difficult."

"I am?" I asked in surprise. "I didn't do anything."

"I'm tempted just by you existing."

I sucked in a sharp breath. I understood that feeling all too well. Worry and concern intruded their way into my brain and forced me to ask, "What if it's just sea goggles?"

His hand stilled. "What?"

"It's what yachties say about being on board a ship. That someone who is like a four on land is a nine on a boat because your options are so limited."

Hunter's blue eyes were so sincere that I didn't doubt his next words. "There are no goggles here. I see you clearly. Land or sea."

Now I wanted to kiss him. "Let's start the movie."

"Need the distraction, do you?"

He understood me far too well.

We began to watch and I did my best to pay attention to the plot. I had always loved this movie, even if I was always outraged on Calamity's behalf that her supposed best friend stole her crush.

I paused the movie. "Do you know what's annoying?"

"Not being able to kiss you?"

"No," I said, although that was very annoying. "If Katie had just told Calamity that she wasn't Adelaid Adams, Calamity still would have brought her back to Deadwood. She didn't need to hide who she was."

He nodded and looked pensive. Like there was something he needed to say. I waited.

"Lucky, there's something I need to get off my chest."

Good heavens, please let it be his shirt, I fervently prayed. Which led to thoughts of his torso in general and how magnificent it was, what it had been like to touch him and kiss him, and the next thing I knew, I was leaning forward and pressing a kiss to his throat.

"What was that?" he asked, both confused and delighted.

"I'm sorry! I shouldn't have done that. I was just picturing you without your shirt—" I covered my mouth with my hands. I seriously needed to shut up.

"And then you were overcome by lust for me?"

"Something like that." *Exactly that.* "I didn't mean to do that. It was completely involuntary."

There were only so many times I could use that as an excuse. Even though it was true. One minute I was thinking about him and the next my mouth was fused to the man's neck. Like a deranged, starving vampire.

What was wrong with me? I had told him we couldn't kiss and here I was, less than twenty-four hours later, doing exactly that.

"Do you have any other body parts that like to do involuntary things?" he asked playfully.

"No!" I quickly exclaimed. I had to head this off immediately before the rest of me started getting ideas.

"Does this mean we can kiss again?"

"Kissing was a onetime thing. Well, I guess technically now it's a one-and-a-half-time thing. But definitely not a two-time thing!"

"One and a half? What was the half?"

I gestured in the direction of his neck. "I kissed you but not on the mouth."

"How is that half a kiss?"

"If I had kissed you on the lips, then it would be a full one."

"So . . . ," he said, his fingers drifting up my arm, leaving tiny trails of fire everywhere he touched. "If I kiss you someplace that's not your lips, it would count under that half that you've already done."

That made perfect sense to me. I nodded.

"If I kiss you on your cheek"—his fingers caressed me there—"or on your neck, on your jaw, your eyelids, your earlobes . . . that still only counts as half?"

"I mean, that's only logical." I sighed as he kissed me softly on the cheek, the stubble from his jaw rubbing against my skin. "You make my brain turn off."

He pulled back. "I'm . . . sorry?" As if he weren't sure how to respond.

"It's a good thing," I told him. "When I'm with you like this, I can just be present and enjoy myself without worrying about the five hundred different ways things could go wrong. You help to quiet that anxiety I feel."

"I'm glad I make you not think," he said, pressing a kiss to the underside of my jaw. "Get ready to do a whole bunch of not thinking."

He kissed his way up, heading toward my ear. He sucked the bottom of the lobe into his warm mouth and I gasped while arching against him, stars exploding behind my eyelids.

"Still not thinking?" he murmured against my skin.

"Totally blank," I said breathlessly, my heart thudding dangerously hard, my lungs constricting so tightly I was worried they might cut off my oxygen flow.

He moved down to a spot I hadn't even realized was sensitive, just behind my ear, toward the back of my neck. I gasped again, digging my fingers into his shirt as zings of pleasure shot up and down my spine. It had me shuddering against him.

"Are you sure you didn't major in anatomy?" I asked as the way he was kissing my throat drove me completely wild. I felt like I was barely hanging on to reality.

"Minored in it," he teased as he ghosted his lips along my collarbone, staying tantalizingly out of reach. "I aim to please."

"That's not what you said before."

Now he was kissing my collarbone and I felt him grin against my skin. "Depends on the situation. And when it comes to you, I'll always aim to please."

And I was so, so glad.

As he continued on his quest to make me not think, I realized that we were brushing right up against that line I had set for us.

Technically we weren't breaking the rule, although most likely we were breaking it in spirit.

Only, once again, I didn't care. This was going to be a problem.

I had told myself it was better to be safe than sorry.

But I was careening headfirst toward sorry.

~

We were tangled up in each other the next morning as Hunter gently kissed my forehead.

"The captain trusts me," I said. "I don't want to ruin that trust."

"I understand that."

"I'm not qualified for this job. He took a big risk on me."

He kissed the tip of my nose. "You're more than qualified. You're the best chief stew I've ever worked with." He let out a puff of air as I poked him in the chest.

"I'm the only chief stew you've ever worked with!"

"But still the best." Now he was running his fingers along my hair, tucking it behind my ear.

"I can't let him down."

"No, you can't."

"Stop being so agreeable!" I protested.

"Sorry." He didn't sound sorry, though. "What is it you want me to tell you?"

"I . . ." I wanted him to say that everything would be all right. That he and I had a future and would find a way to be together. That he wouldn't cheat on me and wouldn't abandon me the first time things got hard.

That he loved me.

Too soon, that voice inside me said.

"I could tell you . . . that this is definitely my lucky day," he said as he kissed my cheek. "Or that every day with you is my lucky day."

"You're not funny."

"I think I have promise."

My phone beeped and I reached for it. I turned so that I was flat on my back, Hunter's head right next to mine.

Rose had texted.

We need that money for Chauncy's vet bill.

I already sent that to you.

That was the down payment. Half up front. We need the other half.

"Is their dog getting plastic surgery or something? Why is it so much?" I glanced at him and he added, "I'm sorry for reading over your shoulder."

I nodded. "It's okay." I didn't mind that he had.

What kind of surgery was it?

I saw the three dots blinking at me but Rose didn't respond. Instead Lily stepped in.

Hey Lucky! Rose was mistaken. We don't need the money for surgery. We actually need it for rent.

Which I already sent you this month.

I know, and we're so grateful and we're totally going to pay you back. But we need it for next month because we're so behind on our credit card bills and they are threatening to send us to collections.

This wasn't sustainable. Hunter didn't say anything but he didn't have to. And even though he kept his opinions about my sisters and their money asks to himself, I could imagine what he might say if I asked him for his input.

He probably would have told me that I wasn't responsible for my sisters. That they needed to grow up and learn to take care of themselves. That I wasn't doing them any favors by continuing to enable them to make poor financial decisions.

With shaking hands I pushed the button to call Lily and put it on speakerphone.

"Hello? Lucky?"

"Hi. Is Rose there with you?"

"She is. I'll put you on speaker. Okay, we're both here. What's going on? Will you be able to send us the money?"

My body started to tremble and I felt his arms around me, strengthening me. "No."

There was a long pause. Then Lily said, "We must have a bad connection. Did you say no?"

"I'm not going to send you any more money. The two of you have to figure out how to take care of yourselves. You're adult women with full-time jobs. I can't afford to keep financing your lifestyles. You need to make better decisions. Learn to budget. Spend less than you earn."

He kissed the side of my head.

"That's easy for you to say," Rose piped in. "You don't have any expenses."

"I know that. But when I did, nobody bailed me out. I had to do it on my own, and both of you can do the same thing."

Then Lily went straight for the jugular. In a weepy voice she said, "You're our sister. We don't have anyone else to turn to."

The trembling got worse and his arms went tighter. "I am your sister and I always will be. But you can't keep asking me to give up on my future for your present. I have dreams and things I want to accomplish and I work really, really hard for it. You should want that for me. I want that for both of you. Because I love you."

There was no response and then my screen changed to indicate that my sisters had hung up on me.

By this point I was sweating and shaking. "That was one of the hardest things I've ever done."

"But you did it. I hope you feel proud of yourself."

"I do, but sad at the same time."

"Which is totally valid," he said. I was grateful that he had let me work this out on my own.

"I also feel a little sick."

"Sometimes that's how it feels when you do the right thing."

I turned my face and buried it against his throat. "I'm just worried that they're going to go out and try to find some sugar daddy or something."

"Hopefully they won't. But now they know you won't be their sugar sister any longer."

I let out a little laugh and stayed there nestled against him for a few minutes longer while he soothingly stroked my hair.

"We better get to work," I said.

"Yep. Back to the grind until we can come back here and be alone together again."

I kissed his neck and we both got out of bed. I got ready first and headed out to the galley in search of coffee before I spent my day making sure the ship was completely perfect.

And hours later, I had done the best job that I could. Georgia had helped tremendously, while Emilie hid in the laundry room, doing very little.

Then it was time for the guests to join us. Everyone changed into their whites and went to the aft deck to wait for their arrival.

Hunter was the last one to come up and he grinned at me. "What's all this comm-ocean a-boat?"

"You just sound Canadian," I told him, and he laughed. I felt Emilie's gaze on me, and if she'd had any superpowers at all, she would have bored two holes into my head with her heat vision.

"Who do we have this week?" he asked. "Crypto jerks? Russian mafia? Head of the UN?"

"The new owners. The Cartwrights."

His face fell just as we heard voices coming up the passerelle. The Cartwrights had arrived.

"What's wrong?" I asked him.

"I will explain everything later," he said.

Something strange was going on, but I couldn't ask him about it here.

The Cartwrights were a middle-aged couple, but in that rich way where they didn't actually look like they were in their fifties. They had their two teen girls with them, Hadley and Harlow, both of whom were on their phones.

The captain was shaking Mr. Cartwright's hand. "Pleasure to have you aboard, Mr. Cartwright, Dr. Cartwright."

"Thank you, Captain. And please call me Hank. This is my wife, Susan, and our daughters."

They all greeted the captain and then moved down the line and introduced themselves to each crewmember. When they got to Hunter, Hank reached out his hand. "Good to see you, son."

Hunter shook his hand. "Dad."

CHAPTER
THIRTY-FIVE

Lucky

Dad?

This was Hunter's father?

Surprise slammed into me and rendered me temporarily immobile and speechless. What was happening?

The women were much more effusive in their affection and they all hugged Hunter tightly, telling him they loved him and had missed him. I stole a glance at Hank and I felt a little foolish that I hadn't immediately made the connection as soon as he had stepped on board.

He was Hunter thirty years from now.

I was in complete and total shock. I might have shaken hands with his father but I couldn't remember. Everything with his mother and sisters was a complete blur.

Then I heard Captain Carl say, "Lucky will take you on a tour of the boat and we'll get your luggage all handled."

I was in no state to do a tour. It was a good thing that I had done it before because I was basically relying on muscle memory as I moved through each room and explained its function.

This was Hunter's family. His *family*. They were the new owners of the ship. This very expensive yacht.

Which meant he was wealthy. Obscenely wealthy.

It also meant his name wasn't Hunter Smith.

Hunter *Cartwright* had been lying to all of us since the very first day he'd come onto the *Mio Tesoro*.

Did the captain know? He had to have known. Why else would he have told me to keep an eye on Hunter? Because he knew exactly who Hunter was.

The owners' son.

His soft, uncalloused hands. The way he hadn't known anything at all about yachting. Law school. He'd never talked about working or having another job besides this one. Being in a fraternity. There had been so many hints that he came from a completely different background from mine.

I thought back to that night with the Carmines, when Hunter had asked whether or not we had a dishwasher, and realized that he probably hadn't meant an appliance—he had most likely grown up with an actual person who had washed his 24-karat-gold-plated dishes by hand.

We went back to the main salon, and with my brightest, fakest smile, I asked what I could get for them. Both girls requested sodas, their mother a dry martini, and their dad asked for a whiskey sour. I invited them to go onto the deck to watch us pull out of port.

They did so and I was grateful for the temporary reprieve. I went over to the bar and started grabbing bottles and glasses.

I had shared so much with Hunter about my life, where I had come from, my struggles.

And while he had been vulnerable with me, I realized now how careful he had been in what he had shared. I'd heard the captain call his mom Dr. Cartwright. What was she a doctor of? What did his dad do? Where did all this money come from?

What university had he gone to? Which law school? My guess was Ivy League on both.

How could he have kept this from me?

Georgia came over to the bar, most likely to help me, and immediately quiet shrieked, "Hunter is rich?"

"I can't believe he didn't tell me." I was still shaken up over it.

"He didn't tell you about the fake-dating thing, either," she pointed out unhelpfully. It was true, though. He had kept things from me before.

"Why would he do this?" I asked.

"I don't know, mate. He obviously had his reasons for it. I can't imagine they were nefarious. Regardless, he's still invited to my future wedding as the groom." At my expression she hurried to add, "Kidding! It was a joke!"

We had a job to do, but all I wanted was to run and find him and make him explain what was going on.

When I didn't say anything, she said, "I'm sure there's a logical explanation. Give the bloke a chance."

I wasn't angry. I was confused and surprised. Maybe the anger would come later. I just didn't know what to make of all this.

Maybe I wasn't surprised because men had always lied to me before.

"You also need to watch out for Emilie," she cautioned.

"Emilie? Why?"

"She went downstairs and doubled Hunter's point value. Now that she knows he's rich, I think all bets are off. Him being a Cartwright was like waving a red flag in front of a bull."

"Great. One more thing for me to panic about."

"I thought you said that Hunter helps you to not worry so much."

"He does," I agreed. "But he's not like a cure or something. When he's around he helps to clear out the noise better than when I'm on my own. He's normally very calming, but today he is the cause of all my anxiety."

"Well, I think you should lock him down ASAP so you don't lose him to Emilie's schemes. The girl doesn't take no for an answer and, I'm assuming, has the restraining orders to prove it."

I wanted to say that if he was weak enough to fall for Emilie, I didn't want him anyway, but couldn't. I might resort to actual hairpulling and eye gouging if either one of them got too close to him. "I don't know how we move past this," I confessed. "This feels like a really big secret to keep from someone that you . . ."

That what? We weren't in a relationship. We weren't dating. We weren't even kissing. I mean, not on the mouth.

What did that make this? A situationship? A boatmance?

"That you're in love with," she finished for me, shaking her head. "You're one of the people that make the universe mad. You beg it to give you a cake and it sends you eggs and oil and sugar and flour and puts you in a galley. But you're running out of the room, upset that you didn't get that cake you wanted. Everything you need is right in front of you, but you have to make some effort here. You asked to be happy and that was given to you."

There was a lot of scary wisdom in what she was saying, which felt a bit odd coming from Georgia. "So in this scenario Hunter is cake?"

Also an apt description because he was delicious enough.

She ignored my joke. "You'd be a bloody dag if you let him get away."

"Georgia!" I protested. "You're supposed to be telling me to not take his crap and that I can do better."

"Maybe. But I think he's the best thing that's ever happened to you. I can see that he's made you happier. More relaxed. Like a better version of you. And that's the truth. If you want something sugarcoated, Andre's got some doughnuts," she said. "I'm going to go down and check on Emilie and make sure she hasn't got Hunter tied up somewhere."

Returning to the deck, I handed out the drinks to everyone. When I got to Hank, he thanked me and said, "I don't normally drink this early. I guess that makes me a bit of an aqua-holic!"

His quip shot an arrow straight at my heart. It was so like something Hunter would have said. Hank took a drink and pronounced, "This is excellent. Thank you."

"You're welcome." There was a weird sense of déjà vu speaking to him. His voice was remarkably similar to Hunter's.

"So, Lucky, do you know what they call an optometrist who buys a boat?" he asked.

"I don't."

"A see captain. 'See' with an *E* on the end." He grinned at me but his youngest daughter let out a loud groan.

"Dad! Leave her alone and stop telling her stupid jokes!"

"I like them," I said to no one in particular, realizing that it was true. I loved every time Hunter would say something ridiculous to me. "Is there anything else I can bring you?"

Everyone said no and I took the chance to run down to the galley and hide out. There was something disconcerting about being around Hunter's family. They all seemed very nice but I was super aware of the fact that I had some weird romantic-y type thing going on with their son.

And even more aware that they were the ones who had instituted the no-fraternizing rule.

Andre was preparing some trays with sophisticated snacks. I asked if I could help and he brushed me off. I waited for him to finish, trying not to fixate on Hunter.

"Did you hear that the itinerary has changed?" Kai asked me as he came into the galley to grab some food.

"I hadn't."

"Apparently we're going to spend the entire trip off the coast of Italy with a two-day stop in Naples."

Hunter had done this. I had told him how important it was to me to go to Italy, especially Naples, and he had arranged it.

While it was probably a little less impressive, given that his parents owned the boat, it was still thoughtful and I knew that he had done it for my sake.

"Here, all done," Andre said. I started grabbing trays and balancing them on my arms. I could have called for help but I didn't particularly want to see anyone else at the moment.

One foot in front of the other, I told myself. I could get through this. I would concentrate on doing my job and eventually I would have that conversation with Hunter.

I threw myself into service, waiting on the Cartwrights. The thing that struck me was not only the resemblance Hunter bore to both of his parents, but how ridiculously in love they seemed to be. They were probably closing in on three decades of marriage but they were acting like they were on their honeymoon. After I'd served all the trays, Susan said, "I'm sure you have so much you need to attend to. Don't worry about us. We are totally fine."

That had never happened before—I was at a bit of a loss. I'd never had guests tell me to go do something else and not run around fetching whatever struck their fancy. It was thoughtful on her part because there was a lot that needed to be done.

I went down to make sure their cabins were prepared by getting their bags unpacked. Emilie should have put away their clothes by herself, but she, once again, had not. She was on her phone.

"This is a serious problem," I told her. I had cut my sisters off financially. I had discovered that I actually had a backbone. I could deal with Emilie, too. "You need to start contributing or I'm going to have to go and speak with your uncle about your behavior and how you don't do what you're told."

She put her hands on her hips and glared at me. "He told me that you're in charge of me, that my actions reflect on you. If you go to him, that won't end well for you, either."

I thought of that phrase Hunter had used—mutually assured destruction. She wanted to threaten my job? I would call her bluff. "Of the two of us, I'm the one he can least afford to lose."

"Go tell him and let's find out," she challenged. "And when I speak to him, I'll be sure to tell him that either you go or I go and I think we both know who he will choose."

Emilie might have been surprised at the decision the captain might make. Not that I could a hundred percent guarantee it, but I was pretty sure he'd keep me. Captain Carl might have been abrasive and demanding, but he had to realize that I was good at my job. The old me probably would have panicked endlessly about this situation but I knew that I was needed on this ship. We had one less stew than we normally did and Emilie was like a barnacle clinging to the hull. Totally unnecessary and weighing the rest of us down. She could easily be let go and we wouldn't miss a beat.

"Fine," I said, my decision made. When I got the opportunity, I would speak to the captain and then we'd see where things ended up. "Start unpacking Mrs. Cartwright's bags and take out any dresses that need to be steamed."

I would stay in here and watch her and make sure she worked. Of course she moved as slowly as was humanly possible, but at least she was working.

When we were nearly finished, Georgia texted me.

Pieter gave Hunter a two-hour break. Maybe you should take yours now, too?

It was my job to schedule all the breaks for the stews. I was entitled to a two-hour break every day. And I would have taken it on a more regular basis if I weren't having to constantly clean up behind Emilie.

Today I would be taking that time. I needed an explanation and I wasn't sure I could wait another twelve hours before I got one.

"Take those dresses into the laundry room and steam them," I said to her. Hopefully she would actually do it and not deliberately wreck any of the clothing in the process.

Although if she did, it would certainly give me some additional ammunition when I went to the captain.

The thought of speaking to him about how awful his niece was caused me more anxiety than the thought of the conversation I was about to have with Hunter.

Why was there such a difference? It was probably because I trusted Hunter. Maybe I shouldn't have, given the lies, but I always felt safe with him. Like he was a good man who had my best interests at heart.

It was the opposite with Captain Carl.

I also believed that Hunter would be honest with me. That he must have had a good reason for covering up his background.

When I got to our cabin, he had apparently been about to get into the shower, as he had his shirt off. He was on his phone. When I opened the door, he glanced up and gave me a half smile.

"Lucky, I'm so glad you're here. I really need to talk to you. To explain."

CHAPTER THIRTY-SIX

Hunter

My family just showing up now was not how things were supposed to go down. They weren't scheduled to visit until the very end of the season. I had planned on telling Lucky about them after I told her that I loved her. When we were in a more secure and stable place and knew what we meant to each other and what kind of future we wanted to have together.

I had tried to tell her a couple of times, but we had gotten interrupted or I had been busy kissing her.

My heart beat like a drum in my chest and there was a sick feeling at the back of my throat. She had every right to be furious with me. This was now the second time I had kept something serious from her.

The first was telling the two other stews that Lucky and I were dating. That had been a harmless lie to keep them away from me. And then I'd completely forgotten that I'd even done it until she had confronted me about it.

She had quickly forgiven me.

Luck might not be on my side this time. I had to swallow down the dread I was feeling.

"Can you put on a shirt?" she asked angrily.

"Yeah." I grabbed one from the closet and slid it over my head. I had an impulse to tease her but I knew now wasn't the time.

Once I was dressed she said, "You know, when you told me you had a hard time with names, I didn't realize you meant your own."

"I can explain!"

"I hope so."

She sat on her bunk and I crawled in after her, making sure to keep my distance. I didn't deserve to touch her right now. This had been a stupid plan from the beginning and she would be well within her rights to tell me to get out of her bed and out of her life.

"Are you even qualified to be on this boat?" she asked.

"I have my STCW and ENG1 certifications."

That seemed to mollify her slightly. "You kissed me under false pretenses."

"What?"

"You're not who you said you were."

"Lucky, just because I used a different last name doesn't change who I am. I kissed you under real pretenses. Because I wanted to."

She closed her eyes against my confession and then whispered, "Were you ever going to tell me?"

The pain in her voice broke my heart. "Yes! I tried a couple of times but we kept getting interrupted or I got distracted. You know how easily I get distracted. Especially by you." I pulled in a deep breath. "And honestly, it was a little harder after your 'I hate rich people' speech."

That had really thrown a wrench in the works.

Again, I felt her soften slightly. "You still lied to me."

"Can we say 'playfully omitted'?" I asked and then let the smile drop off my face when I saw her expression. "I'm sorry. When things are tough I joke."

"I noticed."

I ran my fingers through my hair. I kept messing this up. What was wrong with me? I needed to tell her everything, why this had happened.

"I told you before that I'm a constant disappointment to my parents. Dropping out of law school, partying way too hard, and generally not dealing well with losing Harper."

She nodded.

"My dad in particular took it as some kind of personal affront. He's a lawyer. There is a law firm that my family owns. My father, grandfather, great-grandfather, great-great-grandfather, et cetera, all worked at it. There was a tremendous amount of pressure on me to join the family business. And I probably would have."

"But then you left school."

"And my dad's never let me forget it. I got better, went into therapy, but he still expected me to go back, even when I told him I wouldn't. Then, when I decided I wanted to open up a residential treatment center, I went to him and my mom and asked them to invest. My dad said no, that I never finish what I start."

A sharp wave of pain at how much I felt like a failure, like I was never good enough and never would be, smacked into me.

"They both think I'm lazy and that I'm not willing to work hard. So this was their deal. I come and work on the ship, where no special favors would be given to me because of who I am, and prove that I could do it. Day in and day out, that I won't give up. If after six months I'm still here and doing well, then they said they would invest."

"You don't need your parents' money. You could go to a bank or find someone else to invest in you. You don't need their permission. You're an adult."

"An adult who lives off the money his mom and dad give him," I said, embarrassed. I was in love with a woman who had been helping to take care of her family since she was a teenager, and my parents paid for everything for me. It made me feel immature and useless. I'd never really cared about my parents financing my life until I met Lucky.

"Again, you don't have to," she said.

"It's not like I'd be able to walk into a bank and get a loan. I don't have an income. I'm not exactly a good risk. I don't really have a choice. I have to stay."

The saddest part was that I would give it all up for her, if she asked me to.

But I knew that she wouldn't. She had a dream, too, one she was determined to bring to life. It was one of the things I loved most about her.

I was scared that if I told her how willing I would be to let it all go for her sake, she might respect me less. See me differently.

And I was still trying to be the man she deserved.

Harper would have told me that I was holding on too tight.

She would have been right. I had found something special and I didn't want to lose it.

"I am sorry about lying to you," I said. "It was part of the agreement. My parents didn't want me to be treated differently or to get out of work because they owned the ship. I agreed not to tell anyone who I really was. Only the captain knew."

"Then why is your family here? Coming to the boat and acknowledging you as their son isn't exactly keeping things under wraps."

"The entire season had already been scheduled when they bought the yacht. They didn't intend to come out until that two-week cancellation happened." I didn't have a right to be aggravated by their sudden change of plans, but I was. They hadn't even bothered to text and let me know first.

"And they gave half of that time to Rodney, who I'm guessing they know. It explains why he looked startled when you introduced yourself. Because he knew who you were."

I nodded. "He's a friend of the family. My parents understood how hard this time was for him. They offered to let him come here so that he wouldn't sit home, alone."

She seemed to be considering my words. I wished I knew what she was thinking.

"I'm sorry," I said again. After a couple of minutes had passed, I asked, "What are you thinking?"

"You don't know the whole story about my last relationship. When I found out about my ex and my best friend, he denied it for three hours straight. Said it never happened. That I was mentally unstable. I actually had to show him the picture she'd sent me of the two of them together. Without their clothing. Even then he stormed out, yelling at me for invading his privacy and trying to gaslight him and saying I didn't respect his boundaries."

That infuriated me. "That sounds like someone trying to manipulate you by using therapeutic concepts. I hope you didn't listen."

She waved her hand. "I know I didn't do anything wrong and I'm past all of that. But I really hate being lied to."

And what had I done? I felt like I'd been kicked in the gut. "And then I went and did just that. Another man who lied to you. I don't know what else to say other than I'm sorry and I won't do it again. I promise you."

Another quiet, sad nod. I wanted to take her in my arms and hold her until she felt better. I hated myself for being the reason she was upset. "Do you feel like I betrayed you?"

"You didn't actually do anything to me. And like you said, this doesn't change who you are at your core. The man I know. If I'm being honest, I think part of me expected something like this to happen. Like I've been waiting for it."

Another direct hit to the face. "I should have told you. It was a bad decision. The moment that I knew—" I couldn't tell her that I loved her right now. It might make her wonder whether I'd said it because it was how I really felt or because I was trying to sway her. This was another situation where she needed to make up her own mind.

So I said, "I never want to be the reason that you're hurting or upset."

She twisted her mouth into a line, as if she were trying not to cry. I was going to have to sit on my hands so that I wouldn't reach for her.

"You hiding your last name seems like a silly thing to get upset about," she said, filling my heart with hope. "It's hard to believe that all of this belongs to you."

"Not to me, to my parents. I hope it doesn't matter to you that I come from money."

"I would say the whole thing is mind boggling, but I think my boggle ceiling was hit a while ago." Her voice was a bit lighter. Would she be able to get past this? "But when it comes to your background, if anything, it makes me more insecure."

"Why?" I was genuinely dumbfounded.

"You're basically Prince Charming. The looks, the personality, the goodness, and now the castle and the wealth."

"It's a yacht, not a castle," I said, wanting to tease her so that things would be okay between us again.

"How many houses do you have?"

Ugh. "Do apartments and condos count?"

She made a sound of disbelief, and I hurried to add, "I have zero houses. My parents have . . . more. And if you think I'm the prince, then that makes you my perfect Cinderella."

"This isn't a fairy tale."

I wanted it to be. I wanted the happily ever after. "If I had known what would happen between us, how I would feel about you, I would have told you the truth the first night. I know I can trust you."

She sighed shakily then, as if my words had touched her. I knew how she could catastrophize things, and I again wanted to kick myself for doing something that could make her anxiety worse. I didn't want her to think she couldn't trust me. She had told me how other men had let her down in the past—why hadn't I immediately told her the truth then?

The only thing I could hope for was that she would see me in a different light. That she would realize I hadn't been trying to hurt her but had wanted to protect something that was important to me. That she'd recall the times I had tried to tell her.

I should have tried harder. I'd done my best to make it up to her in some way, asking my parents after they'd come on board to change their plans so that we could visit Italy and give us some time off. I had spent the last couple of hours organizing a surprise for her in Naples. A selfish part of me wanted to tell her, hoping that it would soften her anger, but I knew that I couldn't.

I hadn't done those things to make it all better. I'd done them because I loved her.

She might run. I understood that. I would accept it if she did. I didn't ever want to be the reason that she ran.

Maybe she didn't know how terrible I used to be, but she should know that I was pretty sure I was the reason for the rule.

"My dad is the one who made the no-hookup rule because of potential liability. He always thinks like a lawyer. He wanted to protect himself if something happened with the crew. That, and he wanted me to focus on what I had come here to do. He doesn't trust me. He assumed that I would . . . mess things up. Because of my past. I've . . . dated a lot of women."

"I doubt that. You're wildly unappealing," she said sarcastically.

Another glimmer of hope. "Is there a way for me to make this up to you? I can buy you a pony. Or a bakery." As soon as I'd said it, I wanted to take it back. "Not that I would. I know it's important to you to do it on your own."

"You're right."

Lucky was so fiercely independent and it made me want to accomplish things on my own, too. I couldn't fight off the desire to help her, though. Take care of her. Give her everything she wanted.

"Maybe sometimes it wouldn't be such a bad thing to let someone help you. A rich boyfriend has to be good for something." I hadn't meant to say that. It had slipped out. I had been thinking of her as my girlfriend for so long that it had just happened.

She raised her eyebrows at me.

My brain was screaming at me that this was the worst possible time to be doing this but it was already out there. "I would like to be your boyfriend."

"I . . . I don't think I'm ready for that."

Disappointment punched me in the face. I knew I deserved that. And I could wait. I could be patient. Time would pass and we would get off this boat and I could show her what she meant to me.

Maybe I could do some of that now. "I know you're scared. You have a right to be. But I'm not going anywhere. And I have something for you."

I reached into my pocket and pulled out the box my sister had passed off to me. "I had Hadley bring this."

She was supposed to have brought it several months from now, and while I wanted to be pissed at her for not giving me a heads-up, the fact that she had brought the gift early had allowed me to get over it quickly.

Lucky's hands were shaking when I gave it to her. She opened it and let out a soft sigh. "Oh. Thank you."

I took the necklace out of the box and showed it to her. It was a penguin pendant with a star on its stomach. "It has a star. Because you're my lucky star."

She turned her back toward me and lifted her hair so I could put it on. Now I was the one with trembling hands. My fingers brushed against her skin as I struggled with the clasp and I had to swallow down what I was feeling.

Lucky turned back and took the pendant in her hand, studying it. "No one's ever given me a gift like this before."

It was just a simple necklace. Diamonds would have been my first choice but I knew she would prefer something simple. Again, I was left wanting to punch every dirtbag who had treated her so poorly before. She deserved the entire world. "I'm glad you like it."

"I love it," she whispered.

I wanted her to love me. To forgive me.

To give me a chance.

"Would it be too much for me to ask you to forgive me for this, too?"

I held my breath.

After a moment she reached over to put her hand on top of mine and I felt so much gratitude and relief that I wanted to burst.

I didn't know what I would have done if she'd told me to stay away from her. I was so thankful for her capacity to love and forgive, for her kind and sweet heart. I hated that I'd hurt it.

"Is there anything else you need to confess first? Is this it? Or do you have a wife and child somewhere like François? Do you secretly kidnap puppies and hold them for ransom?" She said it lightly, but I heard the serious part behind it.

"This is everything. I swear it. There isn't anything else I'm lying about."

"Stop doing stuff you have to ask to be forgiven for," she said sternly.

"I promise," I said, raising her hand to my lips and kissing it softly. I would earn her trust back.

"Then we're okay. I forgive you."

I finally did what I'd been dying to do since we'd started talking. I pulled her into my arms and she immediately sank against me.

I promised myself that I would stop screwing up. I would do better. She was the best thing that had ever happened to me and I didn't want to ruin it before we ever really started.

CHAPTER THIRTY-SEVEN

Lucky

Dinner that night was . . . interesting, to say the least. The first problem was that I couldn't find my phone. I checked my cabin thoroughly, but nothing.

The last place I remembered having it was in the primary cabin, when Georgia had texted me about Hunter's break. I told him my fear that I'd left my phone in his parents' room.

He said, "Do you want me to ask them if they've seen it?"

That was the last thing I wanted. I had no desire to come across as incompetent. Especially not to his family. "When they're eating I'll go down and look for it."

I was still a little wrecked emotionally from my conversation with him. I did forgive him. I was touched by his thoughtfulness, the gift he'd given me. And it would have been silly to get so hung up over him hiding his name when he'd done so for a good reason—to keep his job.

Wasn't that why I had been keeping him at bay? It would have made me a hypocrite to be furious with him.

I knew that he was a good man. He wasn't like the others I had dated. This time was going to be different.

In five months. Which seemed so very far away.

When the Cartwrights were seated, I began pouring them some water and asking what they'd like to drink with dinner.

"Anything you have will be fine," Susan said. "I want to hear about you, Lucky. Where are you from?"

Guests didn't typically ask me questions about myself. "East Haven, Connecticut." I refrained from adding "Why?" on to the end of my sentence. "How are you enjoying your yacht?"

"It's always been Hank's dream to own one," she said, looking lovingly at her husband.

Her husband took her by the hand. "Although she is constantly reminding me that a boat is a hole in the water you throw money into."

I smiled and knew how true that statement was. Ships like this were very expensive to maintain. "I've heard it said that the two greatest days of a boat owner's life are when they buy their boat and when they sell it."

Hank laughed. "Probably true. I will have to rename it, though. I was thinking about *Seas the Day*." He spelled out the word so that I would hear the pun. I smiled and shook my head. Like father, like son.

"Did you go to college?" Susan asked me.

"I didn't get the chance," I said.

Hadley, Hunter's eighteen-year-old sister, looked up from her phone long enough to say, "Nice necklace." She had a knowing grin.

"Thanks." I hoped I wasn't blushing. I tucked the necklace back into my uniform.

"Do you have any siblings?" Susan resumed her line of questioning.

"Two younger sisters," I said. "Twins."

"And where is your family from?"

"All over. But my paternal grandparents are from Italy."

Georgia was across the table from me, pouring wine for Hank. She raised her eyebrows and smiled at me in amusement. I understood what she was silently communicating. Nobody was asking her any questions. Just me.

Something flashed across Hunter's mother's face. Understanding? Recognition? She nodded with a look of satisfaction and then asked, "What do you see yourself doing after yachting?"

This was starting to feel a bit like an interrogation. White-lie time. "I love my job so much I can't imagine doing anything else," I said. "I'm going to go check in with the chef. I'll be right back."

I let out a deep sigh when I entered the main salon and hurried down to the galley. Hunter met me on the staircase, blocking my way.

"Found your phone," he said, handing it to me.

"Where was it?"

"On the floor of our cabin."

I frowned. That was weird. I had done a thorough sweep of our room. "Thank you."

"How are things going up there?"

"What did you say to them about me?" I didn't mean to sound so accusatory, but I couldn't help it.

"Nothing!" he said, holding up his hands like he was about to be arrested. "Why?"

"Your mom was asking me a bunch of questions. She seemed keenly interested in me and didn't ask Georgia anything. It felt personal, like she knew something about us."

He dropped his arms down to his sides. "My mom is very perceptive and sees things that other people don't. It's part of what makes her such a great neurosurgeon. Did they do anything else besides interrogate you?"

"Your dad told me what he wanted to name the yacht."

"I suggested *Titanic II*, but that didn't amuse him. I also tried *Knot Pro Bono*, 'knot' with a *K*, but that aggravated him even more." He looked at my grin. "Why are you smiling like that?"

"Apple, tree, something about trajectory."

"I'm not like my dad." He seemed to bristle slightly.

I put my hand on his arm. "I just meant that you both love puns."

"My mom always said that's how my dad won her over."

The fact that he'd probably looked exactly like Hunter when he was younger had probably helped. "They seem very much in love. They act like they're still on their honeymoon."

"You have no idea how annoying that was growing up."

"I would have liked that," I said quietly.

Realizing what he'd said, he took me into his arms and hugged me tightly. "I'm sorry. I didn't mean—"

"I know you were joking," I said against his shoulder. He released me but kept his hands at my waist. "But there must be some part of you that likes that your parents love each other so much."

"You're right, I do. And I've always secretly wanted to have a relationship as strong and stable as theirs." His bright blue eyes sparkled in the low light.

Did he think that we might be able to have a relationship like that? Someday?

My gaze traveled down to his lips and I wished that I could kiss him. He had the best mouth.

"Hey, my eyes are up here," he teased.

And his eyes were filled with an intensity, a fire, that burned me from the inside out.

We stood there in silence, my heart beating so loud I was sure it was echoing in the staircase, and I tried to remember why the rules mattered.

He cleared his throat. "Hey, so I have a surprise for you. We're traveling overnight so that we can get to Naples tomorrow. And my parents are giving the entire crew the next two days off."

That brought me out of my lust-filled stupor. "What? I've never heard of a crew getting time off like that when guests are on board."

"The owners have given their official permission. My youngest sister wants to go explore Monterra, so they're going to grab a train in Naples and spend a couple of days there. Personally, I think she's going to see if she can find one of those teenage princes and get him to fall in love with her." He tugged me forward so that my body was flush with his. "Would you like to spend the day with me?"

"Yes." I didn't care what we would do. Most crewmembers never had plans when they had a day off. We would just go out and explore, sometimes in groups, sometimes alone. I'd love to share Italy with him.

"First thing tomorrow morning, bright and early." He leaned forward and kissed me on the cheek. Then he went around me and back up to the deck.

Another thing he must have arranged with his parents. His mom didn't have to be extra perceptive—the fact that he had asked for this kind of favor, she must have suspected that he had done it for someone's benefit.

And she had quickly figured out that it was mine.

$\sim$

Precisely fifteen hours later, Hunter put his hands over my eyes and had me walk forward. We had landed in Naples and then he had immediately hustled me onto a train. He wouldn't tell me where we were headed.

"Where are we going?" I asked for what felt like the hundredth time, nearly stumbling over a bump in the sidewalk he hadn't warned me about.

He didn't answer but we came to a stop. "We're finally here. Ready?" He pulled his hands away and we were standing in front of a row of storefronts. "Ta-da!"

"What am I looking at?"

"I brought you to Salerno. You are looking at Il Pane. The bakery of Arturo and Giovanna Mascarelli."

I gasped. Salerno? This was where my grandparents had grown up. Where my last name came from. And the bakery where my nonna had worked? "Are you serious?"

He looked so pleased with himself. "I am. My dad has some connections and I was able to find them."

I threw my arms around him, hugging him tightly. "I can't believe you did this."

"I'd do anything for you," he said into my neck. We stayed there for a bit and then he let go of me, taking my hand. "Let's go meet the Mascarelli family."

And it was the entire family. Children and grandchildren, cousins, aunts and uncles. There was an entire horde of Italians waiting to greet me and kiss me on both cheeks before passing me along to the next person. I could understand some of what they said, but not everything.

It made me wish I had paid closer attention when my nonna had tried to teach me Italian.

"Welcome to our bakery," a woman close to my age said. "I'm Maria, and I'm one of the granddaughters. I'm here to translate for everyone. My grandparents are so excited that you've come. They loved your grandmother. And we heard you want to learn to make sfogliatelle? We make the best."

"Please thank them for having me. I'm so excited," I said.

Someone handed me an apron and pushed me toward the kitchen. Giovanna spoke in rapid Italian and Maria translated everything she said for my benefit. And as we started to make the dough, nothing about it was different than what I had been doing. I'd hoped that there would be some special ingredient, some technique that I didn't know and the Mascarellis would show me.

But so far it all seemed familiar.

Giovanna said something and Maria turned to me. "My grandmother is asking what's wrong."

I explained my concern and how I had made them exactly the same way but mine never turned out quite right. Maria translated and Arturo started talking and gesturing wildly with his hands as he pointed at the countertop where we were working.

"My grandfather is asking what kind of flour you use."

"The regular kind."

Maria said this to Arturo and he made a face of disgust and spit on the floor. Then he launched into what looked to be a serious rant, his hands moving as quickly as his mouth.

"My grandfather says you are using American flour and that is the problem. Italian flour is superior to American flour. Our wheat is softer and it is more finely ground to remove all shards of the bran. Our flour is like velvety powder. It's why our pizzas and pasta taste so much better than yours."

I was stunned. Was this the answer? If I had used Italian flour, would my sfogliatelle finally turn out like my nonna's? "I can't believe the answer is that simple."

Hunter said, "I know people who only eat bagels from New York because they think the tap water there is superior. Something about the mineral content."

My heart was racing. I would import Italian flour and then I would finally be able to make my nonna's sfogliatelle the way they were meant to be made.

I hugged him with excitement.

Giovanna began to roll the dough up. Maria turned to me and said, "The dough has to chill overnight. She wants you to come back tomorrow. And you are invited to come and eat with the family now."

"Is that okay? If we stay?" I asked Hunter.

He kissed the tip of my nose. "I want whatever you want."

So we ate with the Mascarellis, and through Maria, Arturo and Giovanna told me story after story about my grandparents, about how they had met and how they had fallen in love. I had heard the stories before, about how my nonno had been hired to deliver for the bakery and how he was late one morning and my nonna had thrown a wooden spoon at his head. It had been love at first sight for him. My nonna said he'd had to convince her and that, even though he hadn't known it back then, she was more than willing.

"My grandmother says that your grandfather always said that Lucia was his lucky star."

At that my heart stuttered in my chest. It felt like a sign from my grandparents. Like them giving Hunter and me their blessing.

"I didn't know that," I whispered back. My nonno had died when I was so young and I had no memories of them together.

Hunter's arm tightened around me. I said to him, "My mom always told me that my nonna had picked my nickname, but I never knew the reason why."

"Now you do."

Even though I couldn't understand most of the conversations happening around me, what I did feel was the love. The love in the food, in the company, and the love I had for Hunter, who had arranged this for me. Who had given me something I had thought was lost forever.

I laced my fingers through his and he kissed my hand while laughing at a story Maria was telling us.

This was turning out to be a completely perfect day. Laughter, family, love, and great Italian food.

I couldn't remember the last time I had felt this happy.

CHAPTER
THIRTY-EIGHT

Lucky

We spent the entire day with the Mascarellis. I felt a little guilty, thinking that maybe we should have left sooner so that they could focus on their daily routine, but they'd insisted that they show me the correct way to make every pastry and bread that their bakery sold.

Hours later, it was finally time to go. We couldn't keep imposing on this poor family. I promised Maria that we'd return in the morning to work on the sfogliatelle and said goodbye to everyone else.

When we got outside Hunter took me by the hand. "Dinner?"

"With you or what do I think about it in general?" I teased, and he smiled.

"I had the chance to chat with Maria and she told me about this local restaurant that I think you'll love."

"Why do you think I'll love it?"

"I'll tell you when we get there."

There hadn't been a lot of nice surprises in my life and I loved that Hunter kept finding a way to give them to me.

The restaurant was small but cozy-looking. Definitely a locals type of place, not at all touristy. The smell of bread, garlic, and tomato hit me when we walked inside, making me feel nostalgic for my nonna's kitchen.

The walls were exposed brick, and strands of white lights had been hung along the ceiling. The tables were covered in white linens and had dark, wooden chairs. We were shown to a quiet spot in the back of the room, drawing the attention of almost everyone as we walked by.

And I wasn't sure if it was because we were so easily identifiable as Americans or if it was because of how insanely handsome Hunter was.

I completely understood the urge to stare at him all the time.

We sat and were handed menus. I opened mine and asked, "So what's the surprise?"

"Maria said they have unlimited pasta here," he said.

I let out a tiny shriek of delight. "Are you serious? All the pasta I can eat?"

He chuckled. "I knew you'd love that. But I'm not sure why you're so excited about it. Olive Garden has the same deal."

"Hush," I said. "Every time you say the words 'Olive Garden' in this country, a real Italian restaurant dies."

That earned me another small laugh.

"They also have pizza, and nothing compares to Italian pizza," he said. "If you want to try some of their other stuff, maybe you shouldn't load up on pasta. That's how they get you."

"That might be how they get you, but not me. I will bankrupt this restaurant," I said, going through the menu and picking out what I would eat first.

He grabbed my hand, grinning at me. "Have I ever told you how much I like hanging out with you?"

I heard the wistfulness in his voice. I knew he wanted more, but I didn't think I was capable of that right now. We were in this limbo state where I was scared of being more serious, we couldn't be together because of the rules, but we also didn't want to stay away from each other.

"I like hanging out with you, too," I said, squeezing his hand in return. It was all I could give him right now.

He started rubbing small circles on the back of my hand with his thumb and returned to reading the menu. "Enjoy your food, but don't get upset with me when your stomach explodes."

"Today Giovanna told me that I can eat all the pasta I want while I'm in Italy and the calories don't count, and I'm not looking for any further nutritional advice at this time."

A waiter approached and spoke English to us, welcoming us. "Do you have any questions?"

"Besides the unlimited pasta, do you have any other specials? Like, for your pizzas?" Hunter asked.

The waiter blinked at us slowly and looked annoyed. "Sì. You buy two pizzas and you pay for both of them."

Hunter shot me an amused glance and placed an order for a large margherita pizza. I said I would have the unlimited pasta, asking the waiter to bring out the fettuccine carbonara first.

When he left, Hunter leaned across the table. "I wanted to ask for pepperoni and mushrooms but I was too afraid he'd get mad."

"He does seem like the type."

I adored this man so much. It felt like it was flowing out of me and I wouldn't be able to contain it.

"Penne for your thoughts," he said. "And that's the pasta kind of 'penne,' not the coin."

"I might tell you my innermost thoughts for a good bowl of penne," I said. "And I was thinking about how much fun I've had today. Thank you for all of it."

"It's about to get a lot better," he said, leaning back as our waiter approached with my dish, setting it down in front of me.

After he left I asked Hunter, "Am I supposed to wait until you get yours to start eating?"

"No, dive in."

Sariah Wilson

I picked up my fork and waited a moment, wanting to take a mental snapshot of my pasta. "You know, I've never believed in love at first sight before, but I'm kind of believing in it now."

He shook his head, amused. "It's good to know where I'm at in the rankings. Somewhere behind pasta and baked goods."

I wanted to tell him that wasn't true, but I had made the mistake of putting the first bite into my mouth. I let out an embarrassing moan. This was amazing.

"Good?" he asked, that fiery intensity there as he watched me take each bite.

And if I'd been eating anything else, I would have stopped immediately and attacked his face, but I was far too distracted by the tiny bites of bliss. "I'm trying to figure out how to convert this into blood and inject it into my veins because I want to feel this good all the time."

"I like a woman who knows what she wants." The timbre of his voice sent tingles and shudders along my limbs.

"I do know what I want. And tonight I want you . . . to pay for dinner."

He laughed. "I'm just glad they brought you out the real thing and not some veggie impasta."

"We're not going to add pasta puns to the repertoire, are we?" Not that I really cared. Just so long as the waiter kept putting dishes like this in front of me.

"Remember that this is just a phase and it, too, shall pasta. And I'm alfredo I can't stop because I know I mac you smile. Personally, I think we should be exploring the pasta-bilities because the pesto's yet to come."

"You are pre-pasta-rous," I said.

"I'm so glad you spaghet-me."

The rest of the dinner continued in the same vein—the waiter bringing me the best pasta I'd ever eaten while Hunter kept up a steady stream of jokes, stories, and puns to entertain me.

If someone had asked me whether things could get better after our day spent at the bakery, I would have said no, but leave it to him to find a way to make that untrue.

Despite eating my body weight in pasta, I still had room for dessert. While I probably should have picked something Italian, I opted for the chocolate soufflé, and it was like a kiss from a chocolate angel. Profoundly delicious.

After we finished eating, he grabbed the bill and paid it. I should have protested and offered to split it but it was part of this perfect day—not having to dip into my savings.

Another gift from him.

He took my hand and we walked along the darkened streets of Salerno. It was like so many other port cities that we had been in—older buildings painted in bright colors, trees, green vines climbing up walls, clean laundry hanging overhead on clotheslines, filling the air with the smell of detergent, which combined with the salt from the sea.

"Did you have a good day?" he asked.

"The best. Thank you so much. I can't even tell you how much I appreciate all of it."

He brought my hand up to his mouth and briefly kissed it. "You don't know how nervous I was today."

"Nervous? Why?"

"I wanted everything to be amazing for you. Your own personal movie montage."

I couldn't believe he remembered that. He was the absolute sweetest. "It was amazing because you were with me. I'm so happy that I got to share all of this with you," I said, leaning against his arm.

He kissed the top of my head. "I don't want it to end. Do you want to go back to the yacht or stay here in town tonight?"

"Stay," I immediately responded. "Someplace nice."

"I can do that," he said, pulling out his phone and searching it. "I found somewhere. Come on."

And while I'd been expecting some quaint little bed-and-breakfast, he led me to a castle on a cliff, overlooking the ocean.

"Hunter, I was kidding about the 'someplace nice' part. I just meant without roaches," I said, feeling a little bit awed as he led me inside.

"I'm pretty sure there's no roaches here. They wouldn't dare." He gave me a wink as he took me over to the front desk. He asked if they had a room available tonight.

The woman at the computer was older, her silver hair tied back in a severe bun. She peered at us from over her glasses. "Two guests for one room? For one night?"

There seemed to be an underlying implication there that he picked up on and then ran with it in a direction that surprised me. "Yes, it will be for my wife and me."

Her entire demeanor changed. A smile lit up her face. "Are you on your honeymoon?"

"We are! We're traveling along the Amalfi Coast and had to stop in your beautiful city. My wife's grandparents are from here."

"Let me see what we have." She typed on her keyboard and then after a few seconds said, "I have the honeymoon suite available, if you would like it."

"We'll take it," Hunter said, handing over a credit card.

A black credit card.

I'd only ever seen charter guests use a card like that before.

Another small reminder of how different our lives were.

But does it matter? that voice inside me asked. *Who cares if you grew up differently? The only thing that matters now is how well you get along. And you love being together.*

It was true. We never ran out of things to talk about. I never got tired of him, never wanted space. I wanted to see him first thing in the morning and last thing at night. I wanted to share everything with him, tell him all my stories and hear all his. I even loved his puns, although I'd never admit to it.

He was my favorite person in the whole world.

And I was madly, desperately, unequivocally, head over heels in love with him.

"Here you are, young newlyweds. We hope you enjoy your stay with us." The woman handed us our key cards. We thanked her and then headed to the elevators.

I pushed the up button and we waited.

He said, "You know, I didn't even ask if you wanted separate rooms. I shouldn't have just assumed—"

I slipped my hand into his. "You didn't have to ask. I don't want to be anywhere except with you."

The elevator arrived and the doors opened and we stepped inside. He pushed the button for the top floor.

"Your wife, huh?" I asked as the elevator doors closed.

"The desk clerk seemed like the disapproving type."

"I don't think I know any men who would pretend to be married. Most of them are trying to avoid the institution at all costs."

The elevator doors opened. "I'm not like most guys."

That was the truth.

Our room was at the end of the hallway. Hunter used the key card and opened the door, sticking his foot at the bottom. "Come here."

I walked over. "What are you—"

Before I could finish my sentence, he had swung me up into his arms. "As your pretend husband, I have to carry you across the threshold."

That made me laugh as I put my arms around his neck. He carried me inside and then set me down near the king-size bed. The room was gorgeous and modern. It was mostly white with bright blue accents to mimic the ocean visible from the massive windows.

The same blue as Hunter's eyes.

I went over to the balcony and opened the doors. The night air smelled of the sea, the breeze was warm, and the stars twinkled overhead.

Including Hunter's lucky star.

He came out and joined me. We stood, staring out at the inky sea.

"I'm grateful that we've had this time together," I said. "Although I don't know how you can prove that you're doing a good job on the boat if your parents give you two days off."

"This wasn't my idea. It was theirs. I told them how hard everyone works all the time and that we don't get a lot of breaks. You especially needed the time off."

"Me especially?" I echoed.

He turned his head to look at me. "You're the one that concerns me the most. I see how hard you work and how you take on the responsibility of two or three people because Emilie won't do her job and I worry about you getting burned out."

I knew that he cared. And everything he did and said showed me how much.

A moment passed between us, charged and electric. He cleared his throat and then went back into the room. I watched him as he went over to look at some papers on the desk. A lock of his blond hair flopped over his forehead as he studied them.

I thought of everything that had happened, all that he had done for me. He had given me back a piece of my nonna, and I didn't know how to thank him for that. My stomach fluttered in anticipation.

Words were inadequate.

I'd told him I didn't want more. That we couldn't date. I didn't want to risk my heart.

But my heart already belonged to him.

I came back into the room and closed the french doors behind me. I walked over to him, mind made up, pulse racing.

"They have some movies we could watch, but they're in Italian," he said. "Do you want—"

I wanted.

I threw my arms around him and kissed him with all the wildness and desire and love that I felt for him.

CHAPTER THIRTY-NINE

Lucky

I felt his surprise, the way his body tensed up. He was the one who put his hands on my shoulders and pushed me back. I saw his throat tighten, the tense line of his jaw.

"Not that I'm complaining," he said in a rough voice laced with want, "but what was that? I'm confused."

"So am I."

"I thought that was supposed to be a one-and-a-half-time thing."

"Two times. Twice seems okay. Two times isn't so bad for breaking a rule."

"I'm pretty sure if you murdered someone two times, it would be bad." I couldn't even laugh at his joke because I was so intent on kissing him again.

His hands moved from my shoulders down to my waist. "You know how much I want to kiss you, Lucky. I'm not sure I'm stroganoff to resist you if this is what you really want. I'm ready to go over to the dock side if you are."

How could he keep making jokes at a time like this? All the blood had left my head and was pooling in other parts of my body, making it impossible for me to think.

"My mom used to say in for a penny, in for a pound," I said. We'd already kissed. What was a little bit more?

I knew I was rationalizing it but I didn't care.

"And we don't have to tell the captain," I added as he pulled me flush against him. "I know the rules still apply even if we aren't on the ship, but what he doesn't know won't hurt him."

Yep, definitely trying to justify what we were about to do.

What I *needed* to do.

Because if I didn't kiss him again soon, I was going to explode. And I already knew that Hunter had the patience of a Christmas ornament still hanging in September. He would wait. I just couldn't do it anymore.

"Have I told you how beautiful you are?" he asked and it startled me.

"You've never said that before."

"I didn't want to scare you off. I was supposed to only be your friend. I thought it all the time, though. I should have told you every day, every minute, every second. Because you are so beautiful that I sometimes forget to breathe."

Which I got because his words were strangling the breath out of me right now.

"Tell me where the boundary is," he said lowly, digging his fingers into my back.

His respect, him saying I was beautiful, along with the way he was looking at me—like I was a bowl of cookie dough—was a lot for my loins to take. I listened to him breathe, and each quick, sharp inhale and exhale only made me more excited.

"Where is the boundary for you?" I asked, realizing that I hadn't asked him and feeling bad about it. I played with the hair at the nape of his neck, letting the short, silky hair there bristle against my fingers.

"I've never had a boundary where you're concerned."

The still-functioning part of my brain realized how bad that was. How easily and quickly things could spin out of control if we let our bodies and emotions take over.

"Just kissing," I said, before I could convince myself to change my mind. This was the only way to make things okay. If we didn't actually take it too far, then it wasn't quite so bad.

Deep down I knew it was untrue, but it made my conscience feel slightly better. "And we shouldn't even be doing that. Your parents are the ones who made this rule. I don't want you to get in trouble or to be the reason why you lose out on getting that residential treatment center to honor your sister."

He leaned forward to nuzzle his nose against the side of my face. "Like I said, I only think my dad made that rule for liability reasons."

"And to keep you on track," I reminded him. One of us needed to be thinking somewhat clearly and very soon it was not going to be me. Especially with him leaving butterfly kisses on my temple.

He stilled. "I'm doing my job. I'm doing it well. And I can multitask."

"You cannot."

"Not usually, no," he agreed. "But I'm pretty sure I can kiss you at night and still tie a good bowline the next day."

He somehow managed to draw me even closer so that his body was a hot, hard line against me. I felt the violent beating of his heart against my chest. It made my body heavy with want, tense with need.

We were alone. We wouldn't be interrupted. No one would walk in on us. Nobody would know what we were about to do.

"Kiss me, Hunter."

He did not have to be invited twice. With a rough groan his mouth descended on mine. Bright, hot sparks exploded along my veins as he kissed me fiercely, fervently, searing both my lips and my heart.

We crashed into each other like two giant waves, and I was plunged into the undertow, being dragged down toward the bottom of the ocean, unable to breathe, but not resisting. I wanted to be fully immersed. To drown in him and never surface again.

There was nothing gentle about this kiss—it was raw with his need. Rougher, edged with frustration and desire. It felt like my lips were connected to every nerve ending in my body, and all my senses seemed to blow up at once.

He ignited me. His mouth was wild on mine, relentless, scorching, and it felt like I was standing over a blazing campfire, bolts of heat being shot through me. The sweet fire continued to race as he threaded his fingers into my hair, tilting my head back to give him better access to my jaw, my throat.

I was panting as he dragged his mouth along my skin, leaving blazing trails in his wake. I had forgotten what an expert he was in this. Like his law school had offered it as a special course and he'd gotten an A.

There was no way I could give this up again. Captain Carl could take a long walk off a short pier.

"Do you like that?" Hunter said the words against my neck.

"Can't you tell?" My eyes were literally rolling back into my head.

He grinned. "You know what they say about making assumptions."

"Is it 'come here and kiss me again'?"

"Yes, that's exactly it," he said before he returned his mouth to mine, hot and urgent, demanding and hungry.

Everything was burning. I was dizzy, breathless, floating, and totally on fire. I was lost to everything except his lips scorching me, his body hard against mine. It was like I had lost all sensation in my legs—as if he'd melted them away.

My stomach swirled and tightened with that same heat and I was suddenly completely out of breath, falling backward. He had backed me up to the bed and I hadn't even realized.

"Is this okay?" he asked as he came down to join me.

I scooted back as he advanced, making room for him. "Yes."

He stalked forward like some kind of predator and it thrilled me. I was more than willing to be caught and consumed. My desire for him made me lightheaded and apparently clumsy—I stumbled a bit moving backward with my elbows.

He didn't seem to notice.

Then I was beneath him and nothing had ever felt so absolutely perfect or right before. Like this was where I belonged. And judging from the soft groans and growls of pleasure he made, he felt the same.

His kisses grew insistent, desperate. And whether that was because of all the time we'd spent denying ourselves or because we knew that this might be our last chance to be alone like this for a very long time, I wasn't sure. But we were frantic for each other.

It was like a fever, this need I had for him. I was shivering, burning, sweaty, slightly delirious, and breaking out in goose bumps everywhere he touched me. I wanted to get closer to him, to see if he was having the same kind of reaction. Would his flesh be slick beneath my hands?

Without thinking I reached under his shirt and brushed my fingers against those hard abs of his and he let out a sharp moan from the back of his throat that had me wanting to explore even more of him. To navigate and discover this new land of Hunter Cartwright and claim it as my own.

As if he could read my mind, he removed his shirt with one fluid motion, barely breaking contact with my mouth while he did so. I would have been impressed if he hadn't made me so mindless for him. He wrapped one of his hands around my throat and kissed the exposed side, forcing me to stay put.

It didn't stop me from kissing what I could reach—his strong shoulder. I wanted to taste his skin and flicked my tongue out and felt him shudder against me in response.

He started murmuring whispered promises against my skin, his warm breath heating me even more. I couldn't make out what he was saying, mostly because I was far too busy running my fingers along every muscle and ridge in his back. There were so many. I could have happily spent all day doing this, noticing the way he would contract beneath my touch, tense up, and then relax.

"Lucky." He breathed my name out, and there was a hint of wonder in it, along with an overwhelming desire that made me feel like I was drowning all over again.

"Do you know how badly I want you?" he asked in a low voice that made me tremble all over. I was past speaking. I wanted him, too—I just couldn't manage to form actual words.

His mouth was on mine again, possessive, as hungry for me as I was for him. This time I was the one letting out soft breaths and moans as he began exploring me the same way I had him. His fingers brushed against the bare skin of my stomach and I quivered in response. My heartbeat seemed to be keeping time to the rhythmic pulse of his kiss.

As his fingers began to climb my rib cage like a ladder, I put my hand on his wrist. "Hunter, wait."

He immediately stilled.

I understood where this was leading. More clothing would come off. It would be so easy and so enjoyable to take the next step. And the next. And the next.

But we couldn't. If I broke the rule so flagrantly, I wouldn't be able to look the captain in the face.

Or Hunter's parents.

Or myself.

And the last one was what mattered most. Captain Carl had asked me to be in a position of leadership, to follow the rules. I wanted to be worthy of that trust. Rules were important.

No matter how very badly I wanted to break them.

I couldn't let things go further with Hunter. Not like this. "We can't."

"You did say only kissing," he said with a wry look. "Sorry for getting a little carried away."

"I did, too." I wanted him to know he wasn't alone in this. That I had happily participated and would be excited to do so at some point in the future when we were no longer on the ship.

He rolled away from me and we both lay on our backs, looking up at the ceiling, trying to catch our breath. My heart still thundered in my chest, my skin was so sensitive that my clothing was almost painful, my lips throbbed, and I felt the aftershocks of the way he'd kissed me throughout my entire body.

"You're really good at that," I finally said.

"I know."

He laughed when I reached over to smack him on his perfect chest and he grabbed my hand, pressing it to his warm skin. "And you're phenomenal at it. You made me forget my own name."

"It's not Hunter Smith, in case you were wondering."

Another laugh and then he pulled me into his arms and I snuggled against him. I wasn't sure this was the best idea, as I hadn't quite cooled down entirely, but I couldn't resist the opportunity to cuddle with him.

"You're the best, Lucky Salerno." He gently brushed his lips against my forehead.

I realized that I'd never had anything like this before. This kind of passion, this intensity, coupled with this sort of tenderness and caring.

It was an explosive combination and I didn't know how long I'd be able to hold out. To keep following those rules.

I loved my job but I knew I loved Hunter more.

CHAPTER FORTY

Hunter

We woke up the next morning completely intertwined. Her back was against my front and I held her tightly. I took advantage of my position to kiss the back of her neck in that spot that drove her wild.

When she started to squirm, I whispered, "Good morning," over her sensitive skin. She let out a sigh of pleasure that made my body tighten. I didn't know if I'd be able to calm down while I held her. Especially not when she pressed back against me like that.

So unfair.

It had been a long time since things had stopped at a vigorous make-out session. It made me feel a little like I was back in high school.

Except Lucky was not a girl and was very much a woman.

She rolled over to face me. "Good morning to you."

I really was the luckiest man who had ever lived. I reached up to trace the curves of her face. "How are you this beautiful this early?"

She flushed in the most attractive way. She really was gorgeous. She might not have believed it yet, but I believed it enough for the both of us.

Something had shifted between us last night. Things were different now. "I like waking up next to you," I said.

"Me too."

"I like kissing you even more."

"Also me too," she said. "And you . . . you're so . . ."

Silly woman. "Pick a word, any word. We could list my incredible qualities in alphabetical order if that would be easier for you. Awesome. Bold. Charismatic. Dashing. Energetic. Funny. Gregarious—"

"Handsome," she interrupted me. That wasn't something she'd ever really said to me. "Not that you need the encouragement, given that you have an alphabetical list of how incredible you are ready to go."

I couldn't help but laugh and be utterly charmed by her. "I knew you thought I was hot."

"Yeah, yeah," she grumbled teasingly.

I didn't know how I was going to resist her. Not able to help myself, I leaned in to kiss her softly and it had the effect of making my stomach quiver.

She needed to know how I felt. How important she was to me.

The most important person in my life.

No more waiting.

It was time.

"Lucky, there's something I want to tell you. I wanted to say it last night but I didn't want you to think that I was only saying it because of the situation."

She gulped. As if she knew exactly what I was about to say.

Then the words that I had thought would be hard to say felt entirely natural. Like I should have been saying it the whole time. "I'm in love with you."

A thousand different emotions crossed her face. Disbelief, concern, excitement, desire, worry, resolution.

And then I saw what I most hoped for.

"I love you, too," she said.

Her words lit me up like stadium lights. My heart grew three sizes and I wanted to run around the entire city shouting that she loved me. That couldn't have been easy for her. My girl was so unbelievably amazing and brave. I was beyond thrilled.

"That's good. Otherwise this would have been really embarrassing for me. 'Up a creek without a paddle' kind of situation," I said. I was teasing but I hoped she knew how happy she had just made me.

This had to change things. We weren't in some disposable situation where we would move on from each other and cause problems among the crew. This was real. This was serious.

We were in love.

My dad wouldn't have to worry about liability. She and I would find a way to make things okay.

We belonged to each other.

"I've never said that to anyone before," I confessed.

"Neither have I. I've been so busy protecting my heart, worried about people leaving, that I . . ." She took a deep breath. "That I've been too afraid to be open and vulnerable. Too scared to care about someone so much that I gave them the power to hurt me."

I felt so honored by the gift she'd just given me. I kissed her again. "Thank you for trusting me. I would never hurt you that way."

"I know." She sighed and nestled in closer to me. "We should get up and go. The Mascarellis are expecting us this morning."

"Are you sure I can't stay here with you like this?"

"There's nothing I'd love more, but we have to go."

It was difficult to leave this room, this safe bubble she and I had created, but we did have a schedule.

We made our way back over to Il Pane and were enthusiastically greeted by just as many family members as we had been yesterday. Giovanna waited for Lucky in the kitchen and had already taken the dough out of the fridge. Maria translated as they moved through the next steps.

When everything was completed, Giovanna took the sfogliatelle out of the oven and handed one to Lucky to eat. She bit into it.

Tears immediately sprang to her eyes and she began to cry. "It tastes just like my nonna's."

I wrapped her up in my arms while she cried happy tears. I was going to order her an entire mountain of Italian flour for her bakery.

My parents were planning on returning by dinner, so we had to head back to the ship. It took a long time to say goodbye, with all the kissing and hugging and promising to keep in touch. They'd adopted us both as part of their extended family. Maria and Lucky exchanged emails and cell numbers, and Lucky promised to contact them as soon as she made her first batch of sfogliatelle.

Giovanna loaded us up with bags of baked goods to take with us, insisting that we were both too skinny and needed to eat more.

When we finally exited the bakery, Lucky surprised me by pulling me into a long, deep kiss that made both of us breathless. "I'll never be able to thank you enough."

I didn't need her thanks. Just her love.

∼

When we got back to the ship, everything felt different. I told my mom to leave Lucky alone. She didn't ask for an explanation and I didn't offer one. When things were settled in a few months, I would proudly bring her home and let my mom ask her every question she had.

Not yet.

There was work to be done on the ship, so Lucky and I had to settle for stealing glances and exchanging secret smiles.

I loved watching her with my parents. She soaked up the stories they told her about me and my sisters. Hadley and Harlow teased her and each other and they all laughed. Lucky fit in so well.

She needed more family.

And I realized as I watched her that someday my family would be hers. They would love her just as much as I did. I was glad that I would be able to give that to her.

I couldn't hang out with them, though. They would be relentless and they would figure out how head over heels I was for Lucky, and

I wasn't going to be the reason that either one of us got fired. I asked Pieter to switch shifts with me so that I would be put back on anchor watch, awake when my family was sleeping.

Lucky's disappointment nearly made me reconsider. I told her, "My family will expect me to hang out with them and I have a job to do."

It made it so that I went to bed as she was getting up for the day. I missed her terribly and settled for kissing her good night / good morning.

I was ready for this charter to be over so that I could have her all to myself again.

And a few days later, it was finally drop-off day and we were leaving my family in Monte Carlo.

They hugged me and kissed me and said they couldn't wait to see me again. I told them I loved them, too. My dad had to pull my mom away so that she would stop hugging me. I glanced over at Lucky. I knew I was fortunate to have this.

I was glad that my parents had set such a good example for me of what a relationship looked like. So that I would know when I'd found the right person.

And I had.

When we got back to our cabin, Lucky seemed more upset that they'd left than I did. "Are you sad about your family leaving?"

"I'll miss them, but I'll be seeing them soon enough. Plus, I have you and you make it hard to think about anybody else," I told her, pulling her in for a kiss that very quickly got heated.

Thomas radioing me finally broke us apart. I'd been down in our cabin for too long.

"I better go," I said regretfully. "Are we going out with the crew tonight?"

"We probably should."

And despite wanting to talk her out of it, I knew it would be better for us to go out. Hours and hours of unchaperoned time could be tricky.

My parents had specifically requested that we be given the night off, despite the fact that we had a charter the next day. They had also offered to cover the cost of our drinks and dinner at a nearby upscale casino.

My dad had been hoping to get a new sports car and I was pretty sure the crew was about to drink him out of it.

So instead I said, "Until tonight, then. You'll be getting my A game. I hope you'll be able to keep your clothes on."

I kissed her one last time and then went to see what Thomas needed.

And despite telling her that I wouldn't lie to her anymore, I just had.

Because I very much hoped Lucky wouldn't be able to keep her clothes on.

CHAPTER FORTY-ONE

Lucky

Georgia convinced me to break into the "dress stash." Guests often deliberately left some of their expensive things behind. One woman had told us, "How can I convince my husband to buy me more dresses if I bring them with me?" We kept them in a closet and broke them out when we were going someplace fancy.

Like tonight. We had decided to go to one of the casinos where they had filmed that James Bond movie. While Emilie and Georgia grabbed dresses quickly (with Emilie shooting me dirty looks the entire time), it took me a bit longer. I finally found one that fit me but it was very short. It would have been short on an average-size woman but on me? It was practically a mini. If I bent the wrong way, the whole world would see my religion.

Hunter didn't seem to mind, though. He couldn't keep his eyes off my legs.

"Are you trying to kill me?" he asked in a strangled voice.

Suddenly I couldn't breathe and my lungs were no longer functioning. "You have to stop," I told him.

"I can't," he whispered back. "I love your legs. Have I ever told you how much I adore those little skorts you wear? How much I imagine kissing every single inch . . . or how badly I want you to wrap them around me." His words heated me up and I was glad we were surrounded by people because I wanted to attack him.

It made me question again how we were going to make it through the next few months when it was all I could do now to keep my hands off him.

"Are you going to play any of the games tonight? Blackjack? Roulette?" I asked while fanning my face, trying to distract us both.

"How could I not when I've got luck on my side? Although you do know what they say—lucky in love, unlucky in cards."

I hushed him and glanced around, glad that no one else was listening.

Georgia leaned over and said to me, "What have I been doing with my life?"

"Chasing boys and the approval of others," I told her, watching Hunter turn to his other side and engage Kai in a conversation. "Why?"

She nodded, seemingly in agreement with me. "Do you know what's odd?"

"Numbers not divisible by two?"

Since she had started drinking before we'd left the ship, she missed my joke completely, while Hunter laughed on the other side of me.

"I think I like Pieter. This guy from Slovakia had been texting me and I find the amount of letters in his last name very charming, but I want to be with Pieter. I blame you and all your happiness. You've rubbed off on me and I hate it."

"I'm . . . sorry?" I wasn't sure what she wanted here.

"My entire dating history has been like Halloween. Men pretending to be someone they're not and they want my candy and then they move on to the next person. Why can't they just be honest? Nobody ever says, 'Hi, would you mind it terribly if I waste the next six months of your life with my lack of emotional intelligence and fear of commitment?'"

I didn't know how to respond to her. It was so unlike Georgia to be introspective and admit to her dating issues and fears.

Fears that I still had, although I was trying to put them aside.

"Then you tell me to give Pieter a chance and he's just like you said—a nice guy—and I have no idea what to do with that!" she said, slamming her hands down onto the table.

"You date him and see where it goes. Although I never thought I'd see you in a real relationship. I thought hell would have to freeze over first."

"And it's possible because we have global warming," she said solemnly and I tried hard not to laugh. "I do worry about sea goggles."

I glanced at Hunter. It was something I still worried about. We were in a casino/hotel full of very beautiful women. Would he take a look around and remember that there was life beyond the boat? More than just me?

Not wanting my mind to go down that dark path, I said to Georgia, "I think you and Pieter are a good thing. You deserve to be treated well."

"As do you," she said before taking another gulp of her wine. "Speaking of, how far have things gone exactly? It's pretty obvious that something has changed between you two for the better."

I knew it! I knew it was obvious. I wondered who else had come to the same conclusion. I glanced around the table but no one was paying any attention to our conversation. "We've smooched a bit. A lot, actually."

"And you're in love."

I didn't confirm it, but I didn't deny it, either, which pretty much was confirmation, given the way she started gloating. "Ha. Called that one the first day."

Panic set in, and somehow, Hunter seemed to sense it. He was deep in conversation with Kai but he reached under the table and put his hand on my knee, squeezing it, making me feel better.

"Are you going to freak out?" Georgia asked, worried.

"I'm okay." I put my hand on top of his and he turned it over so that we were holding hands. He always exuded so much comfort and warmth. Was I sweating? I was worried that I was sweating.

"Yeah, no, you totally look like you're okay," she said and I knew she was teasing me. "A toast!"

That got everyone at the table to stop talking and that anxiety of mine started up again. I was afraid she was about to tell everyone about me and Hunter.

Instead she said, "Here's to alcohol! Helping people make regrettable, life-altering mistakes for thousands of years!"

Everyone else cheered and clinked their glasses together. Hunter made eyes at me over his glass and I leaned in.

I knew I shouldn't ask the question, but it was like I couldn't help myself. "What are you thinking about?"

He set his glass down. "All the ways I'd like to take that dress off you."

A spike of desire struck deep in my gut. "That's not fair," I whispered.

"Not trying to be. Here." He handed me a basket full of bread. "I asked the waitress to bring extra bread for you because you wanting bread is usually a safe bet."

I hadn't even noticed the waitress distributing everyone's dinner. I was ravenous, but not for food.

Food was the only thing I could have, though.

I pretty much attacked the steak I'd ordered. Thankfully, it was one of the best filets mignons I'd ever had. And Andre cooked this sort of thing regularly. I was kind of glad the chef hadn't come out with us tonight and had opted to go to bed early. I felt a little like I was cheating on him with this dinner.

"Is it good?" Hunter asked. He had some kind of seafood platter.

"It's like crack made out of beef," I told him, offering him a bite. And I watched every moment of him taking it from my fork, the way his mouth closed around it, how he slid the meat from the tongs and . . . why did I suddenly feel woozy?

He leaned in close. "You have to stop doing that."

"Doing what?"

"Saying things that make me want to kiss you."

My temperature spiked and I wished, more than anything, that we were alone.

He picked up one of his oysters and offered it to me. "Do you want to try it? I've heard they can be quite the aquadesiac."

"I've never really been into oysters." I ignored his pun and also decided that I wasn't going to tell him that it looked like someone had dripped snot onto a shell. And if it really was some kind of aphrodisiac, I definitely needed to steer clear.

He said, "We've got that charter tomorrow, so think of it as the clam before the storm."

"Oysters aren't clams."

"Yes, but I don't have a pun for oysters."

"You two are like an old married couple!" Georgia declared. She was pretty drunk, and from the looks of things, Emilie was well on her way to joining her.

I was worried that my friend was drawing too much attention to Hunter and me, but then I was saved by Pieter. He came over to her and said, "I think you want to come to the club and dance with me."

"You've been misinformed," she said with a smile but then left with him anyway.

I was acutely aware of Emilie staring at me and tried very hard not to make eye contact. We still ran the risk of her going to her uncle and telling him that she suspected Hunter and I were together. I didn't want to give her any proof.

With Georgia and Pieter leaving, it broke our little party up. Kai stood up and said, "If you'll all excuse me, I believe I just spotted my ride home." He went over to a tall, stunning blonde and began chatting her up.

Following his lead, Thomas said, "That bird right there, the one with the red hair? She looks like a bad decision, doesn't she? I'm off to see if she'd like to have breakfast with me."

It was shocking that those kinds of lines apparently worked for the exterior crew. Following the lead of his friends, François went off to talk to some unsuspecting woman and I wondered whether I had a moral obligation as a fellow woman to warn her.

Emilie stared at us for a bit longer and then stood up dramatically, making her way over to the bar. A handsome man immediately sat down next to her and I let out a sigh. "She's going to make some unlucky guy very uncomfortable tonight."

Hunter chuckled next to me while I realized that the rest of the crew had abandoned us and we were now alone.

The waitress returned with the check, handing it to Hunter. "I guess it's my treat," he said.

"Yes, well, when people find out your parents own a yacht, they'll expect you to cover dinner."

He smiled, pulling out his card, and the waitress immediately returned to run it for him. She came back quickly with the receipt. He signed it and then pulled my chair closer. "Do you want to get out of here?"

I did, which was going to become an issue. But I still said, "Please."

In an apparent hurry to be alone with me back on the ship, he called for a ride instead of walking.

"You don't want to gamble?" I asked. We were in a casino in Monte Carlo. It seemed like we should.

"Everything we've been doing has been a calculated risk," he said. "I don't need to push my luck at the tables."

I thought about his statement as we made our way back to the *Mio Tesoro*. We were putting ourselves at risk, but it was like we couldn't stay away from each other. I loved him so much and all I wanted to do was be as close to him as I possibly could.

A sentiment he shared, as he kissed me on my neck the entire way back.

By the time we got to our cabin, I was so fired up that I was ready to burn this entire ship down. My blood pulsated, blocking out other sounds.

He locked the door. "You told me once that you have to anticipate the needs of the guests. And the crew."

It was easy to see where he was going with this. "I did say that."

"You haven't been anticipating my needs."

"I haven't?" I said innocently.

He fixed me with that hungry gaze of his. "No. You've been very remiss in your duties."

"And what is it you need?"

A lazy, wicked smile lit up his features. "A kiss."

"I live to be of service," I said, stepping forward. He met me halfway, crashing into me. His lips were hot and insistent on mine, and I was immediately plunged into that hazy world of pleasure where nothing mattered except his kiss.

And I didn't know how we were going to keep things PG if he kept kissing me like the world would end if he didn't. He completely overloaded my entire system and it was so difficult to think.

I did finally manage to break away from him, and it was like I was tearing off a piece of myself.

"I love you," he breathed, making my decision to pull back feel like a not particularly smart one.

"And I love you. But we are playing with fire here." We needed to be more careful.

He leaned his forehead against mine, his chest moving up and down quickly. "I'm not just playing with it. I'm like one of those stuntmen in a flame-retardant suit, running around on fire."

I knew exactly what he meant. "What are we going to do?"

"I don't know," he said ruefully. "Maybe we should call it a night before I ravish you."

Yes, please. "Good idea," I breathed out. "The going-to-sleep part. Not the, you know, other one."

He gave me a knowing grin. He kissed me briefly and then went over to the closet, taking off his shirt. I reached for the zipper on my dress and realized that I couldn't quite get to it.

"Need help?"

I had to gulp down the sensations that overwhelmed me as I turned my back to him. He stepped closer to me and I tried hard not to think about what he was doing. He grasped the zipper and tugged it slightly down.

Then he leaned forward and kissed the skin at the base of my neck and I had to put my hands onto the wall to keep me upright. I was trembling, torn between wanting him to continue and scared of what would happen if he did.

He pulled the zipper down oh so slowly, and with every patch of skin that was exposed, he pressed a warm kiss to that spot. It got harder and harder to stand as my knees pretty much stopped working entirely.

Something he seemed to realize as he put his free hand flat against my stomach, holding me in place as he continued his onslaught of unzipping and then kissing.

"This isn't avoiding the fire," I whispered.

"I know," he said in a low tone that made everything inside me burn even brighter. "You are so unbelievably sexy."

His words made my bones liquefy. He released his hand and I had to lean against the door as he crouched to continue his trail of fiery kisses. When he got to the small of my back, something smacked hard into the wall outside our cabin. I heard someone call out in pain.

Without thinking, I unlocked the door and came out into the hallway. Emilie had apparently tripped on her way down the stairs and crashed into the wall.

"Are you okay?" I asked her.

She took in our appearance—him shirtless, my dress gaping in the back, practically sliding off my shoulders, and narrowed her gaze. I didn't know what she thought about Hunter and our fake-dating-but-now-real-dating thing we had going on, but if she had doubted it at all, we had just eliminated that doubt entirely. She went into her own cabin and slammed the door shut.

I turned to Hunter and asked, "Do you think she'll tell her uncle?"

His face was grim. "Let's hope not."

CHAPTER
FORTY-TWO

Lucky

The fear that Emilie would tell the captain stayed at the back of my mind, insistent, and had the effect of cooling my ardor. Which meant I was much more careful with Hunter and didn't let things go too far.

Even though we both really, really wanted them to.

Adding to my anxiety was the fact that our new charter was the absolute worst. The primary guest was a man named Myron in his late fifties / early sixties. He had brought his girlfriend with him, a woman named Amber, who we guessed was nineteen or twenty years old.

He was involved in some kind of cryptocurrency/techno type of company and had brought along his top four twentysomething employees to reward them for their hard work. Their ringleader Brock, Brad, Chaz, and Lance—each one of them jerkier than the last.

François had contemptuously referred to them as "nouveau riche" right after they arrived, and for the first time ever, I heartily agreed with him. In our line of work, there was a definite divide between people who had grown up with money and those who had more recently acquired it.

Old money treated the crew with courtesy and respect. Like we were humans. New money treated us like we were peons at their constant beck and call, degraded us, and generally didn't care how they acted. Like Brock decided their complicated drinks should never go below half-full. I spent almost the whole day getting them fresh drinks, wasting an unbelievable amount of time and alcohol.

It was theirs to waste—they would have to pay for all of it—but I hated pouring money down the sink.

They behaved like it was our privilege to serve them. As if we should be the ones paying them for the honor of being in their presence.

Even Hunter, who was not a complainer, had told me how much the guests were personally annoying him.

"They want the slide out and they use it for ten minutes and then they're done. Thomas actually timed how long they use it because we're all so sick of it. Do you know how long it takes to set up and take down that stupid thing? Hours. I know that it's my job, but use it for more than ten minutes!"

The guests also enjoyed bringing "paid friends" on board. I figured it wasn't my responsibility to worry about what international laws were or were not being broken when that happened, but I was pretty tired of cleaning up the disgusting mess after they were done.

The only thing worse than the men and their unrelenting demands was Amber. She was terrible but I supposed I would be, too, if I were dating a man old enough to be my grandfather. She had a Pomeranian named Bisou, who was also the absolute worst. That little yappy menace peed and pooped all over the ship. I kept telling myself that at least it wasn't cat urine. Nobody had ever trained the dog and she was the most ill-behaved animal I'd ever seen.

"That's not a dog," Hunter said as Bisou snapped at his ankles. "It's a demon in dog's fur."

I was inclined to agree.

The second night at dinner, Amber came out in a red, furry couture dress that had me wondering how many Elmos had been killed to make it. I got the guests all seated and went back down to the galley to wait for Andre to finish up the first course.

He was already aggravated for several reasons, which included the fact that Bisou had stolen the fish he had put out for dinner, the guests had required gluten-free and paleo food, and the primary guest, Myron, had said to "surprise" him for dinner.

"Surprise me" was basically a code phrase for "make what I normally eat but plate it to look different." Which meant that Andre was going to have to try to figure it out on his own with no guidance from Myron.

"Lucky, your favorite guest is having a fit," Thomas called out, observing the monitors.

"What now?" I asked, exasperated. "Is she not having any success luring children into her gingerbread house?"

"Don't know. She's melting down so much that some teenager is going to have to warn the United Nations about it."

"I'd offer to go up and slap some sense into her," Georgia interjected, "but I don't want to get gold digger on my hands."

I couldn't even encourage her to be nice, especially when I wasn't being nice myself. Amber had been upset about everything, and she berated me and my staff constantly.

"You're not going to tell me to behave?" Georgia asked me, clearly surprised.

"How can I? I'm not saying I hate her, but if she was on fire, I'd grab some marshmallows."

"It would be very bad if she was on fire and somebody had to put her out. Her kind melts when they get wet," she said with a nod. "That girl is living proof that money can't buy happiness."

"Yeah, but I'll bet it makes misery a lot easier to deal with," Thomas said, his eyes still fixed on the screen.

With a deep sigh I went up to see what Her Royal Suckiness wanted now.

Amber had pulled linens off the table, sending thousands of dollars' worth of china and crystal onto the floor. Myron was on his phone, ignoring his girlfriend's outburst. The other men, whom Georgia referred to as the Ambassadors of Audacity, were across the room, laughing while they watched the scene play out.

Such a mess. I made a wish that Amber would have to walk on a carpet of Legos barefoot for a month. "What can I do for you?" I asked.

"Clean this mess up!" She flounced into the main salon and sat down on one of the couches.

I retrieved a dustpan and brush and began carefully sweeping up broken glass. Brock wandered over, followed by his fellow cretins.

"Lucky, have I ever told you how much I like your uniform?" He leered at me and I was suddenly aware of how short it was. He added, "I'd like it even better on my bedroom floor."

Ew, ew, ew. I knew that I should say nothing because any verbal interaction might be seen as encouraging this kind of behavior. I continued to clean.

But he kept going. "So are you free tonight or are you going to cost me?"

His buddies laughed at that one and I tried to let their words go in one ear and out the other.

"It looks like you're really on top of things," he continued. "Can I be one of the things you're on top of?"

Brock's goons laughed again. I glanced over at Myron, wondering if he was going to do something about his employees, but he was glued to his phone.

I wasn't a psychic, but my guess was that they were going to have a big lawsuit at some point in the future.

"Where's that sexy Georgia?" one of them asked. "I bet she'll play with us."

Had they taken a special seminar on being gross? Brock came closer to me and leaned down, putting his hand on my shoulder. I wanted to tell him to act like his hairline and take a step back.

Hunter walked into the room, looking furious. He glowered from the doorway and it had the effect of making the other men go quiet. Brock immediately moved away from me.

"I'll be back with the broom," I said as I stood up. "Everyone please stay clear of this area."

I took Hunter by the arm and led him out of the room. "What do you think you're doing?" I asked in a sharp tone when we were out of earshot of the guests.

"That guy was touching you."

"I'm aware. You can't come in and intimidate the guests. Not when we're depending on their tip. I can take care of myself."

I'd never seen Hunter looking so angry while also being overprotective. And honestly? It was kind of sexy. "I know you can."

"And if those slimeballs go to the captain, and they're absolutely the type that would, complaining that you were being threatening toward them? He could fire you." I couldn't let that happen. I would miss him and I wanted him to fulfill his dreams and he had to keep this job to do so. "You have to remember that the customer is always right."

"Even when they're sexually harassing you? That is not okay."

"No, it's not. But it happens."

He stepped closer to me and, in the calmest, most rational voice, said, "If he puts his hands on you again, I'm going to choke him out."

Yep, definitely sexy. "No, you're not. That's felonious assault."

"We're on the ocean." He shrugged.

"Close to the shore, so Italy's laws apply." We were on our way to Portofino.

He dragged his fingers through his hair and growled. "This is going to be my supervillain origin story."

I glanced around, and when I'd made sure that we were alone, I wrapped my arms around his waist. "You can't show your parents you're being a responsible, hardworking adult if you kill one of their charter guests."

He let out an exaggerated sigh and kissed me quickly. "Fine. I'll be reasonable. But if that Brock guy touches you again, all bets are off."

"I kind of like your Neanderthal ways," I said.

"Oh yeah? Wait until I drag you back to my cave," he said, making me forget that we were supposed to be working.

I leaned in, intending to kiss him for real, when I heard the sound of someone approaching. We quickly released one another and Emilie came up the stairs.

"There you are," she said. "I'm sick."

She looked fine. "Do you need to see the doctor?"

"No. I don't think I'll be able to work tomorrow."

With these guests we definitely needed all hands on deck. "Can't you take some medicine? We really need your help." As little as it actually was.

"No." Then she left without another word.

It was like we were playing a game of chicken to see who would crack first. That was it. I had to tell her uncle what she had been doing. Or, more accurately, not been doing.

As soon as this charter was over, I would go to him and say that Emilie needed to be let go. Enough was enough.

If she tried to swipe back at me by telling him about Hunter, well, I'd cross that bridge when I came to it.

"She's sick?" Hunter asked, sounding as incredulous as I felt.

"Allergic to work, most likely," I said. "I can't be shorthanded with this bunch."

"I'll help you," he said. "I'll fill in for her."

"You will?"

He nodded. "I'll ask Thomas if it's okay and then I'll do whatever you tell me to do."

Another spike of want. "Anything?"

His expression was hungry and intense. I was already burning up for him and he wasn't even touching me. "I would say I'm looking forward to working under you but I don't want to sound like those scumbags in there."

"It's okay if you say it," I whispered, and that intensity in his eyes somehow increased.

"Lucky . . ." All the frustration and yearning we both felt was encapsulated in the way he said my name.

"Soon," I told him.

It wasn't fair to say because "soon" was so far off. After this charter he and I would sit down and figure things out. We couldn't keep going like this.

Something had to give.

CHAPTER FORTY-THREE

Hunter

Last night, after I had witnessed one of the tech bros asking Georgia to come and sit on his lap so that he could guess her weight, I'd met up with François and Thomas and we decided that none of the female crewmembers should be left alone with our current "guests." I wanted to call my parents and tell them to be more selective in the charters they accepted and explain to them how terrible these people were.

Lucky begged me not to, because she mistakenly believed my parents would think that she personally wasn't doing a good job. I tried to make her see that that wouldn't happen, but she didn't believe me.

The other guests had gone fishing and Lucky told me that while the succubus and her demon dog were on the sundeck, we needed to clean the primary cabin.

She seemed frustrated, so while we stripped the sheets and comforter from the bed in the primary cabin, I asked, "How are you doing today?"

"I've got ninety-nine problems and these horrible people are all of them." She grabbed the clean, ironed linens and directed me on how to put them on correctly. "If there was an iceberg ahead, I don't think I'd be too upset."

I laughed while she showed me how to fold the corners correctly. She was so sexy when she bossed me around. I said, "I'm kind of surprised we don't have to clean up any Barbies."

"She is really young, isn't she? I hoped they didn't cross any state lines getting here."

I shook my head. "Some people say age is just a number."

"And in his case a high one. That closely correlates with death," she shot back.

"Maybe she's an old soul and he's a kid at heart and so together they're . . . still forty years apart."

She grinned at me. "I'm sure their love will last for many, many days." Then she tossed me a pillowcase.

I picked up a pillow and read the tag. "One hundred percent cotton, nontoxic, organic." I glanced up at her. "What are other pillows made out of?"

"Asbestos, toxins, and inorganic materials, obviously."

I loved how she and I could play around and have fun together, just enjoying each other's company, while still being able to have the serious conversations if we needed to.

Which Lucky was about to do. "Hunter, about last night, I'm sorry for unloading my frustration with the guests on you."

I paused what I was doing because I was confused. "When did you do that?"

"I was angry with you for intervening. I kind of snapped at you. I know your heart was in the right place."

"Lucky, you didn't do anything wrong. You're allowed to be mad if you're mad."

She looked startled. A moment later she said, "If I was ever mad or frustrated, my ex would get angry at me, and even if he was at fault, I always had to be the one who apologized."

I was going to make a list of all the butts I had to kick when we got off this ship. I went over to her, taking both of her hands in mine. "That's not how relationships are supposed to work. It's my job to be there for you when you need me. To support you. And I hope you'd do the same for me."

"Of course I would."

"I'll be strong for you and you'll be strong for me. We'll fill in each other's gaps."

"Okay." She smiled at me. "I don't know if I can trust in people who work through their problems. That doesn't feel like a real thing."

"I promise it is," I said, giving her a quick kiss and then helped get the comforter back onto the bed and also tucked in the corners.

We finished the bed and took a step back to survey our handiwork. "Perfectly made. Do you feel a sense of pride when you look at it?" she asked.

"When I look at it, this is what I think." I put my hands around her rib cage and tossed her through the air so that she landed on the bed with a surprised laugh and a thud.

"Hunter! We're going to have to remake this."

"Then let's mess it up a little first," I said with a wicked grin.

"Are you serious right now?"

"Not the kind of question to fill a guy with confidence."

She propped herself up on her elbows. "How do you want your no? Fast or slow?"

"For the record, I like my yeses loud and drawn out."

"Yes," she said quietly.

"Not as loud as I want, but I'll take it." I crawled onto the bed and stopped at her ankles. I did what I'd told her I wanted—I started to kiss her there and then leisurely made my way up her right leg. She was already making those little breathy sounds of excitement and she made me so ravenous for her. I needed one more kiss and then another and I kept going.

When I reached her thigh, her legs quivered and she grabbed my head and pulled me up to her mouth, no longer able to wait. She was so passionate, so desperate, that only one part of me was currently thinking and it wasn't my brain.

I devoured her, kissing her so thoroughly and deeply that I forgot where we were. I tugged at the bottom of her shirt so that I could get to her velvety-soft skin. I needed to touch her everywhere. I loved that I was the only person allowed to touch her like this. That I was the only one who got to see her this way.

Now she was the one tugging at my shirt, and pleasure skated along my skin as she brushed her fingertips over my ribs, up to my chest, back down to my stomach. Liquid fire torched through me, my muscles rippling everywhere she touched. I loved when she touched me. I craved it. I was a total addict. She made everything hazy and hot.

I moved my lips urgently over hers, and then she sucked my tongue into her mouth and all of my other senses shut off completely. I ground myself against her and she moved with me until we were both sweaty and desperate.

She suddenly stopped and it was like the sun had turned off.

"Did you hear that?" she asked.

My lust-addled brain wanted us to stop talking. "The only thing I can hear is my own heartbeat and those sounds you make when you especially enjoy what I'm doing."

She moved away from me and I didn't want that. She cocked her head to listen and it felt like an invitation to nip at her neck. "All alone," I told her. She was being paranoid.

"Probably not for long," she said reluctantly, letting out a little sigh I understood all too well. "We have to remake this."

I stood up. It was so hard to love her this much and have to keep my distance. "Good thing I'm an expert at it now."

"Okay, Mr. Expert, you fix this while I go start in the bathroom."

She disappeared to go clean and I figured it was probably a good thing to give us a little bit of space. Because the only thing I wanted to do was toss her back on this bed and finish what we'd started.

I straightened out the bed and glanced at some of the red roses in a vase next to the bed. I wanted to do something nice for Lucky. And making the guests happy made her happy.

So I deflowered a bunch of the roses, spreading their petals all over the bed. When I was finished it kind of looked like someone had massacred a flower shop.

Thomas called me on the radio and I hurried out to help him get one of the Jet Skis back on the ship. I was disappointed because I had wanted to see Lucky's face when she saw what I had done.

I ran back to the primary cabin and she was still in the bathroom. It had to have been a big mess.

"Lucky! Come and see what I did for Myron and his not-able-to-legally-drink-yet girlfriend!"

She came into the cabin, and instead of looking pleased, she looked horrified.

"No, no, no," she muttered as she came over.

Why was she upset? "It's romantic."

"It stains unless you freeze the petals first," she said. She tried to pick up some of the petals from the bright white comforter but it was too late. It was stained. It looked like someone had been bludgeoned and then bled to death.

"I'm sorry, I didn't know," I said, trying to pick up the petals. I had wanted to help her and instead I was only making her life harder.

"I have a replacement in the laundry room. We have to get this out of here," she said. I helped her grab it, and the bedding beneath it was fine.

We went out into the hallway and nearly crashed into Captain Carl.

The captain's gaze landed on the blanket. "What's that?" he asked.

"Oh, the duvet from the primary cabin got a little stained." Her voice was high and tight. She was scared.

The captain tugged at the blanket and he saw how extensive the stains were.

"Who is responsible for this?"

I opened my mouth to tell him I was to blame but she jumped in front of me.

"It was me," she said. "I did it."

CHAPTER FORTY-FOUR

Lucky

Seeing the expression on the captain's face, I kept talking, trying to make this okay. "I thought the guests might like some rose petals on their bed and this happened. By accident. I've got another one to replace it with, though."

This wasn't a uniform shirt. It was significantly more expensive. I sensed that Hunter was about to refute my statement and so I took a step back, landing it on his foot so that he would understand to stay quiet.

"This is becoming a pattern, Lucky," Captain Carl said. "I heard about the incident last night in the dining room with the dishes." By that he meant Amber's toddler tantrum she had thrown. "I expect you to keep a handle on the guests and not let them be so destructive."

I blinked in surprise. Now I was supposed to be controlling irrational people? How did he expect me to manage that?

"Understood, Captain," I said. Georgia was right. He *was* an unreasonable tyrant with ridiculous expectations.

Satisfied, he nodded and headed up the stairs toward the bridge. When we were alone Hunter spun me toward him.

"You should not have done that," he said.

"I had to. You need your job. I'm not willing to let you get in trouble. Especially after the damage you caused to the ship when you didn't drop the fender." I was afraid of what kind of information the captain would pass along to Hunter's parents. He might delight in telling them how their son was destroying their new purchase.

"And you need yours," he countered.

"It's okay," I said. "The captain would have blamed me anyways. You're currently under my command, so I'm responsible for not keeping a better eye on you or teaching you properly."

He crossed his arms over his chest. "By that logic, shouldn't the captain take the blame when you mess up?"

"It doesn't really work like that, unfortunately. And it's only my second incident, so it should be fine," I said. "Stop running yachts into docks and don't kiss your temporary boss in beds and everything will be okay."

He gave me a half smile. "I'm not sure I can promise the second one."

Even now, the man flirted.

Then he added, "You should have let me take responsibility for what I did. You don't always have to make things okay for everyone."

I did it because I loved him. Because I didn't want him to miss out on what was important to him.

As if he understood that, he leaned forward and kissed my forehead. "But plank you very much for standing up for me. I appreciate it."

"You're welcome."

"Maybe we should just come clean with the captain," he said and my adrenaline spiked. That was a terrible idea. "I could call my dad and tell him the situation. Tell him that I'm the one who stained the blanket. That we're in love. Explain it so that he understands. We can change how things are."

"You are trying to prove something to your parents, and if you call them, you put everything in jeopardy. You'll be living down to their expectations. I don't want that to happen, for either one of our sakes."

He nodded and smiled, but it didn't quite reach his eyes. "Okay."

And even though things appeared to be fine, I got the sense that I had overstepped in some way. That there was something else going on, some underlying thing that I didn't know about, and it worried me.

~

That uneasy feeling only increased as the day went on. The guests decided that they were going out to Portofino for the evening and had demanded the exterior crew join them. They were currently getting ready for their night out.

Georgia told me that they had asked for her to come as well, but François, of all people, had told them that wouldn't be possible. Maybe he was seeing his own bad behavior in these guests and was becoming a better person.

She and I were sitting in the crew mess having something to eat, taking advantage of this break in our schedule. The fishing expedition had turned out to be a bust. Hunter had texted me about it.

In a twist of bait the only thing they managed to catch was waves. There goes their reely good day.

Apparently in an attempt to compensate for failing so miserably at fishing, they had brought more "paid friends" on board. There was a lot of disgusting stuff we would now have to clean up once they'd left for the night.

Georgia asked, "How is Princess Tiny Terror doing?"

"She made me keep bringing her new ice water because the ice was melting and watering down her drink," I said.

"What about Brock?" she asked. "Still the world's biggest wanker?"

"He plays to his strengths." I twirled the noodles around my fork and took a bite. I was too tired to heat anything up besides ramen.

"I heard what he did to you last night. The way he would have been able to taste pepper spray for the rest of his days if I had been there," she said with a shake of her head. "This group is personally responsible for turning me off of men entirely."

"Don't let a couple of rotten apples spoil the bunch."

"We're talking whole orchards here."

"Only a few more days," I told her. "We're nearly to the finish line."

"Yes, and then we'll probably pick up another terrible group of people." She let out a short sigh and said, "Let's talk about something happy. What's going on with you and your . . . I don't know the right word to use. Fling? Although you don't seem like a fling kind of girl."

I couldn't stop the satisfied grin that settled onto my face. "Oh, I've been flung."

"Really?" she said, sounding very interested.

We were getting into some dangerous territory, and I didn't want to share all the glorious details with her. It was something just for Hunter and me. "We have . . . an understanding."

"Hmm. I think it is very unkind of you to not share what it's like to be with that sexy man. Maybe I should have done your game and then things might have gone differently."

She was joking. She was with Pieter and happy, as far as I knew. But her words struck an insecure nerve. "What do you mean?"

"The whole hard-to-get thing. That's never been my vibe. Although my mother always told me that she'd never met a man who wasn't attracted to the idea of winning over an indifferent woman. Thrill of the hunt and all that."

Was that really what she thought? That Hunter only liked me because I had initially kept him at arm's length instead of drooling over him? I had drooled over him like Georgia and Emilie—I'd just kept that information to myself.

I hadn't been trying to play a game. I'd been desperately trying to keep Captain Carl's rule and protect myself. Not trick Hunter into being interested in me.

"And the whole secrecy thing must just add another level," she continued, unaware of the way I was questioning things. "I know it works for me and Pieter."

"Hunter thinks that maybe we should tell the captain. Be up front about it."

Her eyes went wide with horror. "Don't do that! He'll fire you both. When you rock the boat, you fall out. Leave things alone."

Our radios crackled and then the voices of the exterior crew filled the space around us as they made their plans to accompany the guests to Portofino.

"You do know why they're taking the deckhands, don't you?" Georgia asked, turning down the volume on her walkie-talkie.

"Because we refused?"

"No. Because they're attractive men and they'll lure the women over so that those bloody bogans can brag about their money. The crew will be bait."

"Do you really think the guests would do something that stupid?"

"Gee, what are the odds?" she responded sarcastically. "Obviously they'll do something stupid. But I wouldn't worry about Hunter."

I wasn't worried about him going out with the guests. I knew that he and his fellow deckhands would behave.

Instead I was concerned about all the questions that Georgia had just inadvertently brought up that I didn't have an answer for.

She reached across the table to squeeze my hand. "And if Hunter fails you somehow, I know you might feel like there's no one there for you, but do you know who will always be there for you?"

"Who?"

"Laundry."

I let out a small laugh and she grinned at me. Her questions and declarations had sown some seeds of doubt and I didn't like how that felt. I wanted to be in my own little world with Hunter where nothing mattered but the two of us.

Georgia finished her food and stood up, walking over to wash out her bowl. She came to a halt in front of the monitors and let out the foulest string of curse words I'd ever heard her use.

"Lucky, don't—"

Despite her warning, I looked at the monitors.

There was a camera pointed at the hallway just outside the primary bedroom, and there stood Hunter and Emilie.

And they were kissing.

CHAPTER FORTY-FIVE

Lucky

A rush of white noise filled my head, blocking out all my senses. This couldn't be happening. It couldn't.

I dropped my head down to the table, like I couldn't support the weight any longer. Each beat of my heart was painful, as if a knife were cutting into my chest. My lungs constricted, and I felt like I was going to throw up.

It was like the worst panic attack I'd ever had.

And all I wanted was for Hunter to be here, holding my hands.

But he was too busy kissing Emilie.

Georgia rushed to my side, putting her arm around me. I couldn't hear what she was saying, like my hearing had been turned off.

Had he been telling Emilie the same things he'd told me? Saying he wasn't interested in me or Georgia, that she was the only one for him?

I felt so completely foolish. How did I get taken in by men like this every single time?

Why had he done this? I wouldn't have sex with him and Emilie would? Was that the reason?

This is Hunter, a small voice said to me. *He wouldn't do this to you. He loves you.*

Maybe I had misunderstood what I'd seen. That was possible, wasn't it?

It would be an easier lie to swallow if I hadn't witnessed it with my own eyes.

"Lucky? Are you okay?" Georgia's words finally pierced the foggy, confused haze I found myself in.

"She's supposed to be sick." It was the only thing I could think to say.

"I can't believe this," Georgia said.

Neither could I. It felt completely unreal. Like it was a movie and not actually happening to me.

"There has to be an explanation," I said, finding it painful to speak. Didn't I owe it to him to let him explain?

"I don't know, mate. How well do you really know Hunter? He's lied to you about some important things."

Yes, but there had been reasons for that.

"I don't want to be a downer here but I also don't want you to get hurt. What if this is just a fling for him? Do you know how many crewmembers I've thought I was in love with?"

This wasn't like that. Or, it hadn't been up until about three minutes ago. But what if she was right? What if he and I were caught up in some faux romance because we lived and worked together? How was I supposed to know if this was real or not?

And how could he kiss Emilie?

Somebody stepped into the crew mess and then hurried down the hall.

It was Emilie.

I held my breath, wondering if Hunter was going to come chasing after her.

He didn't.

"Go into your cabin and splash some cold water on your face," Georgia said. "Lay down if you need to. Take a few minutes to collect yourself."

How was I supposed to collect myself when I had been shattered into a billion tiny pieces and scattered all over the floor?

I did as she suggested. My mind was reeling; I was trying to make sense of what I'd just seen. I didn't get into my bed, though. There were too many memories there. I stayed in the bathroom with the door locked.

And I couldn't figure out a way to make this okay. There was no reason or explanation other than Hunter had been cheating on me the whole time and I was so caught up in him that I hadn't realized it.

It certainly wouldn't have been the first time that this had happened to me.

At some point I was going to have to get out of this bathroom and start cleaning. Georgia couldn't do it all by herself and Emilie certainly wasn't going to help—she was too busy sticking her tongue down Hunter's throat.

I wanted to cry but I knew that if I did, I wouldn't be able to stop. I didn't have the luxury of getting to break down and fall apart. There was still work to be done.

"Lucky, Lucky, Captain Carl."

I fumbled with my radio for a second before I could respond. "Yes, Captain?"

"Come up to the bridge."

"Copy." I wondered what the captain wanted now. Maybe he was going to berate me for not letting Brock sexually harass me.

I felt like a zombie as I made my way up to the bridge, numb and incapable of thought. Because remembering what I had seen was too heartbreaking and it was easier to just block everything out.

Captain Carl was waiting for me. "What is this?" he asked, handing me a piece of paper.

I was still so scattered that it took me a bit to recognize what it was. The sCrew List.

My name was on it.

And I had points.

"I don't know—"

"Save it," he cut me off. "I don't actually need you to explain this to me. I can see exactly what it is."

"But I didn't make this. I didn't participate."

He narrowed his gaze at me. "That paper says otherwise."

Suddenly everything came into focus. When Emilie had rushed past us in the crew mess, she must have been going after the list, adding my name to it and giving me points for kissing Hunter.

"And then there's this."

He handed me another piece of paper and I gasped. Someone had taken a picture of Hunter kissing me in the primary cabin. The captain must have printed it out.

I knew I'd heard something. Emilie must have done it.

Then another paper. This one was a screenshot of my texts with Georgia. Where she asked me if I was hooking up with Hunter and I had sarcastically replied that he and I were having sex.

Georgia never would have shown those texts to anyone. Had she been too drunk that night and forgotten to delete them? She had sent them from François's phone. Would he have shown the captain? That didn't seem like something François would do.

But how did the captain have them? Wait, my phone had gone missing and then mysteriously reappeared. Emilie must have taken it. I hysterically thought about the fact that I had always meant to put password protection on it and now it was too late.

"This was a joke," I said, my heart beating so fast it felt like it might actually explode. "That's why there's a smiley face after it. I was kidding. I haven't slept with Hunter."

"There's photographic evidence of you kissing him, which is against the rules."

And I couldn't deny it. He was right.

"You kissing on the primary guest's bed with a fellow crewmember is inappropriate and unprofessional. What if one of the guests had walked in and seen you?"

My face burned with shame. Again, he was right. Most of the guests had been off the ship but Amber could have easily gone down to her room for any reason.

"This is the third strike, Lucky. The last few weeks you have shown a continual pattern of not doing your job properly or within the parameters I've established."

Sweat broke out on my lower back as I realized what was going on. I was at DEFCON screwed. I had lived in constant fear of the captain letting me go, and now here we were. It was happening.

I was being fired.

"I'm afraid I'm going to have to let you go."

There it was. My anxiety had caused me to imagine him firing me so many times that part of me had almost been expecting this. The one time I broke a rule and it was destroying everything.

He got my passport and paperwork, along with an airplane ticket. He said I would fly out of Genoa and catch a connection in Rome back to America. "You can take the tender with the guests and the exterior crew."

Which meant I had to hurry. I was shaking now, so hard that the papers he'd handed me made a rustling noise.

"I'll radio Thomas to grab your suitcase," he said.

And that, more than anything, made this feel final for me.

I'd lost my job.

And my dream of opening a bakery.

And the man I loved.

There was no point in trying to defend myself, either. Even though most of it wasn't true, the main one was. I had kissed Hunter repeatedly in violation of the rules.

I also realized that if I tried to tell the captain about Emilie, I would only come across as bitter and self-serving. He wouldn't believe me. He would have to find out the hard way. The rest of the crew didn't deserve to be stuck with her, but Captain Carl certainly did.

I left the bridge and went down to my cabin. I stood there, not sure of what to do. I had to pack up immediately. I knew that.

This was all my fault. If I had been more honest with the captain from the beginning, maybe things would have turned out differently. If I'd had the guts to tell him about how lazy Emilie was, she would have been long gone and I wouldn't be here, trying to gather up all my belongings.

I had tried so hard to protect everyone, including myself, that I'd only made things worse. I should have been truthful about how I felt and what was happening. The problem was my emotions were a whirling, tangled mess of confusion and I couldn't see my way clear.

Georgia came running in, panicked. "What happened?"

Thomas must have told her. "I got fired. The captain knows about me and Hunter." I shared all the other details, like the list and the screenshots. Her eyes widened with shock as I spoke.

"That's not fair!" she said. "This is partly my fault. I made the list and I encouraged Emilie. I'll go up there right now and straighten this out."

"You can't," I said. "Then you'll lose your job, too. Your grandma relies on your help."

"We've all done so much worse than you," she said in a sad voice, and I could only nod. It felt supremely unfair, but I didn't want anyone else to lose their position here.

Thomas came into the room with my suitcase. I hadn't expected to see it again for a very long time. "I'm sorry, Lucky. We'll miss you around here."

"Thanks," I said. Impermanence. This happened all the time. I knew that even if the crew felt bad now, they would get over it quickly and go on with their lives. Nature of the beast.

"I'll see you on the tender," he said.

Georgia offered to help me pack and I took her up on it. We had so much practice packing and unpacking for guests that it didn't take us very long.

"I don't know how I'm going to do this without you," she said, hugging me tightly. I was glad that my numbness was overriding my other emotions or else I would've probably started crying. I couldn't imagine not seeing Georgia every day.

"I'll miss you," I said, swallowing down the sob that rose up in my throat.

She walked with me to the tender. All the guests and the exterior crew were there already. They had been waiting for me.

Thomas took my suitcase and loaded it onto the smaller boat. The port here required larger ships to stay in the bay near the harbor and be ferried to the pier. It would only be a five-minute ride.

But once I saw Hunter's face, I had no idea how I was going to make it through the next five minutes.

CHAPTER FORTY-SIX

Hunter

Thomas had told me that Lucky had been fired. I couldn't believe that it was true. Queasiness rolled around inside my stomach and my chest felt too tight. Panic and dread pumped through my veins. I didn't understand.

I led Lucky into the back of the tender, away from everyone else. I needed answers. Her face had gone completely pale. "What happened?"

She couldn't be leaving. I didn't want to be here without her.

Her voice sounded numb. "The captain knows about us. And then Emilie told him that I was part of the list, trying to get points, and showed him a screenshot of texts between Georgia and me where we were joking about me being with you. Emilie took a picture of you and me together in the primary cabin."

I wanted to punch something. "This is my fault. I told her I was going to talk to the captain about things she had done, and she must have gone to him as some kind of preemptive strike."

She must have been planning to do this for a while. I'd dismissed her as harmless but she was some kind of criminal mastermind out to get Lucky.

How had I not seen this coming?

"Or she did it because you two were having some lovers' spat," she said angrily.

Now I was really confused. "What?"

"You kissed Emilie. You were cheating on me."

Emilie had kissed me. Did Lucky really have so little faith in me? Did she think I was like every other guy she'd dated? I would never cheat on her. Ever.

And she was accusing me of doing just that.

When I didn't answer she added, "I saw you two. On the monitors."

What were the odds? That must have killed Lucky. It was bad enough that Emilie had pounced on me. I had immediately put a stop to it. I would have told Lucky about it after I'd spoken to the captain.

I understood how this would have crushed her, but a part of me was hurt that she didn't trust me. Hadn't even tried to talk to me about it. If I hadn't been in this tender, she might have left the ship without saying a word to me.

Did I really mean so little to her? Had our situations been reversed, I never could have done that. "Emilie must have set me up."

"You're saying she knew I'd look up at the exact right moment and catch you?"

I knew how far-fetched that sounded but I didn't know how else to explain it. "I have no idea what's going on in that evil mind of hers. But I didn't kiss her. She kissed me."

Lucky made a sound of disbelief.

My heart hurt. "Do you really think I'm the kind of man who would tell you I love you and then turn around and cheat? I would never do that to you."

She looked conflicted. Like she wanted to believe me but she couldn't get past what she had seen. Or the part of her that expected to get hurt.

The part that had been waiting for me to screw up.

Lucky was pushing me away, not the other way around.

"Emilie told me that she didn't think you'd be around for much longer and then said she thought we would be good together and then, without warning, kissed me. I immediately stopped her and said that I was going to report her to the captain. That's why she went to him first."

I wanted her to understand. To know what had really happened. I wanted to beg her not to do this. To not end things between us over a misunderstanding. But half the crew and all the guests stood behind us.

"Did you see me push her away?" I asked.

She shook her head.

"The captain should have fired me, too. I was on the other end of that kiss with you," I said.

That seemed to spur her into speaking. "So that we can both be out of work? I don't want that. I want you to keep your job."

She still cared. She was angry and hurt and confused and so was I. But she still cared about me.

"What about your bakery?" I loved her too much to let her lose it, but there wasn't anything I could do to stop this. It was already done. I would call my parents and make them understand what had happened.

"My bakery was on the line the first time we kissed. It was stupid to think we could keep hiding it. Especially after you told everyone that we were dating."

"I'm so sorry. I wish I could go back and undo that."

There were so many things that I wished I could change.

"And if I can't undo it, I'll do the next best thing," I said. "I'll talk to the captain. I'll talk to my parents. I'll fix it."

"If you do that, you'll lose all credibility with your parents. You're working hard to overcome their negative perceptions. You will wreck that."

"I don't care!"

But she did. "No."

I didn't know what to do. I wanted to leave with her. To throw everything else away and just be with her. But what did I have to offer her? I didn't have a job. Money of my own. I didn't have a place where we could live or a way to support her. I couldn't offer her anything that she needed.

I wasn't good enough for her yet.

The tender was nearly to the pier. It was almost time for us to disembark.

"Do you believe me?" I asked. "I didn't cheat on you. I wouldn't."

"I don't know what to believe," she said.

We had to talk away from all these people.

"Stay in Portofino," I said.

"What?"

"We need to talk this out and we can't do it now. I have to go out with these tools and finish up this charter. But when it's over we can meet up. I should have a couple of days off."

"I—" I saw her hesitation. She wanted to believe me.

But she didn't seem to know whether or not she could trust me.

And that destroyed me.

The boat pulled up to the dock and Pieter hopped out to tie off the lines and keep the tender in place. The crew helped the guests out and Thomas came over to grab Lucky's suitcase and put it on the dock.

She went to climb out and I grabbed her by the wrist. "Please, Lucky."

"I'll think about it," she said.

I hurried to catch up with her as she wheeled her suitcase down toward the street. "I'll call. And text. I will come back here as soon as I can."

She nodded and then went off in the opposite direction of the guests and the crew.

And as I watched her go, I was struck with a sick feeling like this was the last time I was going to see her.

I didn't know where it came from but I wanted to run after her.

Lucky wouldn't like that. She needed to sort things out and I would have to wait. I knew that she would find a way to leave without talking to me face-to-face. She was scared and running.

I didn't know how to fix this. One of the things my therapist and I had talked a lot about was how, after Harper's death, I didn't want to let go of things, especially people. But that if I held on too tight, they would slip through my fingers. I would lose them anyway.

Now I knew exactly what she had meant. If I chased after Lucky, tried to force her to talk to me, I sensed that I would ruin any future we might have. I had to back off and give her the space she needed even if it killed me.

But there was a phone call I could make so that at least one of her dreams would come true.

CHAPTER FORTY-SEVEN

Lucky

"Hunter!"

Turning my head I saw that he was still standing there, watching me go. Thomas was calling for him, telling him to join them. I stared at him for a beat before resolutely spinning around and walking away.

My heart ached so badly that I had to put my hand over my chest. I found a quiet café and ordered tea. I had to figure out what to do next. I could do what he asked. I could stay in Portofino. It would be easy to change the times on my ticket and leave a few days later.

But all I could think about was all the men who had tricked me before. Who had lied to me and used me and cheated on me.

Maybe that was unfair to Hunter, that I was making him bear the brunt of my past heartache and broken trust.

I had lost so much, so many people I loved, and I recognized that I was overly cautious about being hurt again. Was I looking for a way out? An escape hatch to make sure that Hunter couldn't destroy me completely?

There was no way for me to reconcile the man I thought I knew and loved with him kissing Emilie. It was so unlike him.

The problem was that I needed to get away. To see if my feelings were real, to figure out how much of a part proximity and sea goggles had played.

I see you clearly. Land or sea.

His words filled my memory, along with images of all the time we had spent together, laughing, kissing, holding, sleeping.

Loving.

My dull, aching heart lurched sideways, like it wanted to disconnect itself from the rest of my body.

If I waited for him in Portofino, I knew what would happen. He would leave the ship.

I didn't want to be responsible for him losing what he'd been working so hard for. It was bad enough that I already had.

I wished that someone else could make this decision for me. I didn't know what to do. The pain of seeing him kiss another woman still burned in my chest. How was I supposed to sort all of this out?

I needed to talk to someone about this. I couldn't call Georgia. She was going to have to do everything single-handedly on the ship.

Who else did I have besides Hunter?

I texted my sisters.

I need to talk. I think I just broke up with my boyfriend and I lost my job.

They might still be angry with me. But it was Hunter's words that I remembered. That they were my sisters and they would love me no matter what.

I wanted that to be true.

My phone rang and I saw that it was them. Tears filled my eyes and I answered. "Hello?"

"You have a boyfriend?" Rose said. "What happened? How did you lose your job? Are you okay?"

"No." My voice caught and I couldn't speak.

"You should come home," Lily said.

That was what I wanted. To go home. That was where I could figure this out.

"Although you might have to help with Lily. She was in a car accident a few days ago. She broke her foot," Rose said.

"And you didn't call me?" I asked, upset.

"I'm fine," Lily insisted. "Rose is just being dramatic."

"I am not," Rose shot back. "But seriously, Lucky, come home. It's time that you let us take care of you."

This was so unlike how things had been with us in the past that I wanted to sob. "I'm going to the airport now. I'll be home as soon as I can."

Then I hung up and cried at the café table. My heart had been broken so many times in so many ways that I didn't know if it could ever be whole again. Part of me still wanted to wait for Hunter. But I couldn't think. So many bad things had happened in a row that I had to separate them and decide what I would do next.

It was a choice I would have to make on my own.

Then I could decide how to move forward with him.

Whether I even wanted to.

I ordered a car to Genoa from my rideshare app, and balked a little at the cost. I was about to blow through a big part of my savings by going back home. It meant that I would have to start over in trying to save up.

After everything was arranged I texted Hunter.

> I'm going home. I need some time to think. About us. And where we go from here.

It was several minutes before he responded.

> How long?

I was a little surprised. I had half expected him to beg for me to wait. To offer to come with me.

He had to stay on the ship.

I don't know. A month?

This time he responded immediately.

Okay. Take all the time you need. I love you. I'll be here when you're ready.

It was like someone was performing open heart surgery on me with a rusty, dull knife. Every cut was excruciating, the worst pain I'd ever felt. It made me wonder whether I had made a mistake.

My car arrived a few minutes after his last text, and it was a relief to climb inside because it meant I wouldn't try to find a way to sabotage my recently made plans and stay put, waiting for Hunter.

And as the car pulled away from the curb, the desire to stay increased. Hunter had told me once that it was normal to feel sick when I did the right thing and he was correct.

I had to be strong. Distance and separation would be best for both of us.

But deep down I was afraid that I was wrong.

CHAPTER
FORTY-EIGHT

Lucky

On the plane ride home, I considered texting Georgia and having her get the full story from Emilie during the crew's next night off. It wouldn't be hard. After a couple of drinks, Emilie was fond of oversharing. If anything, she would probably be happy to brag about how she and Hunter had pulled the wool over my eyes.

But Emilie's side in this didn't matter.

The only thing that did was whether or not I was willing to believe Hunter.

And honestly? I'd let Georgia interfere too much already. It was her doubts and fears that she'd expressed to me just before I saw the kiss that pushed me toward disbelief.

Not that I'd needed much of a push, with my dating past.

The farther I got from Italy, the more I started to question the conclusions I'd leapt to. Did I really think that Hunter was the kind of man who would lead me on for weeks as some sort of game? Because he saw me as ungettable and thought it would be amusing to make me fall in love with him? While keeping Emilie in his back pocket to pull out whenever he felt like it?

That would have meant he was some kind of psychopath, and that was the last thing Hunter would ever be.

You know him, that voice inside me said. *You know him and love him and he wouldn't deliberately hurt you.*

If he was telling the truth . . . then Emilie had cornered him and forced herself on him, which was not okay.

And entirely within character for her.

I took a car home from the airport in Hartford and thought about what I would do next. The *Mio Tesoro* was not the only superyacht in the ocean. Tomorrow I would email some crew agents and send them my CV. I wasn't going to have a recommendation but that was okay. I could go back to being a second or third stew and just start over with my savings plan.

The car went past my nonna's old bakery. The building had remained empty ever since the bakery had been foreclosed on. I was still going to reopen it. It was just going to take a bit longer than I had anticipated.

When I got to my sisters' apartment, I knocked and heard Chauncy barking. Rose opened the door and her face lit up when she saw me. "Lucky!"

She hugged me tightly, which was so unlike my younger sister that I felt like I'd stepped into a parallel universe.

"Come in, come in!" she said, taking my bags from me. Chauncy jumped up on me until Rose told him to get down. He did so immediately and I scratched him behind the ears to reward him for being a good boy.

Lily was seated on the couch with her foot propped up, in a cast. Definitely broken. "Are you doing okay?" I asked.

"I have to wear this thing for like, six weeks, but I'm fine. Come sit down! How was your flight?"

"Good." I sat down on the couch and asked what had happened with the accident and the twins fell all over themselves giving me the details. Someone had blown through a red light and hit Lily's car.

I was so grateful that she had come out of it with only a broken foot. The twins didn't really remember our dad, so I was sure the accident didn't affect them the same way it did me.

"I'm really glad you're doing okay," I said, my eyes going blurry from the tears that wanted to fall.

"Oh, Lucky!" Lily said, pulling me in for a hug.

I let her hold me for a second and then sat back up, reaching for my purse. "How much?"

She blinked at me, confused. "What do you mean?"

"The hospital bill. How much do you need?"

Rose and Lily exchanged glances, and then Lily put her hand on top of mine. "Zero. We don't need anything."

Now I was the one confused.

"You were right," Rose said. "We took advantage of you. So we're not taking any more money from you. And we're going to pay you back."

"And we really mean it this time," Lily added. "We shouldn't have been so reliant on you. Or expected you to take care of us. We're going to get one of the budget thingies and do that!"

Rose smiled. "We downloaded some financial apps for our phones and everything."

Lily squeezed my hand. "I think having you there like that made it so we didn't miss Mom so much. You're not our mother, though. And it's time we helped take care of you. We are the only family that we have left. So we're going to give instead of always asking. Do you want to stay here with us?"

I had assumed I'd go to a hotel. That probably would've been more comfortable, but I couldn't turn down my sisters' kind offer. My throat burned with unshed tears at their words. I really had thought they wouldn't want to talk to me after I told them I wouldn't send them any more money.

"I'd love to stay with you," I said, my voice tight. "I just hadn't heard from you in so long that I thought—"

"You thought we were upset with you," Rose finished for me. "We're sorry we didn't reach out to you sooner, but we wanted to get our situation straightened out first so that you would know we meant it. Actions instead of just words. Plus, we know how much you worry and wanted to show you that we were okay."

"Car accident notwithstanding," Lily added with a grin.

"Wow," I said, knowing that if I tried to say more, I was going to cry.

"We're growing up, right?" Rose preened, clearly proud of what they were doing.

"You are." Yep, my voice was definitely wobbly.

Lily noticed. "What's going on with you? And what happened with your job? And your boyfriend?"

And even though it felt too painful, the entire story came pouring out of me. Every single little detail.

I cried the entire time, sobbing and talking, snot dripping from my nose. Rose went and grabbed me a roll of toilet paper and handed it to me so that I could keep telling them everything. My throat ached, my eyes burned, but I kept going until I had shared it all.

Chauncy came over and rested his head in my lap. I allowed myself to finally break down, with my sisters there to hug and listen to me.

It made me feel not so alone.

And after I had told them the whole story, they were both quiet. I had expected them to offer me advice or tell me what they thought I should do. In the past they'd always had opinions about everything.

Instead Rose brought me a pillow, blanket, and sheets and helped me make up the couch so that I could sleep there. She showed me where the bathroom was and then helped Lily to bed.

They paused at the doorway. "We'll talk more in the morning," Rose said.

"We're here for you," Lily said with a smile.

I didn't even know what to make of this. That surreal feeling returned, like I had wandered into someone else's life.

But if this was how my relationship with my sisters was going to be from now on? I would very happily take it.

And as I lay down to go to sleep, I realized that the person I most wanted to tell about how things had changed with the twins was Hunter.

~

The next morning I began to contact crew agents to see if there were any openings. I sent out emails with my CV and said I was available for immediate hire.

I heard back immediately from one of the agencies, and the woman there warned me that, at this point in the season, crews were well established. The only way I'd find a new position would be a situation like the one I'd just left—where the former crewmembers were either jumping ship or being fired due to a somewhat toxic environment. I was used to that, though.

She was the only agent who responded the first day. It made me wonder if Captain Carl had called crew agents and told them not to hire me.

Word spread fast in our industry.

I helped take care of Lily, as she was still recovering. She asked me more questions about Hunter and I found that I loved talking about him nearly as much as I loved being with him.

"And do you believe him? That he didn't kiss that girl?" she asked carefully.

"I want to. More than anything. And if I can't believe him, there can't be a relationship. I'm just scared. But I don't know if I'm letting the fear take over and crowd everything else out. I don't want to do that. I want to make the right choice."

"Do you miss him?"

"So much that it's hard to breathe when I think about him too often."

"That kind of feels like an answer," she said.

"Maybe. Or maybe I need to give it more time."

That evening I got a text from a number I didn't recognize.

Lucky?

My first wild, heart-thumping thought was that it was Hunter. That he had borrowed someone else's phone and was texting me. In case I had blocked him, even though I would never do that.

Who's this?

Rodney Whitlock.

The disappointment I felt was palpable. It made me wonder if that was another clue to my true feelings.

How are you?

I'm good. I have something I wanted to send over to you. Can I get your address?

Right. He had wanted to send me his wife's recipes. I gave him my sisters' address.

Thank you. It will be there tomorrow.

My heart skipped a beat. What if . . .

What if what he planned on sending me was Hunter?

CHAPTER
FORTY-NINE

Lucky

When there was a knock on the door the next morning, I was nervous and excited. As was Chauncy, who barked himself silly. I had even gotten dressed up, put on some makeup, and brushed my hair. My face still seemed a little puffy from all the crying that I had done but it would have to be good enough.

But when I opened the door, it wasn't Hunter.

It was Rodney Whitlock.

"What are you doing here?" I realized how rude that must have sounded but I couldn't help myself. I was stunned to see him.

He smiled. "There was something I wanted to show you, if you wouldn't mind going on a quick ride with me."

"Uh, okay. Just give me a second." I didn't have any other plans. I was just waiting around hoping a crew agent would call me.

"I'll be downstairs waiting," he said.

I hurried into Lily's bedroom and let her know that I was going out for a little bit.

"I heard the front door. Is Hunter here?" she asked eagerly.

"No, one of the guests from the yacht. I'll explain later," I said. I grabbed my purse and headed downstairs. I didn't know why I had thought Hunter might come. I'd asked him to give me space and he was the kind of man who would do what I asked.

I also didn't want him to lose his job. If he came here, the captain would fire him and Hunter's parents wouldn't invest in the center. That was the last thing I wanted.

An expensive-looking black SUV idled in front of the apartment building. Rodney rolled down the window in the back seat and waved me over.

I got in and the driver pulled away from the curb.

"I'm happy to see you but very confused," I told Rodney.

"This is a big surprise, isn't it?" he said, sounding delighted with himself.

"And a bit strange. I feel like I should be serving you."

He laughed. "Not this time."

"Can I ask where we're going?"

"Now that wouldn't be much of a surprise, would it?"

His surprise worked, because when he pulled up in front of my nonna's old bakery, I was completely shocked. "What are we doing here?"

"Come and see." He got out of the car and I followed him, intensely curious.

That feeling only increased when he opened the front door and walked into the building.

A wave of memories hit me the second I crossed over the threshold. I hadn't been inside in years. If I closed my eyes, I could smell the yeast and flour, hear my nonna singing a show tune, my mom telling the twins to get down from the table.

I put a hand over my heart. "Thank you."

"For what?" He sounded genuinely puzzled.

"For letting me be here again. How did you know this was my nonna's bakery?"

"It's amazing what you can find out with a quick Google search," he said. "Lucky, I want you to open your bakery."

And I wanted to be able to eat pasta and not gain weight. "I will. When I get the money."

"No, now. I'm going to invest."

My heart sped up and I blinked several times. "What?"

"You're going to open your bakery, and I will be your silent partner, putting up all the capital you need. I think it would make my wife very happy to know that somebody was living out her dream."

"No, Rodney, I couldn't ask—"

"You're not asking. I'm offering," he said. "The ownership will go into a trust, and when I pass, the bakery will be a hundred percent yours. This isn't a loan you have to pay back. I'm investing in you."

"That's too much."

He frowned slightly. "It's my money. I get to decide what to do with it. I don't have any children, and this is the kind of legacy I want to leave behind. Helping people achieve their dreams."

My mouth hung open, unable to believe that this was happening. "I don't want this to be because of Hunter." I didn't want to owe Hunter—I wanted whatever happened between us in the future to be because we chose it. Not because I felt indebted to him.

"It's not for him. It's for you. Because you're the kind of person who would stay up all night with an old man letting him talk about the love of his life. I've seen how hard you work, how diligent you are, how dedicated, how caring, how detail oriented, how talented. I would be a fool to pass up an opportunity to go into business with someone like you."

Now I felt presumptuous and a little bit embarrassed. "I don't really know what to say."

"I hope you'll say yes. Although I should warn you, I do have two conditions."

Unless they involved selling my soul to the devil, which I might seriously consider, given what Rodney was offering, I was going to say yes. "What conditions?"

"The first is that you have to sell those chocolate chip cookies you made me on the yacht because those were incredible. The second is that I want you to name it Lucia's. That was my wife's name."

A shiver passed through me, making my skin break out in goose bumps. "That's my name. And my nonna's name."

It was a common enough name in several countries, so I probably shouldn't have had this kind of reaction, but it was like my grandmother was personally sanctioning the deal, urging me to take it.

"Then it sounds like a perfect name for the bakery," he said.

"Yes," I said. "I'm in."

"Excellent. I'll have my team start drawing up paperwork."

Rodney had a team of people. An actual team, and he had come to East Haven to help me open my bakery.

"You came all the way here just for this?"

"I have some business in New York and made a quick stop to see you. Speaking of, I have to be going to make my meeting on time." He threw me a key and I caught it. "The building has already been purchased, so this key belongs to you."

I held it in my hand, turning it, letting the light hit it. It was one of the most beautiful things I'd ever seen.

"'Thank you' doesn't seem big enough to tell you how much this means to me."

He smiled. "Live your life and be happy. That's all I can ask in return." Then he stood there, as if he wanted to add something else and was wrestling with whether or not he should say it. "Things happen in life. People die. Relationships end. Heartache seems inevitable. But grief is the price we pay for love, and Lucky? It is a price worth paying. I would take an entire lifetime of grief over missing one moment of love with Lucia. You should really think about what's important. What matters."

Then Rodney left, leaving his nuclear truth bombs behind. My heart was beating so quickly.

I needed to face my fears. I had to believe in Hunter, and more importantly? I had to believe in myself.

Which felt a bit easier to do now that I was standing in my nonna's bakery.

No, *my* bakery.

The person I wanted to call and tell was Hunter.

Regardless of what Rodney had said, I knew that Hunter had played a huge part here.

How else would Rodney have known that I was back in the States? I had told him I'd be in touch when I had a more permanent residence again. But he had reached out to me first and asked for my address.

Hunter must have told him.

Which meant that Hunter had found a way to help make my dreams come true.

~

My instinct was to reach out to Hunter immediately. But after the chaos of both my life and my time on the *Mio Tesoro*, I needed true clarity. To let myself come to a decision where I wasn't acting impulsively or glossing over things. I had to take the time to do that, even if I didn't want to.

If time felt sped up on the boat, it seemed to be going in slow motion in regular life. For the next two weeks, I had nothing to keep me busy, especially not compared to my yachting days. Rodney's "team" had been in touch, and there were all kinds of bureaucratic hoops we had to jump through before we could start renovating. I did research on some construction companies that I could contact when I got the green light, looked up the best ways to import Italian flour, gave my sisters' apartment an unnecessary but very thorough cleaning that involved Q-tips and toothbrushes.

Which gave me the free time I needed to think about Hunter. I did what Rodney had encouraged me to do, to figure out what was important and what mattered.

My sisters.

My new bakery.

And Hunter.

I had thought that maybe if I didn't see him every day, my feelings would fade, but if anything, they had only grown stronger. Missing him was a physical pain that I had all the time. Like a giant splinter had become embedded in my skin and every time I moved or breathed I felt it, throbbing and aching. I realized that I had used the nonfraternization rule like a shield. I had justified spending time with Hunter and claimed that I wouldn't cross the line into something deeper because of that rule. That hadn't been the reason why, though. It had been my own fears and insecurities that had held me back. The rule had made it so that I could avoid reality.

I knew that because I'd suffered so much loss—my parents, my grandparents—it had made me desperate not to lose anyone else. It was why I had let my sisters take advantage of me for so long. It was easier to hide than it was to be up front and honest. I had told myself that I didn't need a romantic relationship, didn't want one, but it wasn't true. I wanted to be loved and cared for and to do that in return for someone else.

I was just worried that I'd lost my chance.

There was a Hunter-size piece of my life missing.

I had focused so much on my own hurt, on the way that I had felt betrayed, that I didn't stop to think things through logically. Hunter had been devoted to me for weeks. Both Georgia and Emilie had pursued him and he'd brushed them off. He'd made his intentions with me clear. He had only wanted me, and I had been so caught up with my own issues that I hadn't been able to see that.

He wouldn't have cheated on me. I knew that, too. I fully believed that Emilie kissed him and he had told her to stop and that he was going to report her to the captain.

I also hadn't considered how Hunter might have been hurt by my actions. By me jumping to a terrible conclusion and not believing him. That had been so wrong of me.

Maybe he wouldn't be able to forgive me. Maybe I had hurt him too badly for us to move past this. That thought terrified me, too.

I talked to the twins about him constantly. They let me work through everything and examine it from every angle, but their conclusions were always the same.

That Hunter and I were in love and I'd been a complete fool to push him away.

Lily said, "You've grown a lot and I think Hunter played a part in that. Loving him and being loved by him, it made you change. It gave you a confidence and a strength I haven't seen before."

That was also true. My mind still went to extremes and envisioned the worst possible outcome, but it was better than it had been a month ago. I handled things more easily than I had in the past.

Although I didn't think that I was handling this Hunter thing particularly well.

The more I thought about what had happened with my firing, the worse I felt. While I didn't regret coming home to check on Lily, I should have flown back to Portofino and talked things out with him.

"What if he's moved on?" I asked. "Out of sight, out of mind."

"I doubt that," Rose countered.

"He's not out of your mind," Lily pointed out.

"Maybe he doesn't feel about me the way I feel about him."

"Again, I doubt it," Rose said. "The fact that he's giving you the space you asked for? He loves you."

"You two found something special and you should hold on to it with both hands as tightly as you can. You should call him."

They were right. Or I desperately wanted them to be right. I did worry that he'd forgotten about me. Georgia texted me here and there but I knew how busy she was. She never said a single word about Hunter. I could have called her and asked if he had replaced me with someone new. The captain would have made her chief stew and brought on a new junior stew. Which meant the new girl would share a cabin with him.

What if he had moved on?

I couldn't bear for that to be true. Which I also took as a good sign about my true feelings.

I realized that I had made a huge mistake and needed to rectify it. I had to talk to him. I texted and said:

Can we talk?

I waited for him to answer. I calculated the time difference. I knew he was probably working at that moment but I was too impatient, wanting to hear back from him immediately. So I added:

I miss you. Can you call me?

But hours later, I still didn't have a response. I went to bed that night terrified that I had destroyed whatever it was that we'd had.

CHAPTER FIFTY

Lucky

The next afternoon I took Chauncy for a long walk. I had waited all day for Hunter to send back something. I would have been happy with even an emoji. But total radio silence.

I worried that he might have blocked me. I couldn't imagine him doing that, though. I didn't let myself get sucked into a spiral. Things would work out the way they were supposed to. And if Hunter and I were over, well, my heart would be broken but I would pick myself up and keep going. I had a new and improved relationship with my sisters and the bakery to look forward to.

It didn't stop me from wanting him to be a part of it.

My brain tried to fixate on the fact that I deserved not to hear from him. That I had basically abandoned him and accused him of terrible things and now he didn't want to talk to me. I was not going to allow myself to go down that path. If nothing else, I had learned to redirect myself to more positive thoughts.

Losing Hunter was an awful price to pay for that internal change.

When I entered the apartment, I called out, "Lily? I'm back." I put my keys on the ring and undid Chauncy's leash. He ran into the living room. "I found a recipe for that babka you asked me to make. Of course, first I had to read through thirty paragraphs of the baker's autumn in New York in 2010 right after her boyfriend ended their relationship and how she made this to—"

I came around the corner and saw Hunter standing there.

"Hello, Lucky."

For a full ten seconds, I thought I was hallucinating. That I had missed him so much that my mind was imagining him being here.

But no, he was standing next to Lily, who was on her crutches. He looked scruffy, tired, worn down.

"Hunter?"

He smiled at me and I put a hand over my fluttering stomach.

"So I was just going to take Chauncy for a walk," Lily announced loudly.

I held up the leash. "I just—"

"Come on, Chauncy! Let's go to the park." She took the leash from me, got it on Chauncy, and then hobbled out of the apartment.

Hunter was here. Rodney must have given him the address.

When she closed the door, I said to him, "I thought you didn't want to talk to me. You didn't answer my text."

He put his hands in his pockets. "How could it be a romantic surprise if I gave you a heads-up?"

"Romantic?" I echoed, unable to help myself. My heart surged with hope. It was a good thing that he was here. He wouldn't have flown halfway around the world just to end things, would he?

But if he was here and not on the *Mio Tesoro* . . . "Did you quit the ship?"

"When I got your message I told the captain that I quit, effective immediately. Then I flew home to New York to talk to my parents, and then I came straight here. I haven't slept in like, two days."

He looked like it. "What did you say to your parents?" I was so worried for him and his future. This was the last thing I had wanted him to do.

"I explained everything to them. I told them that you meant more to me than their offer and I left."

"But your dream," I protested softly.

"You're my dream," he countered, his words filling me with lightness and hope. "I told them that if the only way they were willing to fund the center was if I stayed on the boat, I would figure out a way to do it on my own. Plus, I know lots of rich people who are looking for tax breaks."

He was right. I had once sworn that I'd never take out a loan or work with a rich person and yet here I was. There could be another path for Hunter, too. "I happen to know one who has decided he's in the business of helping people achieve their dreams," I said.

He nodded, since he knew exactly who I was talking about, given that he was the one who had sent Rodney to me.

"Thank you for that," I said. "Sending Rodney here."

"You deserve to have your dream, too," he said. "I wasn't going to let you lose that."

I loved him so much.

"Back to what I was saying, when I talked to my parents, my dad accused me again of not finishing what I started. And this time he's right. I don't want to finish what I started with you. I don't want it to ever be over between us."

That fluttering in my belly increased to full-on flapping. "Oh."

"When I first met you," he said as he took a step closer to me, "I could see how hard you were fighting, how you wanted to be stronger than the panic attack, and I admired you for it. I still do admire you. I think you're one of the most amazing people I've ever met. Sometimes I think you can't possibly be real and that I must have made you up."

"I know exactly what you mean."

That earned me a tired but hopeful smile. "You took my breath away that first day and I felt like I haven't caught it since. I also knew that you deserved better than me. But I didn't want to see you with someone else, so I tried to become better for you. Even when you left, I thought I had to open the center and become successful to be good enough for you. But then I realized that the only thing I wanted from you was you. And I hoped that just me would be enough for you."

How could I have ever doubted this man?

"That night I saw you sitting with Rodney . . . it did something to me," he went on. "You are so kind and caring, and even though I'd already been falling for you, that was when I completed the journey. I realized that I was in love with you. You are the kind of person I want in my life. The kind of person I can see building a future with."

This was so much more than I had expected him to say.

Another step closer. "I have a lot of regrets in my life, Lucky. After I lost Harper, I discovered that I have this tendency to hold on too tightly to things that matter to me. I was worried that I was doing that with you, which was why I backed off and didn't chase after you. Made sure to give you space. I wish that I had walked off the boat with you. I hope you've figured out whatever you need to because I want to be with you. And I'm afraid this time I'm going to hold on as tight as I can."

Again Hunter was being honest and up front about what he wanted. He wasn't playing games or making me be vulnerable first. He was putting his whole heart on the line for me. That was how much he loved and trusted me. I had been the worst kind of fool.

"You know nothing happened with Emilie, don't you?" he asked.

"Yes," I immediately responded. I had to take a step back because he was close enough now that it would take very little for us to be touching. And the second he touched me, this would all be over. There were things that I needed to say first.

"I don't like how I reacted," I confessed to him. "I should have immediately believed you. I know who you are and I know that you wouldn't cheat on me. I'm sorry that I didn't realize it right away. That's not how you should treat someone you love."

He startled slightly, as if my words surprised him.

"You gave me your trust so easily and I held back," I said. "Some part of me didn't want to believe in you, in us, and I expected to get hurt. I was always trying to protect myself instead of opening up to what you offered. And so when the worst happened, it was like a self-fulfilling prophecy. Which wasn't fair to you."

I let out a deep sigh, feeling ashamed of my actions where he was concerned. "I wouldn't blame you for being angry with me."

"I was never angry with you," he interjected.

"Georgia accidentally got in my head," I said. "I think she was trying to be helpful, but she made me second-guess everything, including myself. She suggested that the only reason you liked me was because you'd had to chase me, and it messed with my head."

"Lucky, if you'd pulled me into your bed the first night, I would still be here, wanting you. Loving you. I didn't fall for you because you made me pursue you. I love you because of who you are."

My throat went tight, and my chest ached. I wanted to cry. "Well, I need for you to know that I won't do something like that again. I want you to be able to trust in me the way that I trust you."

"I know that's hard for you," he said. "To trust someone else."

"When it comes to you? It's not. I'm sorry that it took me this long to figure it out. I should have met you in Portofino. I shouldn't have doubted you. I'm sorry that I did."

"Your sister told me about them telling you to come home. I know you needed a safe place to land and to think. I'm glad you have them back in your life. I would have come with you if you'd asked. I have missed you so much these last two weeks."

I had missed him, too. "I didn't want you to lose your job, and I think deep down I knew you'd come with me, too."

"My Lucky," he said, reaching for me, and this time I let him. He held me to him tightly, like he was never going to let me go again. "Always sacrificing for the people you love. You don't have to do that for me anymore. I will always be there for you."

I spoke into his shoulder. "We're going to fill in each other's gaps, remember? You sacrifice for me and I'll sacrifice for you. Because we love each other."

His arms tightened around me. "I've been worried for the last couple of weeks that you would realize you didn't love me. You don't know how relieved I am to hear you say it."

I laughed. I couldn't help it. "How could I not love you, Hunter Cartwright? You are practically perfect. Plus, you shouldn't be catastrophizing things and imagining the worst-case scenario."

"You're right," he said in that teasing tone I loved.

I pulled my head back so that I could gaze into those bright blue eyes of his that I loved so much. "I know I'm a messed-up chocolate chip cookie, and I'm hoping that's good enough for you. Or that we can start the recipe over again."

"You are the best chocolate chip cookie ever," he insisted, kissing the tip of my nose. "There's no reason to start over when you came out perfect."

Neither one of us was perfect by any stretch of the imagination, but I supposed that was what love did. It polished over the rough spots so that even good enough chocolate chip cookies seemed like the absolute best.

"I just wish that my heart didn't have so many dents and bruises," I said. "I wish I could have been more open from the beginning."

This time he kissed my forehead. "Those dents and bruises make you who you are, and I love who you are. And I don't ever want to be apart from you again. This was . . ."

"Torture?" I finished.

"Yes," he said. "I hated it."

"Me too. So now what?"

"Right now or in the near future now?"

"Near future now," I said.

"East Haven is not too far from some great places where I could set up the center. Plenty of acreage and farmland." I knew he wanted a lot of land for horses, another thing his sister had loved.

"You're staying here?"

He gave me a funny look. "I'm staying wherever you are and we'll figure the rest out."

"I love you," I said, the feelings washing through me all over again.

"And I love you," he said, grinning. I had missed his smile so very much. It was like the sun returning after a week's worth of rain. "So as far as grand romantic gestures go, how was this one?"

I shrugged. "I don't know. I think it was a little lackloyster."

"Lucky! An oyster pun?"

"I've been saving it for a special occasion." And things didn't get more special than this moment with him. "And I can explain why it was hilarious in case you didn't catch it."

"Are you going to clamsplain your jokes to me now? Or should we just shellibrate the way I've converted you?"

"I'm so lucky that I get to love you," I said.

He nodded, serious. "I am something of an expert on love, did you know that?"

"You are?"

"Yes. And this, right here, is love."

I laughed and shook my head. "Since we've got the near future now sorted out, what about the right now, Mr. Expert?"

"It depends. How long are we going to be alone for?"

My heart sped up, my skin tingling with anticipation. "Rose is at work and Lily walks really, really slowly. So we have time."

A wicked grin. "Good. Because I need to show you just how much I've farfallen for you. I'm tortellini in love with you, Lucky Salerno."

Then he had me flat on my back on the couch so quickly that it took me a second to catch my breath. "I'm setting myself up for a lifetime of nothing but puns, aren't I?"

He nodded as he settled himself on top of me, kissing me slowly, in a tantalizing way that made every cell in my body light up with joy. "You are."

"I guess that makes me the luckiest girl in the world."

Hunter kissed the underside of my jaw. "I'm happy that I'm finally allowed to say that I'm getting Lucky."

That made me laugh again. "I love you more than pasta and sugar."

He stopped and stared down at me, the delight in his eyes evident. "Now that's true love."

"I also love your puns," I said, stroking the side of his face.

He turned to catch my palm and put a kiss there. "I know."

Then he proceeded to kiss me and throw every pun he could think of at me. "Bouy meets gull, harboring strong feelings, setting us up for a true row-mance, after we've been through hull and back. It's been quite an oar-deal, but we both know that you bow-long with me."

"I think you're the only man in the world who could make puns sexy."

He kissed me thoroughly, deeply, leaving me lightheaded. "Are you sure you don't want me to stop?"

"Never," I said. "Because our story has a ferry-tale ending."

EPILOGUE

One year later . . .

Hunter had found the perfect location in Branford near the village of Stony Creek, about ten minutes from our apartment. Since Rodney had signed over the bakery building to me, Hunter and I had renovated the second floor to be our apartment.

And in the midst of all this, he had been working on his facility. Rodney had been more than happy to invest in Hunter's dream. His parents had come around and donated. Hunter had hired some amazing people to help him navigate all the steps, hiring the right staff and therapists/psychologists/experts, coming up with the programming specifics, working on licensing and accreditation, setting up the 501(c)(3) to make it a nonprofit.

Today was the center's soft launch and Hunter had invited everyone out. It was a big celebration and he was a month away from accepting their first clients, who would live here full-time on their road to mental health and addiction recovery.

He had decided to focus on outdoor activities, including equine therapy, and on the arts. A whole section of the converted bed-and-breakfast would be devoted to different mediums—painting, sculpting, drawing—along with a dance studio and all sorts of music therapy options. Singing, playing instruments, composing.

Everything had moved quickly because he was so motivated and because money greased all wheels.

I was beyond proud of him as I watched him cut the ribbon on the Harper Cartwright Academy. Rodney had come, as had all the Cartwrights. Hunter's mother sobbed through the entire ceremony, his dad having to hold her the whole time.

They had been so welcoming to me. Susan had sent many a car for me so that I could spend time with her and Hunter's younger sisters. I loved the entire Cartwright clan, and it felt like I was getting a bonus family.

Hunter was getting a bonus family, too. Rose and Lily cheered loudly as he cut the ribbon. I was so grateful they had come. I had offered my sisters jobs at the bakery but they had turned me down. Thanks to grants, Lily was back in school to get her nursing degree, and Rose had been promoted at her company. They were completely financially independent from me, and our relationship had never been better. They totally adored Hunter, to the point that I thought if he and I ever broke up, they would both choose him.

"Put the phone up higher, mate!" Georgia called out, and I lifted it so that she and the boys could see more clearly. Georgia and Pieter were still together and she was more shocked than anyone else about it. They were madly in love, though. Pieter had texted me last night to show me potential wedding rings so that I could help him pick out which one she would like best.

It was hard to imagine Georgia, of all people, settling down, but I supposed stranger things had happened.

Andre had gone back to São Paulo to open a restaurant where he could keep Preacher on his shoulder while he cooked. François had given up life at sea and returned to France, where he and his wife had welcomed another baby. Georgia had told me that his wife pretty much didn't let him out of her sight, and I didn't blame her. I hoped he would behave.

Thomas and Kai were still on the ship with Georgia and Pieter, and Hunter and I had talked about taking a trip out to the yacht sometime later in the summer. I did worry that it might be a little weird being a guest instead of part of the staff.

Fortunately, Captain Carl was long gone. Hank had fired him the day after Hunter told them everything that had occurred on the ship. Carl had taken Emilie with him.

Everyone on board adored the new captain, an Aussie named Jason who Georgia had immediately labeled a "stern brunch daddy." He was good at his job and treated his staff well. The nonfraternization rule had been lifted.

Hank had renamed the yacht *Seas the Day*, the way he wanted. Hunter still joked about going and writing *Knot Pro Bono* somewhere in small letters so that his dad wouldn't see it.

Hunter's sister Hadley held up one of my cupcakes and then gave me a thumbs-up. I waved back. I was the official dessert caterer for the ribbon-cutting. The bakery had been open for six months and was doing extremely well. I had let Maria and the Mascarellis know that with the Italian flour, the sfogliatelle turned out perfectly almost every time. Giovanna insisted on sending me every recipe they had from their bakery, and their excellence set me apart from other bakeries in the city.

And I couldn't keep my chocolate chip cookies in stock.

The ceremony ended, Hunter posed for pictures, shook hands with important government-type people, and then opened the center for guests to go in and tour. He rushed over to me, picking me up in a big bear hug and twirling me around.

"You did it!" I exclaimed. "I'm so proud of you."

"Thank you. I couldn't have done it without you."

He probably could have, but I loved that he thought it anyway.

"Hey, two of the horses arrived. Do you want to come see them?" he asked.

"Yes!"

He had spent a lot of time picking out the perfect animals to inter-act with the teenagers who would be living here. Gentle and kind, and very loving.

We walked hand in hand toward the stables. The land here was so serene and gorgeous. Green as far as the eye could see, surrounded by tall trees and lush underbrush.

"We got a boy and a girl. A gelding and a mare," he said. "I think we should name them Harry Trotter and Hermioneigh."

"What about Sylvester Stallion and Kolt Kardashian?"

"Al Capony and Britney Spurs?"

We threw a bunch of names at each other that had me laughing, like he always did. It seemed to be his specialty. He had brought so much light and laughter into my life.

He was the best boyfriend. Devoted, caring, and so, so sweet.

Not to mention incredibly passionate. My skin flushed at the mem-ory of last night.

We walked through the garden area that I adored. Hunter had envisioned it as a place where the clients would be able to congregate and hang out. A previous owner had made it like a wild English garden, so there were all types of wildflowers blooming along paths that led to a patio, where Hunter had placed comfortable outdoor chairs and couches. A large white gazebo encased the center, with climbing roses growing up the sides.

As we were about to reach the center, he let go of my hand. "Hang on, gotta fix my shoelace." He knelt down to do so.

"Have I ever told you how much I love this spot?" I said, taking it all in.

"Many, many times. I know you sometimes think I don't listen, but I always do."

I turned back to look at him, and it took me a second to realize that he had on shoes without laces. He hadn't been fixing anything.

He was kneeling with a ring.

My heart slammed into my chest. We had talked about marriage but we had wanted to get our businesses going first.

And now they're going, that internal voice of mine reminded me.

"Lucky Salerno, I am so thankful every single day that my dad is obsessed with boats. Grateful that I got set on a path that led me to you because you are the most wonderful, amazing, spectacular thing that has ever happened to me. None of this," he said, waving his arms wide, "would mean anything to me without you. You not only make my life better, you make it complete. I love you so, so much. Will you marry me?"

"Yes!" I shrieked, throwing my arms around his neck, knocking him to the ground and going down with him. "Oh, sorry. I didn't mean to do that."

He laughed and hugged me tightly. "Good thing I have catlike reflexes and I didn't drop the ring box."

"That would have been unforgivable," I agreed. He slid the ring onto my finger, and it was the most beautiful thing I'd ever seen. After a moment I realized that it was just like my nonna's wedding ring, but bigger and flashier. Which meant that the twins had been involved in this.

"Did she say yes?" It sounded like Harlow, his youngest sister. I lifted my head above the wildflowers and saw all of the Cartwrights and my sisters watching us and waving.

They had all known and kept it from me. I grinned at them.

"She said yes, but don't come over here yet!" Hunter yelled back. "I'm going to kiss my fiancée senseless!"

"Gross!" Harlow called out.

"Fiancée," I repeated. "I like the sound of that."

"I'm going to like the sound of 'wife' even better," he said, pulling me down so that he could kiss me into a mindless oblivion.

When we could breathe again, he said, "Did I tell you I already came up with a theme for our wedding?"

"You did?"

"Yep. It can be 'We Tide the Knot,' and it will all be nautical."

"That makes me a little em-ocean-al," I said, wondering how long he'd been planning this.

"Good, because obviously our vows will have to be made up of all kinds of puns. Like I'll say I love you a yacht and will warship you all of my days."

"Right. I'll say I'm all a-boat loving you."

He kissed me again. "I'm so lucky that you love me."

I grinned at him, amazed that this was my life. That I would get to spend every day after this with him and his terrible puns. I loved him so, so much. And I was the Lucky one. "You're anchorrigible, but there's no one else I'd rudder be with."

AUTHOR'S NOTE

Thank you for reading my story! I hope you liked Lucky and Hunter and enjoyed them falling in love as much as I did. If you'd like to find out when I've written something new, make sure you sign up for my newsletter at www.sariahwilson.com, where I most definitely will not spam you. (I'm happy when I send out a newsletter once a month!)

And if you feel so inclined, I'd love for you to leave a review on Amazon, on Goodreads, or any other place you'd like. Thank you!

ACKNOWLEDGMENTS

I always thank my readers first because I'm so grateful to you for choosing to read my books. There are so many things out there competing for your time, and I'm honored that you would choose to spend a few hours in my world!

A huge thank-you to Lauren Plude—thank you so much for everything and for being a supporter and for all your amazing ideas and suggestions. Thank you to Megan Sakoi—I know it can't be easy to come in and pick things up midstream, but I'm excited to work with you! Thank you to everyone at Montlake. Thanks to Charlotte Herscher for making this so much easier and for making the hard decisions on which chapters to switch to Hunter's POV and helping me find things to cut!

Thank you to the copyeditors and proofreaders (especially Kellie!) who find all my mistakes and continuity errors and gently guide me in the right direction. Thanks to Hang Le for the amazing cover!

For my agent Sarah Younger—you truly are Santa's Number One Elf, and I'm so grateful for all that you do!

For my kids—you make everything worthwhile. I love you.

And Kevin, I'm glad that we got to fall overboard together.

ABOUT THE AUTHOR

Photo © 2020 Jordan Batt

Sariah Wilson is the *USA Today* bestselling author of more than two dozen contemporary romance and romantic fantasy novels, including *A Tribute of Fire*, *The Chemistry of Love*, and *Roommaid*. She happens to be madly, passionately in love with her soulmate and is a fervent believer in happily ever afters—which is why she writes romance. She currently lives with her family and various pets in Utah, and harbors a lifelong devotion to ice cream. For more information, visit her at www.sariahwilson.com.